The Arawn Prophecy

When the author offered an ARC to review his new book, I was curious. Having not read his previous novels, I was intrigued by the premise of combining the genres of Christian fiction, LDS fiction, and horror. I wasn't disappointed.

The story is well crafted and researched. I loved learning about the lives of the Roman legionnaires as I met Marcus. The trials of being a former princess, now defeated as a slave, as I met Maelona. The conflicting emotions of loving a human, but being compelled to kill those who do evil, when I met Branwen. I say met, because that is what it felt like. The characters are easily pictured, well written, and easy to connect with.

The word "Prophecy", as written in the title, plays a major part in the story. Marcus has the Gift of Prophecy, and each chapter begins with one quoted. I enjoyed the challenge of first trying to determine the meaning, and then discovering it as the chapter played out.

Don't let the idea that this is part of a series, or the horror genre, turn you away. There is enough back-story given to catch you up with the extra characters, and Mr. Belt does a wonderful job of letting your imagination fill in the details that constitute the horror. This story is easily read as a stand-alone novel. Bravo, Mr. Belt!

Cydnie Dial - South Jordan, UT

I just watched a great movie—in my head, from reading this outstanding story! Attend the tale of Marcus Scribonius Audaxus, Roman legionnaire extraordinaire! Having suffered the loss of his mother at the hands of wicked men, Marcus joins the Roman army and grows to become a great leader. Also having been baptized by an original member of the Quorum of the Seventy, an elder named Aristobulus who served with Jesus Christ during His earthly ministry, Marcus experiences many great challenges that test his faith, including fighting with extremely wicked men who worship Arawn, Lord of the Dead. Marcus is not only valiant, courageous, humble, faithful, loyal, and full of integrity, but he has a special gift of receiving prophecies that proves to be a great blessing to him and those he loves. His steadfastness, courage, faith, and his love prove to be a great catalyst in causing two beautiful women, a slave-turned-princess named Maelona and a mortal-turned-vampire named Branwen, to fall incredibly in love with him. This love permeates the story and plays a role in tying together the past with the future as the heroes who defeated Lilith (see Belt's "The Children of Lilith") learn all about Marcus and those who nobly fought beside him. These two heroes honor Marcus and his descendants in a final act of selfless love, and then the final prophecy is fulfilled. 'Tis an epic tale of great magnitude and a tear jerker in the end!

John Abercrombie - Bountiful, UT

"The Arawn Prophecy" drew me in and made me feel as though I was part of the story. I joined Marcus Scribonius "Audaxus" as he fought physical battles in the Roman army and struggled with matters of faith and temptation. I joined Maelona as she transformed from slave to princess. As their relationship changed from fear to love, I felt the emotions they were going through. I joined Branwen while she was having her own inner struggles with her feelings for Marcus. I joined them all on their journey to fight the wicked priests of Arawn as they put their fear behind and found the courage they needed to face what could possibly be their last battle. I did not want the story to end! I couldn't put the book down.

Thank you for an amazing, exciting, wonderful journey, C. David Belt!

Carrie Farnsworth - Kaysville, UT

"The Arawn Prophecy" was a beautifully crafted story. I was drawn in by characters so well-written, I could have sworn I was there with them. This was a story built around keeping faith during times that seemed to contradict everything, and rising above and becoming stronger for it.

Kimberly King - Logan, UT

The
Arawn Prophecy

C. David Belt

ISBN: 978-1-5136-4356-4 (paperback)

ISBN: 978-0-4634-1269-5 (e-book)

Cover design: Ben Savage

PARABLES
Walkersville, MD
http://www.parablespub.com
parables@parablespub.com

For Cindy –

my lady,
my princess,
and my queen

If you're going through hell, keep going.

Winston Churchill

Courage is fear holding on a minute longer.

George S. Patton

He treats a flower girl as if she was a duchess.

Eliza Doolittle

Greater love hath no man than this, that a man lay down his life for his friends.

Jesus Christus

Author's note

I used to love the movie *Braveheart*. I mean, I *loved* it. Such an inspiring story of courage! Like great bagpipe music, it stirred my blood. (And to those who might say, "There's no such thing as 'great bagpipe music,'" I say, you have never heard the Tabernacle Choir sing "Amazing Grace" with bagpipes . . .)

I teach classes on Medieval weaponry and armor at writers' conferences and Renaissance faires—"Swords and Spears and Axes, Oh My (Medieval Weapons 101)." I have collected a rather large arsenal of ancient weapons—some are truly ancient, while most are battle-ready, museum-quality replicas of actual museum pieces. I pass the swords, spears, axes, war hammers, maces, daggers, etc. around and allow participants to heft and handle them, while I sing songs and tell tales from history and talk about how those lovely, lethal objects were actually used.

At writers' conferences, the purpose of the class is to allow authors and aspiring authors the opportunity to describe combat with a greater degree of accuracy and, in many cases, to wisely choose which weapons their characters should use in the stories. At the Ren faires, I'm attempting to infuse a greater love of history and a love and respect for the brave men and women who stand between us and the darkness and have done so throughout history.

In my classes, when I talk about the Battle of Bannockburn, I ask, "How many of ye have ever seen the 'entertainment' known as *Braveheart*?" (I call it an "entertainment," because it's a Ren faire and movies didn't exist in whatever time period is being portrayed. Also, I do my classes "in-character" to match my full Scottish garb, including kilt.) In answer to my question, a great number of people raise their hands, including me. Then I ask, "How many of ye ken it's all a pack of lies?"

That elicits a laugh.

Then I list off some of those lies—

"Nobody wore kilts at the time."

"William Wallace was a nobleman, nae a commoner. He was Laird Protector of Scotland, fer cryin' out loud!"

"William Wallace was a Lowlander, nae a Highlander."

"William Wallace did nae cry, 'Freedom!' as 'tis impossible tae yell anythin' when your diaphragm has been removed, which is part of the mode of execution known as drawing-and-quartering."

"There was nae ever any such a thing as *prima nocta*."

"Robert was a true Scottish patriot, nae a craven political maneuver."

"Oh, and the princess? She was six years old when Wallace died and had ne'er been tae Scotland. So . . . *that* did nae happen."

So when, to my dismay, I learned of all the inaccuracies and blatant lies that were portrayed in that beloved movie, I did some research of my own on the screenwriter who wrote the movie (who claims to be a descendant of William Wallace and who I will not name here). When questioned about the nonhistorical nature of the film, he said, "Never let the truth get in the way of a good story."

Well, I simply can't do that. Yes, I know I'm writing fiction, but I want to keep the story as close to the truth as possible. No, "want" isn't a strong enough word. I *need* to stay as close to the truth as possible, otherwise, the story rings false. But, especially in the case of this story, I am fighting Hollywood tooth and nail. Ancient Rome has been depicted many times in film and so, increasingly, has first century Roman Britannia. And the inaccuracies are often stunning.

While I am no scholarly expert on this period of history and this setting, I've painstakingly researched in order to keep the details as accurate as possible. And I've consulted with a former professor of antiquities, a friend of mine in the Tabernacle Choir at Temple Square. In fact, I've talked his ear off. And he has graciously and patiently listened and advised.

So as you read this story, I am going to challenge (and decimate) many of the images that Hollywood has spoon-fed into your minds. (By the way, *decimate* is a very interesting word with Roman military origins. It didn't mean then what it means today . . .) So, please be prepared to set aside many of your preconceived notions.

Here's one example—did you know that there were only eighteen Roman male first names in use during the first century? The main character is named Marcus Scribonius. And in his century (Roman military unit) of eighty men, fifteen other men would have the first name of Marcus. So at this period, one would never refer to Marcus Scribonius simply as "Marcus." One would almost always use his first name *and* his family name—Marcus Scribonius. Only in an intimate setting would he ever be called "Marcus," and then only if there were no other Marcuses in the room.

Another example—the Romans, while obsessed with bathing, did not use soap (and, yes, soap was around at the time). They cleaned their skin by rubbing olive oil onto the skin, and then scraping it off with a flat, hook-shaped instrument called a strigil. I have to admit, when I discovered this little fact, my mind was officially blown. And they washed clothes in urine.

In spite of what you have seen in the movies, the Roman short sword known as the gladius was not used to *hack* at the enemy. It was a thrusting weapon, used to *stab* at the enemy. So there was none of this sword-clashing-on-sword fighting in the Roman army. In fact, legionnaires were not trained in one-on-one combat—they trained and fought only as organized units. And they were extremely effective.

If you have read my other published works, you may recognize certain characters and circumstances, and I hope that will bring you joy. If you have *not* read my other published novels, don't worry—you will still be able to fully enjoy the story.

For me, this has been a fun ride—all of it, including the late nights of historical research. I sincerely hope you enjoy it.

C. David Belt
August 2nd, 2018

Chapter I

"For the father shall fall and the son shall rise in his stead. And many shall slip and die in the blood of their friends."

from the Book of Marcus Scribonius

DCCCXIV *Ab Urbe Condita* (61 A.D.)

The terror began with the fall of his centurion.

Not with the blood-congealing battle cries of the Celts, outnumbering the legion twenty-three to one. Not with the thunder of the enemy as they crashed in wave after relentless wave upon the Roman shield wall. Not with the cacophony of stones and iron-tipped spears as they rained down upon the shields, spearheads punching through like quills from a hundred thousand giant, metal porcupines. Not with the dark red of the blood-soaked ground. Not even with the well-nigh overpowering stench of blood and death around Marcus Scribonius.

No, the true terror began the instant a single Celtic spear pierced Centurion Gaius Aquillius Regulus and drove him to the ground.

Like every other man in the century of eighty-four legionnaires, Marcus Scribonius crouched in front of his commander, holding his shield above his own head, and bracing the man in front of him with his right hand. Marcus Scribonius didn't actually *see* Gaius Aquillius fall. But he *felt* his commander fall. One moment, his mentor was there, behind him, putting his head above the shield wall, acting as the century's eyes and ears, exposing himself to danger, giving them strength. And the next moment, he was not.

Marcus Scribonius turned his head and glanced behind.

Gaius Aquillius lay on his back with a wooden spear protruding from his segmented armor, just below the collarbone. The fallen centurion clawed at the spear shaft with bloodied hands.

And Marcus Scribonius knew he could do nothing to save the man he loved as dearly as he loved his own father. But mourning would have to wait for later.

If there was to be such a thing as "later."

And so, Option Marcus Scribonius Audaxus did as he was trained to do—the only thing he could do. As option of the century, he did his duty—he assumed command.

Lowering his oval shield and drawing his sword, Marcus Scribonius stood, raising his head, armored by a helm with a longitudinal, front-to-back, crest of red-dyed horsehair, above the shield wall. Exposing himself to the enemy. "Man down!" he roared, hoping to be heard above the cacophony of battle. "Stretcher! Man down!" He glanced to his left. Two men—clad in the leather brigandines worn by the support personnel—dashed toward him, running behind the lines of the first centuries of the legion's cohorts. The runners bore a stretcher. Whether they had heard him or not, it mattered little. Marcus Scribonius felt assured they would see his fallen centurion and carry Gaius Aquillius to the physicians.

But Marcus Scribonius had no illusions his beloved commander would survive the day, if indeed the hour.

Put it aside, he thought. *You cannot save him. You have other men to worry about.*

The lives of the entire century were in *his* hands. *Not just the century, the entire Second Cohort.* More than five hundred men depending on him to lead them, to be their eyes and ears. Just as they had depended on Gaius Aquillius.

Marcus Scribonius was terrified.

He turned his face toward the battle.

And beheld an ocean of howling Celts armed with a forest of spears.

The scouts had estimated that Queen Boudicca commanded two hundred and thirty thousand, but to Marcus Scribonius the enemy seemed as numberless as the stones of a mountain avalanche—an avalanche crashing down upon the Romans.

And we have but ten thousand.

Make that ten thousand less one.

Not now. Focus on the battle.

Rippling from the rear like a great wave upon the sea, the Celts surged forward again. In moments, that wave would crash upon them.

"*Testudo*!" he roared, reiterating the call for the "tortoise" formation the century already held. "Hold the formation! Brace yourselves!"

Spurius Orcivius, the *cornicen,* wearing the bearskin pelt and bear head that marked his office, crouched under the back of the shield wall. He echoed the signal on his *cornu*, the circular trumpet of battle.

The testudo shield wall shifted as the century made small adjustments to their shields, ensuring no gaps remained. Legionnaires replanted their hobnailed boots, each man bracing the man in front of him with a stiff right arm and a hand placed on that man's back. Marcus Scribonius knew the men of the front line held their swords ready, pointed toward the enemy.

Screaming like devils, the wave of Celts smashed against them.

But the shields of the testudo held.

"Thrust swords!" Marcus Scribonius bellowed.

The cornicen blew the signal.

As one, the men of the front line parted their shields slightly, stabbed blindly at the horde, then quickly resealed the wall. The mortal screams of newly wounded Celts ripped the air asunder.

With a bestial roar, a single Celt leapt upon the top of the shield wall. Carrying a spear, he danced upon the shields, charging toward the rear. Toward Marcus Scribonius.

Marcus Scribonius braced his feet and raised his sword.

Splattered with blood and naked from the waist up, his foe wore no armor save the "magical" torc around his neck. The bearded man leapt forward, his spear aimed at Marcus Scribonius's heart.

Marcus Scribonius somehow brought his shield up barely in time to deflect the spear, but not the man behind it. The Celt fell upon Marcus Scribonius's short Roman sword, and the weight of the man bore Marcus Scribonius to the ground.

Letting go of his shield, Marcus Scribonius shoved with his left hand and rolled to his right. The mass atop him rolled away and off him. Relieved of the weight, Marcus Scribonius wrenched his gore-washed sword free from the Celt's body.

Blind and deaf! he thought. *The century is blind and deaf!*

Ignoring his dying foe, Marcus Scribonius scrambled to his feet as he grasped his shield again. And once more he stood behind the century, raising his plumed and helmeted head above the blinding, deafening safety of the shield wall and exposed himself to the enemy.

The tide of Celts surged forward again.

"Testudo!" he cried with scarcely a moment to spare, without even a moment for the cornicen to echo the command.

The tortoise held.

He glanced back again. The other five centuries of the Second Cohort stood ready in a long line, shields over their heads. To his right stood the First Cohort with its five double-sized centuries—one hundred and fifty-five men apiece, seven hundred and seventy-five in total. The legion's right flank was also protected by a dense forest to the rear, and on the right by the walls of the narrow, natural bowl in which the legion made its stand. To his left, the remaining cohorts stood their ground, stretching away to the other side of the bowl.

The legate, Gaius Suetonius Paulinus—Roman *propraetor* or governor of Britannia and commander of this cobbled-together legion—had chosen his ground well. The enemy could not approach from the right, the left, or the rear. Queen Boudicca's Celts, all two hundred and thirty thousand of them, could attack only from the front. Boudicca's plan was simple—overwhelm and crush the Romans.

But thus far, the legion had not surrendered an inch.

However, the front ranks were exhausted, and the enemy gave no quarter.

Marcus Scribonius had lost count of how many waves they had repulsed. *No matter how strong we are, they just keep coming. They just keep coming.*

So many of them.

The legion had no opportunity to relieve the frontline centuries. *We will tire, and then we will fall.*

If only the legate would call for the advance. At least then we'd have some relief from –

He heard the signal, echoing from century to century, blown by each cornicen, rolling through the legion.

"Prepare to advance!" he cried, interpreting and echoing the signal.

From below and in front of him, he heard, "About cursed time!" Mettius Canius—the "Ferret"—always somehow at the back of his squad, always at the rear of the formation.

"Silence!" snapped Marcus Scribonius. *The fool knows better than that.* But Marcus Scribonius understood the indecorous legionnaire's sentiment. *It is indeed time to move.*

Then came a new cornu-carried signal.

"Advance!" he shouted.

As one, like a massive wave creeping up a seashore, the legion moved. Without breaking formation, the Romans stepped forward.

And the Celts fell.

The ground, turned to mud by baths of Celtic blood and mired with bodies of dead and dying Celts, caused the barefoot enemy to slip and fall. But the Romans, shod with their hobnailed *caligae* boots, found traction, pushing the enemy back. Each legionnaire on the front line shoved with his shield, then stabbed with his sword—the deadly, efficient *gladius*.

Step. Push shield. Thrust sword.

Step. Push shield. Thrust sword.

Step. Push shield. Thrust sword.

"Hold ranks!" Marcus Scribonius bellowed. His order was drowned out by the screams of the enemy as they turned and fled. But he could've saved his breath. His men held their formation perfectly.

Step. Push shield. Thrust sword.

The Celts fell before them. By the hundreds, by the thousands.

Step. Push shield. Thrust sword.

They had trained the men well—he and his beloved commander, Gaius Aquillius.

For the briefest of instants, the pain and grief made his knees wobble.

Not now. Mourn him later.

He adjusted his blood-slick fingers around the ivory hilt of his gladius—a gift of gratitude from his fallen centurion.

Honor him with a glorious victory.

But it wasn't a glorious victory. The Celts turned to flee, slipping in the blood of their fellows, falling before the unstoppable Roman advance, trapped by their own women and children—women and children watching in horror from the wagons that rimmed the bowl.

No, it was not a glorious victory.

It was butchery. Slaughter.

♦ ♦ ♦

"He's calling for you, Option." Septimus Scribonius stood tall and straight, though his posture could not conceal the fatigue in his voice.

Marcus Scribonius nodded from where he stood, leaning on the shaft of a discarded enemy spear. The rest of the century also stood wearily about. As exhausted as they were, most of them displayed no desire to kneel, sit, or lie on the blood-drenched earth. Even Mettius Canius stood, though he *had* sat briefly, heedless of the gore, until Marcus Scribonius convinced him, with a murderous glare, of the wisdom of taking his feet once more.

"He still lives?" Hope rose in him, making him tremble slightly.

Septimus Scribonius—a friend and distant cousin—nodded, paused, then shook his head. "Not for long."

Marcus Scribonius put a hand on the man's armored shoulder.

Septimus Scribonius returned the gesture of comfort. "You'd better hurry."

Marcus Scribonius straightened and dropped the Celtic spear to the red-brown mud. He didn't feel like keeping the enemy weapon as a war trophy. It was inferior to the Roman *pilum* anyway. "Tesserarius," he said, nodding to the officer of the watch, the next in command, Caeso Lucilius. "You're in charge."

The junior officer, wearing the wolf pelt and head of his office, put his right fist to his chest in salute and acknowledgment. "Yes, Option." Then he lowered his hand. "Give him . . ." The tesserarius's voice faltered. "Tell him of our love. We shall build him . . . a glorious . . ." Caeso Lucilius shook his head mutely, unable to continue.

Marcus Scribonius nodded. "I will." He turned and trotted toward the cluster of hastily erected physicians' tents.

As he ran, he was forced to weave between the countless corpses of the slain. An indecent, horrific number of the fallen were women. No Roman casualties were to be seen. They would have already been removed from the battlefield—the wounded to be tended, the dead already laid out in orderly rows. A few assigned legionnaires moved among the Celtic bodies, pausing infrequently to administer a final stroke to some not-yet-dead enemy.

The stench of blood, vomit, unwashed bodies, urine, and feces hung over the battlefield like a miasmic fog.

Marcus Scribonius ignored the vile odor as best he could, but several times he had to fight the urge to stop and empty his already depleted stomach.

As he drew near to the cluster of medical tents, he headed straight toward the rearmost pavilion, where the wounded officers would be tended. The screams of men suffering amputations and cauterizations punctuated the otherwise eerie silence. Before entering the goat-hide tent, however, out of respect, he removed his plumed helmet and carried it in his left hand. Though his commander was dying, Marcus Scribonius would honor the protocols the centurion required.

He spied Gaius Aquillius on a field bed. Marcus Scribonius knelt at his mentor's side. "I'm here, Centurion."

Gaius Aquillius's flesh hung loose and pale on his grizzled face. The long battle scar running down the left side of his face was the only livid mark on his cadaverous countenance. His breathing was labored, and Marcus Scribonius could hear a gurgling, bubbling sound as the man's chest rose and fell. A great linen bandage, stained with various shades of red and brown, covered Gaius Aquillius's shoulder and half his chest. The centurion's eyes fluttered, then opened. "You"—he swallowed and coughed, and blood trickled from the corner of the older man's lips—"came. I knew . . . you would."

Marcus Scribonius nodded with vigor. "Yes, Centurion. I'm here. The men of the century send their love to you. They . . ." He could not find words to continue.

Gaius Scribonius gave an almost imperceptible nod. "Yes. Well, tell them . . ."

Marcus Scribonius said, "I will."

The dying centurion gave another faint nod. "Did we . . . win?"

"Yes, we did. A great . . . victory."

"How . . . b-bad?"

"The initial reports are"—Marcus Scribonius still struggled to believe the casualty numbers—"four hundred on our side and seventy or eighty thousands of Boudicca's army." *Only four hundred out of ten thousand—but why must one of them be* you? He let his tears fall.

"Boudicca?"

"Fled. Escaped on her chariot. With her two daughters."

"Pursuit?"

Marcus Scribonius shook his head. "Not yet."

"Won't matter. Get her . . . eventually."

"Yes, Centurion. I'm sure we will." He'd heard the stories from Camulodunum. Stories of how the rebellious Celtic Queen Boudicca had massacred the Ninth Legion and how she had treated her *own* people. Tales of a forest of impaled Celtic women. Marcus Scribonius hoped they would catch her. *Rebellion is one thing. Slaughter for the sake of slaughter is madness. Atrocity.*

But Marcus Scribonius also knew *why* Boudicca had rebelled. He'd heard about the horrific treatment Boudicca and her daughters received at the hands of Roman Procurator Decanius Catus and his band of sadistic Roman mercenaries. *May Decanius Catus and his beasts burn in the fires of Hell.* "We'll get her, if she doesn't take her own life first. Her daughters, though . . ."

"Hopefully, they'll . . . escape."

Marcus Scribonius nodded. "That would be . . . merciful, perhaps."

Gaius Aquillius coughed again, and more blood, fresh and bright, bubbled from his mouth. "Your god . . ." His eyes turned toward Marcus Scribonius. "Your god . . . Did he tell you . . . about this . . . about me?"

Tears fell afresh from Marcus Scribonius's eyes. "Yes. I didn't understand it at the time. But now . . ." The words of the prophecy—the words he'd rehearsed over and over in his mind since the battle ended—echoed cold and ghostly once again through his mind. Only after the battle had the meaning of the words become clear.

For the father shall fall and the son shall rise in his stead. And many shall slip and die in the blood of their friends.

The centurion wheezed in a weak approximation of a gurgling laugh. "Should have . . . warned me."

Marcus Scribonius shook his head. "I didn't know. I didn't understand. With my prophecies, it's . . . always like that." *I never seem to understand until it's too late. What good are they?*

Another, weak, gurgling chuckle. "Why'd you . . . have to . . . pick . . . a wretched . . . foreign god? Nothing good . . . ever came . . . out of Judea. Prophecies . . . no help . . . at all."

Marcus Scribonius forced a weak smile. "Why'd you have to pick a wretched Persian god?" The familiar exchange was an old one, oft spoken between the two of them. But at that moment, Marcus Scribonius took no comfort in the old joke. *Our Father who art in heaven, hallowed be Thy name. Why, Father? Why couldn't I save him? I would have given my life for him. If I bore Thy priesthood, I could anoint him even now with consecrated olive oil and lay my hands upon him. I could save him! Even now I could . . . if I but had Thine authority!*

But seeing his beloved commander's weak smile, Marcus Scribonius continued their customary verbal sparring, comforting his commander in their last moments together. "You shower in the blood of Mithras's sacred bull. How foolish is that?"

Gaius Aquillius's smile widened. "You eat . . . bread . . . drink wine . . . and call it . . . his flesh . . . a-and blood. Cursed . . . cannibal." The centurion's eyes closed. His breath began to rattle in his chest.

Marcus Scribonius knew the sound all too well—a death rattle. *If only I'd had the wisdom to interpret the prophecies Thou gavest to me. I could have warned him!*

I could have saved him.

Gently, he brushed the graying black hair off his mentor's forehead. *But no. Even if I* had *warned him, he would have done his duty anyway.*

Forgive me my trespasses, Father. Forgive me my arrogance.

Gaius Aquillius's eyes popped open wide. "Audaxus!" he cried, using the *cognomen*, the third name he himself had bestowed upon Marcus Scribonius. The centurion's hand shot up, gripping Marcus Scribonius by the forearm. The grip was surprisingly strong. "Must tell . . . My . . . son . . ." The grip loosened. The arm fell away to hang limply over the side of the cot. The eyes remained open. Open and unseeing.

The death rattle had ceased.

Marcus Scribonius bowed his head. *Father in heaven, be merciful unto him. Teach him, so that I may be baptized for him.*

He was a good man.

"He was your father?" The quiet voice came from near the foot of the bed.

Marcus Scribonius raised his head and turned his bloodshot eyes to the physician who was clad in a bloodstained tunic. "No. But he was as a father to me. To us all."

"You were his option then?"

Marcus Scribonius nodded. "Yes." *Option. Chosen one. Second in command.* "I was his option."

The physician nodded gravely. "Then may Mithras, or whatever gods he worshipped, take him home."

Marcus Scribonius Audaxus rose to his feet. He placed his crested helmet on his head and buckled the chinstrap. "We will send for his body and armor. But for now, I must see to my men." The weight of the plume—and the office it signified—felt like the burden of mythical Atlas.

Chapter II

"Though thou seekest not after other gods, yet shalt thou seek the lord of the dead. And behold! Thou shalt find him."
from the Book of Marcus Scribonius

The sheepskin pavilion provided shelter from the sun shining in a rare, nearly cloudless sky, but the great tent did nothing to buffer against the reek of more than eighty thousand corpses rotting under that same sun. Neither could the pavilion mute the incessant cawing and croaking of a vast host of rooks and ravens—black carrion birds gorging themselves on the Celtic dead.

The few hundred fallen Romans had already been honored with a mass funeral pyre. No funerary feast had been held in their memory, however, because the train of supply wagons had not yet caught up with the army.

Not that most men could've stomached roasted meat with the putrescence polluting the air. Marcus Scribonius, for one, was grateful their rations of bacon, barley, and *posca*—a mixture of water, wine, herbs, and sometimes honey—tasted nothing like the stench that filled his nostrils.

The army had removed more than half a mile from the battleground, but a fiendish wind kept shifting just enough to carry the reek of decay and the cries of the carrion fowl to the encampment.

The massive pavilion once belonged to Queen Boudicca, but the great tent had become the field headquarters of Legate Gaius Suetonius Paulinus. The legate himself had not yet arrived at the council of war, but the senior officers under his command—tribunes and the *pila prior*—the "first spears" or senior centurions of each cohort—began to assemble.

Marcus Scribonius was the only option in attendance at the council—the only one. When he entered the pavilion, carrying his helm under his left arm, Option Marcus Scribonius Audaxus quickly scanned the tent. And he observed that not a single helm—other than his own—was topped with the longitudinal crest of an option. Of the dozen or so men already assembled, each carried under his arm a helm with the *latitudinal*, side-to-side, crest of a centurion, tribune, or other senior officer.

And as each additional man entered the tent, Marcus Scribonius observed his face. Some of the senior officers he recognized. The pilus prior of each cohort in his own Fourteenth Legion Gemina—those he knew. He'd served with them over the eleven years of his military career. Others, he did not know—the pila prior of the Twentieth Legion Valeria Victrix. Those cohorts had joined the hasty march when word of Boudicca's rebellion reached the army in Cambria. There, Roman forces had been busy quelling what they thought was the last of the Celt and Druid resistance at the Isle of Mona. Marcus Scribonius was likewise unfamiliar with the centurions of the auxiliary units who marched with them.

But whether he knew them or not, they all outranked him.

It would seem, he thought with some bitterness in his heart, *we were the only cohort to lose our commander. The only one.*

Technically, Marcus Scribonius wasn't supposed to be at the council at all, since he merely held the rank of option. But until a new centurion was assigned to his century, he was required to stand in his fallen commander's place. Gaius Aquillius had been the pilus prior of the Second Cohort. And that meant Marcus Scribonius must temporarily stand for the entire Second Cohort—and all six of its centuries—even if he must stand alone.

Marcus Scribonius chose an empty stool next to an unfamiliar centurion. As he sat, Marcus Scribonius gripped the pommel of his sword, so he could lean it safely to rest at his side. He placed his helm on his lap, then nodded to the centurion.

"Have you ever met him?" asked his neighbor. Marcus glanced at the man. Even sitting, the centurion was obviously taller than average and slighter of build. His armor of segmented plates hung somewhat loosely upon him, leading Marcus Scribonius to wonder if the fellow might have been ill lately.

After that forced march from Mona to Londinium and then back here—almost the full journey back to northern Cambria again—all of us are thinner, but . . .

He asked me a question, didn't he? Oh, yes . . . "The legate? The *propraetor?*"

The lanky centurion turned a pair of hard, gray eyes, set in a lean face with full, almost too-red lips, upon Marcus Scribonius. "Yes, the governor. Gaius Suetonius Paulinus. Have you met him?" The repeated question came out as if the man seemed to think Marcus Scribonius was slow-witted.

Marcus Scribonius found himself taking an immediate dislike to the tall, thin centurion. Then he chastised himself. *Now, now. Our Lord said, "Judge not according to the appearance," did He not?* He shook his head. "No. Although, I've *seen* him . . ."

The centurion's full-lipped mouth twisted in annoyance. "We've all *seen* him—that speech he gave before the battle . . ."

Marcus Scribonius nodded. "Good speech. Short. Effective. Inspiring."

"Yes. Yes." The centurion waved impatiently. "But have you *met* the man?"

Marcus Scribonius forced his expression to remain calm. *I already answered you.* "Not personally. He's spoken to my"—the slightest hitch in his voice betrayed the still-raw grief—"my centurion in my presence. The legate is a great . . . tactician."

"Yes"—the man, lifting his chin with the haughty air of a born patrician, nodded slightly—"a great tactician."

A great tactician who is also a butcher.

Two days prior, at the end of the battle, with victory certain and Boudicca's vast army dead, dying, or fleeing, Legate Gaius Suetonius Paulinus had ordered the auxiliary centuries—conscripts all, save for their Roman-citizen centurions and options—to slaughter the defenseless women and children in the Celtic wagons. *I wonder,* thought Marcus Scribonius, *if this man was one of those who led that cursed massacre?*

And what would you have done, Marcus Scribonius, if you had been ordered to commit murder?

I hope . . . I pray *I would've had the courage to refuse such an order and face the consequences. I pray I will* never *have to make such a choice.*

The centurion surveyed the pavilion, his face twisting in disgust. "You'd think we'd have proper chairs for a war council, not these"—he shifted uncomfortably on the Celtic stool—"these wretched things."

Marcus Scribonius shrugged. "It has been only two days since the battle. The supply wagons have yet to catch up with us." *Assuming they were not intercepted along the way.* "Today, they say. Or perhaps, tomorrow."

The tall centurion grunted. "I'm sick of short rations. Nothing but bacon, grain, and that vinegar they dare to call wine. And *barley* at that. Bah!"

The Celts had brought along herds of cattle to feed themselves. However, those beasts, at least, had possessed enough sense to flee after the battle. Even though some had been caught and butchered, fresh meat was still in very short supply.

The centurion gave a low, bitter laugh. "Marius's Mules! That's what we are—wretched pack mules!"

The reference to the policy of Gaius Marius, instituted more than a century before, was not lost on Marcus Scribonius. "We carried what we needed on our backs. As ordered." *Like mules.* "Otherwise, we'd never have reached this battlefield so far ahead of the enemy, never had time to rest, to be ready. Choose the time and place of your battle—basic military strategy. And this choice was brilliant."

The centurion nodded with vigor. "Boudicca never stood a chance. From the beginning, victory was never in doubt."

Marcus Scribonius gave his companion a sidelong glance. *Were you fighting in the same battle? I was scared out of my wits.*

"You seem to be the sole option present. Were you summoned?" his companion asked. "Where is your centurion?"

Marcus Scribonius attempted to swallow the lump that suddenly constricted his throat—with limited success. "F-fallen."

"Oh." The man's countenance drooped. "I am sorry." He paused. "Who was he?"

At this sudden display of sympathy, Marcus Scribonius looked his companion in the face. *Perhaps, I have misjudged him.* "Gaius Aquillius Regulus."

The centurion's expression soured, and he lowered his eyes. "Ah."

Or . . . perhaps not. "You knew him?" *And disliked him perhaps?*

The man shrugged. "He was . . . a kinsman." He looked Marcus Scribonius in the eye and extended his right arm. "I am Quintus Aquillius Lucanus, commander of the Sixth Century, Reserves, Twentieth Legion."

So, he's a patrician, a nobleman. House Aquillius. Reserves—one of the butchers. But Sixth *Century? Not a pilus prior, not the commander of a cohort. So what* is *he doing here?* Marcus Scribonius glanced at the man's extended hand. *Unwise to refuse his greeting.* He clasped Quintus Aquillius's hand. "I am Marcus Scribonius."

Quintus Aquillius returned the handclasp, but the man's grip was far too hard to be friendly. The man raised his eyebrows. "You are the one they call . . . Audaxus?"

Marcus Scribonius's mouth twitched in irritation. *Ridiculous name.* "Yes. Gaius Aquillius bestowed that cognomen on me." *I didn't choose it. I would* never *have chosen it.*

"So I've heard." Quintus Aquillius released his decidedly unfriendly grip. "The Valiant." The corner of his mouth raised in a half-sneer. "And from what I've heard, you earned the name." In contrast to his words, the man's tone carried an edge of contempt.

"Actually, I'd much rather people forgot it."

"It doesn't work that way." The centurion turned his face away, scowling. "Perhaps someday you will come to merit a different cognomen, one that suits you better."

Ignoring the thinly veiled insult, Marcus Scribonius managed to keep his countenance neutral. *It's as if he despises me—hated me before he even met me.*

Wretched dog. Patrician—a noble, yes, but a dog all the same. Pity the man who must serve under such a "noble" cur.

Oh, Marcus, judge not. Judge not.

Wretched, noble cur.

A flap opened at the back of the tent, and a man entered. And all conversation abruptly died. Gaius Suetonius Paulinus—Legate of the Fourteenth Legion Gemina, Propraetor of Britannia—was clad in full armor, including his elaborately plumed *galea* helm. His sword hung at his right hip and his leaf-bladed *pugio* dagger hung at his left. The commander wore his graying brown hair and beard long and full—like a Celt or a Gaul of Germania—unfashionable for a Roman legate, though reasonable, given the dismally cold climate of Britannia. Powerfully built, with a commanding bearing, the legate looked every whit a warrior and a general.

Brilliant tactician. Vastly outnumbered, and yet we emerged victorious. We owe the man our very lives. Truly a soldier's legate.

But then he orders the slaughter of women and children.

Such brutality. Will it quell further rebellion, I wonder? Or incite it?

Eighty thousand warriors dead. And they didn't even bother to count the slaughtered innocents. Just left the corpses to rot where they fell.

Left them to the ravens.

The legate stood silently beside his table for a long moment, his right hand resting on the pommel of his sword, as he surveyed his subordinates. His eyes swept left and right as if searching for someone in particular. Then his gaze fell upon Marcus Scribonius, and his eyes narrowed. A grim smile curled his lips.

He was looking for me*?*

That does not *bode well. Could one of the prophecies apply to this day? This hour?* Marcus Scribonius searched his memory. *Something particularly dark and dire?*

But he could recall nothing to fit the circumstances—at least nothing he understood.

What good is this gift of prophecy? I couldn't save Gaius Aquillius.

"Well done, men," said the legate at last with a decisive nod. His eyes finally drifted from Marcus Scribonius. "Well done. You fought bravely. I am filled with pride. Mars and Mithras have given us a great victory against overwhelming odds." He gave them all a grim smile, then clasped his hands behind his back. "But the war is not over. The rebellion in Cambria continues. Therefore, I will return to Mona with the Fourteenth. The remaining units will begin a punitive campaign against the Iceni, Trinovantes, and the other Celtic clans who joined Boudicca. You will march on Venta Icenorum and ensure she is dead or brought to justice. From there . . ."

Marcus Scribonius groaned within himself. *Punitive campaign. More slaughter.* He was grateful he'd be returning to northern Cambria and the Isle of Mona. *At least that will be* honest *fighting.*

Is there such a thing as honest *fighting?* he wondered for what seemed like the thousandth time. And for the ten thousandth time he wondered, *What are we doing in Britannia? To vindicate Julius Caesar's unsuccessful invasion a hundred years ago? Is that all? Imperial pride?*

Yes, there is tin and copper in Dumnonia and gold in Cambria, but those we could buy at a much lower price than the cost of keeping several legions here. As for the rest? A land of sheep, barley, and cold, wet, miserable weather. Surely these people are no threat to Rome.

♦ ♦ ♦

As the council began to break up, Marcus Scribonius rose from his seat. However, a tribune motioned for him to approach. Marcus Scribonius walked over to the senior officer. *What is his name? I know I heard it mentioned. Marcus Orcivius? Yes, that's it.* "Yes, Tribune?"

"The legate would have a word with you." The man tilted his head toward the governor. "Wait here until the tent clears out."

Marcus Scribonius nodded. "Yes, Tribune."

I suppose I'll find out who my new commander is. But such business the tribune could handle. Why would the legate wish to speak to me personally?

He recalled the words of the lanky centurion. *"Have you met him?"*

I suppose now I will.

He looked around at the remaining occupants of the pavilion. Everyone else was leaving, except the tribune and the legate. And the arrogant Centurion Quintus Aquillius.

He asked if I had been "summoned." And he doesn't command a cohort.

So that must mean he *was summoned to the council.*

No! Surely not!

Not him.

However, in moments, the four of them—the tribune, the legate, the centurion, and the option—were all that remained.

From Gaius Aquillius to this wretched dog.

Marcus, you had better change your outlook. This wretched dog is going to be your new commanding officer.

The tribune tilted his head toward the legate. Then the tribune turned and exited the pavilion through the back flap.

As soon as the three of them were alone, the legate said, "Approach."

Marcus Scribonius and Quintus Aquillius stepped forward and stood at attention across the desk from Legate Gaius Suetonius Paulinus. As one, both men thumped their right fists to their armored chests.

The legate returned the salute. He fixed his eyes on Marcus Scribonius. "I've heard about how you handled yourself during the battle, Option. You showed courage and you led your century flawlessly. You are to be commended. If I could, I would promote you to centurion this day and give you command of your century. But I cannot. Not at this time."

Marcus Scribonius knew very well the reason—he was several months shy of the minimum age of thirty.

"But," continued the legate, "if you keep going the way you are, you will have your own command within the year."

Gaius Suetonius turned his eyes to the centurion. "You shall take command of the First Century, Second Cohort. At least for the time being. Quintus Aquillius Lucanus, I want you to see this as a chance to prove yourself in the field. Of course, given your low seniority, Centurion, the First Century will be relegated to the position of Sixth Century."

"As you command, Legate," replied the man.

Marcus thought he detected a note of chagrin in the centurion's tone. *This is a* promotion *for him—from the reserves to the Second Cohort.* But it seemed to Marcus Scribonius as if the legate's words contained a barely concealed rebuke. *And for us, for my century, this is certainly a great demotion.* Within a cohort, the standing of each century was determined by the seniority of its centurion.

Not much of a reward for valiant service in combat.

And to be stuck with such a wretched commander!

The legate kept his eyes on Quintus Aquillius as he pointed a finger at Marcus Scribonius. "I would advise you, Centurion, to retain this man as your option. He knows the men. They respect him. And he has served with *great* distinction. You are fortunate to have him."

Marcus Scribonius felt his cheeks warming at such praise. An option served at his centurion's pleasure. And he seriously doubted his new commander held him in the least regard.

"As you command, Legate," replied the centurion.

"Now," said the legate as he took his seat behind his table, "grab some stools, men. I have a special assignment for you and your century."

Centurion and option did as instructed.

The legate leaned forward, placing both hands on the table. "These are perilous times, as you both know. We won this battle."

"A glorious victory," said the centurion.

"Hold your tongue," snapped the legate. "And your cursed praise. The gods favored us. If the front centuries had not held . . . If even *one* had given ground . . ." He turned his face pointedly to Marcus Scribonius. "Losing a centurion at a critical point should have been disaster. And I heard about the Celt who leapt atop the shield wall." The legate shook a finger at him. "If you had not dispatched him and gotten to your feet when you did, the whole line could have collapsed." He slapped the table. "We were *that* close to defeat. But you got to your feet. You may have saved the whole army."

Quintus Aquillius shook his head in obvious disbelief. "The men were already braced. Surely, they would have held. I do not doubt the option's courage, but . . ." The centurion's voice trailed off as Legate Gaius Suetonius turned a withering stare upon him—a stare that frightened even Marcus Scribonius. And he was not the target of those hard, cold eyes.

"The only reason you are getting this assignment, Centurion of the patrician family Aquillius," said the legate in a soft voice pregnant with menace and murder, "the *only* reason is because you have never, *never* stood at the front lines. I need men of experience and judgment if we are to hold Britannia. And that is experience you cannot gain in the reserves." Without moving his eyes from the now ashen-faced centurion, the legate addressed Marcus Scribonius. "Option, this inexperienced centurion needs the benefit of your frontline experience. He needs your wisdom and instruction. Therefore, explain this concept to him. Use small, short sentences so he cannot fail to understand."

Why is he humiliating him like this? But Marcus Scribonius did as he was told. "The testudo formation is designed to hold against a superior enemy when—"

"I have no doubt your commander knows what the testudo is used for," said the legate. "Explain to him why it needs a man like *you*. And turn and face him, man."

Marcus Scribonius rotated his body on the stool and faced the man who now stood in the place of his beloved centurion, Gaius Aquillius.

Quintus Aquillius's face had gone from ashen to livid as he turned to face his new second-in-command.

Marcus Scribonius met the centurion's gaze. "The men get tired. Yes, they are holding their shields with the left hand, planting their feet, and bracing the man in front of them. But the arms, the legs get fatigued." The words of instruction from Gaius Aquillius came back to him, falling from his own lips. "And because the shields are locked together, with no gaps between, the men are blind. And that blindness causes doubt. Doubt gives way to fear. Fear is the mother of terror. And terror causes the knees to shake and the arms to weaken. The men need to know *when* the next wave will hit—be it spears or darts or rocks or men. So they can strengthen themselves just before that wave breaks upon them. They need to trust the man who stands as their eyes and ears. Then they will be ready. For if they are not ready, the wave will break them."

The centurion stared at him in silence. Hatred burned is his eyes.

He will never forgive me for this.

The legate nodded. "Very well said. Keep this man as your second, Centurion. He is wise as well as fearless. You will learn much from him."

Centurion and option turned to face the legate.

The governor eyed Marcus Scribonius. "Tell me, lad. Did you enjoy that?"

Marcus Scribonius blinked at him. "My lord?"

A smile played at the corner of the legate's mouth. "Did you enjoy humiliating your commanding officer? Taking him back to school, as it were?"

Marcus Scribonius resisted the urge to glance at the centurion. "No, Legate."

Gaius Suetonius nodded. "Good. Let me give you a piece of advice, Option. *Never* do that in front of the men. If you see that he is in error or lacking in judgment, counsel him *in private*. But never in front of his men. Do you understand me?"

Marcus Scribonius nodded. "Yes, Legate."

"However, in private," continued the legate, "you are to help him, to guide him. Help him to become the centurion I need."

"Yes, Legate."

The legate turned his hard eyes on Quintus Aquillius. "This happened here, in private. At my order. You are to forgive it. And forget it. Never use it against Marcus Scribonius Audaxus. Do you understand me, Centurion?"

"Yes, Legate," came the stiff reply.

He will never forgive nor forget.

"Now," said the legate, producing a roll of parchment, "as I said, I have a special assignment for the Sixth Century, Second Cohort." He unrolled the large parchment to display a map of known Britannia—Caledonia to the north was largely unmapped and untamed. The map lacked many details, especially information about terrain. The legate placed smooth stones on each corner to hold the parchment open. He then planted a finger on the Roman highway running roughly north and south. "We are here." With the index finger of his other hand, he indicated a spot in southern Cambria, southwest of their current position and closer to the western coast of Britannia. "This is where you are headed . . . roughly. You are to take the Sixth Century and march overland. The supply train should arrive before nightfall. You will take your assigned wagons and march at first light. This is an armed reconnaissance mission, men. Observe and report."

The legate paused, and the centurion, apparently having regained some composure, asked, "And what are we to observe and report about?"

The legate looked up from his map and shrugged. "Most likely, nothing. Jumping at shadows." He shook his head, looking back at the map. "But in the current situation, I find myself forced to jump at the shadows."

The legate produced another, smaller scroll. He unrolled it, but kept the contents angled away from them. "I have here a report, the most recent of several, actually, telling of what can only be described as a manifestation of . . . the divine."

Marcus Scribonius blinked. "The divine, sir?"

"Yes." The legate drew the word out slowly, as if doubting its veracity. "The *repeated* manifestation, or I should say, *appearance* of a god. A *Celtic* god, however. Now, normally, this would be nothing. As you know, we allow the peoples of the empire to worship as they please." He chuckled, though the laugh sounded more like a grunt.

"And if we like a god or goddess, we may *adopt* him or her. Jupiter knows it's happened before. Jupiter himself was Greek—Zeus, as you know. Mithras was Persian. Now they are ours, and we are theirs." His eyes flickered to Marcus Scribonius. "At least, most of us are theirs." He shrugged again. "With Mithras, we didn't even go to the trouble of changing his name or recognize him as a foreign manifestation of one of our own gods. We just took him as our own. And he has blessed us. But *this* one . . . This one may be trouble."

The centurion shifted on his stool as if he were suddenly uncomfortable. Such talk bordered on blasphemy—at least, it would in a public setting. "So why is this a problem?"

"It's a problem," replied the legate, "because I don't need another cursed uprising right now. And a god, real or imaginary, a *Celtic* god might inspire an uprising, another rebellion. Especially when the Celts can *see* him. And right now . . . Right now, I have Mona to deal with in northern Cambria. We'll finish that. And with the punitive raids against the Iceni and the Trinovantes and the others, we should secure Roman rule here for the next few centuries at least. However, I fear a god—a *real* god—could, as I said, inspire another rebellion. And if that god himself were to rally the Celts . . . Well, we simply don't need that right now."

There are no gods save the one true God, and His Son, Jesus Christus, and the Holy Spirit. There are no other gods. No other gods.

And you are so certain of that, Marcus? Marcus Scribonius shoved the old, familiar doubt down into the dark recesses of his heart.

One of his prophecies tickled the back of his mind.

Though thou seekest not after other gods . . .

"And who is this supposed god we must find and report on?" asked Quintus Aquillius with a sneer. "Some local, petty Druid sprite inhabiting a rock or stream or tree?"

. . . yet shalt thou seek the lord of the dead.

The legate shook his head, scowling. "No, this is one of their big ones. He is their lord of the underworld."

A cold shiver of fear crawled up Marcus Scribonius's spine, sending tendrils of ice through his brain.

Legate Gaius Suetonius Paulinus leaned forward. "This, men, is Arawn, lord of the dead."

And behold! Thou shalt find him.

Chapter III

"And lo! Thy tribulation cometh, shrouded in red and riding in a wagon."

from the Book of Marcus Scribonius

What if this 'Arawn' is nothing more than an imposter?" asked Marcus Scribonius. *There can be no other gods. It is impossible.* "He may be simply a pretender, a fraud working tricks with colored smokes and sulfur."

The legate nodded. He lowered his eyes and stroked his beard as if deep in thought. "Perhaps. Yes, that would be much better, much easier to deal with. And if he does turn out to be some Celtic *goetia*, crucify him in front of his disciples. That should put a stop to any potential uprising in his name."

He fixed Marcus Scribonius with a hard stare. "You are a disciple of that Judean *magus*, or so I've been told."

Marcus Scribonius noted the legate's choice of words—"magus" rather than "goetia"—the former being a worker of divine miracles, and the latter, a magical trickster. *At least he shows a degree of respect.* "Yes, Legate. It is well known that I am a Christian." *Jesus was not simply a miracle worker. He was . . .* is *the Son of God.*

And crucifixion did not stop Him.

But now is not the time to engage the legate in a theological debate.

Gaius Suetonius Paulinus nodded again. "Then you are uniquely qualified to make a judgment in this case. Perhaps the reports are exaggerated. Perhaps this 'Arawn' is but a man and poses no real threat. Exercise your good judgment. Pontius Pilatus handled the Judean situation poorly. The man Jesus posed no threat to Rome. He led no armed insurrection. But Pontius Pilatus crucified him anyway—just to appease some local priests. He made the fellow a martyr, and now, Jesus's influence has spread even to Rome." He gave Marcus Scribonius another hard stare, then his eyes softened. The legate frowned. "And in the end, Pontius Pilatus's actions did nothing to pacify Judea."

He turned his attention on Quintus Aquillius. "Perhaps . . ." The legate stared at the centurion a moment, stroking his beard once more. "Perhaps, you *are* the right man to lead this mission after all. You served in Judea, did you not?"

The centurion straightened, lifting his chin in a typically patrician manner. "Yes, Legate. But not under Pontius Pilatus. I was but a child when—"

The legate grunted in loud disdain. "But a child? Even now, by Jupiter, you are barely old enough to wear a man's tunic!" He flipped a large hand in the direction of the helmet in the centurion's lap. "Let alone that plume on your helm."

The centurion's countenance reddened, and his jaw trembled slightly, but he said nothing.

He does look young, but not that *young. Perhaps the legate is referring to his inexperience.*

The legate breathed deeply, then exhaled through his nose, as if he were attempting to rein in his blatant contempt for the man. "But regardless, as I said, I need centurions of experience. This is your chance, lad, to gain that experience and prove yourself. Seize the chance! Seize it by the throat. *Be* the man I need you to be, instead of an overpromoted patrician whelp. You have a unique opportunity here. And as I said, perhaps your wretched Judean experience will be of some value on this mission. And, let me say again, you have the best option in the legion to help you and to teach you. Seize the opportunity, Quintus Aquillius. Make the most of it."

Still red-faced, the centurion gave a stiff nod. "Yes, Legate. I will."

The legate nodded. "I trust you will. If Arawn turns out to be a god, return and report to me at Mona. Return . . . if you can. If he turns out to be a man, a magus working miracles in the name of his god, use your judgment." His eyes flickered from centurion to option. "Your *best* judgment. But if he turns out to be a cursed goetia, crucify him. Do you understand?"

As one, both centurion and option answered, "Yes, Legate."

The legate grunted his approval. "Very well. Now, you'll be moving through hostile territory . . ."

As Marcus Scribonius listened to his legate, taking in the details of the mission, several thoughts chased each other through his mind.

My centurion despises me. How will I ever gain his trust? Especially after the legate forced me to instruct *him.*

What about the men? After Gaius Aquillius, how will they serve under such a man?

But one thought filled him with a creeping terror, like a cold serpent slithering up and down his spine.

Return . . . if you can.

♦ ♦ ♦

The racket of army camp life and the grim calls of carrion fowl filled the air, but the silence between centurion and option was thunderous. Marcus Scribonius knew how to hold his tongue, but he also knew that he would eventually need to establish an understanding with his new commander. *Better to speak to him now, here, and not in front of the men.*

Of one thing he was dreadfully certain. *This will not be pleasant. It is said, however, "Better to slip the knife in quickly."*

He waited until a trio of legionnaires, laughing and joking, passed them on business of their own.

Marcus Scribonius and his new commander turned at the end of the row of orderly goatskin tents that marked the encampment of the Sixth Century, Second Cohort. *Fifth Century,* he corrected himself. *They're the Fifth Century. We're the* Sixth *Century now. With our new centurion, the other centuries have been promoted. We've been demoted.*

But it's not the centurion's fault. It's not his fault he's the least senior centurion in the cohort.

Still, it's a terrible reward for the men.

But . . . it's time to "slip the knife in quickly."

"So," Marcus Scribonius began as they walked between the rows of tents, shields, and cooking fires, "you served in Judea."

Quintus Aquillius replied with a simple, "Yes."

At least he didn't bark at me. Not a bad beginning, I suppose.

"I have been in Britannia for the last several years," Marcus Scribonius said, "with the Fourteenth—"

"Yes, yes, I know!" the centurion snapped. "I know all about you, *Audaxus*!" The venom in his voice made the name sound like a curse. He wheeled upon Marcus Scribonius. Quintus Aquillius's right hand gripped the hilt of his sword, and his left hand, the hilt of his dagger. Murder smoldered in his eyes.

Marcus Scribonius took a step back. He resisted the impulse to reach for his own sword. *Surely, he would not attack me here, in front of witnesses?*

The centurion's angry words had attracted the attention of a small group of men sitting or lounging in front of their tent, repairing armor and sharpening swords. They eyed the tall centurion and the option with more than casual interest. One of the legionnaires rose to his feet, holding a gladius in one hand and a whetstone in the other. The man said nothing and made no aggressive move.

If the centurion attacked me, would this fellow come to my *aid . . . or his?*

In his rage, the centurion seemed oblivious to the presence of the other men. "The Hero of Mona! That's what they call you. Do you know that? Of course, you do. Cursed Jewish traitor!" His hand flexed, then tightened around the hilt of his sword. "But I served in Judea. Yes, I did. I know your kind. Traitor Jew."

Marcus Scribonius forced his eyes away from the hand and the sword. Instead, he focused on the centurion's eyes, menacingly narrowed to angry slits. The advice of his dead mentor came to his mind. *"Don't watch the weapon, lad. If your opponent is going to move, you'll see it first in his eyes."*

Marcus Scribonius calmed his rapid breathing. "I am not a Jew. I am a loyal Roman, just as you are."

"You're one of those troublesome Judean rebels. You and your cursed Christus. You may have the legate fooled. But I know your kind. I fought your kind. You are a traitor to Rome."

"Audaxus!" said a cheerful voice. A small crowd of soldiers had gathered around them. "You are well, my friend?"

Marcus Scribonius dared not take his eyes off Quintus Aquillius, but he thought he recognized the voice. *Marcus Lucilius.* Marcus Scribonius didn't know the man well, but their past encounters had been friendly. *Coming to* my *aid.* "I am well. You came through the battle, then. And your century?"

Centurion Quintus Aquillius's grim countenance hardened, then relaxed. Both his hands slowly released the hilts of his weapons. The tension in the air bled away.

"We lost two men," said Marcus Lucilius. "Not too bad, considering how horrible it was at the end."

Quintus Aquillius looked away.

Marcus Scribonius glanced at his deliverer. *Thank you.* He had little doubt, had the confrontation come to blows, that he, himself, would have emerged the victor, but he had no desire to fight his new centurion.

Marcus Lucilius, as well, seemed to sense that the crisis had passed. "I heard about Gaius Aquillius Regulus. I am sorry for your loss." He paused, then grinned, stepping between Marcus Scribonius and Quintus Aquillius. "So, are you the new commander of the First Century, Centurion?"

The new commander turned a haughty expression to the legionnaire and lifted his patrician chin. "I am the commander of the Sixth Century."

"Ah," said the legionnaire as the full import of the words sunk in. "That means a promotion for us! Welcome, Centurion. It will be good to know that you will guard our backs." His right fist thudded to his chest. "It will be an honor to serve with you."

Quintus Aquillius returned the salute. He nodded his head, but said nothing.

An awkward silence congealed around them.

Quintus Aquillius looked about, seemingly becoming aware of the dozen soldiers encircling them, all of them armed. All of them watching him with false smiles that did not touch their eyes. He extended a hand, indicating the way toward the front of the cohort, toward the encampment of his new century. "Option, lead the way." His voice was calmer than it had been during the confrontation, but it still carried an undercurrent of danger.

Marcus Scribonius saluted, fist to chest. "As you command."

The circle of men parted, and centurion and option strode away, silent as before.

However, voices followed them. "That's him? Audaxus? The Hero of Mona?"

"Yes, that's him. The pride of the Second Cohort. You're too young to know, lad, but if it hadn't been for Marcus Scribonius . . ."

The "Hero of Mona" tightened his lips and gritted his teeth. *Stupid, wretched name.*

♦ ♦ ♦

Centurion Quintus Aquillius Lucanus assumed command of the Sixth Century, Second Cohort, Legion Fourteenth Gemina with a speech. A long and pompous speech.

Option Marcus Scribonius Audaxus stood dutifully at his commander's side as the lanky centurion addressed the assembled men of the century.

The men stood in their ranks, fully and formally armored, dutifully paying attention to the centurion's oration—or at least, making a good show of it. Even Mettius Canius kept his eyes on the centurion. However, "the Ferret"—as he was known—was not entirely successful at masking his disdain for the new commander.

That one will be trouble, thought Marcus Scribonius. *But when has the Ferret not been a pebble in my boot?* Of all the men of the century, Mettius Canius was the only legionnaire Marcus Scribonius did not trust.

Marcus Scribonius would willingly place his life in the hands of any of his men, but not in the hands of the Ferret. *Always scheming. Always weaseling his way to the back of the formation, no matter where I place him.*

However, Marcus Scribonius had never caught the man *in the act.* If he could just once . . . Marcus Scribonius quickly shut down fantasies of putting the man on half rations, overnight banishment outside the protection of the camp, perhaps a public flogging . . .

"I have been entrusted with a secret mission," said Quintus Aquillius.

Every man in the century seemed to perk up at that. Many of them mouthed, "Secret mission?"

Marcus Scribonius suppressed the urge to shake his head in disgust. *"I have been entrusted . . ." Not "We have been entrusted . . ." It's not like we won't all be there, sharing the danger.*

"We will wait for the supply wagons to arrive," continued the centurion. "And assuming they arrive tonight, we leave at first light. We will take six wagons with us, not the usual eleven—five for you and one for myself. We will be traveling overland, and at some point along the way, we may need to abandon the wagons. So, you will need to travel light."

This elicited a few quiet groans from the men.

He said, "You will need to travel light." Not "We." The men are tired of light rations. At least, we'll have some wheat once the wagons arrive. Perhaps some better-quality posca. And hopefully, some actual *wine.*

"So," said the centurion, "you need to be prepared to carry everything on your backs, my Mules of Marius."

You are not winning them over. They know what is expected of them. No need to grind their noses in the dirt.

"And some cattle and sheep," the commander droned on, "it is to be hoped. So, we shall have some meat and milk along the way. Perhaps."

That comment gained him a few grins, but not many.

The very air stinks of rotten meat. I know it will be different when we are away from here, but . . .

And only a fool would think we can keep cattle and sheep together. What? Are we to have a small army of cowherds and shepherds with us?

"Details of the mission will be dispensed as needed. So, do not ask questions. Just follow my orders."

How much longer will this go on? If we have to march tomorrow, we should be preparing, resting.

"There will be no discussing the mission, no speculation, even amongst yourselves."

Marcus Scribonius very nearly rolled his eyes at that one. *Truly? Secrecy is one thing, but you truly expect soldiers to refrain from speculation?*

"And definitely no—"

"Centurion!" A runner, in leather armor and bearing a courier's pouch, trotted up to Quintus Aquillius.

The centurion turned his head toward the runner. Quintus Aquillius did not even attempt to hide his annoyance at having his oration interrupted. "Speak!"

The man thumped his fist to his chest. "You are Centurion Gaius Aquillius Regulus, First Century, Second Cohort, Legion Fourteenth Gemina?"

The centurion's visage darkened into a deep scowl. "No. I am his replacement." He growled as if infuriated at his choice of words. "I am his *successor*," he amended.

The runner nodded his head. "Your pardon, Centurion." He saluted, then turned to go.

"Wait!" cried Quintus Aquillius. "Gaius Aquillius is dead. I am his successor and near kinsman. Whatever you had for him, you may give to me." He extended an open hand, ready to receive.

So he is a near relative to Gaius Aquillius . . .

The runner hesitated, then opened his pouch.

Marcus Scribonius could see two scrolls inside, identical in length.

The man pulled both scrolls from the pouch. Each bore the official seal of the Imperial Senate. The runner examined each.

Marcus Scribonius observed the names of the intended recipients—Gaius Aquillius Regulus, Centurion First Century, Second Cohort, Legion Fourteenth Gemina, and Gaius Suetonius Paulinus, Governor of Britannia.

From the Senate? Probably identical in content. To Gaius Aquillius and the legate. But from the Senate?

The runner placed the scroll addressed to Gaius Aquillius in the centurion's outstretched hand. He closed his pouch, saluted, then trotted off, presumably toward the legate's tent.

Quintus Aquillius glared at the sealed scroll in his hand. He muttered a vile curse under his breath. Without looking at the assembled men of the century, he stalked off toward his tent.

After the centurion had disappeared inside the private quarters that had once belonged to Gaius Aquillius, Marcus Scribonius turned to face the men. "Dismissed."

The century dispersed with many a shrug and a mutter.

That was handled badly.

He looked toward the centurion's tent. *What was in that scroll?*

It's almost as if he already knew. He knew . . . and he didn't like it.

Was Gaius Aquillius to be promoted? Called home to serve in the Senate perhaps?

"I guess it was bad news."

Marcus Scribonius recognized the voice of his friend and cousin before turning his head to Septimus Scribonius. "Perhaps." He shrugged. "Who knows? I certainly do not."

Septimus lifted a corner of his mouth in a half-grin. "Secret mission? Do you know what this is all about?"

Marcus shook his head. "You heard the orders. No questions."

Septimus opened his mouth as if to violate that very order. Again. Then he nodded. "As you, or rather, the centurion commands." He chuckled. "He's . . . an interesting fellow, isn't he?" Then his expression drooped. "Nothing like . . ."

Marcus placed a hand on Septimus's shoulder. "I miss him too." He drew a deep breath. "I need you to help me with this. No questions. And encourage the men to do the same."

Septimus nodded slowly. "Yes. I'll . . . do what I can. We do not need to understand. We have only to live and die at his command." He grinned, even as he shook his head. "For the glory of Rome, yes?"

Marcus sighed. "The glory of Rome."

The men deserve to know.

But I doubt I'd be able to convince the centurion to change his mind.

He took his hand from Septimus's shoulder. He scanned the camp. He could no longer see the tesserarius, the officer of the watch. "Septimus, find Caeso Lucilius. Tell him to have the guards wake the men two hours before sunrise. We must be ready to march—"

"At first light." Septimus sighed. "I'll tell him. Any word of the wagons?"

"They've been sighted by the legion watch. Should be here within the hour."

Septimus's face opened into a wide grin. "I'll tell the men that as well. We could do with some real wine!"

"Take care, my friend. And tell the men to take care as well. We need to be ready—"

"Option!" The voice came from the direction of the centurion's tent. Quintus Aquillius no longer wore his plumed helm, but the tall man stooped in the entrance, holding the tent flap open.

Without a word to his cousin, Marcus Scribonius turned and trotted toward his commander.

When he arrived at the tent, Quintus Aquillius stepped aside, still holding the flap for him. Marcus Scribonius entered. He removed his own helm in deference to the bareheaded commander. Then, helm under his left arm, he saluted. "Yes, Centurion?"

Quintus Aquillius's fury was evident in his livid face. "Did you just violate my express order that there be no questions?"

Marcus Scribonius looked straight ahead, forcing his eyes away from the angry eyes of his commander, focusing on the man's chin instead. "No, Centurion. In fact, I was making arrangements to rouse the men two hours before first light so that we may be ready to march."

The tall man gritted his teeth, but said nothing for a long moment—a moment that felt to Marcus Scribonius like an hour.

Marcus Scribonius kept his gaze carefully focused below the man's eyes. *Why do you despise me? What did I do to you? What am I missing?*

At last, the centurion said, "I suppose you know what was in that scroll?"

Marcus Scribonius blinked. *What? How would I . . .* "No, Centurion. I have not the slightest idea."

Quintus Aquillius eyed him as if looking for any hint of deception. "Very well. Send some men to fetch my belongings from my former unit. Tell them to wait for my personal wagon and escort it here, directly to me. Do you understand, traitor?"

At that, Marcus Scribonius met his commander's eyes. "I understand, Centurion." *But I don't understand. I don't understand why you think I would know what was in that senatorial scroll. I don't understand why you hate me so. Is it because I'm a Christian? Is that it?*

"You don't like it when I call you traitor, do you, Audaxus?"

"I am a loyal citizen of Rome. My faith does not change that."

"Who is your king? Nero or Jesus?"

"My earthly monarch is Nero Claudius Caesar Augustus Germanicus. I serve the emperor faithfully. My record—"

"I know all about your cursed record! You were fortunate. Smiled on by the gods. The very gods you have turned your back on. *Audaxus*! What a pitiful joke. You were about to tell me your heavenly king is this Jewish goetia, no? You cannot serve two masters, Audaxus."

Marcus breathed through his nose, forcing himself to remain calm. "My record speaks for me. The legate has no problem with my religion."

"The legate is—" Quintus Aquillius's mouth worked as if he were chewing on something particularly vile. "The legate is not your direct superior. He does not understand the Judean problem, the Judean threat to the empire. He does not understand . . ." The centurion eyed him for a moment, then turned away. "See that my wagon is delivered to me. See to it personally, Audaxus."

"As you command, Centurion."

"You are dismissed."

Marcus Scribonius put his fist to his chest.

The centurion did not return or acknowledge the salute.

Marcus Scribonius turned and exited the tent.

He searched his memory for a prophecy that might apply to the latest events of the day, but could find nothing.

♦ ♦ ♦

The wagons arrived at dusk. The herds of cattle and sheep arrived shortly thereafter.

As the news of their arrival spread, cheers filled the camp. It took another hour before the wagoners and their cargoes could be directed to the various centuries of the legion.

And within another hour came the smell of cooking fires and roasting meat. The wind had mercifully shifted, allowing a respite from the stench of the battlefield. Soon the sounds of revelry, of men enjoying some actual wine, drowned out the ceaseless caws and croaks of feasting carrion birds.

Marcus Scribonius was not among the men enjoying a well-earned celebration. Aristobulus, the elderly Christian missionary—of the original Seventy sent out by Jesus Himself—who had introduced Christianity to Marcus, taught him that he should never drink to excess. *"Be filled with the Spirit, not with wine," Aristobulus said. "'In wine is truth,' goes the saying, but the only truth is in Christus."*

But a caution against too much wine was not what prevented Marcus Scribonius from rejoicing with his men—he didn't have to drink to excess to share their festive mood. No, that was not the obstacle to his joining in the celebration.

The obstacle was a broken *soleae ferreae*—a horse's shoe. Or in this case, a mule's shoe.

Marcus Scribonius had led a small squad of legionnaires to retrieve the belongings of their new centurion from Quintus Aquillius's old tent among the encampments of the reserves. That being accomplished, Marcus sent the legionnaires back to camp. The centurion's personal wagon, however, had not as yet arrived at the reserve encampment. And the centurion had ordered Marcus to see to the delivery of that wagon personally.

And so, he waited.

He waited as the wagons arrived with their precious cargo. But when the wagons for the reserves rolled into camp, Quintus Aquillius's personal wagon was not among them. After diligent inquiries among the wagoners, Marcus Scribonius discovered the reason for the delay.

"The wretched mule broke its shoe," said a surly wagoner, a Germanian, judging by his heavily accented Latin. He pointed at an iron shoe attached to and encasing the foreleg hoof of his own mule. "A *fabro* is making the fool beast a new one. He should be along shortly."

"Shortly" stretched to yet another hour. By the time the wagon, pulled by the newly reshod mule, lumbered up to the reserve encampment, the sky was black as coal and studded with starry diamonds. Marcus Scribonius hailed the wagoner. Marcus Scribonius wore the longitudinal plume of his office, so the driver would perhaps be more likely to accept his authority.

The wagon slowed, and the wagoner hunched forward as he peered into the torch- and campfire-lit night. He uttered a curse in Celtic, then cried in Latin, "Out of my way! This is the personal wagon of Centurion Quintus Aquillius Lucanus. Out of my cursed way or I'll have the mule tread you down!"

"Yes," replied Marcus Scribonius. "Your master sent me. He has been reassigned—promoted. He now commands a different century. I am his new option. If you would follow me?"

The wagoner uttered another curse in Celtic.

Marcus Scribonius knew a little of the local language, enough to catch something about "Roman goat lovers."

But the man nodded his acceptance. "Lead on then, Option."

Marcus Scribonius turned, showing the way and taking caution to keep to the right of the path. *No need to let the fellow make good on his threat.* And no need to step in the piles of manure that littered the paths between the camps. From time to time, he glanced back to ensure the wagon was following.

As he walked, he searched his memory, as he had done all evening, for a prophecy to fit the arrival of his new commander. In his mind's eye, he unrolled the scroll that he himself had written, seeing the carefully recorded prophecies, seeing them as if the scroll itself were open before him. Gaius Aquillius had once commented on

Marcus Scribonius's ability to accurately recall virtually everything he had ever read or heard—*"Perhaps it is a gift from your god,"* Gaius Aquillius said. However, Marcus Scribonius's gift of memory had been with him from his youth—long before he met Aristobulus. *It could still be a gift from God.*

This gift of prophecy, however, did not start until after my baptism, not till after I received the Holy Ghost.

In his memory, he continued down the scroll. *Trial. Tribulation.*

Tribulation.

In his mind's eye he read,

And lo! Thy tribulation cometh, shrouded in red and riding in a wagon.

No, that can't be it. He's already here. He didn't arrive in a wagon, nor is he shrouded in red.

The ghost of a smile rested on his lips. *Unless you count him being red-faced today.* He sighed.

How about this one?

Thy near kin shall despise thee, though he has seen thee not. For he knoweth thou shalt stand in his room.

That seems promising. Perhaps. The part about "though he has seen thee not." But Quintus Aquillius is not my near kin. Not even close. He's a patrician of House Aquillius. And I'm from a plebian family.

Maybe his mother was a Scribonius?

Could it be? Is he ashamed of his mother's parentage perhaps? Is that why he hates me?

You are grasping at smoke, Marcus.

But the rest of it . . . "thou shalt stand in his room." I could very well inherit command of the century, next year, when I turn thirty. That could fit.

I'll have to ask around, find out if his mother was a plebian, a Scribonius.

Marcus Scribonius raised his hand and halted. "This is the place."

He turned about, and the wagon halted.

The century sat or stood around their ten cooking fires—one for each *contubernium,* each unit of eight men. "Audaxus!" one cried, standing and lifting his wine. Others stood, echoing the greeting.

"Join us!" called Caeso Lucilius, the tesserarius.

"Soon," Marcus Scribonius replied with a smile. "I need a few men to help unload the centurion's wagon. Any volunteers?"

The nearest contubernium rose as one, all eight men setting down wine cups. Other men rose as well, but seeing that enough volunteers had stepped forward, sat down once more.

Marcus Scribonius felt gratified to note that none of them seemed the least bit unsteady on his feet. *Good thus far . . . But the night is young.*

He went to the back of the wagon, reaching it before the men. And stopped, dead still.

In the back of the wagon crouched a cloaked and hooded human figure.

Marcus Scribonius drew his sword.

"Who are you?" he demanded out loud. "Stand and declare yourself!"

The figure stood slowly, silently. It rose to its full height, though the head was bowed.

"Show me your hands!" Marcus Scribonius was suddenly aware of the presence of many men standing beside and behind him. In moments, the entire century stood with daggers drawn. At least a dozen men pushed ahead of him, protecting him with their bodies. The men of the watch, the guards in full armor, had drawn their swords.

The figure, the intruder, lifted hands from within the cloak. Empty, weaponless hands. Small hands at the ends of slender arms.

"Move aside," Marcus Scribonius said to the men in front, the men shielding him.

Obediently, they parted, but they kept their daggers ready.

Marcus Scribonius took one step toward the wagon. "Show me your face!"

The small hands pulled the hood back, revealing a bowed head.

Even in the light of the fires and torches, Marcus Scribonius could discern the color of the long, curly hair that shrouded the face. Red. Like a Celt.

"Show me your face!" he repeated.

The head raised, and the hands parted the red hair.

"A girl!" One man said it, and the murmur spread throughout the century.

"She's mine!" Quintus Aquillius strode forward, into the light. He was unarmored, but he carried his sword in his hand. "Keep your cursed hands off my slave!"

The men of the century backed away from the wagon.

From between the parted veil of red curls, a pair of eyes stared at Marcus Scribonius. Green eyes—soft and haunted.

My tribulation has come.

Chapter IV

"Beware of pity, for in pity lies thy peril."
from the Book of Marcus Scribonius

He has a woman? Here?" Caeso Lucilius, the tesserarius or officer of the watch, stared at the commander's tent—the tent into which the centurion had taken the slave with the red curls and the haunting, emerald eyes. "How can he have a whore *in* the camp? It's against regulations."

Similar murmurs and questions rolled like waves in a pond, throughout the gathered men.

Marcus Scribonius stared at the tent as well. "Quiet, all of you! He'll hear you."

"But a whore!" Agrippa Corfidius, the vexillarius or standard bearer, shook his head. "The legate would not allow it."

"Who says he knows?" asked Nonus Sestius. "You all saw. She was hooded and cloaked. And besides, a centurion is allowed a body slave."

"She's no body slave." Mettius Canius licked his lips. "She's a whore." The hunger in the Ferret's voice was unmistakable.

Marcus Scribonius shook his head. "Not a whore. A whore gets paid for what she does. A whore can come and go as she likes."

Quintus Aquillius was part of the Twentieth Legion. Perhaps the legate does not know.

Septimus Scribonius spat loudly. "He's a cursed patrician. They can get away with anything. At least Gaius Aquillius never used his family status to do something like—"

A scream cut him off.

Then the voice of their new commander, barely muffled by the tent, followed. "I saw you! Making eyes at him."

Another scream followed.

"You want him?" the centurion cried, seemingly unconcerned that the entire century could hear. "Well, you're wasting your insignificant charms on that one. He's a cursed Christian. He won't touch you. Oh, no, he will not. But the rest of them? You know what will happen should you fail to please me."

"Please! No! I didn't!" The voice was high-pitched, and the Latin bore the accent of Cambria. "I didn't!" Another scream.

That time, Marcus Scribonius heard the slap. And the one that followed.

Our Father who art in heaven. Please make him stop. I can do nothing. Nothing. Please make him stop.

At last, there was silence from the tent.

There was silence as well from the gathered men.

After a moment, however, the Ferret muttered, "No more than the whore deserves."

Marcus Scribonius fought down an almost irresistible impulse to strike the man. "Mettius Canius, you never seem to know when to keep your mouth shut." He glared at the Ferret. *I have not forgotten your lack of discipline in the battle.* "Your mouth may cost you dearly someday."

Mettius Canius met his glare. His mouth twitched. Then he lowered his eyes. "Your pardon, Option." He turned and slunk off, pushing his way through the rest of the men.

Marcus Scribonius noted that none of them took any pains to allow him passage.

The celebratory mood had dampened like a fire smothered with a wet blanket. Without a word, the men unloaded the contents of the wagon, setting the goods outside the centurion's tent.

Marcus dismissed the wagoner to return to his assigned century in the reserves—Marcus's century had their own wagons and drivers. He turned to the men and said as gently as he could, "We have an early start tomorrow. Best to make some preparations tonight and rest." It was no order, merely a friendly suggestion

The men began to disperse. They retrieved their wine cups. Some of them, the lucky ones who hadn't spilled their wine when the commotion started, drained their cups.

Marcus Scribonius stood watching the centurion's tent, listening for further sounds of abuse. He heard none.

So, she is to be my tribulation? How? She is his slave. I can do nothing for her. Is she to tempt me? Is that it?

Marcus thought of those haunted, emerald eyes. Of the wild, red hair.

And he shook his head.

She looks like one of the Witches of Mona. A shudder of revulsion ran through him.

The legion had crossed the water on hastily constructed flat-bottom boats. They formed in their ranks, and before them stood the horde of the Celts. The Druid priests raised their hands to the heavens and called down curses on the Romans.

The legion had seen this before. They did not fear the Celtic gods or their priests. The Romans prepared to advance.

But then came the witches.

Like the Furies, the witches were dressed all in black, their red hair wild and disheveled, sticking out in all directions. They stood in front of the Celt horde, brandishing torches. And they howled and shrieked like demons.

And the Romans, to a man, were paralyzed with crippling terror.

Their legs trembled as if the earth itself were quaking beneath them. They lowered their shields. The sea was behind them. And shrieking demons before them.

They were trapped.

Marcus Scribonius – not yet an option, merely a legionnaire – trembled along with the rest.

Our Father . . . Save me. Protect me. In Jesus's name!

Celtic spears and stones thundered upon them.

Hundreds of men fell, their screams of mortal agony mingling with the shrieks of the witches. The centuries and cohorts disintegrated into a terrified rabble, legionnaires scattering in all directions, many casting down their weapons and fleeing toward the boats.

Marcus Scribonius, trembling with fear, brought his shield up in time to deflect a shower of stones. In his terror, words he had recorded several days before came to him.

Fear not the witches, for they have no power. Fear them not, for thou shalt deliver thy legion.

They have no power! *But that denial did not strengthen his knees nor dampen his fear.*

Fear them not . . .

"They are just women!" he whispered, though he did not believe his own words. "They are not witches. They cannot be witches." Then he shouted, "They are not witches! They are simply women! Fight them!"

He glanced in the direction of his centurion, Gaius Aquillius. And the breath in his lungs congealed as he saw a trio of Celts bearing down on his beloved commander.

Marcus broke ranks and charged the attackers. "They are just women!

Fight them!" He threw his remaining pilum—he had dropped the other spear when the witches appeared. The pilum felled one attacker. Marcus placed himself between the two remaining Celts and his centurion. "Fight them!" he cried. "They are not witches! Fight!"

He parried with his shield and thrust with his sword. One Celt went down.

But the other was upon him, slashing with a falcata, an inwardly curved sword of the Celts.

Marcus twisted, trying to bring his shield to bear. But the Celt hammered the shield with a blow that ripped it out of Marcus's hand. Off-balance, Marcus raised his sword to ward off the next blow.

The heavy falcata broke off Marcus's sword, a hand's breadth from the hilt.

Marcus drew his dagger as the Celt raised his sword for a killing slash. Marcus sidestepped, thrust with the leaf-bladed dagger, and drove it into the man's gut and up through the diaphragm.

The Celt wheezed, unable to scream.

Marcus withdrew his dagger and stabbed his foe once more.

The Celt fell to the ground.

Marcus bent and retrieved his own shield and the Celtic sword.

"They are just women and fanatics! They have no magic. Fight them!"

Others took up the cry. "Fight them! Fight them!"

Gaius Aquillius himself, suddenly finding his courage, bellowed, "Form up!"

Romans picked up discarded weapons and shields, and the legion assembled into their ranks once more.

And the tide of battle turned.

Official accounts of the assault on Mona told that Legate Gaius Suetonius Paulinus had given a speech to rally his troops. However, every man who was there knew the truth.

It was the courage of a lone legionnaire that rallied the legion, that turned a rout into victory. For that act, Marcus Scribonius had been promoted to option. For that act, Centurion Gaius Aquillius Regulus had bestowed upon him the cognomen "Audaxus"—the Valiant.

Option Marcus Scribonius Audaxus was hailed as the "Hero of Mona." He was lauded as fearless.

But what no one would believe, what no one could accept, despite his many denials, was that Marcus had been as terrified as the rest. Even when he fought to save his beloved commander, he was trembling with fear, barely able to make his quivering muscles obey him.

Marcus did not feel like a hero.

He felt only shame that he, in spite of his declared faith in Jesus Christus, had shaken in fear and doubt before the Witches of Mona.

Our Father who art in heaven, hallowed be Thy name. In Jesus's name, forgive me my doubts. Strengthen my faith. And whatever trial this slave-girl will be to me, help me to face it without fear, without doubt. Or rather, help me to face it in spite *of my fears and my doubts. Lead me away from temptation.*

He paused. *Temptation? To lust after such a creature? Surely not.*

He shuddered at the thought.

What then? How shall she try me?

"You should take your own advice, my friend." Caeso Lucilius stood beside him. As tesserarius, officer of the watch, Caeso Lucilius carried the wax tablet of his office. On the wax of the tablet would be inscribed the challenge-phrase and password-of-the-day, and the schedule of those who would stand guard in shifts throughout the night. "Pack up and get some sleep."

Marcus Scribonius nodded. "You should do the same."

The tesserarius chuckled. "As soon as I have finished assigning the guards." He paused. "Mettius Canius is on the list. He has the last watch."

Marcus Scribonius scowled. "Who is with him?"

"Marcus Vivanius. I've told him to keep half an eye on the Ferret."

Marcus Scribonius nodded his approval. "Good choice." He sighed. "Good night." He removed his helm and began loosening the leather thongs on the front of his armor as he headed toward the tent of the junior officers.

Inside the tent, he found Agrippa Corfidius, the vexillarius or standard bearer, and Spurius Orcivius, the cornicen, already filling their field packs and preparing to turn in for the night. Upon seeing Marcus, the vexillarius gave him a wry grin. "Our new centurion—he's a pompous one."

The cornicen shook his head and chuckled. "Pompous. And a fool. Like as not, he'll get us all killed on this secret mission of his."

Agrippa held up a hand. "I'm not asking, of course, about the mission . . . but I can assume *you* know all about it?"

Marcus nodded. "And that's all I'm going to say."

Agrippa grinned at him. "I'll be content with that. And with the knowledge that when the time comes, you'll know what to do to bring us all back alive."

The plumed helmet in Marcus's hands felt suddenly very heavy.

He removed the rest of his armor and arranged it next to his bedroll, laying the armor so that it was ready to be donned quickly in the morning. He stuffed his meager belongings into his field pack, including the Celtic falcata he'd taken at Mona.

As his fingers brushed the long and narrow wooden box inside his pack, a tingling started in his brain and rushed down his spine.

Unbidden, words formed in his mind.

He pulled the box from his pack, opened it, and retrieved the scroll inside. He rapidly pulled out his small, portable writing desk. He took a quill and sharpened it with his dagger. He unstopped the ink bottle, dipped his quill, and began to write at the bottom of the scroll.

The life of the slave shall be in thine hand. Beware of pity, for in pity lies thy peril. Above all, thou must preserve and deliver the slave.

Marcus stared at the drying ink. *Beware of pity?*

But he did pity the girl. *In pity lies my peril? She's enslaved to that dog. How can I not pity such a creature?*

He stoppered the ink bottle, then scattered sand to dry the fresh prophecy. He blew away the sand and rolled up the scroll.

"Another one?"

Marcus Scribonius looked up to see Caeso Lucilius standing just inside the tent entrance.

Marcus Scribonius shrugged as he put the book back into its protective box. "Yes."

"Anything to help us?" asked the tesserarius as he knelt on his own bedroll. "Anything we should know?"

What should I tell them? He wasn't shy about sharing the prophecies, but he was never certain what they meant or how they were to be used. "I think I need your help. All three of you."

As one, the others assented. They knew him, and their trust in him was firm.

"What do you need?" asked Spurious.

"I must protect the girl," Marcus said.

Agrippa's eyes widened in surprise. "The slave?"

Marcus nodded slowly. "Yes."

"Protect her?" Caeso asked. "From what? From whom? Her master?"

"I"—Marcus shrugged, growling in exasperation—"do not know." *I never know! How am I supposed to heed Thy commands, Father, if I cannot understand them?*

Caeso shifted uneasily from foot to foot. "You cannot protect her from her master. She is his property. He can do with her as he wills." He lowered his voice to a barely discernable murmur. "Even if she shouldn't actually be in the wretched camp."

"Let us assume," said Agrippa, absently stroking the head of the bear pelt—the symbol of his office, lying next to his bedroll—as if he were stroking a pet dog, "at least for now, that we are not required to protect her from the centurion."

Marcus noted that the vexillarius—the standard-bearer—had said "we," rather than "you." Warm affection for his faithful brother-in-arms spread through him. *He does not believe in the same God, but he believes in* me.

"But from what, then?" asked Spurius. "Wolves? Bears?"

"The men?" Caeso glanced meaningfully at the entrance of the tent and the men encamped beyond. "I mean, she is a woman, even if she does look like a demon witch. And some of the men are . . ." A grin lifted one corner of his mouth. "By Mithras, we all are." He chuckled, then looked at Marcus with tilted head and lowered brows. "Maybe, not *all* of us."

"But," said Spurius, "it would go badly with any man who touched her. I doubt our new commander would tolerate it. By Mithras, it's as much a protection for the *men* as for her."

"Agreed." Agrippa appeared to realize with a start that he was petting the bear skin. He lifted his hand from the fur, placing the hand instead on his dagger. "And . . . wherever we are going on this cursed *secret mission*"—he gave Marcus a sidelong glance—"and no, I'm not asking . . . it's going to be deep in enemy territory. We're going to need every man we've got."

For a long moment, silence reigned in the tent. They glanced from one to another. And Marcus Scribonius was certain they were sharing the same thought.

Every man – including the Ferret.

Caeso tapped the wax tablet in his hand. "Very well, then. I'll spread the word among the watch tonight—no man is to touch the slave. They are to guard her at all hazards."

Marcus smiled and nodded. "Thank you, my brothers. I . . . Your loyalty . . . humbles me"

Caeso grinned. "You are blessed by the gods. Or at least, by *your* god." He pointed with his tablet at Marcus's scroll box. "You keep on recording those divine scribblings of yours. You and they have saved us all."

Caeso lowered his gaze.

Silence filled the tent like a smothering fog.

And once again, Marcus was certain they were all thinking the same thing.

All . . . except for Gaius Aquillius Regulus.

♦ ♦ ♦

Marcus Scribonius could not sleep, but that was not unusual. Around him, the other three officers—vexillarius, cornicen, and tesserarius—snored in three distinct pitches and rhythms, reminding Marcus of a trio of croaking frogs. He had seen a performance of *The Frogs* by Aristophanes, done in the original Greek. The chorus of the eponymous amphibians had greatly amused him, as much as they had annoyed the Dionysus character in the play. "Brekekekèx-koàx-koáx," Marcus whispered, recalling the croaking chant. He could recite the entire play, of course, not just the chorus. His eerily accurate memory of all things he'd ever read or heard had served him well.

But when the time came for sleep, his mind often buzzed—or croaked—with words he could not suppress. And that night, he could not quiet his thoughts.

He lay upon his bedroll, staring at the candle guttering in the solitary lantern, suspended from the rope running along the apex of the tent roof. Soon the candle would be out.

I should change it.

"Brekekekèx-koàx-koáx." With a bone-weary sigh, Marcus arose from his bed.

By the time he replaced the dying candle with a fresh one, he discovered, to his further annoyance, that he needed to visit the latrine.

He knelt on his bedroll and buckled on his belt—a legionnaire never appeared in public without his belt. The belt made the difference between wearing a man's tunic and a woman's dress. He straightened the five leather strips hanging in front. He ran his finger down the center strip, feeling the brass letters there. "Christus." He touched the brass image at the top of the leftmost strip, lovingly tracing the lines of a tiny female face. "Mother." He did not bother to touch the image at the top of the rightmost strip, feeling no urgent need to affirm his loyalty to the emperor.

He laced up his boots with their hobnailed, hard-leather soles and their open sides. He knew better than to venture out with his feet unprotected. He had no desire to march dozens of miles in the morning on a foot lamed by a stone or thorn.

Then he stood, straightened his dagger, and trod as silently as a cat toward the tent door.

Once outside, he spotted the two guards on duty standing on either side of the century's camp. He approached the nearer, fully armored soldier.

The man drew his sword and uttered the challenge, "Rocks and mountains."

Marcus raised a hand and responded with the password-of-the-day, "Willow."

The guard nodded, sheathing his sword.

In the darkness, Marcus couldn't recognize the man. The light was insufficient to show the man's distinctive belt with its five adorned strips, and his face was hidden within the shadows of his helm. But the challenge had been given and the proper password accepted.

And so, the guard resumed his slow patrol of the camp, taking no further notice of Marcus.

Marcus slogged away toward the ditch that comprised the latrine.

He thought briefly of Gwynn, the century's tanner, then dismissed the thought. *This is one pot of piss Gwynn can do without.* Besides, he didn't want to wake the man.

Clouds obscured the moon and stars. The only lights were occasional muted candles burning inside some tents.

The air was still and heavy with the scent of wood smoke, unwashed bodies, the droppings of grass-fed beasts, and the acidic stench of latrines. Mercifully, the reek of the distant battlefield did not carry to the camp.

The carrion birds had quieted for the night, but Marcus could hear the lowing and bleating of cattle and sheep. A mule snorted nearby.

Otherwise, the camp was quiet.

"Brekekekèx-koàx-koáx," Marcus croaked softly.

Nothing answered—not even a frog.

After he had completed his visit to the latrine trench, he turned back to camp.

Father in heaven, hallowed be Thy name.

I know that I am not always grateful . . . that I do not express the proper gratitude unto Thee for the gift of prophecy. Open my mind, Father. Show me Thy will. I will perform it. I will perform the task set before me.

I thank Thee, Father, for loyal comrades. I thank Thee that they trust in me.

No. That is wrong.

Forgive me my arrogance.

They trust in Thy *word.*

But he knew that wasn't exactly true.

A mule brayed.

Marcus was fully alert as he turned his eyes toward the sound.

He couldn't see the beast, but he heard it, as iron-shod hooves tramped the earth. The mule snorted again. And to Marcus's ears, the animal sounded agitated.

He attempted to pierce the darkness, gazing intently in the direction of the sound.

There!

The mule, a black silhouette in the blackness, pulled at its tether.

And there was another dark shape—low and crouching.

Marcus drew his leaf-bladed dagger. "Rocks and mountains."

The shape froze. And did not answer.

He tried the challenge-of-the-day once more, louder that time. "Rocks and mountains."

Silence.

Marcus started toward the intruder, his tread slow and cautious, his senses—sight, hearing, and smell—heightened by fear. In the darkness, he could not judge the distance to his target—a dozen paces or perhaps twice that. *Should I raise the alarm? Could be a wolf. Or a dog.*

Or a Celt.

"I can see you." However, he was no longer certain that he could discern one shadow from another. He thought he could still see the mule, so he kept moving in that direction. "Stand and identify yourself."

The only response was a snort from the agitated mule.

"Stand and identify yourself."

A black shape arose in front of the mule's silhouette—a head and shoulders.

"Identify yourself."

"I d-do not know the password." A high, female voice, speaking Latin, but with a Cambrian accent.

The girl.

"Please," she said. "I needed . . . the latrine."

"Show me your hands." Marcus was near enough—he hoped—to see any weapon.

The slave raised her hands. "I have nothing. Please. D-Do not k-kill me. I meant no harm."

As Marcus closed the distance, he began to see her more clearly—not enough to make out the details of her face, but he could see she wore a hood and cloak. And her hands were empty. "Lower your hood."

She complied. The outline of her wild, curly hair could be seen.

But her face was still darkness. He could not see her eyes, could not discern her intent.

"He—He does not give me the password. He never gives me the password. A-and I cannot read the tablet. I cannot . . . read."

Marcus kept the dagger ready and took one more cautious step. He was within a couple of paces. Finally, he could make out some details of her face. He could see her eyes, wide and shining in the darkness. He caught the glimmer of wetness on her cheeks.

"I'm sorry!" Her voice was low, but carried the intensity of fear. "I needed to use the latrine!" She was trembling. "That's all. I wasn't running away. I wasn't!"

Her obvious terror relieved Marcus's own fear. "Have you . . . are you finished?"

Her shoulders sagged as if with relief. She nodded. "Yes. I was on my way back."

He extended his left hand, but he kept the dagger in his right. "Give me your hand. I'll escort you back to camp." *Back to your master.*

She hesitated, then placed her hand in his.

Her hand was small. Soft.

Soft hands? Not accustomed to manual labor. Was she a noble of some kind before . . .

. . . before her capture?

He turned, and they walked toward camp. He glanced at her, taking in her height. *At least a head shorter than I am.* "How old are you?"

"T-twenty winters." Her hand trembled in his.

"What's your name?"

"Maelona."

"That's . . ." *Odd.* ". . . a pretty name. It's Celtic? Cambrian?"

She nodded.

"I'm Marcus Scribonius."

She said nothing.

"I'm named after the Roman god of war. Marcus."

No response.

"Maelona. Does it have a meaning?"

She hesitated. "It means . . . It means . . . Princess." Her tone conveyed bitterness. And soul-deep humiliation.

"I see." *Soft hand. Soft and warm.* "Are you? Are you a princess?"

"I am a slave."

"I meant before . . ."

A tremor ran through her. "There is no before. Before is dead." Her voice dropped to a bitter whisper. "They are all dead."

They? "Who? Your family?"

"My entire clan. All my people."

Her entire clan? Perhaps she speaks the truth. Perhaps she has no place to run to.

Marcus knew all too well that the clans of Cambria warred among themselves—or they had before the Romans came and brought civilization. If the girl's whole clan had been destroyed—most likely by the Roman army—then no rival clan would take her in. She would be killed or kept as a slave.

"I'm sorry," he said at last. "Was it us? Did we kill your family?"

She shrugged, but gave no other answer.

They walked in silence, her small, soft hand warm in his, clinging tightly.

"See?" From behind them. "I told you." The voice was slow and heavy with drink. "A woman . . . in the camp!"

Marcus pivoted toward the voice and pulled the girl behind himself, his dagger held low and ready.

Four of them—unarmored, but with their daggers drawn and glinting in the dim light.

One of them laughed—a low, wicked sound. "Come here, whore. Let us sample your wares. See if you're worth the denarii."

Marcus whispered, "Can you make it back to camp?"

"No! I-I think I'm lost!" She pressed against his back, trembling like a newborn colt on shaky legs.

Marcus's own legs threatened to give way. "Rocks and mountains!"

"Willow," came the reply.

"Come on, lad," one them said in a voice that sounded slightly more sober. And vaguely familiar. "Share the cursed whore."

"Stay back," Marcus said. "I'll raise the alarm."

A low chuckle. "No, you won't! You've got a woman in camp. They'll take her, cut her throat, and you'll be flogged." Another low, evil chuckle. "Or worse."

Marcus knew they were correct, of course. His threat of raising the alarm had been an empty ruse. He could not protect the girl that way.

But four of them? Even if they're all the worse for drink, I cannot defeat so many.

Not while protecting the girl.

Our Father who art in heaven . . .

The four dark shapes moved toward him, daggers flashing in the night like lethal, silver leaves.

Marcus pulled his right arm back, ready to thrust his dagger into the belly of the first man to come within range.

One of his attackers cursed, pausing. "Stop!"

The others hesitated.

The first man pointed at Marcus's groin, at his belt. "Audaxus!" he hissed.

The other three muttered oaths, naming various gods. "Audaxus!"

"Run!" They turned and ran or staggered away, scattering into the night.

Marcus stood, trembling and breathing heavily. *Father, I thank thee.*

He felt two thin arms encircle his waist, a body pressed against his back. She trembled and clung to him like a frightened child. "Are they gone?"

Marcus swallowed, not trusting himself to speak, not wanting to betray his fear.

The girl whispered something into his back, her face pressed against this tunic, but he could not catch the words.

"Wh-what did you say?"

Still clinging to him, she repeated, "Why did they run?"

He laughed then. Softly. "They recognized me." He gently pulled at her trembling hands, loosening her grip.

"In the dark? How could they? Did you recognize them?"

Perhaps. One. I cannot be certain. "One of them . . . He saw my belt." He took her hand and pulled her to his side. He pointed with his dagger at the center strip. *Idiot. She cannot read.* "On the center strip." They began to walk back toward the camp once more. "It is customary to put emblems on these strips. Brass emblems or letters. My mother's face. The emperor's face. The name of my God."

She looked up at him with soft eyes, made softer by the darkness. "Your god? The god of war? Marcus?"

He shook his head, turning his attention back to their path, looking around, scanning for other foes in the darkness. Anywhere . . . but at her eyes. "No. Marcus is a form of Mars. And he is not my God. I worship the one true God. And His Son's name is on my belt."

We were saved by the name of Christus. Perhaps, it was a miracle?

I have never seen a miracle. Does this qualify?

"Do all you Romans worship this god?"

"No. I am alone in the legion. Perhaps, alone in the entire army in Britannia. They saw the name of the Son of God, and they knew me."

"And they fled?"

"Yes."

She kept silent for a long moment. "Your god must be truly terrifying."

Marcus chuckled at that. "That is not how I think of Him."

She leaned her head on his arm, her curls pressed against his sweat-cooling flesh. "He said I could trust you."

Marcus stopped, looking down at her—ignoring the gooseflesh on his arm. "Who? My God? Christus?"

She sighed, lifting her head off his arm. "No. My master. He said, of all the men in the army, you were the only one who would not . . . touch me."

The centurion? Quintus Aquillius? "I doubt he meant it . . . as a compliment."

She laughed softly. "No, he did not."

"Rocks and mountains!" A guard of the watch had appeared before them.

"Willow." Marcus hailed him. He could see the man's belt and recognized the emblems of . . . "Nonus Sestius."

"Option?" Nonus Sestius pointed at the girl. "You are . . . abroad?"

Marcus Scribonius shook his head. "It's not what you think. The girl needed to visit the latrine. I'm just making certain she returns safely."

Nonus Sestius nodded. "Yes, Option."

Marcus released Maelona's hand, sheathed his dagger, and pointed in the direction of the centurion's tent. "I will see to it that the tesserarius informs you of the challenge and password every day."

Maelona nodded mutely, then hurried off to her master's tent.

Marcus watched her go.

"Scrawny thing, that one," said the guard. "Certainly, too thin by far to be beautiful. And that hair! Like those cursed Witches of Mona! Was she one of them, do you think?"

Marcus shrugged, staring at the tent as the girl disappeared inside. "I don't know. Possibly."

"Still . . . a man could get used to it, I suppose, if he were lonely enough."

Marcus turned his attention to Nonus Sestius. A shudder ran through Marcus. *A Mona witch?* "I pray I never get that lonely."

The guard chuckled. "By Venus, no!"

"Spread the word. No one is to touch her."

Nonus Sestius saluted. "As you command, Option."

"She got past you tonight. See that you are more observant in the future."

Nonus Sestius stiffened, then saluted again. "Yes, Option. It will not happen again."

Marcus returned the salute. "I trust that it will not."

The guard relaxed. His gaze went back to the centurion's tent. "Imagine being tempted to lie with one of those demons . . ."

Marcus shuddered.

♦ ♦ ♦

But later, as Marcus Scribonius lay upon his bedroll, sleep finally claiming him, his last conscious thoughts were of a pair of eyes like emeralds. Soft and haunted. And of a lithe body pressed against his back—of soft, tender arms encircling his waist—of a small hand in his, with skin too soft to be familiar with manual labor.

The soft skin of a princess.

He shivered as he recalled the feel of her curls against his arm.

Maelona.

And then he dreamed.

She stood before him, clad all in black. A breeze whipped her red hair, so that it swirled about her head like flames. And in each hand, she held a blazing torch, the fire unaffected by the wind. On her shoulder perched an enormous raven.

Maelona opened her mouth and howled the words of prophecy.

And lo! Thy tribulation cometh!

Then the breeze ceased, and the firebrands vanished. Maelona's black robe transformed into a cloak, the hood casting her face in darkness. However, her eyes shone like blazing emeralds from the shadows.

The raven spread its mighty wings, flapping them once. The wings curled down, the tips resting on Maelona's shoulders. Black feathers became hands, the bird's body stretched, becoming a man in the full armor of a centurion—Quintus Aquillius Lucanus. The centurion stood behind his slave, his hands resting possessively on her shoulders. His fingers curled around the base of her neck. The message was clear. He alone had the power of life and death over the girl.

Maelona's eyes fixed upon Marcus. Tears glinted at the corners.

A massive snowy owl fluttered down from the cloudy sky. It perched on Quintus Aquillius's shoulder. Blood dripped from its cruel beak, staining the white feathers.

The owl spread its wings, opened its beak, and spoke—not with a screech or a hoot, but with the honeyed voice of a woman—*Beware of pity, for in pity lies thy peril.*

Marcus awoke with a start, the images of the dream still clear in his mind.

A princess. In the hands of that dog.

Beware of pity? How can I not pity such a wretched, defenseless creature?

Chapter V

"Thine adversary layeth a snare for thee. He diggeth for thee a comely pit."

from the Book of Marcus Scribonius

To all appearances, the Ferret could've been marching in full gear for at least twenty miles under a blazing Roman sun. And yet, the century had barely covered two miles under a gray overcast, cooled by a light, refreshing breeze. Even worse, Mettius Canius had somehow worked his way to the back of the column.

Again.

Marcus Scribonius, marching in his customary place behind the column, sped up. He extended his *hastile*, the six-foot staff of his office as option, and thumped the Ferret in the shoulder.

Mettius Canius grunted with shock. And perhaps a little pain.

I didn't hit him that hard. Not as hard as he deserves, at least. "Get back in position."

Mettius Canius murmured a curse.

"Now!"

The Ferret nodded. "Yes, Option."

Without slowing, but with many a grumble, the men in front of him parted slightly, allowing Mettius Canius to push forward, back into his assigned place in the middle of the third contubernium.

The century marched five men abreast—five contubernia of eight men each, followed by five more contubernia—eighty men in total. The centurion rode a magnificent black horse at the head of the column. The other three junior officers marched at the front of the century. Vexillarius Agrippa Corfidius, wearing the lion pelt and head of his office, proudly carried the standard of the legion. To the standard-bearer's left, Cornicen Spurius Orcivius wore the bear pelt and head of his office and bore his circular cornu, the signal horn of battle. And to his left marched Tesserarius Caeso Lucilius, the officer of the watch, wearing his official wolf pelt and head. Caeso's wax tablet, inscribed with the challenge and password-of-the-day, as well as the duty roster, dangled from his belt, attached to a leather thong.

Before their departure that morning, Caeso promised to personally inform the slave-girl of the challenge and password. "I will see to it," he said to Marcus Scribonius.

"Did Faustus Vivanius have anything to report?" Marcus Scribonius asked.

"About the Ferret?"

Marcus nodded.

Caeso Lucilius leaned in and whispered in Marcus's ear. "He said that Mettius Canius reported for duty on time. But the man was obviously the worse for drink."

Marcus nodded. "Let's keep this to ourselves. I may need to use it sometime."

Caeso grinned, resembling the wolf's head above his helm. "Sometime, yes. That man is a danger to us all. He deserves . . . whatever he gets."

"Yes, but it's always little *things. Not enough . . . He's just sneaky enough to avoid . . . what he deserves."*

"And Nonus Sestius confirmed that the Ferret was out of camp the same time you were escorting the slave-girl back to camp."

Marcus nodded again. Then it could have been him. I thought one of them sounded familiar. Still, it is not proof Mettius Canius was there. If I were allowed to wager, I'd bet ten denarii . . . *But Marcus was neither a gambler nor would he punish a man without being absolutely certain of the man's guilt. "I suspected as much. Thank you."*

Caeso Lucilius laid a hand on his friend's shoulder. "I've spread word through the men. No one is to touch her. Well, our noble centurion has already ordered as much, but I added that each man is to protect her with his life."

Marcus eyed his friend with concern. "Did you give a reason?"

The tesserarius shook his head. "Do not worry. I didn't mention your prophecy. But the fact that she belongs to the centurion should be all the reason they need."

Marcus nodded again. "Once more, my friend, my thanks."

"But" added Caeso, "I don't trust the cursed Ferret with . . . anything. Not even to dig a proper latrine. Or to fill it."

Marcus chuckled at the joke.

Marcus Scribonius dropped back to his normal position at the rear, where he could ensure the men marched in line. *If I could only catch the*

Ferret in the act . . .

He wheeled and marched backward for a few steps, trusting in the smoothness of the Roman road. Another part of his responsibility as option was to keep an eye on the baggage train.

The six support wagons followed the column in a line. And behind them marched the remaining noncombatant support personnel—one fabro, who doubled as engineer and blacksmith, one *capsarium,* who would dress their wounds in the absence of a physician, and two *calones,* or soldiers' slaves. Of the two calones, one performed the duties of tentmaker, tanner, and butcher, and one led the three cattle allotted for the mission—two milk-producing cows and one ox to be butchered as needed. With the six wagoners, they amounted to ten men—one nonfighter to each contubernium.

Each legionnaire marched in full armor, with a cooking pot dangling from his neck and clanking against his segmented breastplate, his shield strapped to his back, and his two spears—the ingenious square pila—over his shoulder. None of them, as yet, were forced to carry their portion of the heavy leather tents and tent poles. For the time being, the tents rode in the wagons and would continue to ride there, unless the century was forced to leave the road and travel overland, abandoning the baggage train.

Marcus and the other junior officers carried their packs and gear on a *furca,* a pole carried across the shoulder, but their spears rode in the second wagon, along with their extra rations of bacon, wheat, olive oil, salt, and posca. The other four wagons contained additional rations and the tools of the support personnel.

Only Centurion Quintus Aquillius, astride his horse, carried no pack, gear, or supplies. He wore his armor, of course, with his sword hanging against his right hip from a baldric. Most legionnaires wore the sword at the left, but the centurion and the option wore their swords on the right hip as a mark of rank.

All the centurion's possessions rode in the first wagon—including Maelona. When the century marched away from the legion's camp, she rode in the wagon, hooded and cloaked, and curled up under a blanket. To all appearances, the slave-girl was nothing more than another bundle among so many others—the commander's chair, his table, his bedding, his tent, his rations—certainly not a *woman* somehow smuggled, against regulations, into an army camp. Once safely out of sight of the legion, she sat up openly at the back of the wagon.

Her hood was pulled back, and she sat facing backward, toward the trailing wagons and the cattle. Marcus could not see her face, but he could see her red hair, blown and bounced about by the breeze and the jolting of the wagon.

Marcus turned around, facing forward once more. However, his thoughts still dwelt on the girl with the disturbing red hair.

How did he get her into the camp? Surely, others must be aware of her presence, even if she took steps to hide herself.

Is it simply the fact that the centurion is a patrician, the highborn son of powerful family? Is he abusing his family name to take liberties? Is that it?

The legate obviously despises him, said he was "overpromoted."

And the horse! He should be marching along with the rest of us. How did he contrive that?

Gaius Aquillius had been the head *of the same family—head of House Aquillius. And I never saw him exercise such noble privilege.*

He was a true soldier's commander.

Marcus swallowed the lump that suddenly formed in his throat. *I miss you, my mentor.*

The cornicen blew his horn, giving the signal for a halt.

The century stopped almost immediately. The wagons took a bit longer to slow and halt. The four support personnel at the rear walked a bit farther, till they were safely in the company of the soldiers. Although no danger presented itself at that moment, none of them relished the idea of a Celtic arrow striking from behind a tree or a rock.

Then came the cornu signal to take their ease. The men set their gear down, lowered their packs to the ground, and sat. Wineskins were unstopped, and men drank their posca with the gusto born of carrying eighty pounds of gear on their backs. Then began the low murmur of comradely conversation.

Marcus Scribonius set his gear—except for his hastile—on the ground, but he did not sit. He took a few greedy gulps from his own wineskin, then walked up the line of sitting men. He halted when he found the Ferret.

Mettius Canius lay sprawled on the road, panting like a dog on the verge of death. His eyes were closed as he gasped, sucking in air. He had not even bothered to shed his helmet. The armpits of his red *tunica*, clearly visible, were soaked with sweat.

It has been a hard march, but not that hard—not for a legionnaire.

Marcus stepped between the men as they sat, talked, and rested. He extended his hastile and thumped it on the Ferret's segmented breastplate.

Mettius Canius jerked, uttered a particularly vile oath, and opened his eyes. The Ferret's eyes snapped open wide. He stared at Marcus in shock. Then those eyes narrowed to angry slits.

"Mettius Canius," Marcus said softly, "I need a word with you."

Still flat on his back, Mettius Canius grunted. He closed his eyes. "Go on then. Nobody's stopping you."

"Alone," Marcus said, his voice still soft, but pregnant with menace. "Now."

The Ferret muttered something unintelligible, but the tone was enough to convey blasphemous and malignant intent. He rolled onto his side, his armor grinding against the road. He got to his knees, then heaved himself to his feet.

Marcus motioned toward the open grass to the west of the road.

Mettius slogged his way in that direction, heedless of the men in his way.

Several legionnaires were forced to move to avoid being stepped on or kicked by the Ferret's hobnailed boots. Mettius Canius removed his helmet, then carried it in his left hand at his side, next to his dagger and his sword.

Marcus followed. He watched, not the man's weapons, but his right hand. As long as the right hand stayed at the man's side, he wasn't about to draw.

Even the Ferret wouldn't be so stupid as to attack me in front of the men. Broad daylight is not his style.

When they were a dozen paces from the road and away from the ears of the century, Mettius Canius suddenly dropped to his knees.

Marcus turned his head away from the sound of the man emptying his stomach. He waited until the sounds of retching ceased. Then he said, "Are you done?"

Mettius said nothing.

"On your feet, then."

The Ferret got up slowly. He turned around, wiping his mouth with the back of his hand. He was pale, his face drenched with sweat, his eyes red-rimmed and bloodshot.

He's sweating. Good. Marcus well knew that if a man stopped sweating, he was in danger of heat exhaustion. *He's not going to pass out then.*

Marcus fixed the Ferret's red-streaked eyes. "You were drunk on duty last night."

Swaying on unsteady feet, Mettius glared back at him. "Who says so?"

Marcus gestured with his left hand, waving at the Ferret's pale, dripping face. "Your eyes. Your stumbling gait. Your pale face. You are barely able to march today."

Mettius's lips curled in a snarl. "I *am* marching, curse you!"

"You're not keeping up."

"I am now!"

"You put every man in the unit in danger with your dereliction of duty."

Those words caught Mettius's attention. Dereliction of duty was punishable in various gruesome and brutal ways—including death.

Marcus paused, a deliciously wicked grin curling one side of his mouth. "I know it was you last night."

Mettius flinched. "What're you talking about?"

"With your three friends. Attempting to rape the slave-girl. Drawing weapons on your senior officer."

The Ferret's jaw dropped. His mouth worked as if he were trying to find words to say—words of defense, words of denial. His eyes flickered back and forth, as if seeking for an escape.

His left hand went to his sword.

Marcus shifted the hastile to his left hand and placed his right hand on the pommel of his own sword. "Don't be stupid." He paused again, allowing the wicked smile to spread across his mouth. "Or go ahead. Draw on me. Maybe you'll get lucky."

Incredibly, the Ferret's face paled to an even more deathly shade of white. His hand dropped to his side. "I-I-I— I had an itch."

Marcus nodded, still grinning like a wolf. "I see. Very well. I will be merciful. This time. I never forget anything. You know that."

The Ferret nodded, but kept his peace.

"However, you foul up again—today, or any time for the duration of this mission—and I might forget to be merciful."

Mettius Canius nodded more vigorously. "Yes, Option."

"Now, get back in your place. And stay there."

The man thumped his right fist to his chest. "Yes, Option." Then he stumbled off in the direction of the road and the rest of the men.

"Stop right there!" The voice came from the centurion, riding toward them on his horse.

Mettius Canius froze mid-stumble. He turned toward Centurion Quintus Aquillius Lucanus.

"What's going on here?" shouted the gangling commander. His skinny legs appeared even thinner in comparison to the stout muscles of his mount. "You! Option!" He pointed at Marcus Scribonius. "Report!"

Marcus stood straight as a spear. "The legionnaire appeared

unwell. I was ensuring he was fit to march."

"He's drunk!" The centurion snapped his head toward Mettius Canius, who was doing his best to stand steadily on his feet—and not quite succeeding. "You're drunk!"

The Ferret shook his head in vehement denial. "No, Centurion! I'm . . . My stomach . . ."

"One night's banishment!" The centurion pronounced sentence. "Now, get back in line!"

Mettius saluted, then stumbled quickly away.

Banishment? In enemy territory?

The centurion steered his black horse toward Marcus. When he was close enough to look down on his junior officer, he said, "Option, I expect you to discipline my men, not coddle them. Are you an option or a wet-nurse?"

"I had taken care of the situation, Centurion."

Quintus Aquillius grunted in disgust. Then he spat, barely missing Marcus's boot. "Not well enough."

"If I may speak freely, Centurion? We are in private." *The legate counseled you to listen to me . . . in private.*

The mounted man bared his teeth, his lips writhing. "Curse you. May all the gods curse you and your Judean goetia." He paused, taking a deep breath. "Speak."

"Banishment, sir? Making him spend the night alone, outside the camp, in hostile territory? Is that"—Marcus searched for a word that might be least provocative—"safe? We may need every sword—"

"One night's banishment. That's final. See to it."

Marcus saluted. "As you command, Centurion."

A triumphant smile split the man's face. "Very good. Just remember who *does* command in this century."

Marcus nodded. "Yes, Centurion."

"Now, *Audaxus*"—Quintus Aquillius sneered at the hated name—"I have a special duty for you."

Marcus waited, but when the commander didn't continue, he said, "Yes, Centurion?"

The man's sneer went from mocking to virulent. "You are to watch over my slave."

Marcus blinked. "The girl?"

Quintus Aquillius nodded. "Yes, the girl. I don't like that she is at the rear, unguarded. You are to march beside my wagon. Keep her safe. Talk to her."

Marcus raised his eyebrows in shock. "Talk to her?"

"She can talk. She's not a mute. Talk to her. Keep her company."

What? Why is he doing this? "But— But my duty. My place. I'm supposed to keep the century in line."

The centurion waved dismissively. However, his feral grin remained. "You've trained them well. You still have that responsibility. You may . . . march forward and deal with that as necessary, but the bulk of your time you will spend guarding my property. Is that understood, Option?"

Marcus saluted. "Yes, Centurion." But he did not understand. He understood only that his commander had an ulterior motive.

The gangling man spurred his horse, turned the beast, and rode away. He cupped a hand to his mouth and shouted, "On your feet!"

And Marcus, who had spent the entire break on his feet while his commander had spent it in the saddle, was left to stare in mute puzzlement at the retreating horse and rider. In his mind, he saw words on the scroll glowing as if on fire.

Thine adversary layeth a snare for thee. He diggeth for thee a comely pit.

Maelona? She is the "comely pit?" Comely?

Surely not.

Marcus could think of many words to describe the skinny woman with the frightening, demonic, red mane and the haunted, green eyes—terrifying, pale, repulsive, witch-like, pitiful . . .

Beware of pity . . .

Yes, pitiful. She is that. She may be many things. But she is not comely.

But at the memory of the previous night—of a small, soft hand in his, of curls brushing against his arm—his skin prickled.

♠ ♠ ♠

"Why do they call you Marcus Scribonius?"

Marcus gave the girl a dubious glance. She rode in the first wagon, facing backward. But her eyes were turned to Marcus.

She appeared genuinely curious, but Marcus couldn't divine the thrust of her question. He shrugged slightly under the weight of his *furca* and pack. "Because it is my name, perhaps?"

The girl looked away. She blinked, and her mouth curled in a thoughtful frown. "I see. But . . . why not simply *Marcus*? That is your name, is it not? Why Marcus *Scribonius*? Roman names are so long." She brushed back a stray wisp of red hair.

Marcus suppressed a shudder and forced a smile. *Not a witch.* "I see. There are . . . very few Roman names. And my name, Marcus, is a common one, you see. There are"—he counted quickly—"sixteen men in this century alone with the *praenomen* Marcus. So normally, we use the praenomen and the *nomen*—the first name and the family name—together. It is so habitual to us, I suppose we don't think about it. In intimate settings, such as with close friends or family, we might simply use the praenomen . . . assuming there aren't two of us . . . two of us with the same name, I mean. Two men named Marcus, for example."

He grinned sheepishly. *Why does my tongue tangle when I'm around her? She's* not *a witch.* "I suppose it would get very confusing." He put a hand to his mouth, cupping it as if he were about to shout to the men of the column. "Marcus!" he said at a normal volume. "Come here! And sixteen men all come running."

She laughed then. And suddenly, she didn't look scary at all. She didn't look like a witch. She looked like . . . a young woman. A young woman with a pretty smile.

Then the smile disappeared. She ran her fingers though her red hair.

And the witch returned.

She shrugged. "My people . . . we have many names. I have never met another Maelona." She pursed her lips, tilting her head to the side. "I think it would be . . . strange to meet another Maelona. Perhaps, if we had the same name, we might have the same face, the same eyes, the same hair." She scrutinized his face. "Do all the Marcuses look alike?"

It was Marcus's turn to laugh. He shook his head. "Not a bit."

"Why not use different names? Why so many . . . Marcuses?"

He shrugged. "That is . . . simply the Roman way."

"Well"—she favored him with a mischievous grin—"the Roman way is a foolish way." Her green eyes seemed to twinkle like emeralds. "Don't you think so?"

Marcus found himself grinning as well. "Perhaps. Perhaps, when I return to Rome, I will address the Senate about it—propose a new law."

A puzzled expression appeared on her face. "What is . . . 'address the Senate'? What does it mean?"

"It means to talk to our . . . council of elders."

She shook her head, showing continued incomprehension.

"Our wise old men?"

She nodded. "Oh. Senate? Council of wise old men? I think I understand now."

"Your Latin. It's very good. How did you learn?"

"I listen, and I learn." She bowed her head. "I must learn to . . . *be.*

To live." She threw back her head, sending her mane of curls bouncing in the light breeze. Her small nose—so much smaller than a proper Roman nose—wrinkled. "You say my Latin is very good, but I don't know . . . so many words."

Marcus smiled. "I know so little of your tongue. It would be a useful thing to know." *Useful for a conqueror to know the tongue of the conquered. On this journey, the closest thing we have to a translator is Gwynn,* Marcus thought, referring to the tentmaker, one of the two calones. *And Gwynn's Latin isn't half as good as this girl's.*

Maelona's countenance brightened. Then she bowed her head as if to hide her face. She gave him a sidelong look. Suddenly, she appeared very shy. "If you like," she said slowly, "I will teach you."

Marcus nodded. *Bold as a whore one moment, and shy as a virgin the next.* "I would like that." Then he frowned. "But would your master permit it? I do not wish to get you punished." *Watching over the girl is one thing, but this . . .*

She smiled and bit her lower lip. "We could teach each other. As we . . . travel." Then she lowered her head even more and looked at him through long lashes—emeralds flashing through a soft curtain of autumn reddish-gold. "We could meet. At night. Outside the camp. In the woods." She paused. "Alone."

Marcus pictured her face, pale in the moonlight, floating in a pool of soft, red curls . . .

No! What are you thinking, man? She's a cursed witch.

No, she's not. She's a just woman. A girl.

Taken, enslaved, and . . . humbled against her will.

Her family slaughtered.

Reduced to nothing more than a whore-slave to that arrogant, noble dog.

Beware of pity . . .

Thine adversary layeth a snare for thee. He diggeth for thee a comely pit.

"No," he said, yanking himself from the dangerous reverie. "That would not be wise." He stared at her with narrowed eyes. "Did *he* put you to this task? To entice me?"

She shook her head violently. The blood drained from her face, and her skin turned white as chalk. "No! I . . ." She extended a small hand toward him.

He shrank away from her outstretched, pleading hand.

Tears spilled from her eyes. "Please! You don't know . . . You can't imagine what he'll do to me! Please, even if you won't . . . touch me . . . Please say you'll meet me in the woods tonight! Say you'll meet me!"

Marcus looked away from her, forcing his eyes on the century ahead. "You can tell your master you failed. I will not be enticed. Not by any woman. And most certainly not by one of you cursed Mona Witches."

She gasped, withdrawing her hand. "How did you . . . How did you know?"

Marcus scowled. *And to think I almost let myself be deceived.*

Pity? Pity can rot in Hell. "I didn't. Until now."

But in that moment, it came back to him. He *had* seen her. At Mona, screaming and brandishing a pair of torches.

They traveled in silence, Marcus marching and Maelona riding, for perhaps a quarter of a mile, Marcus doing his best to ignore the former witch. *Think of that, only of that. Her face, contorted in demonic rage, howling curses at the legion. Curses at me.*

". . . at Mona."

Marcus realized with a start that Maelona was speaking again—speaking low, barely loud enough for him to hear over the grinding of the wagon wheels, the creaking of the wagon itself, and the steady clattering of the mule's iron shoes.

"I was struck," she continued, not looking at him, and not seeming to care if he were listening or not, "on the head. When I awoke, I was covered in blood. I was lying among them—my father, my mother, my brother. My little brother, barely able to carry a spear or a knife. My whole family. My entire clan. All gone. Slaughtered like diseased cattle. I was left for dead. I was taken then. Forced by . . . so many. I lost count."

Maelona turned her tear-streaked face toward him. The tears were dried, but they left rivulets through the dust on her cheeks, uncovering the light-orange freckles. "I had saved myself, you know. A princess must preserve herself. For marriage. To join clans together. But my clan is gone. And I am a princess no longer. I am only a slave."

She turned her face away from him. "Later, I was sold. To him. I live only so long as I please him. And I have failed to . . . please him."

Marcus could marshal no anger, no disgust toward the girl. Not even lust. All he felt for her was pity. "I will do what I can to protect you. But I cannot do what you ask."

"Because your god forbids it?"

He gave her a curious look. "How . . ."

But she kept her eyes on the receding road. "He said you cannot touch me. He said it was not . . . it was not because you desired men or . . . boys. I did not know such a thing . . . It must be a Roman custom. He said your god forbids it. That you were like me . . . like I *was* . . . Untouched." She shrugged slightly. "He said you would . . . He said if you touched me, if I could . . . entice you . . . He said it would destroy you."

She bowed her head, her dead eyes on the ground. "I do not wish to destroy you. Because you were kind to me." She turned her eyes to him again. "Please. You do not have to touch me." Her lip trembled, and fresh tears fell from her pleading eyes. "Just meet with me. *Say* you touched me. Please?"

Marcus felt as if his heart would tear itself apart in his chest. *Would it be so bad? To pretend?* "I cannot. I cannot be false. My men know me. They know who I am and the name of my God. They know what my God requires of me. I cannot lie. And I must avoid even the *appearance* of evil. I must—"

Her chest heaved, and her mouth gaped as if she were struggling for breath. "Am I so hideous? So . . . undesirable? That to touch me, to even appear to have touched me would be . . . evil?"

"No! You are beautiful. You are very desirable." But to Marcus, at least in that moment, she was neither beautiful nor desirable. She was not even frightening. She was only *pitiable*. "But I cannot. I will not. I will do everything I can to protect you—you have my promise on that. But I will not *lie* for you. And I will not lie *with* you."

He turned his face forward. He locked his eyes on the road.

She said nothing more.

And Marcus was grateful, for he knew in his heart, if she uttered another word, begged him one more time, he would have pledged to do anything—anything for her. Not out of desire.

Out of pity.

Our Father who art in heaven, hallowed be Thy name. Help me, Father! In Thy Son's blessed name, help me. Help me to escape this snare, this comely pit.

♦ ♦ ♦

The comforting sounds and scents of military camp life surrounded Marcus Scribonius. The sounds of the laughter and ribald jokes of men enjoying a well-earned rest after marching more than thirty miles in full gear, the braying of tethered mules. The smells of wood fires, cracked wheat and bacon frying in olive oil, seasoned with a bit of precious salt, the scent of spilt posca, even the scent of newly dug earth for the latrine. The tents had all been raised. The guards were posted—four men, not two, per watch, since they were in the field.

Most of the men removed their armor. The four men of the watch did not, of course. Nor did Marcus Scribonius or any of the other junior officers, because they still had duties to attend to.

The century had camped a few dozen yards from the road, near a small pond too small, probably, to contain fish—though a few of the men were trying their luck with improvised lines and hooks tied to the ends of spears—but large enough to supply water. Water was hauled into the camp, and a dozen men stripped down to wash themselves with water heated in their individual pots. Even a field bath was an unexpected luxury after so many days of forced marches and weary battle.

Heated water was carried to the centurion's tent by the *calo* Gwynn—but not by Maelona. Marcus, so far at least, had not seen the girl perform any camp duties. *Perhaps, Quintus Aquillius prefers her hands to be soft. Perhaps, she's bathing him now.*

Marcus imagined the gentle touch of those soft hands on his own skin, washing away the grime of weeks of hard army life. Soft, small hands soothing, massaging hard, knotted muscles. The feathery touch of red curls as they whispered against his weary flesh . . .

Stop it!

He forced his eyes away from the centurion's tent.

He stood at the edge of the camp, watching the men. As option, it was his duty to oversee the order of the camp, to see that the tents were laid out properly, that the men behaved themselves.

All was as it should be within the camp. And he took pleasure in that. They were good men. Good soldiers.

Outside the camp, a hundred paces away, the Ferret had laid out his bedroll and built a small fire. Marcus Scribonius doubted Mettius Canius would be able to sleep, at least until he was overcome by sheer exhaustion. A lone soldier would be easy prey for a wolf or a bear . . . or a vengeful Celt. Banishment was a severe punishment. Even if the Ferret survived the night, he would be all the wearier on the march the next day.

So Marcus had quietly requested of the tesserarius that the guards keep half an eye on him. At least twice an hour, a pair of them would casually extend their rounds to check on their errant comrade. As much as Marcus despised the man, he didn't want the Ferret dead. *There are far worse punishments, of course – and it isn't as if the man doesn't deserve them – but banishment under these circumstances is extremely, dangerously unwise. We cannot afford the loss of one man – not even Mettius Canius.*

Is this what we're to expect from our new commander? Inexperience, perhaps. But gross stupidity?

Drunk on duty—Mettius Canius put us all at risk. But this banishment— He'll be so exhausted tomorrow, he'll end up with the same punishment again. Or worse.

That can't be good for morale.

Even if the rest of the men despise the Ferret as much as I do, another such punishment won't endear our new commander to them.

And the presence of the girl. That will cause even more trouble.

It's not her fault, Marcus.

None of this cursed situation is her fault.

And to be honest, it's not all the centurion's fault either. He wasn't even with us at Mona.

He just bought *her later. After she'd been . . .*

Marcus tore at his dinner with his fingers, shoving a chunk of bacon into his mouth. He chewed and swallowed it quickly, barely tasting it. He was ravenous, and he ate his food with a savagery better suited to a wolf tearing into its prey than a soldier enjoying a well-deserved meal. He was surprised, when he downed the final bite—surprised that he had consumed it all. His belly still ached as if it were empty, and his tongue was unsatisfied. He took a draft from his wineskin, forcing himself to savor the taste of the sour posca.

At least the centurion had listened to reason concerning the ring of stones.

Near the end of the day's march, they spotted a ring of standing stones. Such rings of large stones, rough-hewn—or even unhewn—and irregularly spaced, dotted Britannia. Quintus Aquillius halted the century, ordering that his tent be erected at the heart of the circle.

Even as the two calones and the first wagoner started unloading the first wagon, in preparation for erecting the commander's tent, Marcus Scribonius quietly approached the centurion.

"Your pardon, Centurion, but if I may suggest . . ."

Quintus Aquillius gritted his teeth, but he nodded. "Yes, Audaxus?"

"These sites are as temples to the Celts. While it's not uncommon for travelers to camp nearby, camping at the center would be . . . inappropriate. Provocative." Marcus pointed at the tentmaker, Gwynn. "Observe the calo there. He's a Celt. He seems quite agitated. It might be more prudent, even better defensibly, for you to be nearer the men, Centurion." As an afterthought, he then added, "It would be better for morale *if our commander were with us—physically, I mean."*

The commander stared at him. Then his jaw relaxed slowly. He nodded.

"Very well. See to it."

Appeal to the man's vanity. That seems to do the job.

Marcus Scribonius saluted, fist to chest. "As you command, Centurion."

When he informed Gwynn of the change in location, the tentmaker grinned, showing a mouthful of irregular teeth with more than a few gaps. He wiped sweat from his brow, and Marcus Scribonius suspected that sweat was due less to fatigue than to fear. "Thank you," the slave muttered. "This was your *doing, I'd guess."*

Marcus clapped the man on his muscled shoulder and winked at the calo. "I think it would be unwise to say as much to him."

Gwynn winked back. "In the wagon, with my supplies, I have a beautiful new sheet of fine vellum for your book. It's yours. Free this time." He looked up nervously at the stones surrounding them. "The next one after that – full price, of course – but this one . . . In gratitude for your wisdom, Option."

Marcus laughed. "My wisdom is worth far less than your fine parchment, Gwynn. But I thank you. I am *running out of room."*

Gwynn hefted a bundle of tent poles and leather onto his shoulder. "And what does your God tell you about this . . . new fellow?"

Marcus shook his head, unable to suppress a sly grin. But he said nothing.

"Do you know what those are?" the slave said as they walked back to the wagon. He had pointed with his free hand at the three long mounds, covered with long grass, lying a dozen paces from the farthest stone.

Marcus also pointed with his hastile. "Those bumps in the ground?"

The tanner nodded. "Yes."

Marcus shook his head. "No."

"Those are barrows. Tombs of the dead. Chieftains, mostly, or ancient kings or queens, gone on to the endless feasting in the halls of Annwfyn, the Underworld. The kingdom of Arawn."

Marcus shivered, and not with the creeping chill that preceded the setting sun. Arawn. *"Are those . . . barrows . . . Are they entrances to Annwfyn?"*

Gwynn shook his head. "Yes, Master. But only in a manner of speaking. For the chieftain, yes. Or the king or queen. They enter the Underworld through the barrow. And there they stay. But for the living? No. And any living thing which violates the barrow, any mortal man or woman, becomes trapped – stuck between the world of the living and the world of the dead. They become a barrow tanad. Cursed forever – neither living nor dead. They sometimes emerge at night, seeking to lure the living to join – "

Marcus allowed himself a nervous laugh. "There are no such things as tanads, my friend. You are either dead or alive. Or resurrected. But you cannot be stuck in between. At least, that is what my God tells me."

"Are you so certain, Master?"

Marcus nodded, but in that setting, within those stones and staring at the burial mounds, he suddenly felt quite unsure. "I am certain." There is but one God and His Son and the Holy Spirit. There are no other gods. All the rest is . . . fantasy. *However, he could easily imagine bloodless hands clawing their way out of an earthen mound . . .*

He tore his eyes away from the barrows. "Still, it was wise to . . . choose a different campsite." He shivered again.

"Yes, Master. You are most wise. That new one, the new Centurion, he . . ."

"No! Do not forget your place, calo. And do not forget mine. He is my commander. Our commander. Never forget that."

"Yes, Option."

Marcus nodded and forced a smile. "I will take you up on that offer. Soon. I need to stitch a new sheet onto my book." Then he left Gwynn and the cowherd to their tasks.

As Marcus walked away from the ring of standing stones and the barrows, he managed to keep his pace slow. He managed not *to scurry away like a frightened child fleeing a haunted shrine at night. He even managed not to look back, not to look behind, not to check for a ghostly figure emerging from a barrow, following him . . .*

In camp, Marcus was able to put such thoughts and irrational fears behind him. In camp, there were many things to distract him. And soon his attention drifted. But he found himself staring, not at the barrows, not at the ring of standing stones, not at the camp and the men, and not at the lonely campsite of Mettius Canius, but at the woods beyond. The quiet, secluded woods. He found himself imagining a walk in those woods, in the moonlight, with a soft hand in his.

No! This is madness.

He ordered *her to entice me. To get me to break the commandments, the Law of Chastity.*

To betray my Savior? To lie with her, *of all creatures? Of all women on the face of the earth? A witch?*

He *is my adversary. Not her. She is merely the "comely pit."*

"No!" A slap. A scream. Coming from the centurion's tent.

"Stupid whore! One task! One simple task!" Another slap.

Another scream. "No! Please! Please!"

Quintus Aquillius shoved open the entrance of his tent and emerged, dragging Maelona by the arm across the ground. His face was flushed with anger, his teeth bared in bestial rage.

"No! No!" she begged, but her master gave her cries no heed. She didn't fight him, but she did not help him as he dragged her toward the center of the camp. "Please! No!"

The men gathered round but gave the centurion and his slave a wide berth. They said nothing, though they exchanged astonished glances.

The centurion released the girl then stepped aside. "I warned you, whore."

The slave-girl sobbed, gasping and choking as if the air were thick, unbreathable. She curled herself into a quivering ball.

Quintus Aquillius stood, feet apart, with one hand on his hip, near his dagger. With the other hand, he pointed at the girl at his feet. He raised his voice, addressing the men. "My slave has displeased me! As punishment, she is *yours* for the night. All of you! You will each take her and use her." He turned eyes blazing with hatred on Marcus Scribonius. "Do you hear me? *All* of you will take her. *All* of you. As many times as you wish, but it will be *all* of you. That is my command."

None of the gathered men moved. However, out of the corner of his eye, Marcus Scribonius could see the Ferret running toward them. In moments, Mettius Canius had pushed himself through the crowd to the front.

The men looked to one another. Then as one, each legionnaire turned his eyes, not to the centurion or the girl, but to Marcus Scribonius.

They have all heard. They know the warning – protect the girl.

"Me first!" The Ferret was already lifting his tunic and untying his *subligar* loincloth.

Marcus Scribonius uttered a sound – half growl, half grunt.

And Mettius Canius froze, his *subligar* at his feet. He locked eyes with Marcus.

Marcus let his own eyes bore into those of the vile man. *Do it, make another move, and I'll kill you.*

The Ferret stared back, his eyes widening with confusion, and then with terror. He lowered his eyes in defeat. He muttered something about "banished." Then he bent, gathered his loincloth, and slunk away.

"Well?" cried the centurion, nearly apoplectic with fury. "Go on! I command you!"

And yet no one moved.

"I command you, damn you all!"

The girl, still trembling, but no longer sobbing, gazed up at Marcus Scribonius with wide, green eyes.

Marcus took in a deep breath. He breathed out slowly, trying to calm himself. *Challenging him. In front of the men.*

"Option!" The centurion's voice had risen to a pitch bordering on hysteria. "Line up the men! Decimate them! I will not tolerate disobedience. Do you hear me? Line them up and *decimate* them!"

Gasps ran through the men.

Decimate them? Stab one in ten . . . in the gut? He can't be serious.

"Centurion," Marcus began, fighting to keep his voice level and properly subservient, "if I may have a word?"

"NO!" Centurion Quintus Aquillius Lucanus stomped a foot like a little boy throwing a cyclopean tantrum. "YOU MAY NOT HAVE A WORD!"

Never in front of the men.

But he had no choice. "Sir, we need every man we've got. We're in hostile terr—"

"I know where we are! Damn you! Kill them, gut them now! Or I will do it myself!" The gangling commander drew his dagger and stomped toward the nearest legionnaire—Agrippa Corfidius, the standard bearer.

Agrippa did not draw his knife, but he did take a step back.

Marcus moved between them, presenting his own body for the enraged centurion's blade. He seized the centurion's wrist in an iron grip. Marcus locked eyes with the commander.

Hatred blazed in Quintus Aquillius's eyes—hatred for Marcus.

Marcus whispered, "Don't make me hurt you." Then more loudly, he said, "Sir, you must have a fever. Perhaps, it is from bad wine." He paused. *Take the chance I'm giving you. Please.* "Perhaps, you should lie down and sleep it off."

Quintus Aquillius jerked his arm, trying to free it, but Marcus held it firm.

"I will kill you," the centurion growled.

"Go sleep it off," whispered Marcus, as he stared into his commander's bloodshot eyes. "I will take care of things out here."

The centurion jerked his arm again, but with less force that time. Then the tension drained out of the arm like water out of a broken cup. Still he glared at Marcus. "This is not over," he whispered. "*I* command here. Not you."

Marcus didn't nod. He didn't dare move his head or shift his eyes. *If he's going to move, I'll see it in his eyes first.* "Yes, Centurion." A moment longer, then he released Quintus Aquillius's wrist.

With a trembling hand, the centurion sheathed his dagger. "Yes," he said so all could hear. "Bad wine." He took a step back, nearly treading on the girl. He turned his venomous eyes on her. "As I said, she's yours for the night. Take her. Use her as you will. If you don't, there's not a real man among you."

And with that, he turned and walked—with whatever small shred of dignity he could still muster—into his tent.

Marcus released a shuddering breath.

He gazed down at Maelona.

And she gazed up at him, eyes wide with wonder and moist with fresh tears, her mouth agape.

He bent and extended a hand. "Come. I will watch over you tonight."

Tentatively, haltingly, she reached up and took his hand.

So soft. So small. So vulnerable.

Marcus pulled her to her feet. He desperately wanted to hold her, to pull her to himself and protect her. But he didn't. He kept her at arm's length.

He noticed that the other junior officers stood around them like a trio of guards—Agrippa Corfidius, Caeso Lucilius, and Spurious Orcivius.

The four of them—option, vexillarius, tesserarius, and cornicen—exchanged looks, but it was Caeso who spoke first, addressing the girl. "You can have our tent for the night. We will—the four of us—stand guard."

Spurious added, "We can sleep outside, one at each wall."

Marcus nodded, profound gratitude swelling his heart. He smiled at the girl. "Come. You can have my bed." And then he hastily added, "Alone. I'll . . . wrap up in some spare blankets. Outside."

Maelona ripped her hand free of his. She threw her arms about him, locking her hands behind his armored torso.

And she sobbed.

Marcus Scribonius couldn't feel her body pressing against his, not through his armor, but he could feel her quaking. He could hear her sobs, her shuddering breaths. He at last put a protective arm around her. "You're safe. No man here will touch you."

She sobbed all the more.

"Come," he said. "Let's get you some food and posca."

🌢 🌢 🌢

Marcus slept at the entrance to the tent under the open sky. Or rather, he *tried* to sleep. He rested, certainly—he would need his rest for the march in the morning—but so far, sleep had eluded him. Again.

He tried not to think of the ring of stones and the barrows.

He tried very hard not to think of a pair of haunted, green eyes. Eyes that had looked to him as a savior.

Instead, he stared at the stars. The clouds had at last dispersed. There was no moon, but the stars and planets shed a glorious, soft light.

Jupiter was the brightest, with just the hint of yellow. Mars shone with a reddish hue.

At least they are not green.

And allowing his thoughts to stray at last to a pair of pleading, green eyes, slowly, his own eyes closed.

But even with his eyes closed, he could still see the stars. Two stars, brighter than the rest, seemed to glow like emeralds in the Milky Way. Green eyes in a pale face, floating in a sea of softly shimmering red.

And in his dream, Maelona took his hand. Hers was a soft hand—small in his, almost like a child's. And she led him. "We shall teach each other," she whispered. She led him—not toward the woods but toward the ring of standing stones, glistening in the starlight.

No. Not toward the stones—toward the burial mounds, the barrows.

She turned to face him. Her lips . . . her lips were the color of rose petals. And her wings . . .

Why would Maelona have wings? But in his heart, even in the midst of the dream, Marcus knew the woman with the white, feathered wings—like those of a great snowy owl—was not the slave-girl, not Maelona.

Nevertheless, he *knew* her. He had known her all his life. Known her and desired her and loved her.

"Join me, my love," she cooed in a silvery voice like that of a dove. "Join me, and we shall live together forever."

♦ ♦ ♦

Not far from the Roman encampment, the ring of standing stones caught the starlight. In the granite, quartz flecks sparkled dimly. A dozen paces outside the ring, the three burial mounds lay in darkness, the long grass colorless in the night. At the end of the largest barrow, the grass undulated—though there was no wind to stir the long blades. Only at the end of that mound did the grass wave. Then the turf heaved outward, as if the earth itself were opening, as if a hole had opened in the barrow. A hole . . . or a door.

And out of that door crawled something—a low shape, pale and ghostly. It straightened, standing upright—woman-shaped, it was, like the corpse of an ancient queen wrapped in the white cerements of the grave.

The ghostly shape sniffed the air and let out a long, shuddering breath. Then it turned and walked away from the barrow, not toward the main camp, but toward a smaller campsite, where a solitary man huddled, all alone in the night.

Chapter VI

"From a borrowed tomb shall death arise, daughter of the queen of night. With white wings shall she fly as an eagle to her prey. And she shall send the little thief to everlasting judgment."

from the Book of Marcus Scribonius

An owl screeched.

Mettius Canius squealed like a frightened rat. Then he cursed himself.

He'd drawn his sword hours before, but he shifted and tightened his grip on the hilt, palm slick with sweat in spite of the chill.

With his left hand, he ran trembling fingers over the lacings and pins of his armor, then checked the chin strap of his helmet. For the hundredth time, he repositioned his shield as it rested against his back. No cursed Celt arrow, flying silent and unseen out of the blackness, would strike him in the back.

The armor made him sweat, and the cold made him shiver. But he wouldn't light a fire. He wouldn't make himself an easy target in the night.

Mettius Canius was not a praying man—not usually. He believed in the gods, but was not particularly devoted to any of them.

There was Mithras, of course, official god of the Roman army, but it had been several weeks since he'd been able to shower in the sacred blood of Mithras's bull. Although the ritual sacrifice and showering was a common practice before going into combat—especially in Legio XIV Gemina—there had been no opportunity lately, not since well before the second assault on Mona. He'd been washed clean of his sins then, but not since. Not lately.

To tell the truth, Mettius Canius wasn't sure he believed the blood really washed away all past misdeeds, but if there was one thing Mettius believed ardently, devoutly, it was that a man shouldn't take chances. If Mettius had to march into battle and face death, he wanted to do so with a clear conscience.

And sitting alone in the night, unable to see anything beyond a few paces, Mettius wished very much that he could be sinless once more. Since his last crimson shower, he had . . . done things. He'd shown cowardice in battle, taken two women—but only two—by force. Both of them were Celts, so they shouldn't matter, but . . . And then there was the incident with the slave-girl. He and his friends hadn't succeeded, but Mettius had also drawn a weapon on an officer—and worse, the cursed option had recognized him, even in the dark.

And the cursed man was still holding it over his head.

Might have to get rid of him.

Mettius almost smiled at the idea of slitting Marcus Scribonius's throat—from behind, of course—and dumping the body in the latrine.

Wouldn't work. Have to bury *him in the filth. And I'd come back smelling like filth.*

No. Have to bide my time, wait for the right—

A huge black bird, a raven, flapped to the ground no more than five feet in front of him.

Mettius squeaked again. Like a mouse. He pointed his sword at the carrion bird.

The raven—blacker than the night and as large as a vulture—cocked its head as if sizing him up. Then it began to walk. It took a few steps to Mettius's left, looked at him again, then turned and walked slowly to the right. It stopped, turned to him, flapped its massive wings once, then folded them against its body. It croaked. And then it simply stared.

Mettius had heard tales of ravens attacking sheep. And if a sheep, why not a man—a man all alone in the night?

He poked with his sword in the direction of the ominous creature, but he couldn't reach it. "Go away! I'm not for you, curse you!"

The bird seemed to shrug in response.

But it stayed put.

Man and death-bird stared at each other in what felt to Mettius like a battle of wills, a battle of the mind.

And the raven was winning.

"Go a—"

Somewhere in the darkness, an owl screeched again.

Mettius yelped and almost dropped his sword.

The raven turned and walked away into the darkness, blending into the night, and was soon lost to Mettius's sight.

Mettius panted like a frightened rabbit. *An omen. A bad omen.*

This is all the cursed slave's fault.

The whore.

He'd forced many women in his short life. So many, he'd lost count. *The women – they don't matter. Not a one of them. They deserved it, the whores. All women are whores. They wanted it. They ought to thank me, curse them.*

Some of them – no, most of them probably do, in their hearts.

But some of them, the ungrateful ones, they could be trouble. They could pray to the gods for revenge.

Do women's prayers matter? Do they?

Do mine?

Even so, Mettius prayed . . . just in case. He lifted his hands—one holding his sword—and prayed to Invidia, Goddess of Vengeance. Just in case. *Holy Invidia, stay Thy hand. They were just Celts. They were the cursed enemy, Goddess. Don't punish me for them. Please.*

He pictured the goddess, hovering over him, her wings spread, a sword in her hand, ready to strike.

They were the enemy. They don't matter, do they, Lady Invidia?

They don't count. They don't pray to Thee as I do.

I used to pray to Thee every night and day – each time mother took that cursed staff to me. And Thou didst answer my prayer for vengeance – yes, Thou didst – that night Thou didst strike mother down. Right as she was beating me with the rod.

So I serve Thee. I pray to Thee.

I love Thee. Of all women, I love only Thee.

And I have given Thee no cause to . . . No, I have not.

And women – their prayers don't matter. Do they?

But there was still the matter of his sister.

And the Vestal Virgin he'd taken.

She'd screamed so. And he had reveled in her screams. But she'd seen his face, so he'd been forced to slit her throat. *But it was her own fault.*

He'd nearly been caught with that one. In fact, he wasn't entirely certain he might not yet be taken and punished—if he were still in Rome. His sister—she'd kept her silence. But the Goddess Vesta—She might not look lightly upon the desecration of one of Her priestesses. *Even if the virgin was a slut. She wanted it. She enjoyed it.*

That's why she screamed.

Even so, Mettius had fled Rome. He enlisted in the army where he would travel far and wide and would never have to return to Rome, never have to be under the eye of Vesta again. The Goddess didn't leave the City, didn't leave Her temple—or so Mettius had been told.

In the army, he joined the Cult of Mithras. It was the thing to do, if you wanted to go unnoticed. And he'd been washed clean. Many times. Absolved from his sins—if they were sins at all. *So, they don't matter. I'm clean of them. As if it didn't happen.*

It never happened.

In the army, he found fresh prey, and plenty of it.

If you could tolerate the damned red hair.

Though his prayers had been silent thus far, he cleared his throat before continuing. *Please, Lady Invidia. Let not Thy sword of vengeance smite me. Because we brought along a bull. Well, not a bull, precisely. An ox. But that's close enough. In a few days, a week at most, I'll wash in the blood and be cleansed again. So, please, Goddess. Spare me. A few days more. That's all.*

Curse the slut. That slave. All her fault. Wouldn't even look at me. Thinks she's too good for me. Damned whoring Celt.

She deserves it.

"It's not my fault!" he cried aloud.

I'll get her. I swear by Jupiter, I'll have her.

Have to stuff a rag in her mouth so she won't scream.

His palms began to sweat again at the thought. His breathing quickened. He licked his lips.

But she'll scream for me.

"Lady Invidia," he said, hastily turning a lascivious grin into a properly penitent and mournful frown, "have mercy. Have mercy on me. Please, Lady Invi—"

And then he saw her.

Out of the night, she walked toward him. White she was, pale as snow under moonlight. Her long hair hung limp, but in the light of the stars it appeared Celtic red. Her white robes seemed to shimmer with a faint light of their own. White wings spread out behind her. She rose a few feet into the air.

But she had no sword in her hand.

She's going to spare me!

"Lady Invidia!" he cried, tears of relief streaming from his eyes. "I thank Thee, Goddess!" He dropped his sword and knelt, reaching for her in supplication.

She approached, her own hands reaching for him. Hands like claws—thin, and skeletal.

"Goddess?" When her face resolved out of the darkness, horror seized his gut like talons of ice and iron. And the fear twisted, freezing the breath in his lungs.

Her face—skin stretched so tight, her face appeared to be a skull—a skull with green eyes deep in hollow sockets.

Thin, almost fleshless lips opened, revealing sharp teeth.

She was on him before he could scream. Strong, bony hands seized his shoulders.

There was pain.

And then there was ecstasy—pleasure so sweet, he moaned as he communed with the divine. "Invidia!" His breathing became rapid and shallow . . . and difficult. He couldn't draw in enough air. His heart pounded in his chest as if his ribs could no longer contain it. But he didn't care. "I love you!" he gasped. The joy of her presence overwhelmed him.

And then came darkness.

🌢 🌢 🌢

"Option!"

Marcus Scribonius woke with a start. He clambered out of his blanket and lumbered to his feet. For a moment, he didn't know where he was. *Outside. Where's the tent?*

Behind me.

Maelona. Sleeping inside.

Supposed to be guarding her.

His eyes focused on the man who stood before him. A man in full armor. The man who'd awakened him. A guard of the watch, holding a torch and a drawn sword.

Septimus Scribonius, his friend and distant kinsman.

"What?" Marcus shook his head to clear away the dust of sleep. "What is it?"

"Mettius Canius. He's dead."

Marcus blinked like an owl. "Dead?"

"You'd better come and see." Septimus, pointed with his torch in the direction where the Ferret's campsite lay. The light of the torch cast eerie shadows across Septimus's face, and his expression shifted between anger and fear.

Shouldn't have left the man out there. Should have defied the centurion.

Must go.

But Maelona! I can't leave her unguarded. The other three – they're still here.

But this is *the entrance to the tent.*

"Wait a moment," he said, as he squatted and lashed on his boots. When he was shod, he stood again. "I'll go, but I need you to stand guard here."

Septimus raised an eyebrow. Then he nodded in understanding. "The slave-girl?"

"Yes. Guard her at all costs. The other three officers are sleeping outside the tent too—one at each side."

Septimus nodded curtly, showing a bit of impatience. "Yes, I know. The guards . . . It's not as if we haven't noticed what you're doing."

"Of course. Quickly, now. Tell me about Mettius Canius."

The mixture of anger and fear returned to Septimus's face. "I found him. When I went to check on him. He was just lying there. In a heap. Not breathing. He was armed, but . . . his sword is on the ground. And there's no blood on it. And . . ." His voice trailed off.

"What?" Marcus prodded. "What is it?"

Septimus no longer appeared angry—only the terror remained. "I saw something. It was just standing there, a few paces away, in the darkness."

"Some*thing*? Not some*one*?"

Septimus nodded. Then he visibly shuddered. "It looked like a-a woman—all dressed in white. She was wrapped up in . . . It reminded me of a burial shroud. I don't know why. The thing . . . It looked at me for a moment—right in the eye. Green eyes. Like the girl in there. I could see them—the eyes—even in the darkness. I-I couldn't move. I was . . . I don't know. I was . . . afraid."

Marcus put his hand on his friend's armored shoulder. "We all have moments of fear."

Septimus looked him in the eye for a moment as if he were considering the impossible. Then Septimus shook his head decisively. "Not you. You are Audaxus. You have no fear. And I am . . . ashamed." He lowered his eyes.

If you only knew, my friend. I'm almost always afraid.

But I can't show fear. Not in front of my men.

Septimus muttered something Marcus couldn't catch.

"What did you say?"

Septimus shivered as if he were chilled to the bone. "She . . . It sprouted wings. Wings! And then it . . . flew away. Into the sky." He shook his head. "I'm not drunk. Just my ration of posca—no more than that. I swear by Mithras."

Marcus stared at the man, looking for signs of drunkenness. Or madness. And he saw none. "Wings, you say? It . . . flew away? Like a bird?"

Septimus nodded slowly, breathing heavily through his nose.

"Like a-a goddess. Perhaps . . . Invidia, Goddess of Vengeance. Is that it, Marcus? Are we cursed? By the gods?"

There are no other gods, no other goddesses. There cannot be. He took the torch from Septimus. "No. We are not cursed. Not by the gods. There is only one God and His Son, Christus, and the Holy Spirit. There are no others." *Are you so certain of that?*

Septimus's expression hardened, but the fear remained. "I know what I saw. A woman with wings. She must have been a goddess. Or . . . a demon. And she killed Mettius Canius. She struck him down."

Marcus gave his friend one nod, one dip of his head—not in agreement, but in acquiescence. "Let's not argue right now. I need to go see Mettius Canius."

Septimus put his fist to his chest. "Yes, Option."

Marcus nodded at the tent. "Watch over her. But stay outside. Leave her alone."

"I will defend her with my life."

Marcus gave his friend the ghost of a smile. "You're a good man, Septimus Scribonius. Take a moment and wake the tesserarius. He's on the other end of the tent. Just him, mind you. I don't want you to wake the whole camp." *Especially not the centurion.* "Have Caeso Lucilius double the guards immediately." Marcus hesitated for a moment, then added, "Tell him about the woman you saw."

Septimus saluted again, a faint, grateful smile on his lips. "As you command, Option."

Marcus returned the salute. Then he strode off, into the night. As he walked, he transferred the torch to his left hand, then drew his dagger.

"The wind is hot!" A guard of the watch called the challenge to him.

Marcus didn't recognize the voice, but he did recognize the strips on the guard's belt—Marcus Lucilius. Marcus Scribonius responded with the password-of-the-day. "Olives."

The guard, Marcus Lucilius, said more softly, "You heard? About the Ferret?"

Marcus Scribonius nodded. "I'm on my way there now. Wake the capsarium. Get him out there too."

Marcus Lucilius saluted, then trotted off to rouse the combat nurse from his sleep.

When Marcus Scribonius reached the campsite, he found Mettius Canius, just as Septimus had described him. The Ferret lay in a heap, as if he had fallen—or been dropped. He was fully armored. His sword lay on the ground a pace away from the body. And there was no blood on the blade. There was no blood anywhere—not on the ground and not on the body.

He didn't defend himself. Or he didn't have a chance to.

But how did he die? If this bird-woman killed him, how did she do it?

The dead man's eyes were open, staring sightlessly at the stars. The eyes were not yet glazed over.

Marcus sheathed his dagger, knelt beside the corpse, and felt the man's neck.

Still warm.

But no pulse.

Marcus planted the torch in the ground. He drew his dagger again and held it a finger's breadth from the man's nostrils and mouth. After several moments, he examined the dagger by torchlight. The polished blade showed no hint of mist.

Not breathing.

Marcus sheathed the dagger again. He pulled the eyelids down, covering the dead eyes. Then he examined the body for wounds or injury. He could find nothing. He stripped the corpse of its armor. He laid Mettius out on his back. He removed the man's tunic. By the time he'd removed the subligar, leaving Mettius naked, the capsarium had arrived.

Marcus gave the challenge—as he would to anyone approaching from the darkness, especially a man without a torch—and the combat nurse, a man by the name of Gaius Publicia, responded with the password.

Gaius Publicia looked awful, his hair in disarray, his eyes bleary. The man had barely taken the time to lace up his boots.

He knelt on the other side of the nude corpse. "What killed him?"

Marcus shook his head. "I don't know. I'm hoping you can help me find out."

The capsarium wiped hastily at his sleepy eyes, then he nodded. "Let's get to it, then."

Together, they thoroughly examined the body.

But they found nothing. No wounds. No bruises. Nothing. No sign of violence. Mettius Canius was simply and suddenly dead.

The nurse shook his head. "It's as if the gods struck him down."

Stop saying that. There are no other gods. There are no other gods! "Put his clothes back on him." He stood. "I'll send some men from his contubernium to carry him and his gear back to camp."

"Yes, Option." Gaius Publicia did not salute, but he hastened to comply with the command.

Marcus left his torch with the capsarium, and headed back to camp, trying not to stumble in the dark.

He's dead, and it's my fault. Why didn't I defy the centurion? My fault.

No, it's not my fault.

I didn't kill him. And neither did the commander.

But I don't believe in a bird-woman. I don't know what Septimus saw, but it was not a bird-woman. Or a goddess.

Marcus looked up, scanning the star-washed night sky.

And saw something passing across the Milky Way. Something with wings.

Marcus stopped and stared at the winged shape. And the words of a prophecy came back to him, piercing him like a dart to his brain.

From a borrowed tomb shall death arise, daughter of the Queen of Night. With white wings shall she fly as an eagle to her prey. And she shall send the little thief to everlasting judgment.

The words were visible in his mind, as clearly as if they were written on the stars, instead of on his scroll.

The winged shape circled in the sky. Like an eagle. Like a vulture circled above a dying man.

Death. Daughter of the Queen of Night. With white wings.

Mettius Canius – the Ferret.

And "ferret" means "little thief."

Sent to everlasting judgment.

He ran back to camp.

And found the camp swarming with men. Men donning their armor, preparing to defend themselves and each other.

Green eyes. Septimus said she had green eyes.

He reached the officers' tent. Septimus stood before it, faithfully guarding the entrance, sword drawn.

"Stand aside," Marcus ordered.

Septimus obeyed.

Green eyes. Death has arisen. My tribulation. Marcus drew his dagger. "Maelona!"

The flap of the tent flew aside, and Maelona shot out like a bullet from a sling. Her green eyes were wide with terror. "What's happening?" She saw the dagger. And she froze. "What's going on?"

Marcus looked at her – at her green eyes. Then he raised his eyes to the stars.

The winged shape still circled over the camp.

Not her. Not Maelona.

Marcus shivered. With fear or relief, he wasn't certain.

But he sheathed his dagger.

Maelona threw herself at him, wrapping her arms around his chest. "What's happening?" she repeated, quivering against him.

There was no breastplate between them—only a thin tunic and her ragged gown.

Marcus put one arm protectively around her. And held her trembling, warm body against his.

He couldn't help himself.

Not her. Not Maelona.

His mouth suddenly dry, he said, "A man is dead."

"Dead?" Her voice rose to a high-pitched squeal. "Dead? How? Why?"

Marcus shook his head, realizing with a start that he now held her with *both* his arms. Her body was so warm, so soft. So vulnerable. So comforting. "We don't know."

From a borrowed tomb . . .

Suddenly, along with the prophecy, he remembered Gwynn's words from the evening before. *A barrow.*

A barrow tanad? Gwynn said nothing about wings, but . . .

"You're safe here," he said, unwrapping his arms from around her and gently prying her away from himself, "but I have to . . . have to see to something. Go back into the tent."

Reluctantly, and with a pleading, teary gaze, she obeyed him.

Marcus retrieved his sword from the ground where it rested with his armor, near his blanket. He unsheathed the weapon and left the scabbard and the armor behind.

He commandeered a torch from another legionnaire, then set off in the direction of the stone circle. And the barrow mounds.

As he tromped through the darkness, fear twisted his bowels into knots and danced up and down his spine. Marcus forced his trembling knees to obey him.

Our Father who art in heaven, hallowed be Thy name.

Heavenly Father, give me courage. Help me, Father. I'm so afraid. I'm so terribly afraid.

He continued to pray as he went, and he did not stop praying until he had reached the barrow, until he'd seen exactly what he'd known, what he'd feared he would see.

A hole at the end of the burial mound. A black, gaping maw in the earth, large enough for a man to crawl out of the grave. A man . . . or a woman. Or a woman with white wings.

From a borrowed tomb shall death arise . . .

Chapter VII

"With a knife of gold has the evildoer shed the blood of many. And for the innocent blood spilled shall his blood be required by his own blood."

from the Book of Marcus Scribonius

Tell me about barrow tanads," Marcus Scribonius demanded of Gwynn. Marcus resisted the urge to shake the man.

The Celt slave had been waiting for him at the edge of camp, well within the light of the torches and campfires. Gwynn carried a knife in each hand—neither of them long enough to be a dagger. The blades were mere tools he used when butchering cattle or cutting leather.

Marcus glanced at the knives briefly. He'd been watching for a "knife of gold" for months, ever since receiving the extraordinarily cryptic prophecy—

With a knife of gold has the evildoer shed the blood of many. And for the innocent blood spilled shall his blood be required by his own blood.

But neither knife was made of gold.

Gwynn, noting the direction of Marcus's glance, pleaded, "Forgive me, Option! I heard the alarm, and . . ."

Marcus shook his head dismissively. "Right now, we need every blade we've got. I know you wouldn't turn those on us." *I hope.* Still, Marcus was glad of the sword in his own hand.

The Celt nodded, chuckling nervously. "Of course not, Master. I wouldn't. Never!"

"So tell me, man. Tell me what I need to know."

"It was a barrow tanad then?" Gwynn's eyes widened with fear. "A barrow tanad killed him?"

Marcus forced his expression to remain neutral. "One of the barrows is open. The one in the middle, if that makes any difference."

Gwynn shook his head. "No. Why would it?"

"You tell me. One of my men is dead, Gwynn. I need to know what killed him, how it killed him. The body is untouched. No wound. No blood. No sign of violence. I need to know how to fight this thing. What are we up against?"

A bead of sweat appeared at the slave's temple. "I . . . I don't know. By the gods, I don't know. How does one fight a ghost?"

How indeed? And yet, we're on a mission to find a god. "There are spirits, Gwynn. Evil spirits, but the spirits of the dead don't linger on the earth."

"Not *dead*, Master. Not *living*. In between death and life."

"Impossible." *How can you be certain?* Something *killed him.* "But *something* came out of that grave."

Gwynn looked as if he were unsteady on his feet, as if he might faint. His lip trembled. "The tanad does not leave the barrow. It lures the living inside. That's what my people say, Master."

"Perhaps it's not a tanad after all."

"I'm sorry, Master! I simply don't know!"

Marcus nodded as he patted the man's shoulder. "It's not your fault, my friend." *But how do I fight what I don't understand, what I cannot even put a name to?* "Get back among the soldiers. You'll be safe there."

Gwynn did not appear reassured by those words, but he nodded and retreated toward the center of the camp.

Marcus scanned the skies.

Look as he might, he could find no sign of the winged shape. *I can't name it and I can't see it.*

It could be anywhere.

Marcus knew what must be done.

He dashed to the officers' tent.

Septimus Scribonius stood at the entrance, but Maelona stood behind him, wide-eyed and trembling.

At her feet lay Marcus's armor.

The three other junior officers were busy donning their armor.

Marcus quickly nodded to his kinsman, Septimus. "I'll take over here, with the girl." He knelt, laid aside his sword, and began assembling the four distinct sections of his chest armor, the *lorica segmentata.*

Septimus knelt beside him. "Let me help you with that."

But Marcus waved him off. "Alert the men. I want them all assembled and ready to fight. Even the noncombatants."

"Are we under attack then?"

Marcus hefted his armor onto his back, pulling the upper sections over his shoulders. "A man's dead. Now go."

Septimus snapped to his feet, saluted, then trotted away.

The other three officers came around the corners of the tent, surrounding him, as they finished lacing up their own breastplates.

Marcus hooked the front of the shoulder plates onto the uppermost segments of the semicircular bands surrounding his torso. "Has anyone seen the commander?"

Caeso Lucilius shook his head. "I'll check on him. Maybe he really is drunk. Must be nice to have real wine. Commander's privilege, no?" He laughed, but the laughter carried no mirth—only concern, mingled with a touch of fear. The tesserarius put his helm, wolfskin and all, over his head and tightened the chinstrap. He saluted. "With your permission, Option." Then, without waiting to be dismissed, he hurried away in the direction of the centurion's tent.

Spurious Orcivius had just secured his bear skin over his helm and shoulders and was assembling the three sections of his cornu. "Do I sound the alarm?"

Marcus hesitated. "Give the centurion a moment to get here." *I've humiliated him enough already.* Marcus pointed at the cornicen and Agrippa Corfidius, the vexillarius who had just finished fastening on his lion skin. "Get to the center of the camp. Have the men ready."

They both saluted, then trotted off.

Marcus stood. Then he cursed himself for a fool. There was nobody left to help him lace up the back of his armor. Normally, soldiers and officers helped each other with this task, but he'd just sent his comrades away.

Nothing for it. I'll just have to take it off and lace up the back first.

As he was about to pull the pin at the top of his armor to remove it, he felt the steel bands across his back being shifted and pulled together.

"I'll do this side," said a voice from behind him—soft and high, speaking in heavily accented Latin.

"Maelona?"

A soft chuckle. "Who else? A witch?"

Not funny. "Thank you." He suppressed a shudder. *Not funny at all.* "How do you know—"

"My master requires me to dress him each morning. I know all about taking care of your Roman armor."

Marcus nodded. *I suppose you would.* He started lacing up the front of the plates, tying each pair of plates together with distinct, separate leather thongs. "Thank you."

They worked in silence for the next several moments.

When the armor was secured, he was about to reach down for his sword and its sheath, when he found the girl had already retrieved them. She had sheathed the sword. With her small, delicate hands, she lifted the strap of the baldric toward his head.

"The left shoulder, yes?" She asked, her green eyes shyly avoiding his. "So the sword is on the right? Like a commander?"

Marcus nodded, then bowed his head.

She lifted the baldric strap over his head and laid it on his left shoulder. Then she quickly bent down and retrieved his plumed helmet. She held it as if she would place it on his head.

He took it from her instead. "Thank you." He donned the helm and tightened the chinstrap.

Maelona disappeared inside the tent.

Marcus huffed in exasperation. "Maelona! We have to—"

She reappeared and presented him with his staff of office. Her eyes gleamed in the torchlight, shining like emeralds, as they met his. Although she did not smile, she appeared pleased.

Marcus gave her a wondering smile as he took the hastile. "You are a marvel."

She lowered her eyes. "I am a slave."

Marcus nodded. He grasped her hand. "Come."

Together, they hurried to the center of the encampment.

Most of the men were already assembled by the time they arrived. Some were still finishing up the process of donning their armor. In accordance with their training, they were gathering in their contubernia.

Marcus let go of the girl's hand. "Stay behind me, but not too close. I may need room to fight."

She nodded silently, then stepped behind him, out of his sight.

And he tried to push her out of his thoughts.

Marcus quickly scanned each contubernium, checking that each had eight men. One, of course, did not. *Mettius Canius is dead.* The other nine contubernia seemed whole.

Then he searched about for the other junior officers. Vexillarius Agrippa Corfidius stood next to Cornicen Spurius Orcivius. The lion-headed standard-bearer did not carry the standard—that pole was firmly planted in the ground—but the cornicen held his horn ready.

Where's Caeso and the centurion? Marcus peered in the direction of the commander's tent. He spotted two men—one in armor and one not—coming toward him. The armored man wore a wolfskin and was supporting, almost dragging the other man.

Drunk? In the field? The fool drank undiluted wine?

Tesserarius Caeso Lucilius was indeed dragging Centurion Quintus Aquillius Lucanus.

The centurion seemed barely able to move his feet. He wore no armor—only his tunica and his belt. He wore his boots, but Marcus suspected Caeso had been forced to lace them up for the commander. Quintus Aquillius's head hung down. His arm draped loosely across the shoulders of the tesserarius.

A wave of disgust welled up in Marcus Scribonius, contempt for his commander. Marcus was about to ask Caeso Lucilius if the centurion was indeed inebriated, but the tesserarius's disgusted scowl and shake of the head confirmed Marcus's assessment.

Caeso stopped a yard away from Marcus. "What do you want me to do with him?"

Marcus could smell the wine. It was on the commander's breath, on his tunic. Marcus gritted his teeth and suppressed an urge to growl in frustration and fury. *He banished Mettius Canius for being drunk, and now that man is dead.* "Get him to the center, with the other noncombatants."

Caeso nodded. "Yes, Option."

"And take the girl with you."

"No!" Maelona stepped from behind him. "I want to stay with you! Please let me—"

"Do as I say," Marcus snapped. Then he softened his voice. "You'll be safest at the center."

Maelona bowed her head, the mass of bushy, red curls hiding her face. Obediently she moved to stand beside Caeso. And the three of them—the tesserarius, the insensate centurion, and the slave-girl—left Marcus.

Marcus followed them with his eyes. Then he spied the huddle of civilians at the center of the camp. He counted them quickly, knowing there should be ten of them, at least until Maelona joined them.

But he could count only nine. He could not see Gwynn.

No! "Tesserarius!"

Caeso half turned back toward him. "Option?"

"One of the calones is missing—Gwynn, the tentmaker. Find out what you can."

The tesserarius nodded. "Yes, Option."

Gwynn? Where are you?

Marcus turned his face to the night sky.

The winged shape once again soared across the stars. And it was larger than before.

It's lower! Closer.

"*Orbem formate*!" Marcus roared as he dashed toward the civilians huddled around Caeso Lucilius. "To me! Now!"

The men came running. Fully armored or not, they came with shield and sword.

"Orbem formate!" he cried again, calling for the century to form the circular *orbis* formation around him. "Noncombatants at the center!"

Marcus planted himself next to Caeso Lucilius. On the ground behind them lay the centurion in wine-induced oblivion. Maelona stood next to her master. The other civilians—the six wagoners, the capsarium, the fabro, and the herdsman—all huddled in a knot. All of them, except the slave-girl, carried small knives.

The legionnaires formed concentric rings around them, sword and shield at the ready.

"Any sign of the calo?" Marcus asked, not taking his eyes off the thing flying, silhouetted against the Milky Way, as the winged shape circled above them. *Like a carrion bird—a vulture.*

"I was told," Caeso replied, "Gwynn went to talk to you."

"I talked to him. I sent him back inside the camp."

"Nobody's seen him since—at least none of the other civilians."

First Gaius Aquillius. Now Gwynn.

He's missing. Doesn't mean he's dead.

But in his soul, Marcus believed his friend was dead.

"Is that it?" Caeso's voice carried an edge of fear, but it also bore the determination a soldier requires to face the unknown. "What is it?"

"I don't know."

Caeso pointed at the sky. "It's getting larger!"

It is! "It's coming!"

A ripple ran through the century as each soldier adjusted his shield, holding it a little higher, a little tighter. Marcus dropped his staff and drew his own sword.

The winged shape dropped from the sky, shooting toward the ground. In the twilight space between the blackness and the furthest reaches of the torchlight, but well within the encampment, it hovered—wings spread and flapping furiously. The very beating of the wings seemed to express rage. The invader was woman-shaped and white—white wings, white robe. The wings seemed to glimmer with the light of the stars, but caught none of the yellow glow of the torchlight. The hair was not white, however—it was darker.

And in her hand, she held a long, dark sword.

Invidia?

No! No other gods or goddesses!

And yet, there she was.

She did not approach, but she shouted in perfect Latin, "Bring me the evildoers!"

No one moved, though a murmur of fear rolled through the men.

The word she used – "evildoers" –

With a knife of gold has the **evildoer** *shed the blood of many.*

Evildoers? But where's the knife of gold?

"Bring them out to me," she cried, "and the rest of you may live!" Her voice was the voice of thunder—the voice of vengeance.

Not Invidia!

No other gods!

Marcus's knees trembled, threatening to send him toppling to the ground like the broken idol of some fallen god.

The winged woman drifted closer, farther into the light. Her face was contorted in fury, her green eyes blazed like flaming emeralds, and her red hair floated around her head as if tossed by the tempest of her wings. "Bring the evildoers to me, or you will all die!"

No other gods! Seizing control of his terror, Marcus Scribonius bellowed, "NO!"

The blazing, green eyes focused on him, searing into his soul.

"Open up," he said, fighting to keep any tremor from his voice. "Let me through."

None of his men moved, whether from fear or a desire to protect him, he wasn't sure.

"Let me through," he repeated, more loudly this time.

"No, Audaxus," said Septimus Scribonius, behind him.

"No, Audaxus," said another. And another. And another. The denial came from every quarter.

"Obey me," he said.

"But the goddess!" said one of the men. "Invidia!"

"Open up," he said, gripping his sword all the tighter. "She is no goddess." *Are you certain?* And Marcus knew he was anything but certain. "And even if she is, she has no claim on me." He gritted his teeth, clinging to that thought. "Vengeance has no claim on me. Open up. Make way."

Slowly, reluctantly, the men parted, making a path for him.

"I'm coming with you," said Septimus, now standing at his shoulder.

Marcus's heart took courage, swelling with love for his friend and kinsman. "No. Guard the girl."

Marcus stepped forward. He heard Maelona cry out, an inarticulate wail of terror and pleading. And her concern, her fear, strengthened his knees. He carried his large oval shield, but he had no illusions that the wood, steel, and leather would protect him. He gripped his sword, but he doubted it would be of any use against the horrifying, supernatural creature before him.

He passed through the opening in the orbis formation. Without looking back, he knew the legionnaires would be closing ranks behind him. There were whispers of "Audaxus" as he passed—even murmurs of "No, Audaxus"—but the men let him through.

Vengeance has no claim on me.

There are no other gods.

She is not Invidia.

And then he was alone. He stood with the century behind him and the winged woman before him.

But he was alone.

He hesitated. *No claim. No goddess.*

And I am not alone.

Our Father who art in heaven, hallowed be Thy name.

Give me courage.

In Jesus's name. Amen.

And he advanced toward the woman.

As he closed the distance, she became more distinct to his eyes. She hovered a few feet above the ground, glaring at him with green eyes. Her lips were pulled back, exposing gleaming white teeth. Her hair was an untamed mass of red curls—like Maelona's—tossing, waving around her head. In spite of his terror, Marcus had the fleeting, insane impression that, were her countenance not twisted in anger, she might be truly beautiful.

Her vast, white wings, like the wings of a swan or a snowy owl, beat the air.

But there was no wind.

Marcus could see the wings, but they did not stir the air. And they made no sound.

Her sword was dark and long, but as Marcus closed the distance, he could see that it was too long to be useful in combat. And it was covered in rust.

Iron. Heavy. Brittle. Like a ceremonial sword. A burial sword.

Her robe was indeed white, but it was also muddied and stained.

Because she came out of the barrow.

She is no goddess. She is a monster of the grave.

She said nothing as he approached, but her eyes bored into his.

He felt a tugging, a pulling at his mind. He felt a nearly irresistible urge, a need to obey the vision before him, as if he would do anything to please her. His step faltered, and he nearly dropped his sword and shield.

No! he screamed in his mind. *No!* Or was it, *Yes, Thy will be done?*

"No," he said aloud. It was barely a whisper. "No," he said again, a bit louder. "NO!" he roared. "These are *my* men! And you shall not have them!"

The woman—Marcus refused to think of her as Invidia—appeared to be startled and confused. The mask of fury disappeared, and her eyes grew wide and round.

Then those emerald eyes narrowed again, piercing his like daggers into his soul.

And he felt the tugging at his mind again, sapping his will.

"Give me the evildoers!" she roared. "They are mine!"

Of course, my lady! Anything you desire!

No. No. "No." He pointed his sword at her heart, though he knew he barely strike at her feet. He wished he had his spear, but he did not believe a spear could harm her either. "These men are mine!"

"But there is evil among them. And the blood of the evildoer is required—"

"NO!" *And for the innocent blood spilled shall his blood be required by his own blood.* "They are mine!" he cried. "If there is evil among them, then they will answer to Roman justice. Not yours. If there is evil here, it is you!"

She glared at him, but the pull of her will, the sapping of his own will evaporated. She looked past him, at the century. "Give the evildoers to me, or I will kill you all."

"No!" Marcus cried, drawing her malevolent eyes back to his. "I am their champion! Now fight me or depart!"

"I will have you all." Her voice was ice. "All. One by one."

And then she was gone, flapping away—not high against the starlit sky as before, but low to the ground. She did not fly in the direction of the barrow and the stone circle, but away, out of Marcus's sight.

Marcus's knees wobbled. He lowered his sword and his shield. His head sagged forward as if the weight of his plume was too great for him to bear even for a moment longer.

I thank Thee, Father in heaven. Mighty Father in heaven. Lord Jesus is mighty to save.

He turned, staggering, lurching, back toward the century, toward his men.

And found them right there.

The entire host of men had advanced to stand behind him.

As one, they raised their blades to the heavens.

And they cheered.

"Audaxus! Audaxus! Audaxus!"

Breathing heavily, as if he had marched for a hundred miles, Marcus sheathed his sword.

He raised his hand and shook his head. "No! Stop this!"

The cheering quieted, but one voice cried, "Audaxus! He has faced down a goddess!"

This brought a sporadic renewal of the accolades, but there were also murmurings. "He defied the goddess! He defied Invidia! We are surely cursed!"

"No!" cried Marcus. "She was not Invidia! She was no goddess! I don't know what she was. But she did not come from heaven. She came from the grave! From the grave, I tell you!"

Another round of murmurs rolled through the men, but they were interrupted by a yell of outrage.

"Out of my way, you dogs! Out of my way, curse you!"

The men parted, revealing Centurion Quintus Aquillius. The commander, awake at last, staggered forward, toward Marcus. Quintus Aquillius was unarmed but for his dagger. He had drawn the leaf-bladed weapon and he thrust it at a man who apparently hadn't given the drunken centurion enough space. The blade glanced harmlessly off the soldier's breastplate, but the soldier jumped back with a cry.

All the while, Quintus Aquillius glared at his true target—Marcus Scribonius. And even in the light of the torches, the centurion's bloodshot eyes burned with loathing. And murder.

"You've taken it all!" he bellowed. "Everything!"

Marcus was exhausted, bone weary. He was too weary to hate the man who so obviously and unreasonably hated him. Quintus Aquillius was still Marcus's lawful commander, and Marcus Scribonius would serve him as best he could. Even if that meant defying him. "I have taken nothing from you, Centurion."

"You have. You've taken everything. Curse you, Audaxus. My command. My men. Defied your commanding officer. Why not a goddess, eh?" He stabbed at a random legionnaire, but the man was wise enough to be well out of the drunken centurion's reach. "Mutiny.

Blasphemy. Crucify you for this."

Quintus Aquillius stumbled. "Crucify . . ." He toppled and crashed to the ground like a dead and rotting tree pushed over by the wind. The breath rushed from his lungs. His dagger fell to the earth, out of his reach.

He rolled onto his back. And lay still.

Marcus bent and retrieved the fallen dagger. He knelt beside his commander. He observed the man's chest rise and fall.

The centurion's lips moved. Marcus leaned in to see if he could catch what Quintus Aquillius was saying.

"Name. My name. My place. Property."

Someone else knelt beside Marcus—Maelona. She placed a delicate hand on his arm, just above the elbow. "Audaxus," she whispered. "The Valiant." There was reverence in her voice—a reverence that Marcus did not feel he deserved.

Quintus Aquillius's eyes fluttered open. They fixed on the girl. "My . . . property." His eyes shuttered closed once more. "Crucify." He exhaled slowly and then began to snore.

"What are your orders, Option?" Caeso Lucilius, the tesserarius, had spoken, but Marcus knew that every ear was listening.

"Get a blanket for him. See that he is watched over. Kept comfortable. He is still in command. I am merely his option." He raised his voice, so all could hear him. "Quintus Aquillius Lucanus still commands this century. He is not himself at the moment, but he still commands. Do you hear me?" He waited for his words to sink in. "Everyone stays here, in the center. Tesserarius, I want two men in each contubernium to stand watch in shifts for the remainder of the night. The rest of you get some sleep, but you sleep here, in armor. We're missing a man."

"Who's missing?" asked Caeso. "Mettius Canius, yes. But I thought all others were accounted for."

"The calo. Gwynn, the tentmaker."

"I didn't realize he was missing."

Marcus shook his head. "Not your responsibility. Anyway, make enquiries, but I don't want anyone to go looking for him in the dark." *He's probably dead.* "Nobody is to leave the group. Not even to visit the latrine. We stay together and in plain sight."

"Yes, Option."

"At first light, we can go looking for him. We'll bury Mettius Canius then. No time for a pyre. We'll strike camp and march, but not until daylight. Even then, we stay together."

"So," said the tesserarius, "you don't think she's gone." It wasn't a question.

"No. But I have . . . a feeling she'll leave us alone for the night."

Caeso knelt beside him, on the side opposite Maelona. "A prophecy?"

"No." Marcus listened inside for confirmation from the Holy Spirit. And felt it. "Just a feeling."

The tesserarius nodded. "Good enough for me. But, in the morning . . . whither do we march? Back to the legion?"

Marcus shook his head. "They're marching back to Mona, in the opposite direction from where we're heading. That puts them two days' hard march away. We'll be in as much danger going forward as we would be in retreat. No, we have a mission. And we're going to fulfill that mission. Or die in the attempt."

"A mission—that you still can't tell us about." Caeso shrugged. "For the glory of Rome." His words were soft, lacking in conviction.

"For the glory of Rome," Marcus affirmed. "And because it is our duty. We gave our oaths."

"Yes, Option." Caeso laid a hand on Marcus's armored shoulder. "You know the men might not do it for duty, for their oaths, or even for Rome. But after tonight . . . after what you did tonight, these men would follow you into Tartarus itself. I know I would."

Into Tartarus? Into Hell? Into Annwfyn?

We seek the Arawn, lord of the dead.

Marcus gave his friend a grim smile. "They might have to."

♦ ♦ ♦

"Option!"

Marcus bolted to his feet, rubbing sleep from his eyes. "What is it?" He struggled to focus on the man who'd woken him. The light was still the dim twilight before dawn. "Nonus Sestius?"

"Yes, Option. The tesserarius said to wake you."

Marcus rubbed his arms to drive the chill from his bones. *First light. Should've been up by now.* "What is it?" He tried not to sound irritated—it wasn't Nonus Sestius's fault that Marcus had overslept.

"They found the calo, Gwynn."

"Is he . . ."

Nonus nodded quickly. "Dead, Option."

Marcus bowed his head. He was about to offer up a silent prayer when he spied Maelona.

The slave-girl, wrapped in a blanket, was lying next to where he himself had been lying a moment before. She was awake and looked at him with wide eyes, blinking away the fuzziness of sleep.

Sleeping beside me?

"She begged me to allow her," said Septimus Scribonius. He sat next to her, but he was fully armed and alert. "One of us has watched over her all night as you ordered. My turn last. But she begged to be able to sleep beside you."

Maelona was unwrapping herself from her blanket.

What will the men think? He glanced at Septimus's face, but saw no grin, no wink. *Still . . .*

The girl favored Marcus with a shy smile.

Marcus did not return the smile. His jaw hardened, and his eyes narrowed in irritation. "Stay here."

She opened her mouth as if to protest, then snapped it shut. She lowered her eyes.

Marcus adjusted his helm and breastplate to straighten them and to ease the discomfort—the plates of the lorica segmentata had dug into his left side as he slept. Then he adjusted his sword so that the baldric hung properly over his shoulder. He turned to Nonus. "Take me to him."

As they strode quickly to the edge of the camp, Marcus heard the braying of mules.

"They found him near the wagon," Nonus explained, "the one with his tools and skins."

Marcus spied the capsarium, Gaius Publicia, kneeling on the ground, examining the corpse. A number of men had gathered around, but all gave the combat nurse and the corpse a respectful distance.

Gwynn was naked and lying on his side. His limbs were bent in awkward positions. His clothing—including his Roman boots—lay in tatters in a heap near the body.

The body was stiff when they found him. The capsarium was probably forced to cut the clothes off to examine the body.

Marcus knelt next to the capsarium. "How did he die?"

The combat nurse, apparently finished with his examination, turned his face to Marcus. He scowled and shook his head. "The same as the Ferret."

Marcus sighed. "The man is dead. Let's use his proper name."

Gaius nodded. "Apologies, Option. It is the same as Mettius Canius. No wounds. No bruises. Not even blisters on his feet. You'd think he'd have a blister or two, but . . . I apologize again. I have no idea what killed him." He shuddered. "No, *she* killed him. The goddess. Invidia struck him down."

Marcus growled. "Not a goddess."

The capsarium shrugged. "I have no other answer, Option."

"But why? She spoke of evildoers. Gwynn was a *good* man." *He was my friend.*

With a knife of gold has the evildoer shed the blood of many. And for the innocent blood spilled shall his blood be required by his own blood.

Shedding the blood of innocents with a golden knife? And Invidia is thought to be Roman or Greek, not of Gwynn's "own blood." Perhaps the prophecy doesn't apply to him at all. "What evil had he ever done?"

Gaius Publicia sighed. "That I can answer. I found *this* on the corpse." The capsarium stuck his hand under the pile of rags that had once been Gwynn's tunic.

And he pulled out a golden knife.

The breath caught in Marcus's throat.

The nurse placed the knife in Marcus's hand.

In spite of its relatively small size, the weapon was very heavy, as only gold or lead is heavy. Marcus turned the golden knife over, examining it. The golden hilt was shaped roughly like a man, with head, arms, and legs.

The capsarium shuddered. "You know what that is, don't you?"

The knife, already heavy in his hand, felt suddenly even weightier. "Yes, I do—the ceremonial dagger of a Druid priest. Used for human sacrifice." *For shedding the blood of innocents.*

And whatever Gwynn's killer is, she is not Roman. Or Greek.

Green eyes, red hair. She was a Celt . . . somehow . . . a Celt.

Of his own blood.

Chapter VIII

"Death cometh in the night. And lo, she cometh for thine enemy. Deny her a second time, and thou shalt save thine own soul."

from the Book of Marcus Scribonius

"You're a dead man, Audaxus. A walking corpse." The centurion rode his powerful black stallion, walking the beast uncomfortably close to Marcus Scribonius. Rivulets of sweat ran down Quintus Aquillius's pale face. His hand trembled as it gripped the reins. Even from atop the animal, the stench of vomit wafted down to Marcus's nostrils. The man swayed in the saddle, often precariously. But somehow, Quintus Aquillius managed to mount and stay atop his horse. At least, so far.

Marcus Scribonius had seen men who could imbibe prodigious quantities of strong wine, inebriating themselves during the night to the point of unconsciousness and yet, come the dawn, were still able to perform their duties—at least to a nominal degree. Marcus marveled at such a talent, but he neither possessed it himself, nor did he admire it in others. And so, rather than respond to the taunting of the man riding alongside him, Marcus kept his eyes firmly on the marching column of legionnaires in front of him.

"When I have completed my mission," Quintus Aquillius continued, "when we have returned to the legion, I shall call for a tribunal. And I shall see you crucified." He paused, belched, then leaned to the side and retched. Again.

How can the man have anything left in his belly? Marcus wondered. *Perhaps he's still drinking, even as he rides?*

Quintus Aquillius straightened, wiping his mouth with the back of his hand. "No, maybe crucifixion is too good for you. You'd probably take some deranged pleasure in meeting the same fate as your Jewish goetia. No, I have a better idea. I shall order the century to beat you to death with their fists." He laughed. "Don't you see the irony, Audaxus? Your own cursed men beating their cursed hero to an unrecognizable heap of mangled flesh and shattered bones. Don't you see the beauty of it?"

Marcus kept his eyes straight ahead. *He's trying to goad me as if I'm some cornered dog, trying to provoke me to anger. To what end? So I'll draw sword on my commanding officer?*

Does he truly think me that much of a fool?

"Answer me, curse you!"

Marcus took a deep, calming breath. "If such a tribunal were called, what would be the charges against me?"

"Insubordination. Failure to obey my orders. Inciting a rebellion."

"The only order I have *ever* refused in my entire military career, Centurion, was an unjustified order of decimation. You cannot command me to execute random soldiers who have done no wrong."

"They disobeyed my orders! They deserved death!"

Marcus turned and tilted his head. He wanted to look his commander in the eye, to stare him down, but that wasn't feasible while Marcus was marching, not with the other man mounted on a warhorse. So Marcus settled for what he hoped was a withering glance. "No one can order a man to commit rape."

The centurion swayed in the saddle, then caught himself. "It's not rape. Not when she's a slave. She's my property, and I can do as I like with her."

"Yes, Centurion, you can." *And there is nothing I can do to stop you.* "But no one else can. You, yourself commanded that no man touch her."

"But I said—"

"And if they had touched her when you gave a conflicting order, you could have had them punished or executed for violating your first order. You could have them punished for taking liberties with another man's slave. You put the men in an impossible position." *You put* me *in an impossible position. I was ordered to advise you in private, but you left me no choice. You forced me to humiliate you in front of the men.*

"But she's a Celt! She's the enemy."

Marcus gritted his teeth in frustration. "No, Centurion. She is a slave, but—"

"A prisoner of war, taken in time of war."

"Yes, and lawfully sold as a slave, but—"

"And if I say to take her, then—"

"Have you forgotten, Centurion, that it was rape that started this war? Have you forgotten Boudicca and her daughters?"

"She rose up in rebellion! They—"

"Boudicca tried to *legally* protect her people and her daughters' inheritance from a greedy procurator who overstepped his authority. And for that she was stripped naked in front of her people, tied to tree, and brutally flogged. And her young daughters were raped by dozens of mercenaries. And because of that—"

"How dare you presume to lecture me on—"

"My pardon, Centurion. It was presumptuous of me to assume you did not know."

"I know . . ." The man wiped his mouth again, and Marcus Scribonius realized the only reason the centurion had given him time enough to speak was due to the man's difficulties with his stomach. "I know, but I simply don't care."

How does one argue with that?

"As for *other* charges," Quintus Aquillius continued, "there is the matter of a legionnaire's death after you banished him for a night"—he paused—"in enemy territory."

Marcus turned wide eyes on his commander. "*I* banished him? *I*? That was *your* order! I advised you against it. Strongly."

The lanky centurion chuckled. "Oh, no. I distinctly remember that *you* decreed the banishment. And there are no witnesses to dispute me. There are only you and me. And who would take the word of a mere option over that of his commanding officer?"

It's true. The only other witness was Mettius Canius, and he is dead.

"And," continued the centurion, "there is one other charge. You have slept with my slave."

Marcus shook his head in disgust. "I did not. And you know it. You sent her to seduce me, and it didn't work."

Quintus Aquillius laughed again. "She slept at your side last night, did she not? Such a tender scene. The whole century witnessed your appropriation of my slave's affections."

Marcus's breath caught. He felt as if he had been kicked in the chest by the centurion's black horse. *Is that what she was doing? Begging to remain close to me, just so she could incriminate me? All at her master's command?*

Curse me for a fool. I believed her.

I pitied her.

Beware of pity, for in pity lies thy peril.

The centurion's laughter mocked him. "You actually thought she cared for you! You are a fool. And when we return—"

But whatever Quintus Aquillius had intended to say was cut off by a violent fit of retching. In his efforts to remain atop his mount, he must have kicked his horse's flanks. The animal lurched forward, causing the centurion to sway perilously in the saddle.

Marcus noted that, by the time Quintus Aquillius got his mount under control, he had reached the front of the column of soldiers. The centurion did not attempt to turn his horse around in order to ride back and further torment Marcus.

But there was no need. The dagger was already in and cruelly twisted.

She played me for a fool.

Well, I shall let her know that I am a fool no longer.

He slowed his pace, allowing the first wagon to catch up.

The girl was asleep, curled up in the back.

Marcus thumped the side of the wagon with his hastile. The mule pulling the wagon brayed and kicked. The wagoner cursed.

And the slave-girl woke with a yelp.

Sitting up with a jerk, Maelona looked about wildly until her wide eyes alighted on Marcus. She smiled, but the smile quickly faded from her lips as her eyes met his. "What's wrong?"

"What's wrong? Do you mean, perhaps, other than losing two men last night? One of the dead men was my friend—a man I trusted. Or do you mean, perhaps, discovering that my friend had once been one of your cursed Druid priests—a monster who'd murdered countless innocents in your cursed rituals? Or do you mean, perhaps, having to face a flying she-demon? Or perhaps, do you mean finding out that you *tricked* me, played me for a fool at your master's bidding?"

Maelona recoiled at his sharp words as if he had struck her with his staff. "I-I didn't. What do you mean? I don't—"

"Are you saying your master didn't order you to attempt to seduce me? To get close to me? To make me feel . . . sorry for you?"

Maelona's lip trembled and her eyes filled with tears. "Y-you know he did. But I—"

"And last night, you insisted, no you *begged* to sleep beside me." Marcus let out a bitter laugh. "Do you know what you have done? To me? To my . . ." *To my heart?* "To my-my . . . reputation? In the eyes of my men?"

Tears spilled from her eyes, running down her cheeks. Her eyes pleaded with him, but Marcus Scribonius was too far gone in his anger.

"My men know me!" he snarled. "They know what I believe, how I try to live my life." He pointed at his belt and the leather strip in the center. "They know whose name I bear. They trust me. Or they did."

Maelona buried her face in her hands and sobbed.

"You wanted me to feel sorry for you, to pity you. Well, I did. You succeeded. May your master reward you handsomely for it." Marcus growled. He was angry, but he wasn't certain who enraged him the most—the slave, her master . . . or himself. "What a pathetic fool I was."

Maelona's only reply was a shuddering sob.

❖ ❖ ❖

At their first break in the march, Marcus dropped his *furca* and pack. He quickly strode up the column legionnaires, who were seated or reclining, as he checked for any sign of trouble. They were frightened, all of them.

Marcus was frightened too.

He was frightened for his men, for their safety. And for his own safety, of course. But something else worried him all the more.

He could find no explanation for what he'd seen, what they'd all seen in the night. He'd used the word "demon," but there was another word that wormed its way through his thoughts—Goddess.

She had wings. She flew.

And a sword.

But she can't be Invidia. Invidia always carries a pair of scales.

And Invidia is not Celtic. The woman was obviously a Celt.

She spoke Latin.

But she was as red-haired and green-eyed as Mae—he wouldn't even *think* her name—*as the slave-girl.*

And that sword! It was rusted. It was iron—not steel. And old iron at that. Very old.

Marcus used his gift of memory, of precise recall. He recalled exactly the shape of the blade and the handle.

The blade was leaf-shaped—bulging thicker toward the end before narrowing to the tip. At least three feet in length, the blade was far too long to be wielded in combat, particularly if it was made of iron.

At that length, it would break.

And it would be too heavy.

Not for a goddess, it wouldn't.

The handle, as he examined it in his mind's eye, was anthropomorphic—man-shaped—with legs below the handle and arms and a head above it.

A Celtic weapon! And a ceremonial one, at that.

It came out of the barrow, out of the grave. Buried with a chieftain, no doubt.

She came out of that barrow.

From a borrowed tomb shall death arise, daughter of the Queen of Night.

So the tomb wasn't hers. The sword wasn't hers.

Daughter of the Queen of Night? I don't know what that means, but . . .

She can't be Invidia!

He wheeled and marched quickly back toward the end of the column, toward the first wagon.

"Option!" A legionnaire, Marcus Tarquinius, stood and beckoned to him. "May I have a word, sir?"

Marcus Scribonius held up a hand. "Give me a moment." But he did not slow his pace.

Marcus Tarquinius got to his feet and carefully stepped between the other men. "But it's important!"

"Then follow me," Marcus Scribonius called over his shoulder. "I have an urgent matter as well."

Marcus Scribonius didn't look back, but he was certain the man was following after him. His entire focus was on the first wagon and the devious woman inside.

As he approached her, he saw the unruly mass of red curls turn, revealing the pale, freckled face of the slave-girl. Her eyes were wide, and fear was written plainly on her countenance.

The wagoner, lying stretched upon the ground, clambered to his feet. Apparently divining Marcus's mood, the man hid behind his mule. The animal snorted, but seemed unmoved by Marcus Scribonius's furious, stomping approach.

The girl cowered, covering her head with both her arms as if she expected a blow from Marcus Scribonius's hand. Or his staff. But she made no sound.

Maelona's obvious terror stopped Marcus Scribonius a pace short of the wagon. He could hear Marcus Tarquinius stumble behind him as if the fellow was trying to avoid a collision.

She thinks I'm about to strike her. The realization stunned him. *Why would she think that?*

Because violence has been her lot for years now. "I'm not . . . not going to hurt you."

Maelona continued to cower, but she said nothing.

"I wouldn't hurt you. I've never . . . never struck a woman. Never once in my life. Not even in battle. If I had to defend myself or my men . . . I suppose I could, but . . . I have never . . . I— I'm sorry I frightened you." He took a cautious step toward her.

Slowly, she lowered her arms. "Why not?" Her voice was a

whisper. "It's what you Romans do."

Marcus shook his head. "No. My mother—she taught me to never strike a woman." He paused. "My God—He teaches that a man should never do violence to a woman. A man should speak . . ." *Father in heaven, forgive me. In Jesus's name. Amen.*

And a quick prayer is going to absolve you, Marcus Scribonius? It has been years since you partook of the broken bread and the wine.

He took a deep breath. "A man should speak kindly and respectfully to a woman. And I have not. I have sinned."

He stepped around the corner of the cart until he was standing before her. Then he knelt, removed his plumed helmet, and bowed his head. "I beg your forgiveness, Maelona."

She said nothing, but she climbed out of the cart. She knelt beside him.

And she wept. "I . . . I b-b-beg your forgiveness as well. But last night . . . I did not . . . I only . . . You make . . . You made me feel safe. I only wanted . . ." Her body shuddered with another bout of uncontrolled sobbing.

Marcus Scribonius reached toward her, about to lay a hand on her shoulder. But he pulled back before he could touch her. "I . . . believe you."

She wept, drawing in great, hitching breaths, but she nodded. "If you d-did not c-come to b-b-beat me . . ."

Marcus swallowed the lump that had formed in his throat. "I need your help."

She lifted her head, showing him bloodshot, green eyes and a tear-streaked face. "What?"

His lips curled in a gentle smile—at least he hoped it appeared gentle and kindly. "I have a question."

"What is it?"

"Do your people have a goddess of vengeance? A goddess who punishes . . . evildoers?"

She nodded slowly. "Yes. Andraste."

Marcus's mouth was suddenly very dry. "Does Andraste . . ."

Maelona shook her head. "No, she does not have wings."

Marcus Scribonius almost laughed with relief. *Not a goddess. Celtic, but not their goddess.* "Do any of your goddesses have wings?"

She shook her head again. "Not on their backs. Not like . . . what we saw last night."

Marcus Scribonius nodded, smiling widely. "Thank you. Thank you."

Not a goddess. There are no other gods. No other gods.

Maelona smiled as well, cautiously, but it was a smile nonetheless.

Marcus reached forward, slowly so he wouldn't frighten her. He wiped away her tears with his thumb—first one side of her face, then the other. "Thank you."

Maelona's smile widened. And to Marcus Scribonius, it seemed as if her countenance glowed, as if the sun had emeralds for eyes and was shining only for him. And in that moment, for the first time, Marcus Scribonius saw beauty in the face of a witch of Mona.

"Option." The voice came from behind him.

Marcus Tarquinius. Marcus Scribonius had forgotten about the man. "Yes?"

"If I might have a word, Option? In private?"

Marcus nodded. He gave Maelona a brief, parting smile, then he donned his helm and rose to his feet.

He turned to face the legionnaire. He pointed with his staff to the side of the road. "Give me just a moment, and I'll follow you."

Marcus Tarquinius nodded, then he turned and walked quickly away.

Marcus Scribonius turned back to Maelona. "May I help you back into the wagon?"

She blinked at him in surprise and wonder. "Help me?"

Marcus chuckled. "Yes, help you into the wagon. Lift you up."

"Lift me up?" She did not seem to understand.

Is she so unused to simple courtesy? Marcus mimed his intentions, pretending to grasp her about the waist and hoist her up and into wagon.

She put a hand to her mouth as if to cover her embarrassment. "I have to . . ." She pointed to the high grass—on the opposite side of the road.

A nervous laugh escaped Marcus. "Yes, of course." He pointed the opposite way. "I have . . . the same need. And I must speak with someone."

They parted with awkward nods, and Marcus Scribonius walked over to join Marcus Tarquinius.

The legionnaire would not meet the option's eyes.

"What is it?" Marcus Scribonius asked. *He seems upset.*

Marcus Tarquinius began to breathe rapidly. He wrung his hands.

"Go on. Tell me."

"It's *me,* Option." He lifted his eyes and finally met Marcus Scribonius's gaze. "*I'm* the evildoer. *I'm* the one the goddess wants. I'm putting the entire century in danger!"

Marcus Tarquinius? The "evildoer?" I would trust you with my life. But I trusted Gwynn too. "What have you done?"

"It was years ago. When I was barely seven. My cousin . . . We were playing out on the rocks, north of the City. I got angry at him. It was a stupid, childish quarrel. I pushed him. He fell." He shook his head, his eyes brimming with tears of anguish. "I killed him. I didn't mean to do it. I just pushed him." He bowed his head. "I have told no one of this. Not till now."

Marcus Scribonius laid a hand on the man's shoulder. "It sounds as if it was an accident. You are not—"

The legionnaire pulled away from Marcus Scribonius's comforting hand. "It's my fault!" He looked his superior officer straight in the eye. "She'll come for me. Tonight. You must give me up to her. Perhaps my sacrifice will be enough."

Marcus Scribonius narrowed his eyes and set his jaw. "I will not give you up. Not to that demon. Besides, I know you. I know all my men. You're good men, every last one—"

"But the goddess! Invidia must—"

"No. She is *not* Invidia. She's *not* a goddess. And she will not have—"

"But we all saw her!"

Yes, we did. I have never seen a miracle. Not once. But this? This was true magic. How do I convince him? How do I convince myself? But suddenly he had the answer. "Did she have a scale in her hand?"

Marcus Tarquinius blinked, and his mouth worked as if he was trying to form words.

"Did she have a scale in her hand?" Marcus repeated. "Invidia is said to carry the scales of justice."

Marcus Tarquinius shook his head—a small, quick movement, but it was there. "N-no."

Marcus Scribonius laid a hand on the man's shoulder once more and gave him a firm nod. "Then it wasn't Invidia."

The legionnaire's eyes widened in wonder. The corners of his mouth lifted. "Not Invidia?" Then his countenance fell once more. "If not a goddess, then what was she?"

Marcus Scribonius shrugged. "I don't know. A demon, perhaps. But I will die before I give one of my men to her, whatever she may be." He gave the legionnaire a grim smile, full of determination. "We will stand together."

"So she's coming back?"

"I think so. She seemed . . . determined." He shook the man's shoulder. "But we stood against her last night. We will stand against her tonight if need be."

Marcus Tarquinius smiled then. "Yes, Option. We will. Together. We have Audaxus as our leader."

Marcus Scribonius shook his head in vehement denial. "No. Quintus Aquillius commands here, not Marcus Scribonius."

The legionnaire paused, eyeing the option. He nodded, and one side of his face twitched.

And it seemed to Marcus Scribonius as if the man had winked at him.

"As you say, Option."

Marcus Scribonius nodded in the direction of the column. "Now get back into place. We march again soon."

Marcus Tarquinius chuckled, but that small laugh bespoke profound relief.

As the legionnaire strode briskly and confidently back toward his spot in the column, Marcus Scribonius ran his eyes up and down the ranks of his men. *She'll be back. I know it. Tonight. And I know just who she's coming for.*

He nodded grimly. *For once, I know what a prophecy means* before *it is fulfilled.*

Death cometh in the night. And lo, she cometh for thine enemy.

I know who my enemy is.

Deny her a second time, and thou shalt save thine own soul.

And I have denied her – Death – once. So I have to protect my enemy, save him from the demon. Yes, that's what she is – a demon. Not a goddess.

I have to deny her a second time.

And after that, will she go away and leave us in peace?

But that's not what the prophecy says. It says I shall save my own soul. Doesn't mean I won't be killed.

Fear gripped him, a tremor running from his boots to his helm.

What about my men?

What about Maelona?

♦ ♦ ♦

"Let me relieve you," said Septimus Scribonius as he grasped and straightened Marcus Scribonius's leaning spear, "just for an hour or two."

Marcus shook himself. He realized he'd been about to fall over where he stood. The spear had been the only thing keeping him upright. "Must've dozed off." He shook himself again, then looked back at the entrance to the centurion's tent.

All seemed well, as far as Marcus could determine. A lamp still burned inside. He was almost certain he could hear the commander snoring.

Marcus lifted his head, turning his gaze to the sky.

He could see no winged shape moving across the overcast curtain of night. *Nothing but stars last night, and nothing but clouds tonight.*

She could be up there anywhere.

Septimus, fully armored and fully awake—as were at least one man in four throughout the century that night—shook Marcus's spear again. "You were about to fall over, Option. You marched all day. And none of us got much sleep last night. You're exhausted. Just like the rest of us."

Marcus wiggled the spear until Septimus let go of it. "I'm well enough."

Septimus laughed. "You were falling over, Marcus. I mean, Option. You are asleep on your feet."

"I must do this. I have to protect him."

"We're *all* protecting him." Septimus made a sweeping gesture with his arm. At the centurion's order, the entire century was encamped in a circle around his tent. Septimus lowered his voice to a whisper. "Not that he deserves it. He's—"

"Stop it," Marcus growled. "Never say that again. Do you hear me?" He lowered his own voice. "He is your commander, and I won't tolerate it."

Septimus nodded and put up a placating hand. "Yes, Option." He narrowed his eyes and fixed Marcus with his stare. "But you need to rest."

"No. I must do this myself. Myself."

Septimus gave him quizzical look. "One of your prophecies?"

Marcus nodded.

Septimus sighed in defeat. "Then I shall stand watch with you." He grinned wickedly. "If only to prop you up."

Marcus chuckled. "I'll be glad of the company." He sighed, and his sigh gave voice to a profound weariness that went as deep as his bones. "And the support."

Septimus planted his spear in the ground beside his kinsman's. And both men leaned on their weapons.

Septimus let out a sigh of deep fatigue. "Don't you think she'd be here by now? If she's coming at all?"

"She's coming," Marcus said. "I know she—"

The woman dropped from the sky, striking the ground a dozen feet in front of them. The instant her feet touched the earth, her wings vanished as if they'd never been there. But her iron sword did not vanish. The rusted weapon was very real. "Give him to me! Give me the evildoer!"

Septimus threw his spear.

Moving faster than a striking viper, she snatched the spear out of the air. She cast it aside with a bestial snarl.

Marcus threw his spear as well, and she dealt with that missile as deftly and contemptuously as she had the first.

Marcus and Septimus drew their swords and raised their shields.

The demon rushed forward with inhuman speed. She slashed with her sword at Septimus. The rusty iron blade sheared through the top of Septimus's shield as if the wood, leather, and steel were nothing but a sheet of parchment. Then she seized Septimus by the throat and flung him through the air.

As terrified as he was for Septimus, Marcus focused on his foe.

Marcus thrust with his sword. And the gladius pierced her side.

The demon screamed and jumped back. She placed a hand over the wound. Blood flowed from between her fingers.

She dropped her weapon. The brittle iron snapped, breaking in half as it struck the ground.

Marcus stabbed again, aiming higher.

In spite of her wound, she dodged the thrust. She glared at him, her eyes emerald daggers in the torchlight. "Marbhaidh mi thu airson seo!"

That's not Latin. Marcus thrust again.

But the woman easily moved out of his reach.

She pulled her hand away from the wound. And though Marcus could clearly see the rent in her gore-stained robes, her flesh was clean, unmarked.

The wound had vanished.

Her lips curled back from white teeth. "I will kill you for this!" she growled in perfect Latin.

"Audaxus!" The cry came from behind her.

"Audaxus!" cried another man. And another.

The chorus rose up all around them. "Audaxus!"

All the men of the century surrounded them. Armored or not, they were there, carrying a shield and a sword or spear. "Audaxus!"

"Stand back!" Marcus shouted. *She tossed Septimus as if he were a girl's wooden doll.* "She's mine."

The men obeyed, keeping their distance. But they stood ready to attack.

"Why are you protecting him?" The woman glared at Marcus. She bore no weapon, but Marcus was certain she could snap him in two with her bare hands.

Before he could answer, the tent flap opened, and Maelona burst forth. She rushed into the space between Marcus and the woman in white. "Chan eil! Na cuir cron air!"

The woman turned her furious eyes on Maelona. "Seas a thaobh!"

Maelona shook her head in a flurry of untamed curls. "Chan eil! Tha e na dhuine math!"

The demon's wings reappeared, and she rose several paces into the air. She scowled at Marcus. "He is evil. The coward in the tent is a murderer, and I shall have him. I *must* kill him. He is evil blood!"

Marcus heard cries of fear from the men, echoing his own terror.

Marcus pulled Maelona aside, then thrust her behind the meager shelter of his own body. "He is my commander," he said. "Take my life for his." Marcus became aware of the presence of Quintus Aquillius at the mouth of the tent.

Marcus shifted his body, attempting to shield the centurion as well. "My life for his!"

The flying woman's eyes grew wide. "You would sacrifice yourself for that evil one?"

Marcus stood a little taller, coming out of his fighting stance. He pointed his sword at the demon. *A demon who bleeds.* "My God, Jesus Christus, gave His life, His blood for sinners. Take my life, if it will save this man's. Or any man's . . . or woman's! I stand for them! Take me!"

The flying woman lifted her head, raising her chin haughtily. "I will have him. Two times you have denied me. You shall not deny me a third."

She shot up into the sky.

And then she was gone, flapping away into the night. In moments, Marcus lost sight of her.

She's not a ghost. She's not a goddess.

She bleeds. She bleeds!

"Audaxus! Audaxus!" The cheer rolled through the century, and each man held his sword high in exultation. Then one soldier, somewhere in the crowd, lowered his sword and slapped it against his shield. The sound of steel thumping against the convex wooden shield repeated, over and over in a steady rhythm. Other men lowered their swords and joined the synchronized pounding. And between each thunderous stroke was the cry, "Audaxus!"

THUMP! "Audaxus!"

THUMP! "Audaxus!"

THUMP! "Audaxus!"

"Stop!" Marcus cried. "She could come back at any moment!"

But his cries went unheeded, drowned out by the accolades.

THUMP! "Audaxus!"

THUMP! "Audaxus!"

He searched dark skies black as coal dust. *Where is she?*

"AGAIN!" The angry shout came from behind him. "AGAIN!"

As he spun round, he heard Maelona scream, "No!"

Marcus caught a glimpse of red hair. Then he saw the snarling face of the centurion.

But he did not see the dagger.

The blade pierced his abdomen just below his armor. The thrust was angled up, through his gut and puncturing his diaphragm.

Loathing and fury blazed in the gray eyes of Quintus Aquillius as he twisted the dagger, then withdrew it.

Marcus couldn't breathe. He couldn't pull in air.

He dropped his sword and shield, and his hands clawed at his wound in a desperate and futile attempt to hold in his blood, to somehow force his lungs to breathe.

"Mine!" screamed the mad centurion. "All mine, curse you!"

The cheering and pounding had ceased.

As Marcus sank to his knees, as he fought to cling to the red life spilling between his fingers, he watched through a haze of pain as the winged woman returned.

She swooped down upon Quintus Aquillius. In one swift motion, she ripped his head from his body and tossed it aside.

Without touching the ground, she spun about. She thrust her hands under Marcus's arms. Then she lifted him into the air and flew with him into the darkness of heaven, just as the moon broke through the cloud cover.

Blackness flooded Marcus Scribonius's mind.

And he knew no more.

Chapter IX

"Life and death are in her mouth. Beware, lest she claim thee as her own."

from the Book of Marcus Scribonius

Her hands.

Inside him. Pushing. Prodding. Rearranging.

Her face. Over him. Over his belly. Over his wound. Her hair. Red curls. Hanging down.

Her lips. Stream of water.

No. Not water. Drool. Falling. From her lips. Into him. Into his belly.

Moving her head. Hair tickling his face. Lips. Over his. Blowing. Into his mouth.

Lungs. Filling with air.

Air.

Blessed air.

Blowing again.

Air!

Lifting her head.

"Breathe!" A woman's voice. Not Maelona's. "Breathe, curse you!"

He obeyed. Pulling air into his lungs.

It hurt. There was pain, but there was also . . . pleasure—coursing through him.

"Good," she said. "Good. Now, keep on breathing on your own while I put the rest of you back together."

He nodded. Or attempted to. *So weak.*

But he kept on breathing.

It felt good to breathe. Breathing was right.

Forgot how to breathe. Why?

Dagger.

He felt her hands pushing into his gut again. Her head was over his belly once more.

And she was drooling again. The stream of spittle caught the moonlight as it fell from her lips, into his wound.

Her hands worked inside him. Pushing, prodding, rearranging.

But it felt good. His entire body hummed like the strings of a lyre with pleasure.

But then came the itch.

He groaned. *Itches!*

"It will pass," she said. "I know it itches. It's just the Healing. There was so much damage. It was the only way." She drooled some more, shoving his innards around as she did. "I must make certain everything is as it was. I'm no physician, but I have seen inside a body or two. I think I can get it all back together."

He felt her pull his skin, his torn flesh together with her bloodied hands. He couldn't see the wound. He couldn't lift his head. But he could see that he still wore his armor. She hadn't removed it. *Why not?*

No time. I was dying.

She drooled on the wound.

And the itch returned. *The itch!*

And then it was gone.

And so was the pain.

Only the pleasure remained.

Her face was over his again, green eyes pouring into his like wine for his soul. "You shall live." She smiled. And she was beautiful. So like Maelona—but without freckles.

"H-how?" he croaked.

"In time, you shall learn. In time, you shall learn all. But not now."

"Why?"

Her smile lessened, but it did not vanish entirely. She shook her head, and the mass of hair waved around her face, framing it as if in a shadow of crimson. "I have never seen such courage. You would have laid down your life for your men, even for your enemy."

"You . . . killed him."

She nodded, and the smile was gone. "I must kill the evildoers. I must send them to the next life unshriven. I must. It is my . . . destiny. My . . . compulsion." Her smile returned. "With the innocent, however, there can be pleasure. Pleasure . . . and love."

She leaned over his face and kissed him.

The first kiss was sweet, almost chaste. The second kiss was passionate.

Marcus was helpless to resist her, even if he'd wanted to resist. And he wasn't sure he wanted to.

She lifted her face again. Her eyes, though cast in shadow, seemed to glow.

Marcus saw passion there. And lust. Physically weak though he was, he was not immune to that lust. But he saw something else in those lovely eyes. Something that terrified him.

Hunger.

She bent as if to kiss him again, but he stopped her with the only weapon he could muster—questions.

"Who are you? What are you? Where am I? Where are my men?" *Maelona. Where is Maelona? Is she safe?* But he sensed he must not ask about the slave-girl.

She smiled. Her lips, even in the moonlight, were red. Beckoning him.

She sat up. "I am Branwen. Like the goddess."

"G-goddess?" *There are no other gods!*

She chuckled. "No. I am named after the goddess. But I am no goddess. Not in the way you mean it."

"What are you then?"

"I am a Daughter of Lilith. *She* is my goddess. And in time, you shall come to worship her as well."

He shook his head. It was easier. His strength was returning. "No. I worship God the Father, His Son, Jesus Christus, and the Holy Spirit. There are no other gods."

She shrugged. "I have never heard of these gods you name. For me, there is only Lilith."

I know that name. From where?

It came to him. Aristobulus—reading to him from a Hebrew scroll, from the Book of Isaiah, translating into Greek for him. *"There shall Lilith repose, and find for herself a place to rest."* Marcus had asked the elderly Jewish missionary who Lilith was, and Aristobulus had shrugged and replied, "A night-demon."

Daughter of the Queen of Night.

"But what are you?" Marcus asked again of the creature who called herself Branwen.

She gave him a smile then, full of secrets. "I am a Daughter of Lilith. That is all I will tell you and all you will know." Her smile widened hungrily. "Until you are ready. Then you will know *all*."

Suddenly, Marcus wanted to know nothing more—nothing more about the lovely, terrifying night-demon who had saved his life. "My men," he said.

She looked at him hard and thoughtfully. "When I carried you away, they were safe. I killed only the one tonight—the evil one."

"But Septimus Scribonius. You tossed him. Is he—"

She shrugged. "Oh, that one. Let me think." Her lips drooped in a thoughtful frown. "When we flew away, there were none of your men lying on the ground anywhere—except the evil one." A satisfied grin appeared on her face. "And the evil one was lying in two pieces." She shrugged again. "So the first one I tossed aside. He must have been on his feet."

Marcus closed his eyes. *Father in heaven, please let it be so. In Jesus's name. Amen.*

He opened his eyes again. "I must go. I must see for myself. He is my friend, my kinsman."

"You must rest. You will regain your strength. My . . . spittle has healed you. Even the blood"—she paused, sighing—"even the blood will be replenished and made stronger. But you need more time." She smiled again. "And we need more time together."

He shook his head once more. The tingling pleasure had faded, vanished. "No. My men." He tried to sit up. And found that, even as weak as he was, he could manage it. "I must return to them."

"I saved you." Her eyes seemed to smolder with anger. "You owe me your life."

He nodded. "Yes, and I am grateful. But I have my duty. To my men."

She shoved him back to the ground. "Your duty is to *me*."

She ripped Quintus Aquillius apart. She could do the same to me. Marcus could not suppress a shudder. *She could rip me apart.* "You said"—he swallowed down the bile of fear—"that you admired my courage. I need to see to my men."

She bared her teeth—and for the first time, Marcus could see that two of those teeth were long and pointed. "You will stay with me."

"And if I did?" He forced himself to meet her blazing eyes. "If I abandoned my men, would I still be the man you admire?"

She paused, breathing heavily. Her lips relaxed, and Marcus was certain he observed the sharp teeth retract, becoming no more prominent than the other white teeth in her mouth. Her eyes softened. "You are . . . a fool. You are a contradiction."

She pulled away from him but remained sitting on the ground. She turned her face away. "Go then. They are searching for you. I can hear them. They must love you greatly."

Marcus forced himself to his feet, swayed a bit, then discovered, to his surprise, that he had strength to remain upright. "I thank you for my life, Branwen. I am Marcus Scribonius."

Still facing away from him, she said, "Marcus Scribonius Audaxus. Yes, I know. I have ears. Far better than yours, mortal." She stood as well and turned to face him. "You owe me for your life. Someday, I shall claim it. I shall claim *you*." The hunger had returned to her eyes.

No! Please, God, no! Save me! He trembled. "M-my men. Spare my men. And those under my protection. You have what you wanted—the evildoers. Spare the rest. No matter what happens to me, no matter what you do to me, please spare the rest."

"Are you offering yourself? Your life?" She took a step toward him. "Your very soul?"

Marcus fought to control the tremors that shook him. He fought valiantly.

And lost.

She can see my fear.

"M-my l-life, yes." He gathered his flagging courage, wrapping it around himself—like the steel armor he still wore. "But my soul belongs to Christus. He has paid for it with His holy blood." *Lord, grant me courage.* "But my life? If it will save my men and the rest, I offer it."

Her gaze hardened a bit. "Even the woman?"

He nodded. "Yes, she is under my protection."

"Do you love her?" Branwen's question carried danger, and her eyes were daggers.

"No. I do not. I . . ." *Pity her not.* "I pity her. I will protect her."

Branwen's dangerous gaze didn't waver. "Pity can lead to . . . other things."

"I will protect her with my life."

Her lips twitched. "You *will* come to me. You will *choose* me. And I *will* have you."

"Leave my people alone."

She hesitated. "Very well. You have my promise. I will not harm them."

"You will not . . ." He searched for the right word. It was there, in his mind, but he could not grasp it. He feared not only for their lives, but for their souls.

She sighed in exasperation. "Very well then. I will not *corrupt* them either. They shall be sacrosanct. Is that enough for you, Marcus Scribonius Audaxus?"

Corrupt. That is the word. He nodded. "Yes, my lady Branwen."

She blinked at him. "*Lady* Branwen? Yes. Someday, I *will* be your

Lady Branwen. And you will be mine—my lord Audaxus. By your own choice." She waved a dismissive hand at him—a hand still stained with Marcus's blood. "Now go, my brave Audaxus."

White wings sprouted from her back, and she shot into the night sky like an arrow. Briefly, she was silhouetted against the Milky Way.

And then she was gone.

Marcus allowed the tremors to take him for a moment. With quivering fingers, he checked himself over. He still wore all his armor, including his helm. His tunica and his subligar had dagger-sized rents in them, just above his left hip. And one of the strips of leather had been severed from his belt—the left one—the one bearing the image of his mother.

The wound itself, however, was completely healed—his probing fingers couldn't detect so much as the trace of a scar. It was as if he had never received a fatal wound at all.

She saved me. Branwen saved me.

But at what price?

Life and death are in her mouth. Beware, lest she claim thee as her own.

But she has already claimed me.

At least my men . . . and Maelona . . . They are safe from her. She gave her promise.

But of what value is the oath of a demon?

He stumbled through the darkness, toward the torches of the camp.

"Audaxus? Audaxus?"

He could hear their voices.

He waved. "I am here!"

Judging from the number of wobbling torches, the search party comprised easily half the century.

As they came into view, Marcus could see Tesserarius Caeso Lucilius leading, but at his side was Septimus Scribonius—alive and walking.

Heavenly Father, I thank Thee! I thank Thee! He's alive!

Marcus waved again. "Over here!"

Septimus, who carried no torch, broke from the group. He ran toward Marcus. Septimus threw his arms around Marcus and lifted him off the ground. "Alive! Thank Jupiter, Juno, and Mithras! You're alive!"

Marcus laughed. "Yes, I'm alive. Now put me down."

Septimus set him down gently, then stepped back, his eyes wide with concern. "But your wound! I heard—"

"I'm . . . unhurt."

"The goddess—"

Marcus shook his head vehemently. "She's no goddess." *She's a demon.* "But she healed me."

"Healed you?"

Marcus chuckled. "I'll need a new tunic, a change of subligar"—*and I lost my mother's image from my belt-strip*—"but I'm unharmed."

Septimus raised both hands to heaven. "Thank the gods!"

Caeso Lucilius raised his torch and cried, "Thank the gods!"

"Hail, Audaxus!" cried someone.

The others took up the cry. "Hail, Audaxus!"

Marcus shouted, "Stop!"

The cheering died down.

Marcus suddenly realized that he was very tired. He felt as if he would fall over at any moment. "Let us return to camp."

"But the . . . the winged woman?" cried Caeso.

"She won't bother us anymore. She is no threat to us." He lowered his voice, and whispered, "But double the normal watch all the same."

Caeso saluted. "Yes, Option."

Marcus returned the salute. His fist felt like lead. "Let's go." He took one step forward, then stumbled and nearly fell.

Septimus was at his side in an instant. Septimus lifted Marcus's arm and put it over his own shoulders. "You *are* hurt."

Marcus leaned with gratitude on his sturdy cousin. "No, just tired. Almost dying can have that effect, I suppose."

As they walked toward camp, the rest of the men marching around them like an honor guard, Septimus said, "You know what I think, cousin? I think you *did* die. And you have returned from the land of the dead to the land of the living."

"Please," Marcus said, "do not say such things."

But others had heard it. And began to repeat it. "Back from the dead."

"See what you've done?" Marcus muttered. "I'm not—"

A figure came running toward them out of the darkness.

Maelona.

She carried a bundle as she ran, heedless of the uneven ground.

A few of the legionnaires drew their swords, but Marcus said, "No." Then he commanded, "Halt."

Caeso Lucilius echoed the command, and all the soldiers obeyed. They halted, and they sheathed their swords.

Maelona dropped to her knees in front of Marcus. She dropped the leather-wrapped bundle to the side. Then she encircled her arms around Marcus's legs, just above the knees. She turned her head and pressed it against his thighs.

And she wept. "I thought . . . My master!" And she wept all the more.

Marcus looked around at the men. Some were watching. Others looked pointedly away.

Marcus laid a hand on her head, resting it on her curls. "I'm . . . sorry about your master."

She shook her head against his knees. Then she looked up at him. "No! *You* are my master now. I'm so . . ."

No. I don't want a slave. I don't want you to be my slave. "I'm not—"

"Please, Master!" she wailed. "Don't give me to . . . to your men!"

"I'm not . . . I wouldn't . . ." *She's not my slave. She belongs to the heirs of Quintus Aquillius, whoever they may be. I can't free her, not legally. But I can't abandon her either.* He reached down and gently brushed a curl of hair from her face. "We'll discuss this in the morning. But I will not . . . You are not . . . You are under my protection."

She buried her face in his knees. And sobbed.

Then she pulled back, releasing him. She wiped at her nose with her fist.

Maelona picked up the bundle and unwrapped it. She held up his sword, with its scabbard and baldric. She stood and offered it to him.

Like a slave to her master.

He bent his helmeted head, and she lifted the baldric strap over his plume and set it upon his left shoulder.

He stood straighter, taking his arm from around Septimus's shoulders.

Maelona adjusted the scabbard so the sword hung straight down. "Over the right hip," she said, "like a commander." She then knelt and retrieved something small and thin from the empty bundle. She bowed her head and held it up as an offering with both hands. "This was cut from your belt, Master."

Marcus took the strip of leather from her hands. Just below the place where it had been severed was the tiny brass image of a woman's face—his mother's. He pulled the brass face to his lips and kissed it.

Tears fell from his eyes. "Thank you."

He knelt in front of the slave-girl. "Thank you. You don't know what this means to—"

She threw her arms around his neck, pressed her face against his breastplate, and sobbed. "Please k-keep me. Please d-don't sell me or give me away."

You're not mine to keep or to save. Pity smote his heart. *Pity her not.* He put his arms around her anyway. *But what am I going to do with you?* "I will protect you. I will . . ."

Suddenly, exhaustion consumed him, swallowed him like the night. "So . . . tired." He felt the world slipping from him, and he surrendered to oblivion.

Chapter X

"Thou shalt stand in the room of thine enemy, and his name shall be cut off. Beware, for thy tribulation shall be bound to thee, and thou shalt likewise be in bondage. Deliver thyself from bondage."

from the Book of Marcus Scribonius

Red curls tickled his face, catching in the unshaven stubble of his cheeks. Soft eyes, as green as emeralds, gazed at him with a love, a desire so intense, it hovered on the border between pleasure and pain. Plump lips brushed his—teasingly, like two feathers—gently prophesying of sweet passion to come. Skin, fair as moonlight on freshly fallen snow, promised forbidden delights of the flesh.

To think red hair and green eyes once filled me with fear. Why would it ever have been so?

Because it was not her *hair,* her *eyes.*

Another kiss, and then came a soft, intimate night whisper— "I have chosen you. And you have chosen me."

"Yes," he whispered in reply, "I choose you. I am yours—body and spirit. And you are mine."

Branwen smiled then, displaying gleaming white teeth. Two of those teeth lengthened, became sharper—the fangs of a predatory beast. Her pink tongue licked her ruby lips, sensually, hungrily. "The time has come, my love. You shall be blood of my blood. And flesh—"

"NO!"

Marcus woke with a start. As he sat up with a lurch, something warm and weighty slid off his bare chest.

Someone's arm.

And that someone lay with him in the bed. Naked flesh against his flesh.

He scrambled out of the bed of piled furs and away from the other occupant. He gaped at the woman lying there.

Maelona. Naked.

Naked and staring at him with the bleary gaze of one jolted from slumber.

Marcus averted his eyes. "What are you doing here? Why—" Suddenly aware of his own nudity—even his *subligar* had been removed—he snatched a woolen blanket from the bed and hastily covered himself.

He snuck a glance at her.

The red-haired woman grinned at him with obvious amusement. "Have you never seen a naked woman before?"

Marcus looked pointedly away. "Of course, I have." Marcus had been raised in Rome after all. "But never . . . in my bed." He waved in her general direction. "Cover yourself. Please."

"You have never . . . Surely . . . You have *never* coupled with a woman?" Her question sounded guileless to his ears.

"No!" Marcus felt heat rising to his cheeks. "And I have never . . . coupled . . . with anyone." *We didn't, did we? Surely, I would remember such a thing. Wouldn't I?*

"But I am your slave. My body is—"

"You are *not* my slave!"

"But I *am* a slave. If not yours, then whose property am I?" The pitch of her voice rose, warbling as if in fear. "To whom do I belong?"

Marcus heard her moving. He risked another glance and saw that she was crawling—still uncovered—toward him. And though she crawled, there was little of submission in her manner. She was a lioness, stalking her prey.

And Marcus was the prey.

He backed away quickly. "Cover yourself."

"Yes, Master." In spite of how she had moved, her voice carried fear, as if her body acted according to its training and not according to her heart.

"I'm not . . ." For the first time since he awoke—in bed with a naked woman—he realized he did not know where he was.

A low-burning lantern perched upon a small table revealed that he and Maelona were in a tent. But it was not the officers' tent he shared with the other junior officers. This tent was larger and housed a single pile of bed furs.

"The commander's tent," he said aloud. From the corner of his eye, he could see that Maelona had finally wrapped a blanket around herself. *God be praised.*

But a part of him, he knew, was *not* grateful, not filled with reverential thoughts.

At least I can now gaze upon her without guilt.

But not entirely without lust.

Father in heaven, give me strength. In Jesus's name. Amen.

He noted that the light of morning was not yet peeking around the edges of the tent door. *Still night.* "How much longer until dawn? And why have you brought me here? To this tent?"

She bowed her head, her face entirely hidden by her unruly hair. "They brought you here. Your men. That you might rest. You are the commander now." She paused, then lowered her voice a little. "Do I not please you? Am I merely . . . a *witch* to your eyes? A Mona witch? Is that all you see?"

"It's not that."

She pulled at her hair with one hand. "It is my hair! My red hair. My green eyes. My small Cambrian nose. My pale, spotted skin. To your eyes, I am hideous!"

"No. You are . . . I have come to . . ."

She bowed herself to the ground and beat upon her head with both her small fists. "I'm too old! I am used up. You will throw me away and . . . all the men will use me . . . and I will be sold to a brothel or forced into hard labor. Or have my throat cut. I know what happens to women . . . like me . . . when they are all used up."

Her body began to shudder with soft, pitiful sobbing. "Please. Keep me. I will do anything . . . *anything* you demand. I *can* please you. I am . . . experienced. I beg you. Let me try. Only please, please don't cast me away."

Marcus almost went to her then, almost gathered her in his arms. *Protect her. Hold her.*

He felt as if his thundering heart would rip itself apart.

If I do that, if I give in to pity – be it pity or . . . something more – I will be lost.

"Maelona."

At the sound of her name, she quieted her weeping, but she did not look up.

"Maelona, look at me. Please."

She raised her head. He could see her peeking at him from under pale, red eyelashes.

"Please," he repeated. "Let me see your face. I want you to . . . I want you to meet my eyes. I want you to see me when I tell you this."

Hesitantly, she raised her head. Her bloodshot eyes met his, and Marcus could see that those eyes were almost lifeless, devoid of hope. "Yes, Master?"

He attempted a reassuring smile, but she gave no reaction. *She is defeated, condemned, awaiting a pronouncement of doom.* "You are under my protection, Maelona. But I am *not* your master. You are property of the heirs of Quintus Aquillius."

A sudden thought struck him, diverting his thoughts. *What have they done with Quintus Aquillius's body? With his head?* He was certain the remains of the centurion were not in the tent.

"Yes, Mas—"

"Until an heir can be found, I will guard you. At night, you will sleep in my tent—"

Her eyes brightened, and she sat up at those words.

"But *not* in my bed."

Her shoulders sagged.

"Maelona, can you ride a horse?"

She blinked at him, then shook her head.

So much for that idea. I'll be stuck riding that creature. A warhorse like that will not be content to be led. "Very well. I cannot free you—not legally. However, if you were to wander off, I would not pursue you. Do you understand me?"

She nodded, but fresh tears welled in her eyes. "My family is dead. My clan is dead. Whither could I go? Any rival clan would kill me or enslave me anew. I have nowhere to go." She wiped at a tear rolling down her cheek. "I was a princess. I was not trained to be . . . anything else. I am good for nothing else . . . except to please a man . . . until I am too old and ugly to do even that."

She bowed her head again. "I am twenty. I am already old and hideous."

Marcus shook his head emphatically. "No! You are . . . very desirable."

She raised her face again, and her eyes were full of hope once more.

Oh, no. "Maelona, you must understand. I am a Christian, a follower of Christus. I cannot . . . *be* with a woman unless she is my wife." He hastened to add, "And I cannot marry as long as I am in the army."

Her face lit up. And despite the tears and the swollen, bloodshot eyes, and her non-Roman features, she was beautiful.

"And-and as long as you are a slave . . ." *I'm making it worse! I'm not proposing marriage!* "Maelona, I don't want you to misunderstand me. I'm not . . . I cannot . . ." *This is impossible.* "Maelona, I—"

"I have something to show you!" She leapt to her feet, wrapping the blanket more tightly around herself.

Marcus took the opportunity to better secure his own covering.

Maelona scurried over to the desk. She snatched a long object from the table and turned back to him, holding both the object and the lamp. She beamed as she knelt and presented the thing to him.

It was a scroll. With a broken senatorial seal.

"He was so very angry about this!" She giggled. "My master . . . my *former* master—he wanted to burn this. He told me to do it. But I fooled him. I hid it."

Marcus unrolled the scroll.

Maelona held the lamp higher. "I don't know what it says," she added, sounding very much like a young girl gossiping with a friend. "I can't read, but I know it concerns *you*. He cursed your name when he read it. Each time he read it. And he read it many times."

Marcus began to read.

And his heart ached at the sight of the name in the salutation at the top of the letter.

Gaius Aquillius Regulus.

Marcus's eyes were suddenly moist.

"What does it say?" Maelona bounced with unrestrained excitement.

Marcus shook his head in wonder. And long-overdue comprehension. *No wonder he hates . . .* hated *me.*

"What does it say?"

Marcus attempted to swallow the lump that had formed in his throat. "It's a senatorial decree. Of adoption. I have been named his heir. The heir of my previous centurion. My beloved mentor." His hands trembled as he recalled his mentor's words from his deathbed. "He called me his son."

I had no idea. No inkling.

He looked up from the scroll, focusing on nothing . . . except the memory of Gaius Aquillius's face. "I didn't know."

"What does it say?"

"Gaius Aquillius Regulus, my commander before . . . He has named me his heir. The Senate has ratified the adoption." His eyes returned to the scroll and he read further. "It names me as head of House Aquillius. My name is . . . changed. I am . . . Marcus Aquillius." *I didn't want this.* "It specifically disinherits . . . Quintus Aquillius." He read on. "All lands and property . . . forfeit."

Thou shalt stand in the room of thine enemy, and his name shall be cut off.

He accused me of taking everything.

And he was right.

"What does that mean? You are a lord now?"

Marcus blinked at her. "A lord? I suppose. I'm head of an important family. A patrician family. A nobleman."

"And you are a wealthy man now?"

"I suppose that's true too."

She clapped her hands and laughed. "I am very happy for you, my lord."

"Don't call me . . ."

"Aren't you a lord now? Isn't that what you said?"

He shook his head. "It's worse than that." He rolled the scroll closed again. "According to this decree . . ." *Beware, for thy tribulation shall be bound to thee, and thou shalt likewise be in bondage.* "I am now . . . your master."

Maelona's eyes opened wide, and her jaw dropped. "I belong . . . to you?"

He nodded. "Yes."

Maelona squealed in delight, like a little girl presented with a new toy. She leapt to her feet, rushed to the desk, and carefully set the lamp upon it. In an instant she returned, knelt, and threw her arms around him. The blanket barely covered her body.

She clung to him and exploded with fresh tears.

Instinctively, protectively, he enfolded her in his arms. "It's okay. You're safe. Please, don't cry."

She shook her head and clung to him all the tighter. She blubbered, and Marcus could catch only snippets of what she said—"Master" and "happy" and "please you."

Father in heaven . . . Help me!

Her weeping quieted, and as it did, her embrace took on an entirely different character. Though she made no overt move—no kisses or caresses—she pressed her body against his.

Marcus felt the blood pounding in his veins, throbbing in his ears. The flesh of her arms and her hands was so soft, so warm. The scent of her filled his nostrils.

Father, help me please. I don't know how to—

He heard an intake of breath that was neither his nor Maelona's. He snapped his eyes toward the sound.

And his own breath caught.

Branwen stood just inside the flap of the tent. She no longer wore the dirty cerements of the grave, but instead a Celtic gown of blue linen. Her eyes were ice, emerald daggers of fury. She was at once beautiful and terrifying.

Marcus quickly pushed Maelona away, and the girl uttered a terrified squeak. Marcus lurched to his feet, then quickly stepped to place his body between Maelona and the night-demon. He glanced around for a weapon, spied his own armor and weapons, as well as that of the dead centurion. But both sets of arms were at least two paces away—well out of reach.

A sword wouldn't stop her anyway. I wounded her, but she healed herself so rapidly.

If she attacks, there's nothing I can do.

She could rip off my head as she did with Quintus Aquillius.

And as terrified as he was, his overriding fear was, *I can't protect Maelona.*

Branwen glared at him murderously. Her eyes flickered between Marcus and the girl behind him.

Once again, Marcus had no weapon to use against the lovely and fearsome Daughter of Lilith. No weapon . . . except words.

"My lady Branwen. Why are you here? You gave me your promise."

Branwen bared her teeth with a snarl, and Marcus could clearly see the predator's fangs. "I did. I gave you my word. But I am not here to kill. I am here"—her eyes narrowed to slits—"to claim what is mine."

Marcus could feel Maelona's hands on his back, trembling. "Me? You spoke of choices—of how I would *choose* to be yours. And now you come to claim—"

"No. You *will* come to me. You will *choose* me as I have chosen you." Her eyes remained cold, but her mouth relaxed. The fangs receded, became mere human teeth once more. "But *you* are not what I have come to claim."

"What then?"

"The sword of the evildoer." She pointed at the armaments of Quintus Aquillius. "It is mine by right of combat."

His sword? "Why . . . would you desire a sword?"

Her eyes softened, the fury vanishing. "I . . . need a sword. To defend myself."

"From whom? Who could *you* possibly fear?"

"Others . . . of my own kind." She shivered. "And, Audaxus, there are other things, dark beings that walk the night. And they are far more dangerous than I. And I will not face them unarmed."

More dangerous than she? Tremors of fear ripped through his body. Cold sweat erupted on his skin.

He pointed at the sword. "Take it then. Take what is yours."

She nodded in acknowledgement. Then she walked unhurriedly toward the dead man's armaments. She knelt and picked up the scabbarded gladius. She stood, tall and stately, like a queen. Branwen placed the baldric over her left shoulder so that the sword hung at her right hip. The hint of a smile played at the corners of her lips. "Like a commander. Is that not what you said, girl? But he is not for you, little whore. *I* Healed him. *I* saved his life. You are nothing to him. He will use you and discard you like the dung you are."

With that, the night-demon strode toward the tent door.

Anger flared in Marcus. "Branwen, stop."

She turned toward him, "Yes, Audaxus?" She fixed him with her eyes.

Marcus felt her tugging at his thoughts, clawing at his will. Mentally, he batted away the siren call of her mind. "Branwen, if you truly think that of me, you do not know me at all. And Maelona is not a whore."

Branwen's lips curled in a contemptuous sneer. "What is she then?"

"Maelona is a princess."

Branwen laughed. "Oh, truly? I thought she was a slave. You are a slave, are you not, girl?"

Maelona said nothing.

Marcus, however, met the night-demon's stare. "The circumstances have changed. *My* circumstances have changed. I am the new head of House Aquillius. Maelona's master was of House Aquillius. He is dead . . . at your hand, Branwen. All that was his is now *mine*. Maelona was his slave, his property. She is now *mine*." *Deliver thyself from bondage.* "And as my first official act as head of my new house, I grant unto Maelona her freedom. She is a slave no longer."

Marcus heard Maelona gasp.

"And," Marcus added, "she is still under my protection."

Branwen's expression soured. Her lip twitched. Then she gave a low chuckle. "You surprise me, Audaxus. I have walked the earth for almost two hundred years. I thought there was nothing in this world that could surprise me anymore. But you, Marcus Scribonius Audaxus . . . or, I suppose, it is Marcus Aquillius now . . . You, Marcus Aquillius Audaxus . . . you surprise me."

And with that, she slipped out the door and into the predawn twilight.

Branwen was gone, but one thing she'd said lingered in Marcus's mind, seizing his gut with icy fingers of mounting dread.

Dark beings that walk the night . . . far more dangerous than her—far more dangerous than Branwen herself.

Is that what we are marching off to face? A dark being of the night, more terrifying, more dangerous than even a Daughter of Lilith?

But deep in his soul, Marcus knew the answer to his own question.

Yes. We go to face Arawn, lord of the dead.

Chapter XI

"Thy gift shall turn to ash."
from the Book of Marcus Scribonius

As soon as the sun rose, Option Marcus Aquillius Audaxus ordered that a funeral pyre be built for Centurion Quintus Aquillius Lucanus, the late commander of the Sixth Century, Second Cohort, Legio XIV Gemina. And while those funerary preparations were being made, Marcus convened a quick war council with the other junior officers. While there was never any question as to whether or not they would continue their mission, Marcus felt that the others deserved to know the true nature of that mission.

As was the custom for a fallen commander, at least one who had served the gods of Rome, the head and body of Quintus Aquillius had been accoutered in his armor—although no one questioned the absence of the centurion's sword—and laid upon the pyre. Tesserarius Caeso Lucilius, as the highest-ranking devotee of the Roman gods, offered a prayer to Pluto. Marcus Aquillius offered a silent prayer to his God. And the funeral pyre was lit.

As the scents of wood fire and smoke—and burning human flesh—permeated the camp, Marcus assembled the men of the century and formally addressed them. He stood in the back of the centurion's wagon, so the men could see him clearly. Beside him, sat Maelona. She had joined him in the wagon with reluctance, but she came willingly when Marcus told he was making a request and not a command. He'd already informed the other officers, but he explained the mission to the men as well. "So now you know everything I know. And in light of the marvels and the horrors we've witnessed in the last two nights, I know you're afraid. I'm afraid as well."

This was met by murmurs from the men—whispers of "Audaxus."

"Courage," Marcus continued, "does not mean that you are *not* afraid. Only a fool has no fear. And there is not a fool among you. Nor is there a single coward. I have every confidence that you will all serve with courage, in spite of your fear."

At those words, the men, one and all, seemed to stand a little straighter, a little taller.

"I don't know what we will be facing when we get to our destination. This Arawn could be a fraud, a goetia. I hope that is all he is." Marcus shook his head slowly. "But in my heart, I believe we will face something unknown. We may be confronted with forces we don't understand, forces that would make weak the knees of lesser men. But you are not lesser men. You are the best Rome has to offer. I will stand with you against the unknown and the terrifying. Will *you* stand with me?"

Almost as one, the men drew their swords and raised them to the skies. "Audaxus!"

Marcus shouted, "No!" He raised his own sword to the heavens. "Not for me. For the glory of Rome!"

"For the glory of Rome!" came the cheer.

Marcus sheathed his sword. He waited as the century responded in kind. "Now," he continued, "I must speak to you of one other very important matter."

He turned to Maelona and extended a hand to her.

She looked at him with confusion and trepidation, but after a long moment's hesitation, she took his hand and allowed herself to be pulled to her feet.

Marcus released her hand, then he turned back to his legionnaires. He then drew the senatorial scroll from his belt. He held it aloft. "Before we left the legion and started out on this mission, Quintus Aquillius received this letter. You all saw the messenger deliver it. It is a senatorial decree of adoption. I am now the heir of Gaius Aquillius Regulus." Many of the men grinned. Others nodded. "I tell you this, not to boast, but to give legitimacy to what I tell you next. With the death of Quintus Aquillius, I became the sole owner of the slave, Maelona. I declare that she is a slave no longer. She is a free woman. Before she was a slave, she was a princess. She is now a princess once more. You will afford her all the courtesies due to a woman of royal blood."

Murmurs began anew.

"She is also my guest and a guest of this noble century. As long as she is under our protection—and she is free to come and go as she chooses. As long as she is with us, no harm or dishonor will come to her. You will guard her with your lives as I do with mine. Do you understand?"

There were sporadic utterances of "Yes, Option."

"Do you understand me?" Marcus repeated, raising his voice.

"Yes, Option!" they cried as one.

Marcus nodded. "Very good. After consultation with the other officers, it has been agreed that I will occupy the commander's tent. The princess will share that tent."

Some grins blossomed on the faces of the men. A few of them chuckled or ribbed their fellows.

"None of that!" Marcus bellowed. "I wish there were some more suitable accommodation I could make for her. But there is no other place I can put her and ensure her safety at night. I know this looks improper, as if I intend to take liberties with her. But I have no choice." He paused. He removed his helmet. "You know me. You all know me. You're my brothers. We have fought together, bled together. You know what I stand for, whose name I bear. Please, I beg of you—as my brothers—trust me that I will . . . hold to my principles. I will not betray my God. I will not take liberties with the princess. Please . . . trust me."

Several of the men nodded.

Tesserarius Caeso Lucilius—now effectively second-in-command—saluted. "Yes, Option!"

The men thumped their fists to their breastplates. "Yes, Option!"

Marcus placed his plumed helm upon his head once more. "Thank you. And I ask that, should I fall in battle, you will all—each of you and all of you—take my place to ensure that the princess is honored and protected in my stead. Do I have your promise?"

"Yes, Option!" they cried.

Marcus saluted his men. "Very well, then. Strike camp and prepare to march. Dismissed!"

As the century dispersed and each man went about his duty, Marcus turned to Maelona. He had expected to see a smile on her face.

Instead, she frowned. "Did you mean what you said?"

He nodded. "Yes. Every word."

"And you trust them?"

"With my life. And yours. And your honor."

Her frown deepened into a bitter scowl. "I have no honor. It was stolen from me. By Romans. By men like those."

Marcus shook his head vehemently. "Not all Romans are the same. These men are honorable. They are brave. They are *not* evil." He paused. "Branwen, the night-demon, she killed all the evildoers. All that are left are—"

"Romans," she said. "You Romans took everything from me. I have no honor, no virtue. I have no people. I have no family." She sank down into the wagon. "I have nothing." She grasped at the tattered woolen dress she wore. "Nothing but these slave rags."

"You have your freedom."

She shook her head. "Freedom? Freedom to go where? I have nowhere to go! At least when I was a slave, I knew what I had to do . . . to survive. Now I don't know what to do."

Marcus knelt beside her. "You're safe with us . . . with me."

"Safe? As long as I'm with you, perhaps. But when we return to the legion? You said yourself, there is no place for a woman with the army. What then? I cannot stay with you then. And I cannot go. I haven't the skills to live in the woods or in a cave. The best I can hope for is slavery again. A-And a kind master. There is no other life for me."

Marcus searched about, grasping vainly for any idea, any plan. "I am a nobleman now. I have resources. I could send you to Rome."

"To Rome?" Her eyes were wide with terror. She grasped a handful of her red mane. "To be gawked at? A curiosity? A freak? You may be head of a noble house now, and that is all well and good for you, but if you were to send me to Rome, no one would know you—who you are, other than by name. And no one would know me. I would be . . . lost."

Marcus couldn't think of anything to say.

Angry tears fell from her eyes. "Do you know what you've done to me?"

"I was . . . I only wanted . . . to help you."

She uttered one bitter laugh. "That's the worst of all. I believe you. Your intentions were . . . honorable. You were attempting to be kind. You showed me . . . pity."

Pity her not. "I'll find a way. Maelona, I promise you—I will find a solution. I'm sorry. I—"

Maelona rose and clambered out of the wagon. She did not look at him. "When you find that solution, please let me know. But for now, I must . . . prepare for the day's travels." She looked at him then, and her eyes shone like cold, green stars, glistening with bitter tears. "So, tell me, Commander, may I still ride in the wagon with the other baggage?"

Marcus's jaw dropped. "Of course, you may ride in the wagon, but you are not—"

"Thank you, Commander." She spun on her bare heel and strode off toward the commander's tent. As she stomped away, she wiped furiously at her eyes.

The stench of burning centurion filled Marcus's nostrils. The smoke choked him, tasting like ashes on his tongue—like the ashes of his good intentions.

Interlude I

"The unwilling shall deceive the penitent, and she shall be filled with joy. And she shall remember fear."
from the Book of Marcus Scribonius

July 2017 A.D.

Yer intentions were good, laddie, but these"—Moira MacDonald Morgan held up a pair of well-worn canvas sneakers—"are my *gardenin'* shoes. They're nae for walkin' about."

Her husband, Carl Morgan, gaped at the shoes he had packed in Moira's luggage. "You're kidding me." Then he looked at his wife in dismay. "You are kidding, right?"

Moira tried her best—she truly made a valiant effort to give him a stern look as she shook her head. But upon seeing the expression of consternation and horror on her husband's face, she burst into gales of laughter. "Nae, laddie," she managed to say at last, "I'm nae jokin' with ye. These truly are my gardenin' shoes."

Carl sighed, threw up his hands, and plopped down on the small stateroom sofa. "I'm so sorry. I thought I had everything planned just perfect!"

Moira dropped the totally unfit-for-walking sneakers onto the queen-size bed. *'Tis barely queen-sized,* she thought, *but then again, everything is a wee bit compact on a cruise ship.* She navigated the narrow space between the bed and the dresser, then over to the sofa. She didn't stumble—not precisely—but as steady as the Disney cruise ship was, the waters where the English Channel met the North Sea still managed to rock the massive boat a bit.

And Moira had never been the best of sailors. *'Tis a century since I was last on the water.*

She paused at the porthole which, at that moment, provided nothing more than a view of the choppy waters. Even so, it was lovely—made all the lovelier by what that view represented. Then she sat down beside her husband, whose lips were pursed in an irritated pout. She put an arm around him, and then, not satisfied with that degree of closeness, she scooted up into his lap. She put her arms around his neck and kissed his cheek.

His cheek was rough with stubble from the long flight. When they'd first married, Carl never had to shave—their former, mutual condition prevented his beard from growing at all. But that was in the past. At times now, Moira enjoyed the manly feel of his rough cheek. At other times, it was annoying and irritating to her tender lips. This, however, was one of those moments when being close to her husband was important enough to ignore a day's growth of irritating beard.

So she kissed his rough cheek again.

He answered her kiss with a grunt. "I'm sorry."

She laughed. "Ach, laddie, ye did well! 'Tis an anniversary gift beyond my wildest dreams."

"Yeah, but I packed the wrong shoes. How are you supposed to go hiking around the British Isles in crappy, old sneakers?"

She smiled at him. "I'll make do. And at the first opportunity, I'll buy some proper walkin' shoes."

He finally turned his face to her. "Are you sure it's okay?"

Moira rolled her eyes. "Okay? 'Tis positively perfect! But ye, laddie! Ye are such good *liar*! How am I ever tae trust ye again?"

He favored her with a grin and a wink. "Christmas and birthdays! And now anniversaries! You gotta admit, this was my best one yet!"

She narrowed her eyes in an expression of mock severity. "Ooh, laddie, that it was." She sighed. "Are ye sure the wee ones, our precious bairns'll be all right while we're gone?"

He laughed. "Winnie was *so* excited to help. I gotta tell ya, she was the perfect coconspirator. She was thrilled to babysit the kids. And don't worry. She's got your Primary classes covered for the next four weeks too."

"Four weeks? I thought the cruise lasted only thirteen days."

Carl gritted his teeth and growled at himself. "Oh, well, I guess once the cat's out of the bag . . ."

"Wait . . . there's more to this wee"—she counted up quickly—"sixth—nae—*seventh* honeymoon? A cruise? A *Disney* cruise, nae less . . . and there's more?"

His grin was so wide, it was infectious. "I, uh, thought, once the cruise was over, we'd take a week, see London for a day or two, then rent a car and drive up to the Highlands to . . . I mean, if you want to, that is . . . to see your old village. Your birthplace."

Moira froze. *My village? Home? So many memories . . . terrible, horrible memories.*

But there are good memories too. Of the before *time.*

"Sweetheart? Moira? Are you okay?"

Moira shook herself. She smiled then. "Aye, my love, that'd be grand." Her eyes were suddenly moist. "Ye are a wonderful man—a wonderful, bonnie laddie. D'ye ken that?"

He winked again. "Anything to see my bride happy."

She kissed him then. She put her lips next to his ear. "And I *am* that. Perfectly happy."

She kissed him again. "Ye are a wily *liar*, though."

He grinned from ear to ear. "Had you going, didn't I?"

She pulled back, but remained in his lap. "Let me see now." She counted on her fingers. "First we're goin' for a night at the Anniversary Inn in Salt Lake. But nae! Ye missed the exit. 'But we're goin' a wee bit further north,' ye say. 'Takin' the other exit,' ye say. Then 'tis the airport. 'We're goin' to New York. A Broadway show,' ye say. 'Which show?' says I. '*Tangled, the Musical,*' ye say. But nae! 'There's too much luggage,' I say, 'for just a weekend.' 'Just wanted ye tae have *options*,' ye say. 'But why do we need our passports?' says I. Then ''tis nae a *Broadway* show, 'tis a *London* show,' ye say. But nae! When we get off the plane at Heathrow and collect our luggage, ye take me down to catch a Disney Cruise Lines motor coach to Dover! 'Twelve-night cruise o' the British Isles,' ye say. 'But they do indeed have *Tangled, the Musical,*' says I. And ye tell me 'tis indeed performed aboard this very vessel. As if that somehow justified the other lies. Ye would think that'd be enough. But nae! Here we are, aboard this lovely ship, and ye say there's more? A week or so drivin' around Scotland? Tae visit my ancient village? My birthplace? I've more than run out of fingers. When does it end, laddie?"

Carl was nearly choking with laughter by the end of her mock tirade. "That's it! I promise. Last surprise." Then his expression sobered. "You are . . . happy, right?"

Moira smiled. "Deliriously happy, my bonnie laddie! Ye are takin' me home."

He opened his mouth and attempted a nearly tuneless rendition of "I'll Take You Home Again, Kathleen!"

But she put a finger to his lips. "Carl, my love, ye ken ye cannae sing a lick. Besides, that's nae a Scottish song. 'Tis Irish."

He grinned impishly. "Actually, it's a *Star Trek* reference. 'The Naked Time'—Lieutenant Kevin Riley—in Engineering . . ." He opened his mouth and began again. "I'll take—"

Only one way to stop him!

And so, Moira smothered his face in kisses.

But a small knot of dread settled in her stomach. *I'm goin' home.*

Back to where it all began.

Back to where I chose damnation.

Chapter XII

"They are gathered as new lambs in the spring. And they are cast into the flames so that the wicked might honor the lord of the dead."
from the Book of Marcus Scribonius

DCCCXIV *Ab Urbe Condita* (61 A.D.)

It wasn't that Marcus Aquillius Audaxus disliked horses or that he relished the idea of marching for thirty miles or more with eighty pounds of gear. No, the problem was that, astride the massive black beast, Marcus felt removed, segregated from his men. They marched, and he rode.

In short, he felt as if he were cheating.

If he thought Maelona could have handled the stallion, he would have insisted she ride it. But the former slave was adamant that she didn't know how to ride. And this was no pony such as the Celts used—this was a Roman warhorse. The stallion had spirit and required a firm hand—a very firm hand. It took Marcus half the morning's ride to learn to control the beast properly. Marcus understood that, as far as the horse was concerned, Marcus was on trial—the stallion was testing him, evaluating him, deciding whether or not to accept Marcus as his new master. And if the animal found Marcus lacking or fearful, he would never submit to Marcus's will. He might allow Marcus to ride, he might carry Marcus, even allow Marcus to direct him—most of the time—but horse and rider would never become one, never trust each other. The relationship would be a constant struggle for mastery.

Marcus was unsure if he had passed the test. There had been some missteps to be sure—some misunderstandings and struggles between Marcus and his new mount—but the stallion seemed to have grown calmer, more willingly obedient.

And, at least, Marcus had managed to keep his saddle. That in itself was a victory of sorts.

I don't even know the animal's name. He patted the horse's neck. "What's your name, boy?" he asked for what felt like the hundredth time.

The stallion, however, as with all the times before, stubbornly refused to answer him.

Riding the horse did allow him the freedom to move up and down the column, to check for problems—much as he had done before on foot with his hastile. But on horseback, Marcus could do it more quickly, more efficiently—and without the hastile.

I don't have to strike these men to get them to stay in formation. A simple word is sufficient.

The hastile itself rode in the first wagon with Maelona.

She hadn't spoken to him since she rebuked him that morning.

And that rebuke stood like a wall of stone between them, a wall slowly getting higher and more impenetrable.

Her words still stung, but Marcus saw the truth in them. *I have put her in an untenable situation. She has no place in this world.*

And once we return to the legion . . .

How did Quintus Aquillius do it? How did he keep her? Where *did he keep her?*

Not that I want to keep *her . . . not like that. But he kept her safe* somewhere.

Marcus thought about asking her, but regardless of where she'd been housed and kept as a slave, she was a slave no longer. *If I ask her directly, she'll probably think I want to send her back to . . . to her previous existence.*

Besides, she's not speaking to me.

How he wished he could ask his mother for advice.

Marcus loved his mother dearly. He missed her. The blow of her death had driven him to join the army.

But she was the only woman Marcus had ever been able to decipher. The rest—Maelona included—baffled him.

Barely a few hours before, she had been solicitous—*desperate*—eager to please him, seemingly desiring to be with him.

Now, she acts as if the very sight of me makes her angry.

Father in heaven, what should I do? How can I protect her? How can I reach her?

I care for her. I want her to be happy. That's truly all I want.

I want Maelona to be happy.

The full implication of those words struck Marcus like a spear to his heart.

I want Maelona to be happy.

It's not just pity, not anymore.

I love her.

But that realization gave him no joy, no warmth, no comfort, because she was correct—in freeing her, he had destroyed her.

But the prophecy . . . I was supposed to give her freedom. I'm certain that's what it meant.

Deliver thyself from bondage.

But now, I'm bound to her in a different way.

The horse snorted and reared slightly. Then it settled back into a gentle walk once more.

Marcus patted the animal's neck. "Easy, boy. Did you see a snake or something?" Marcus scanned the ground about them, but saw nothing. "Easy, boy. I wish I knew your name."

Marcus chuckled. *Perhaps there's another way to tame the wild beast—to tame both of them.*

Marcus turned the horse and rode quickly to the back to the column, to the first wagon.

The mule drawing the wagon shook its head at the approaching horse and rider, then it snorted. It seemed to miss a step in its steady gate, causing the wagon to jolt and the wagoner to curse.

Maelona turned her head toward the commotion.

Upon observing Marcus, she turned her face away once more and went right back to ignoring him.

"I need your help," Marcus said as he turned his mount, so he could ride beside the wagon.

The mass of curls didn't move, the face inside continued to stare toward the wagon behind them.

"What's the horse's name?" Marcus asked. "Do you know? I can't just keep calling him 'boy' all day."

Maelona glanced at him briefly, but that was her only reaction.

Very well. "You see, the problem is when I say, 'Good boy,' 'Well done, boy,'" Marcus shrugged. "I'm certain he expects me to say something else. It's insulting, I think. He's a proud warhorse, and I'm just the stupid man who sits on his back, keeps yanking on his reins, kicking his flanks, and telling him to go here and there. And I won't even call him by his proper name! So please, not for my sake, but for his—what's his name? I know you're angry with me—and you are justified in your anger—but what about the poor horse? What wrong has he ever done you?"

A smile flirted with the corners of her mouth. Her eyebrows lifted in amusement. "Gaius."

As happy as he was to have made a breach in the shield wall of her silence, Marcus wasn't certain he'd heard her correctly. "Gaius? After the legate? The governor?" *That would be horribly disrespectful.*

She shrugged, then gave an almost imperceptible shake of her head. "No. Your . . . new father."

My new . . . "Gaius Aquillius?"

The red mane bounced.

Marcus realized she must have nodded. "He named the horse after . . . the head of his family?"

She nodded again. "I think my mas— I think Quintus hated him." She raised her head and looked at Marcus for the first time. "I think Quintus was in the process of renaming the beast."

Marcus chuckled. "Let me guess . . . Marcus. Am I right?"

She favored him with a mischievous grin. "It didn't work. The beast refused to take to it."

Marcus laughed. He leaned forward and patted the horse's neck. "Good boy, Gaius."

The horse nodded its head.

Marcus grinned. "I think he likes it. Hello, Gaius. I'm pleased to finally meet you properly."

Gaius the Warhorse nodded again.

Marcus nodded his own head toward the princess in the wagon. "Thank you, Lady Maelona. It appears Gaius appreciates it."

The princess shrugged again. "I didn't do it for that awful beast."

"What?"

"I said, I didn't do it for the wretched horse." She paused. "You asked . . . what wrong has that creature ever done me? Well, he bit me. On my . . . my backside. Hard." She lowered her voice. "I couldn't sit down for days."

A laugh burst from Marcus.

The horse snorted nervously. But it didn't kick.

Marcus patted the animal's neck. But he did *not* say, "Good boy, Gaius."

"It's not funny," Maelona muttered.

"No, it's not," said Marcus, trying to control his mirth. "Not really. I'm sure he's sorry. Aren't you, Gaius?"

The horse snorted.

Maelona bared her teeth at the animal. "See? He is a horrible beast!"

Marcus couldn't help but laugh again. "I don't think he has any idea what we're talking about."

Maelona growled. Then she resumed her silence.

They rode together like that for a bit.

And the silence between them seemed to grow again. The breach in the shield wall was being filled up once more.

"So" —Marcus cleared his throat—"if you didn't do it for him, for the horse . . ." He let the words hang in the air like the hovering dust of the road.

Maelona's head moved as if she were speaking, but Marcus heard nothing.

"I'm sorry," he said. "Did you say something?"

"I said" —Maelona's voice raised, then lowered again—"I did it for you."

"You . . . uh . . ." Marcus swallowed the lump in his throat. Or rather, he attempted to. "My lady, I . . . need to speak with you." He looked meaningfully at the wagoner. However, Maelona was not looking at Marcus and didn't notice. "In private. Please."

He reached a hand down to her. "Please?"

She looked at his hand, then at the horse, her eyes widening with horror.

"Please?" he repeated.

Tentatively, her face twisted in a grimace, she grasped his hand.

"No, take hold of my arm, please, not my hand."

She nodded, took hold of his forearm, and squeezed her eyes shut.

Marcus took a firm hold of her arm and hoisted her up and into his lap.

She tried to settle there, but to no avail—she couldn't find a safe or comfortable way to sit on the Roman saddle. She growled in frustration. "Hold still," she said. She grasped Marcus's neck and deftly clambered around him until she was able to sit behind the saddle.

Then she put her arms around his armor, but she couldn't maintain a firm hold. So she lowered her arms until she had grasped him about the waist, below his breastplate. She sighed. "There. That should work."

Marcus chuckled in surprise. "That was . . . amazing! I thought you said you couldn't ride."

"Not a monster like this," she said into his back. "A proper pony, yes. I know how to ride a pony. My brother and I used to ride like this—him in front, or me in front—it made no difference. But this horrible beast scares me."

"I understand. He's a lot to handle. Spirited."

Maelona tightened her grip about Marcus's waist.

And Marcus dared to hope her action was not entirely due to fear. "I'm sorry . . . about your brother. Your parents."

Maelona said nothing.

And Marcus let the silence between them build once more until it felt as heavy and thick and cold as a wall of stone, not merely a wall of shields.

But he didn't know what he could possibly say. *We killed them.*

"It was war," Maelona said at last. "People . . . die in war. Good people. People we love."

Marcus felt his throat tighten, choking off words. *Gaius Aquillius.* He managed to force out, "My commander. My . . . mentor." *My father. I didn't know. He was trying to acknowledge me, even with his last breath.* "We have both . . . lost people."

She sighed. "You wanted to speak with me." Maelona's tone was neutral, like that of a woman bargaining over the price of fish in a marketplace—not wanting to sound too eager to buy, not wanting to pay too much for what she needed.

Marcus cleared his throat. "Yes, I . . . Yes. I'm sorry. I've bungled things . . . badly."

She said nothing.

"I need your help, but I won't force you to do anything for me. You are not my slave."

Still she said nothing.

Surely, she can feel my blood pounding. "You are not my slave, my lady, but as far as is possible, within the bounds of my duty to my God . . . a-and to Rome . . . I am *yours.* Your slave. Your servant. I will do anything you ask . . . within those bounds." *Curse my clumsy tongue.* "I'm not saying this very well, but . . ."

"Please," she said. "Just stop talking." She squeezed him more tightly.

A long moment passed in silence. And then she spoke. Her words were soft—muffled and unintelligible.

"What? I didn't hear—"

"Even though . . . Even though I'm ugly?"

Marcus very nearly laughed out loud, but he fought the laughter down, subdued it. "Maelona, you are not . . . You are beautiful. Lovely. I'm . . ." *Don't say it. She's not ready. And it cannot be.*

"Would you marry me? Take me as your wife?"

The question stunned him. "I . . . I cannot."

"Why not? I would be under your protection. Forever. It would solve the problem."

She's not asking– It's not because she loves me. She doesn't. She simply needs my protection.

Not that it matters. "You are under my protection now."

"Until the end of the . . . the mission. After that, I will be taken and sold to a brothel. Or to the tin mines of Dumnonia. As your wife—"

"I cannot marry. Not now."

"Because of your god?"

"No, that's not it. My God encourages marriage, unless one is a missionary. And I'm not."

"Then why not?"

"Because of my oath. I'm a soldier, a legionnaire. I cannot marry until my enlistment is over."

"And when will that be?"

"Fourteen more years."

Maelona pulled back a little. She still maintained her grip on him, but it had loosened a bit. "How do you . . . raise more warriors? If the warriors cannot marry . . ."

Marcus shrugged. "Many men take mistresses—local women. There are many children born. And when the enlistment is over, some men marry the women. Or abandon them. Them and the children. It is not honorable, but . . ."

"Will you take me as your mistress then?"

He sighed. "Coupling is forbidden outside of marriage. By my God."

"Stupid god."

Marcus laughed. He shouldn't have, and he knew it. "No, my God teaches that coupling is special—sacred and reserved for marriage."

"But you cannot marry."

Marcus sighed again, but he had no other reply.

"It seems to me," she said, "that the Roman army is no place for a . . . What do you call yourselves? Your cult?"

"Christians. And . . . being in the army . . . has its challenges." *Like falling in love with a woman I can't marry. A woman whose family I helped to kill.*

"What about your night-demon?"

Marcus felt the breath congeal in his lungs. "Branwen?"

"She wants you. She can take you."

"She . . . she said I have a choice."

"And will you choose her?"

For a brief and horrifying moment, Marcus wasn't certain of the answer. "No. What she offers . . ." *What is it she offers? To become like her?* The thought terrified him, but a small part of him—a deep, dark part of his soul—was not entirely repulsed by the idea. *No!* "I will not . . . I cannot choose it."

Maelona leaned against his back once more, tightening her hold on his waist. "But you want her? You desire her?"

Marcus shook his head vehemently. "No." *Yes. She frightens me. But she's also . . . so . . .*

"Do you think she's beautiful? Desirable?"

Marcus swallowed hard. "Yes. She is that—beautiful and desirable."

"She will come back tonight. And every night. Until she persuades you. Until she ensnares you. And then you *will* choose her."

"No." And he meant it. *Because, of all the women in this world, I would choose you. You and only you.* He thought it, but aloud he said, "I will find a way." *To what? To marry you?*

"If I . . . worshipped your god . . . Would you marry me then?"

Marcus smiled. "It would certainly make things easier between us. We would be . . . of like minds. But—"

"Then I will worship your god, your Christus."

"It's not that simple."

"Will you teach me? Teach me the prayers and the oaths and the sacrifices? I will learn."

"Yes, but . . . as I said, it's not that simple. You must also *believe*."

"Your god will be my god. Yes. Then you will marry me. And then you will keep your promise."

"My promise?"

"To protect me."

"But my oath to Rome . . ."

"My mas— Quintus said, a commander could allow it. A centurion could allow it."

"Maelona, I'm not—"

"I was kept with his baggage, but I could stay with him. At night. Because he was a commander. And he desired me. Do you desire me?"

Marcus ignored the question. "I'm not a commander. I'm not a centurion. I'm merely an option. And when we return to—"

"You command these men, do you not? You wear the sword on the right hip. You wear the horsehair on your head."

"It's only temporary. I'm the commander for now, only because . . ."

"Because that . . . *dog* is dead."

Marcus nodded. "Yes, but—"

"So while you are the commander, do it. Take me. As your wife."

"Maelona, I don't have the authority."

She squeezed his waist. "But I would please you. I am skilled. You said I am beautiful. Do you not desire me?"

Marcus groaned. *Yes!* "Maelona, I can't. I simply . . ." He let his voice trail off.

Maelona said nothing.

But Marcus could feel her quiver. *She's weeping.* "Don't weep, my lady. I'll find a way. I promise. I'll find a way." *But how?*

Our Father who art in heaven . . . How? Show me the way!

And to his mind came the words of the Savior. *I am the way, the truth, and the life.*

Is that it? If she becomes a believer? But that doesn't solve the problem. I still can't marry, not and keep my oath.

"You s-said," Maelona managed, choking on her tears, "that I was a *free* woman."

"Yes. You are."

"Then I will w-weep if I ch-choose."

Marcus smiled. "If you choose. But I do wish you wouldn't. I want you to be happy." *I love you. With all my aching heart.*

But it would not be kind to tell you that – not when I cannot marry you.

"I-I p-promise," she said, "I will learn the w-ways of your god. You will . . . teach me?"

"If you wish. I cannot baptize you, however."

"What is . . . baptize? And why do you deny me this . . . this baptizing?"

Marcus laughed. "I'm not *denying* you—"

"You deny me marriage. You deny me the protection of marriage."

"That's different."

"It is because I am impure, because I am . . . spoiled."

Marcus placed his free hand over her hands. He gave her hands a gentle, tender squeeze. "Maelona, that is not your fault. You were taken against your will."

"But it is true. I am ruined. Unfit for marriage. You have kept yourself from women, from coupling. Your god forbids it. So p-purity is important to you. And mine is lost. Forever."

He squeezed her hands again. "Maelona, it was not your fault. And it doesn't—"

"I hated my . . . I hated *him*."

"I know."

"But even so . . . there were times . . . when I . . . had . . . pleasure. And when that would happen, I hated him even more. I hated myself." She sobbed. "I am soiled. And so you do not want me."

Marcus's heart almost broke then, upon hearing her confession and the desolation in her voice. *She has lost everything. Pity her not. But it's not just pity. Not anymore.* He almost made a confession of his own. Instead, he said, "Maelona, listen to me. My God, well, the Son of my God . . . His blood was shed, He gave His life so that we could all be . . . *pure* again. No matter what we have done. We can be pure again."

"You believe this? Truly?"

The incredulity in her voice brought a smile to his face. A little smile. "Yes. Truly."

"But I am no longer a maid. That cannot be restored. Never."

"Once you are pure again, you start over. You are as pure as the day you were born."

"Truly?"

"Truly."

"And the loss of my maidenhood?"

"It doesn't matter. Not to me."

"I will learn the ways of your god." Her voice was stronger, steadier. And she was no longer weeping. "I will be pure again, as you say. And then you will marry me."

Marcus groaned with frustration. "I already told you—"

"You said . . . you *promised* you would find a way."

"That's not what I meant." *But—curse me for a besotted fool—it's what I want. More than anything in this world.*

"Please," she said. "It is the only way."

"Maelona . . ."

"You *will* choose me."

Her words—her *choice* of words—sent a tremor of fear through him. *She sounds just like . . .*

"You will choose me. Not *her*."

Choose Maelona, not her—*not Branwen.* But in his heart, Marcus knew Maelona was correct about one thing—Branwen *would* return.

He was also convinced of something else—in spite of Branwen's proclaiming he was free to choose, she would hammer at his defenses. And he was not entirely certain those defenses would hold.

Her eyes, so like Maelona's, but so different. Maelona's gaze is haunted, vulnerable. When Branwen looks at me, fixes me with her eyes, she pulls *at me.* I want *to . . . do anything she asks. No matter how wrong, no matter how terrifying. Branwen's gaze is . . . compelling. Her lips . . . so inviting. Her skin so fair.*

And she saved my life.

She also killed three men.

Whatever else she is, she is a murderess.

A murderess . . . or an executioner.

She claimed all her victims were evil. Gwynn was a Druid priest. He carried the sacred gold knife – slaughtered innocent people in the name of his gods.

Maelona's gods . . .

"Do you like this beast?" Maelona's question snapped him out of his thoughts.

Marcus grinned, though he knew she couldn't see it. "Do you mean Gaius here?"

"Yes." The word conveyed a mountain of contempt.

Marcus patted the horse's neck. "I barely know him. He's a bit of a handful. But he does make it easier to move up and down the column. Normally, an infantry centurion would not—"

"You take too much on yourself."

"What did you say?"

"You, yourself, told me that my Latin was very good. I think I said it correctly. You take too much on yourself."

Marcus found himself grinning. *Last night she was a slave. Now she's criticizing me? Is this the* true *Maelona?* "What do you mean?"

"You are attempting to be the centurion and the option. I have seen this. You ride up and down the . . ." She seemed to search for a word, then settled upon, ". . . the line. Here you are the option. But you also ride ahead, leading, looking for trouble, searching the road. There you are the centurion. You cannot be both option and centurion."

Marcus chuckled. "So all that time you were sitting in the wagon, pretending to ignore my very existence . . . all that time you were watching me. Observing me? Judging my style of command?"

Maelona said nothing, but her hands shifted against his waist.

It doesn't mean anything – her watching me. It doesn't mean she loves me, not as I love her. It is only because she needs my help, my protection. Protection I cannot provide. "I thought you were angry with me."

"You are a fool."

Yes, I am. An utter fool. In love with a woman I cannot have.

And I didn't even know I was hopelessly besotted until this very hour. "You are not the first woman to say so."

"Have there been . . . many such women?"

Marcus laughed then. Loud and heartily. "No. For me, there has been only one woman in my life."

"Your mother." It was not a question. It was a statement of fact.

"H-how do you know that?"

"The woman on your belt . . . the woman's face on your belt." She tugged gently on the stump of the severed strip with one hand. "If there is only one woman in your life, she must be your mother."

Marcus felt warmth spread from the top of his head to his belly—where Maelona's hands pressed against him. "Yes, you . . . after . . . after Quintus Aquillius stabbed me . . . my belt strip . . . my mother's face. You recovered it for me. You don't know how much . . ." Marcus could no longer find the words. "Thank you, my lady."

He thought about the severed strip, tucked away in his pack, in the baggage wagon where Maelona had been riding.

"Your men need to rest." She pointed at a pond to the left of the road. A handful of sheep grazed nearby, but no shepherd was to be seen. "There is water for the cattle, the mules, and . . . the horrible beast."

"Oh, now you are telling me how to lead the march? Who commands this century?" He tried to sound stern and indignant, but he couldn't hide his mirth.

"Please," she said, "call a halt. And let me down."

"Your counsel is good."

"Of course it is."

Marcus chuckled. *Of course it is.*

And so he called for a halt. He let her down, into the wagon. When she let go of his arm, as he released his hold on her, he was struck with a pang of loss.

Besotted fool.

Once in the wagon, Maelona clambered down and strode quickly away into the high grass, presumably to relieve herself.

Marcus dismounted. He delivered Gaius the Warhorse into the care of the herdsman, a Grecian calo by the name of Demetrius, instructing the man that the animal be watered and allowed to graze for a bit.

Marcus then went in the opposite direction from Maelona and attended to his own needs.

Afterward, he inspected his troops as they rested.

Marcus found that he was sore. His thighs and his knees hurt, though he had not been marching. *Not accustomed to riding—not anymore. I can march dozens of miles a day, but riding for long stretches . . .*

He shook his head. Still he was grateful for the mount. *Gaius. And he tried to change the name to Marcus.* He chuckled. *You bear a proud name, Gaius the Warhorse. Still, I fear you would be a liability in a fight. I need to be on the ground, with my men.*

Are we going into a fight? Into combat?

This is merely a reconnaissance mission, isn't it?

If this Arawn is a goetia, we will crucify him and put down any potential rebellion.

Crucify him.

Like Jesus.

But he's not Jesus. He is not a god or the son of a god.

He's a trickster, raising a following. A goetia. Nothing more.

As Marcus neared the front of the column, he called to Nonus Sestius. "Follow me."

"Yes, Option." The legionnaire got to his feet and followed Marcus to the front.

They found the three junior officers—Cornicen Spurius Orcivius, Vexillarius Agrippa Corfidius, and Tesserarius Caeso Lucilius—resting and talking in low voices. The three junior officers had all temporarily removed their lion, bear, and wolf skins while resting, but the three of them all wore their helms—they were all prepared to fight at a moment's notice.

Marcus smiled as he observed Agrippa absentmindedly stroking the head of his bear pelt. Agrippa noticed the grin and the direction of his commander's eyes. He stopped petting the bear head, his face flushing red. It was an unconscious habit. No one teased him about it—no one would dare—but it embarrassed him all the same.

Spurius asked, "Is something amiss?"

Marcus shook his head. "Yes, but not with any of you. I have . . . received some good advice. It has been pointed out, by our *guest,* that since the passing of our *noble* centurion, I have been attempting to perform the duties both of centurion and option. As I am *not* a centurion, I am not in the position to *officially* appoint a new option. But I have a proposal."

The three junior officers exchanged curious looks. Grinning mischievously, Caeso Lucilius said, "So now you're taking military advice from our lovely guest, are you?"

The other two officers grinned as well. Even Nonus Sestius was smiling.

Marcus grimaced. *Should have left that detail out.* "Good advice is good advice, regardless of the source."

Spurious sighed, tapping his breastplate—over his heart. "And so pretty a source . . ."

Agrippa chuckled. "We're just teasing you. Go on. What's your proposal?"

Marcus forced a serious expression onto his face. "I wish to make a couple of *temporary* field promotions. With your support and approval."

The three of them exchanged sober looks, then nodded as one.

Marcus returned the nod. "I can't guarantee an increase in pay, not for either of those affected. And I can't guarantee that the promotions will remain when we return. But, if you are willing, I would ask that Caeso Lucilius be the acting option—the pro*option,* my second-in-command—and Nonus Sestius here to take over your duties as tesserarius. Effective immediately."

The tesserarius chuckled. Then the other two officers laughed as well.

Marcus said, "What's so funny?"

Caeso, still chuckling, shook his head. "We were just discussing this very question. We thought for certain you'd want Septimus Scribonius as *protesserarius,* but otherwise, we were about to make the same suggestion." He winked. "But I'm sure it was more . . . *pleasing* coming from the . . . princess."

I really wish I hadn't mentioned Maelona. "Well . . . then, I suppose . . ." He turned to Nonus Sestius. "Are you willing to serve as protesserarius? Even without the pay-and-a-half?"

Nonus grinned. Then he saluted. "Yes, Option!"

Marcus grinned. "Then so be it."

Caeso Lucilius stood and handed his clay tablet and wolf pelt to Nonus Sestius. "They're yours." He turned to Marcus with a grin. "So, Option, where's the cursed hastile? If I can't have a plume, at least I'll have the staff. I have to admit that I'm looking forward to thumping this sorry lot into shape!"

Marcus laughed. "Give a man a little power . . ." His expression sobered. "Like I said to Nonus Sestius, I can't promise you the increase in pay—double pay in your case—that should come with the staff."

Caeso Lucilius's expression sobered as well. "I'm not doing it for double pay. I'm doing it because Audaxus asks it of me." He put a hand on Marcus's shoulder. "I told you, we would follow you into Tartarus. That *is* where we're going, isn't it?"

Marcus nodded grimly. "Perhaps. The Celtic version of it, at least. This Arawn is most likely a goetia."

Caeso shrugged. "Perhaps. But after what we've seen on this cursed mission . . . I can believe in anything. Even a 'lord of the dead.'"

"What do your prophecies say?" Spurius Orcivius asked. "Anything about this Arawn?"

Marcus gaped at the cornicen in shock.

Spurius's eyes grew wide, and his jaw dropped. He snuck a furtive glance at Nonus Sestius.

Nonus shook his head and waved a dismissive hand. "The prophecies? You four are not so skilled at keeping secrets as you might suppose. I doubt there's a man in the century who doesn't know of the prophecies of Audaxus." The corner of his mouth lifted in an impish grin. "It's not simply your legendary bravery, noble Audaxus. That's not the only reason why we . . . why the men trust you the way we do. We know your god guides you. You are our centurial oracle."

"But . . ." *They know?* "The prophecies . . . they are only for me."

"Yes." Caeso shook Marcus's shoulder. "For you and those under your personal care." He swept a hand toward the century. "And that is all of us. *We* are under your personal care. You will not—you never have—led us amiss."

Marcus's plumed helmet suddenly seemed too heavy for his neck. "But three men are dead."

"Yes," said Agrippa as he rose to his feet. "The Ferret, a cursed Druid murderer, and that worthless, arrogant pup of a centurion. All 'evildoers' according to the goddess—"

"She's no goddess," Marcus protested, though his protest lacked emphasis. *They all know about the prophecies.*

Agrippa shrugged. "Very well, the night-demon then. She said they were evildoers. And when that cursed Quintus Aquillius murdered you, she flew away with you and brought you back to life. That sounds like a goddess to me."

There are no other gods! "She's not—"

"So what *do* the prophecies say?" asked Nonus.

Marcus took in a deep, calming breath. *They know. They're all looking to me to save them. I've already lost three men.* "The prophecies say that I shall seek the lord of the dead . . . and I shall find him."

"Sounds like a god to me," said Agrippa.

Marcus looked from the cornicen to the other junior officers. "And that doesn't frighten you? Because it scares me almost to death."

Nonus placed a hand on Marcus's free shoulder. "We will follow you, Audaxus. And if death is the fate your god has chosen for you, then we will die with you. But we will die on our feet, sword and shield in hand, our bodies between you and the lord of the dead." He lowered his voice as he shook Marcus's shoulder. "Hail, Audaxus." He'd spoken the salute softly, apparently wishing to avoid starting a cheering chorus throughout the century.

Spurius joined the others, placing his hand atop Caeso's on Marcus's shoulder. "Hail, Audaxus," he said in a quiet voice.

Agrippa followed, placing his hand atop Nonus's. "Hail, Audaxus."

Caeso said, "Lead us into Celtic Tartarus then. You lead, and we'll follow. Hail, Audaxus."

Marcus nodded, feeling as if the plume might snap his neck. He swallowed the lump in his throat.

I'm going to get them all killed.

The men . . . and Maelona too.

"So," said Agrippa, "I suppose that makes you *procenturion*."

Marcus shook his head. "No. I will not take that title. I am still the option, chosen by Centurion Gaius Aquillius Regulus. I am the option—*his* option. I will not take unto myself a title I have not—"

"Option! Option!"

Marcus spun around. He could see Demetrius, the herdsman, waving a hand and calling to him.

The Greek stood near the pond. The stallion, the ox, and the cows stood nearby, drinking or cropping the grass. The wagoners were there as well, watering their mules. The sheep that had been at the pool's edge had moved a stone's throw away and huddled together.

"Option!" the *calo* yelled again. "Come quickly!"

Marcus gripped the hilt of his sword and sprinted toward the herdsman. He noticed that all four of the junior officers were at his heels.

"What is it, man?" Marcus cried as he approached.

The wagoners had gathered around Demetrius. All seven men wore pale countenances. One of the wagoners knelt in the grass, retching.

The scent of animal dung and human vomit filled Marcus's nostrils.

The herdsman pointed frantically at the ground.

Another scent, an all-too-familiar stench, assaulted Marcus—the smell of dried blood and the reek of rotting meat.

A naked corpse lay on the grass, her arms spread wide. Her belly was sliced open.

"Get the capsarium," Marcus said, pointing to Nonus Sestius. "Tell

Gaius Publicia I need him, but there's no hurry."

♦ ♦ ♦

"I'm no midwife," said Gaius Publicia after he'd finished his examination of the body, "but she was with child, probably very close to her time. The infant was cut from her womb. And this was no attempt to deliver the baby and save the mother. No, this poor woman was sliced wide open."

Marcus knelt beside the *capsarium*. "So what are you saying?"

"I'm saying she was murdered, and the child stolen."

Marcus wrestled with the sudden urge to join the retching wagoner. "What else can you tell me?"

"She fought them." Gaius Publicia pointed to her wrists and ankles. "See the bruising? Her lips are torn. Perhaps she was gagged at some point."

"No," Marcus said. "A hand was forcibly held over her mouth."

The combat nurse eyed him and raised an eyebrow. "How do you know?"

"I've seen it before."

Marcus found her – his mother.

He found her when he came from working in their family's small vineyard.

She was naked. Her gown had been ripped from her. Her mouth was bloody, her lips torn. Blood – so much blood – had pooled between her legs.

And Marcus easily deduced what must have happened.

Bands of patrician youths were known to prowl the city, usually at night, ravishing women, young and old. But no such gang had ventured so far outside Rome, and not in the sunshine. At least not until that day.

Even had someone – a servant or even a neighbor – seen them, been able to identify them, they would have been untouchable, as the sons of noblemen.

And they had taken his mother. Taken her virtue and her life.

They probably hadn't meant for her to die, but the assault was so brutal, so violent . . .

Marcus wept.

He covered her with his own robe to hide her shame.

He kissed her forehead.

And he buried her.

And then he left Rome.

Marcus pointed to some shredded clothing lying nearby—a torn woman's gown. "Cover her. We'll bury her before we move on. Nonus

Sestius, organize some men to attend to it."

"Yes, Option." The new protesserarius saluted, turned, and strode away.

"Perhaps, she was tending the sheep," suggested Agrippa, "even in her condition."

Marcus nodded. "Away from home with the sheep. That would explain why no one has found her before now. It must have been days since she was killed, judging by the smell. But where is the husband? Or her family? Surely, she was not alone, not so near her time."

"Over there, perhaps?" It was one of the wagoners who spoke. He pointed toward the cluster of sheep. "I once saw a dead shepherd boy. He died in the field, alone. The sheep would not leave his body."

The capsarium shrugged. "I'll take a look."

"They stole her baby?" Caeso, a combat veteran who'd seen his share of death, was pale, his face sweating. "Who would do such a horrible thing?"

"Another woman, perhaps?" suggested Agrippa. "A woman who desired a child? I have heard of such things."

"No," said Marcus, shaking his head. "There were at least five of them. One who held the ankles, two for the wrists. One to hold her mouth to silence her screams." He frowned. "I suppose one of the men holding her wrist might have been able to do that. And one to cut the child from her. So, at least four."

"Option!" The voice belonged to the combat nurse.

"Spurius," Marcus said, rising to his feet, "stay with her." He walked quickly toward Gaius Publicia.

Agrippa and Caeso followed in Marcus's wake, hands on sword pommels.

The capsarium was kneeling near the sheep. The animals themselves were feeding on the grass.

"I think this was her husband," said the nurse. "The cause of death is obvious."

Indeed it is.

The corpse's throat had been slashed with a single, violent slice. The cut went so deep that the spine was visible.

"A single cut," observed Gaius Publicia. "No bruises. No obvious signs of a struggle. Perhaps he knew his attackers. Or they took him by surprise." He pointed at the man's belt. "His pouch is unopened. They didn't even rob him."

Marcus nodded. "All they wanted was the baby."

The capsarium looked at the small flock munching grass a few yards away. "They didn't even steal the sheep."

Marcus shook his head. "No. Look at his tunic. It's fine cloth. He had some wealth. I think this small family had a much larger flock. The attackers *did* steal the sheep—or most of them. These animals are the ones that got away."

"So," said Agrippa, "they took the baby and many of the sheep. There must have been quite a number of them."

"I'll fetch some men," said Caeso. "We'll bury this poor fellow next to his wife."

"This is a savage land," said Agrippa, adding a curse for good measure. "A savage land with beasts in place of people."

"Rome," Marcus said, "has her share of beasts."

Marcus felt a sudden urge to see Maelona, to hold her, to ensure that she was safe. "Stay with him."

Agrippa saluted. "Yes, Option."

As Marcus turned his eyes away from the corpse, a glint of something shiny caught his eye. "What is that?" He took a few steps closer to the corpse and knelt beside the mutilated neck and the head which was turned at an unnatural angle. He shifted his own head from side to side, staring intently at the exposed spine.

And saw it again. Clearly. A fragment of gold, embedded in the bone. Gritting his teeth and fighting an urge to empty his stomach, he reached into the decaying wound, closed his thumb and forefinger on the tiny, shining object, and pulled. His fingers slipped. He tried again, wiggling the object until it came free.

He wiped the object on the grass, taking great care not to lose it. Then he brought it closer to his eye.

Gold—triangular in shape, about the size of his thumbnail, and sharp on one side.

Marcus knew exactly what it was. "This is the tip of a knife blade. A sacrificial knife. The golden knife of a Druid priest."

Druids did this—slaughtered this man and wife. Stole their child.

Marcus closed his fist around the knife tip, careful not to cut himself.

Why take the child? To raise it . . . as a priest? Their priests are all male. How would they know if the child was a male or female before they ripped it from its mother?

No. They must have taken it for some other purpose. For some dark ritual.

A tingling—starting at the top of his head and traveling quickly down his spine—caused Marcus Aquillius Audaxus to quiver. He knew that feeling well.

It's coming.

Words of a prophecy—new and terrible—seared into his mind.

They are gathered as new lambs in the spring. And they are cast into the flames so that the wicked might honor the lord of the dead.

Marcus strode back to the first wagon, silently repeating the words of the new prophecy so he would not forget them. But there was no need.

Marcus could never forget anything—especially not words of prophecy.

Maelona sat there. When she saw him approach, she appeared to shift around.

Marcus got the impression that she was hiding something under her ragged gown.

She smiled at him, but the smile vanished as she saw the grim expression on his face.

Marcus reached for his pack. "Pardon me." He opened the pack, and removed the long box containing the scroll, the small writing desk, his quill, ink bottle, and sand bottle. With well-practiced actions he quickly recorded the dark and sacred words on the vellum of the scroll.

Maelona peered at the words. Marcus knew she couldn't read.

"What is that?" she asked. "What does it say?"

Marcus sprinkled sand on the ink, waited a moment, then blew the excess away.

"What does it mean?" Maelona asked.

Marcus stared at the scroll. Anger flared inside him. The anger turned to a burning rage. *They are sacrificing infants to Arawn. Burning children alive! Slaughtering anyone who gets in their way.*

The image of his mother flashed before his eyes. He shook his head to clear it.

"It means," he said through his teeth, "that this is no longer a reconnaissance mission."

He turned his eyes on the girl, and she flinched, recoiling as if she was suddenly afraid of him.

"Tell me," he said, forcing calm into his voice—an icy blanket of control to smother the flames of righteous fury—"please tell me about Arawn."

"A-Arawn?" Her eyes were round with fear and her voice trembled. "What d-do you w-want to know?"

"Everything. Tell me everything."

"Yes. But why?"

"Because, god or demon or whatever cursed thing he is, I'm going to march straight into Annwfyn, and I'm going to kill him—him and his cursed priests."

Chapter XIII

"Thou shalt meet a man on the road. And thou shalt offer him an ox and ask a bull in return. If he agrees with thy poor bargain, fear not to go with him. Thy companions shall find rest. Yea, and the humble prayer of faith shall be answered."

from the Book of Marcus Scribonius

Arawn is the lord of the dead." Maelona sat in the back of the wagon, fiddling with her red curls, while Marcus sat on the road itself. "He is king of Annwfyn. But you know all this. He has three hounds. Three white hounds with red ears. Arawn has a wife as well, but I do not remember her name."

Marcus would have preferred they sit in the grass at the side of the road—he had even suggested it—but Maelona had demurred, then adamantly refused when he pressed her. At first, he had thought her refusal to budge from her sitting position might be due to a . . . female concern. *She could be sitting on wool.* He'd observed Celtic women handle their condition in that manner. *But she was with me on the horse not that long ago.*

However, Mother said it can start without much warning.

But if she's sitting on wool, her skirts would be spread around her, not under her.

And so, he sat on the road, lower than she was. It occurred to him that forcing her to look down on him, and him to look up to her, might help to allay her fear. His anger—his fury at the priests of Arawn—She'd seen it in his countenance, and it had frightened her.

"Please," he said, showing her a gentle smile, "go on. Anything you know might be of help."

She nodded, looking at him from under her lashes. She smiled then—a shy smile.

He loved her shy smile. "I'm sorry," he said. "I didn't mean to scare you."

"What has occurred?" she asked. "Something has happened to

upset you. That is why you were angry. Not angry with . . . me." She lifted her face and looked at him directly. "Please tell me. Share your burden with me."

I love you, woman. Marcus shook his head. He glanced past her, to where he knew the two corpses were being interred. "I'd prefer not to go into detail, but we found a woman and a man murdered up ahead."

She turned to look, lifting up slightly.

Marcus noted that there was no woolen pad beneath her spread skirts. However, he did see a glint of metal. *What is she hiding?* He thought of the golden knife point he'd stowed in his pack. *It wasn't gold. But she's hiding something.*

A knife?

She turned back to face him. "You're burying them?"

Marcus nodded.

"Why would you do this?"

Marcus blinked at her. "Do what?" *Does she think we killed them?*

"Why would you bury them? Are they Romans?"

Marcus shook his head. "No. They are . . . They *were* Celts, probably Cambrians."

"But they are your enemies."

Ah. "We are not . . . The Celts are not our enemies."

She laughed with scorn. "How can you say this? We are at war!"

"We are at war only with those who are in rebellion. We have treaties. Most of your kings and queens—"

"Tell that to my brother! Tell that to my father and my mother!" Her pale cheeks reddened, and her green eyes narrowed with rage. "We had no cursed treaty!"

Marcus met her gaze. "You said it yourself. It was war. I wish we were not at war with . . . *some* of the peoples of Britannia. But we are. I myself have questioned why we are here, in this land. But we *are* here. I serve my emperor. You serve . . . *served* your king. We have treaties and—"

"You speak of this land as if we were all one people, one clan! But we are not! We are our own families, our own clans, our own lands. And this land is ours, not yours!"

"But we bring peace, roads, prosperity, civilization—"

"Peace?" she spat, tears streaming down her face. "*Pax Romana*? Peace at the point of a sword! The peace of blood!"

Marcus returned her glare for several long moments. Then he softened his gaze. He bowed his head. "The truth is, my lady . . . The truth is I don't know why we are here. I have asked myself this many,

many times. I just don't know. All I know is that I serve my emperor. I believe in the dream of Rome. One world, many peoples, but one world. I know we have not always . . . not always . . ."

His own hot tears surprised him. He dashed them away. "I'm sorry. I'm sorry about your mother, your father . . . your little brother. I didn't kill *them*—at least, I don't think I did—but I was *there*. I fought at Mona. I killed many of your people. I'm sorry." A great sob hit him, taking him unawares, like a fist to his gut. "I lost my friend. My mentor. My . . . father."

Suddenly, she was in front of him, kneeling, throwing her arms about his neck.

And she wept.

He put his arms around her, pressing her to his breastplate.

And he wept.

The moment lasted no more than the time it took to draw a dozen shuddering breaths. But Marcus felt as if it had been an hour—a comforting hour of unanticipated solace. Two enemies comforting one another for loved ones lost.

"Forgive me," he said, his lips as close to her ear as her hair and his helm would allow.

"I do," she said. "I do forgive you."

"Maelona . . . I will find a way." *I love you.* "I will find a way to protect you."

"There is only one way."

"Maelona, I cannot . . . You know I cannot marry you."

"You will find a way. You have given me your promise."

"Maelona . . ."

She pulled out of the embrace.

He let her go as well, but his heart ached.

Maelona put a hand on each of the cheek-guards of his helm. She turned his head toward herself, fixing her bloodshot eyes on his. "I know you will find a way, because you are Audaxus. Your men believe in you." She smiled. "I believe in you."

Then she tilted her head, drew his face to hers, and kissed him lightly.

It was not a kiss of passion, but it was sweet. *I love you.*

"What did you say?"

Marcus's eyes flew open wide. *Did I say that aloud?*

With her small hands, she shook his helm. "Say it again."

"I said nothing. You kissed me and . . ."

She smiled, and it was as if the dawn of the first day in Eden shone in her countenance. "I have something for you."

She got to her feet, turned, and reached into the wagon. "I started working on it this morning. When I was still angry with you. It needs another stitch, I think. Stitching leather is so difficult. And I am out of . . . *thin string* for stitching."

She whirled, knelt in front of him, and held out something long, thin, and brown—brown with a glint of brass. "I know I cannot work in leather properly, but it should do for now. I can add another stitch later."

She placed the leather strip into Marcus's hand. It was sewn at one end to create a loop—a loop into which a belt could be inserted. And near the loop was the brazen image of a woman's face.

His mother's.

Maelona's smiled, her eyes filled with joy. "I took it from your pack. I hope you will forgive me for the—What is the word?—the impertinence."

His eyes went from the tiny brazen face of his mother to the beaming face of the woman kneeling before him. "You did this for me?" He chuckled. "Even when you were angry with me?"

She shrugged, still smiling. "Yes. I was angry. But that doesn't change how I . . . Does it please you?"

He nodded. Vigorously. "Yes! Yes, it pleases me."

She stood. "Here. Rise. Let me put it on you."

Marcus obeyed.

Maelona unbuckled his belt and removed it. She slid the dagger's scabbard from the belt and handed the sheathed weapon to him. "Hold this." All the while she grinned. She slid the remains of the damaged loop from his belt, then slid the new one—rough in comparison to the other four—onto the belt. She put out a hand for the dagger, and once he surrendered it, she slid it back onto the belt.

"Lift your arms," she said, and he complied. She put her arms around his waist, encircling it with the belt. Then she buckled it, adjusted the position of the dagger on his left hip and the position of the strips so that they were centered in front, hanging over his groin.

Then she stepped back and admired her handiwork. "It . . . looks a bit different. It's about the right length. Not straight enough. And a bit wider than—"

He took her in his arms and kissed her—a sweet, tender kiss. Oh, how he was tempted to kiss her more passionately! He lifted his face and said, "Thank you, Princess Maelona. You have no concept of how much this means to me."

Her face still tilted up toward him, she sighed and smiled. "I think I do."

"Thank you. I . . ."

She wriggled her arms free of his embrace, reached up, and pulled his head toward hers—but not for a kiss. Instead, she pulled his ear toward her lips. "I love you too."

I did say it aloud.

"Now," she said, taking hold of his hand, "what else would you like to know about Arawn?" She led him toward the grass at the side of the road.

Back to the war. "What does he look like? Tell me about his rites and sacrifices."

She released his hand, but she favored him with a sly smile, full of feminine secrets. They sat in the grass, facing each other. "You do understand," she said, "that I have never seen him. I only know what my father and mother told me." A shadow of pain erased her smile for a moment. "Some say he wears a great black cloak and a hood, embroidered with gold. Some say he wears the skull of a stag over his head with great . . ." She gestured over her own head with both hands.

"Antlers?" he suggested. "Horns?"

She shrugged, then nodded. "Antlers on a stag? Yes?"

"Yes."

"Yes. Arawn is pale of skin. His hair and beard are black. I . . . don't remember anything else." She flushed. "I was never . . . particularly devout."

"And his sacrifices?"

She shook her head. "He requires no sacrifices. He collects the souls of the dead and takes them to Annwfyn, the . . . world under the world, where there is endless feasting and joy. Sometimes, he ventures forth with his hounds on the Wild Hunt to collect wandering . . . dead. Ghosts? Wandering ghosts."

Marcus narrowed his eyes in doubt. "No sacrifices? No blood? No . . . infants?"

"Infants?" She pursed her lips. "I do not understand. We make no sacrifices to Arawn. He is a benevolent god. He asks nothing of us. And besides, he is no longer my god. Christus is my god now."

"But this woman"—Marcus gestured toward the burial party—"her belly was cut open. Her infant taken."

"Her infant?" Maelona recoiled in horror as if his words had conjured up terrifying visions. "But why? Who would do such a thing?"

"Druid priests. Your cursed priests. With their cursed golden knives."

Maelona shook her head in vehement denial. "No! We do not do such things!"

"But"—*I must tread carefully here*—"you do perform human sacrifice to your gods. Do you deny this?"

"Yes, I deny it. Some priests . . . to Cernunnos. Not to Arawn. But the sacrifice is an adult. A-and willing."

Marcus shook his head slowly, deliberately. "Not all are willing. What about captives taken in war? Are they not sacrificed?"

"Some clans. Some clans do this. We do not." She bowed her head. "We *did* not. Among my people, we sacrificed animals, grain, fruits, wine. Never people." She narrowed her eyes, and they burned with emerald fury. "We are not all the same—not one people."

Marcus nodded. "No, you are not. Not all the same."

Her eyes softened. There was still anger, but it wasn't directed at Marcus. "There was one man—his name was Conwy—he declared the gods required more. But my father—he drove that horrible man and his few followers out. We did not all serve the gods in the same way."

"Of course not." He reached for her hand. "I believe you."

Although she did not pull away, she did not respond. She lowered her eyes and nodded. "I have not served the gods, not since my . . . humiliation. I prayed to them . . . at first. But they did not answer me. Never." Then she took his hand. Raising her eyes once more, she said in a voice of conviction and solemnity, "I reject the gods of my land. I will serve only Christus." Then her tone softened. "But I do not know how. You will teach me?"

He nodded, tingling at the warmth of her soft hand in his.

"Yes." She nodded with a fierce smile. "And then I will be pure once more. And you will desire me—in spite of my stolen maidenhood. You will desire me once I am pure again."

I desire you now. He laughed softly. *Maelona, if only you knew how much.* "This purity. It comes with baptism. And I cannot perform it."

"Again, you deny me this . . . baptism?"

He shook his head and lowered his own eyes. "I have not the authority to perform it. Only one of our priests can do this. And I am not a priest—I am merely a believer, a member of His Church."

She withdrew her hand. "And this is the real reason why you will not marry me. As I said before—it is because I am impure. I cannot be . . . baptized. That is the word, yes? Baptized? And so, I cannot be pure again."

Marcus groaned in frustration. "I cannot marry because of my oath to the army. That and no other reason. I wish I could make you understand!"

Her eyes blazed once more. "I am not stupid. I understand. It is *you* who does not understand. You say you love me—yes, you did say it—but you do not love me enough to *act*. You are the commander. Give yourself permission! I will make you a good wife." Tears spilled from her eyes. "I love you. Please . . ."

"Maelona, I—"

"Option!"

Grateful for the interruption, Marcus turned his face to the welcome intruder. Marcus couldn't identify the voice or the face within the shadow of the helm, but his sharp eyes discerned the trident of Neptune, the thunderbolt of Jupiter, and the sword of Mars on the man's belt strips—the marks of Caeso Lucilius—even without the wolf skin. And of course, Caeso carried the *hastile*.

Marcus stood. "What is it, Prooption?"

The new prooption stopped a couple of yards short of Marcus, Maelona, and the unhitched wagon. He pointed down the road. "A rider approaches. A Celt. Should I assemble the men?"

Marcus took a couple of steps to the side, so he could see the road ahead.

A single rider on a pony trotted toward them. The rider held his hand—his right hand—upward in greeting. He didn't bear any obvious weapons, though Marcus was certain no man would venture out alone on the road without a dagger or perhaps a sword. His legs were not bare in the Roman fashion—he wore the breeches and long tunic of a Celt, but otherwise appeared to be no threat. *Open right hand without a weapon. He wants to speak with us.*

"No," Marcus said, answering Caeso. "Leave the men to their duties. Come, Prooption. Let's see what this fellow wants." He turned quickly to Maelona. "If you will pardon me, my lady."

Maelona looked pointedly away from him. *Angry with me again. I wish I could make you understand.*

I wish . . .

Then he turned away from the woman and his impossible wishes. Marcus and Caeso Lucilius strode toward the rider.

"The man is a Celt," said Caeso, whose hand rested on the pommel of his sword.

Marcus noted with some amusement that the prooption had switched the gladius to the right hip, in token of his new—albeit temporary—rank. Marcus said, "We are not at war with all Britannia—only with the rebels. Remember that."

"Yes, Option," Caeso replied. "It's sometimes difficult to tell a good Celt from a bad."

Marcus cocked an eyebrow at that. *Just as it is not always easy to tell a good Roman from a bad.* "Well, the fact that he comes alone and with an open hand is a good sign. Still, while I talk to him, keep your eyes open. I'll watch him. You watch everywhere else."

Caeso grinned and nodded. "As you command, Option."

The rider slowed his pony to a halt, but he did not dismount. He was a grown man, but young—no more than twenty. He was lean, but his hands looked strong, and his face was tanned. *He works in the sunlight and the fresh air.* His hair was red—but it was a lighter red, much lighter than Maelona's. Or Branwen's. It was a red such as could be seen even in Rome. Marcus wondered for the briefest of moments if the man had Roman blood—then he dismissed the thought. *Not all Celts look like Maelona. Or Branwen.*

Why is the night-demon in my thoughts of late? Simply because Maelona mentioned her?

Put that thought away. Now.

Marcus raised his right hand, empty, palm exposed. "Hail, friend."

The young man nodded his head. "Hail, Option. Where is your centurion? I wish to speak with him." His Latin bore no accent, as if he had spoken the language all his life.

"I command here," Marcus said, deliberately not mentioning the loss of his centurion. *No need to expose weakness.* Out of the corner of his eye, he observed Caeso twisting his head about, scanning the woods in the distance, on either side of the road.

"Yes, I see." The rider sat a bit taller in his saddle as he lowered his hand. "I am Emrys, Vilicus to Spurius Aquillius."

He's a vilicus—a steward over a large estate? And his master is yet another *Aquillius? How large is my new family? This family I'm supposed to be ruling over?* "Well met, Emrys," replied Marcus, lowering his hand. "I am Marcus Scri— Marcus Aquillius, Option, Sixth Century, Second Cohort, Legio XIV Gemina."

The Celt nodded stiffly. "My master raises cattle. And as I said, I am also his Magister Pecoris and have the charge of all his livestock." The man's voice was haughty, full of self-importance. "His villa is located two miles south of here. He wishes for news of the war." He pointed to a solitary, low hill—a "tor"—as they were called in Britannia. "I spotted you from the hill."

"What were you doing on the hill?" asked Caeso. The prooption's hand had never left his sword. "Spying? Watching for troop—"

Marcus laid a hand on his friend's sword hand.

The Celt followed the movement with his brown eyes. "I was watching for the army, at my master's command. As I said, he desires news." His brow furrowed, and he swallowed visibly. "Is this all . . . all that remains of the armies of Rome?"

He thinks we are survivors, retreating. "No. The forces of the Legate Gaius Suetonius Paulinus, Propraetor of Britannia, have prevailed against the army of Boudicca and her rebels. The legion suffered minimal casualties. The rebel losses were . . . decisive." Marcus nodded his plumed head in the direction of his men. "My century and I are detached from the legion on a special mission."

Emrys's shoulders sagged, and he nodded his head. He wiped away tears. But when he lifted his face, his countenance was bright, his smile broad. "Thank the gods! That is good news. Good news indeed! We thought . . ." He shook himself, still smiling. The Celt dismounted from his pony. He extended a hand to Marcus. "My master will want to know all the news. He supplies cattle to the army. I know he would be pleased to entertain you and your officers at his villa this evening."

Stop for the night? We haven't covered near enough ground today. Only two more miles? We need to go at least ten more.

Apparently seeing Marcus's hesitation, the servant said, "My master will provide a feast for you and your officers, and he will provide a few sheep for your men to feast upon. And wine. He will provide fine wine for all. And he will provide lodgings for you, Option, for the night."

Marcus smiled. "And you are authorized to make this offer on his behalf?"

The Celt raised his chin. "I am the vilicus. My master trusts me with everything. I was given the instruction to make such an offer to the Legate and to his staff—if they had survived. My master cannot afford to feed an entire legion, of course, but he assuredly can feed a single century. He is a generous man and a loyal citizen of Rome." He gazed at Marcus with an intensity that made Marcus uneasy.

He wants me to accept the invitation. He needs *me to accept.*

Is this a trap? A deception?

Our Father who art in heaven, should we go with this man? Marcus listened with his heart.

Instead of the calming assurance of the Spirit, however, words of an older prophecy—received and recorded more than two years prior

—came into his mind.

Thou shalt meet a man on the road. And thou shalt offer him an ox and ask a bull in return. If he agrees with thy poor bargain, fear not to go with him. Thy companions shall find rest. Yea, and the humble prayer of faith shall be answered.

"A few sheep for my men?" mused Marcus aloud. He scratched his nose as he had seen his mother do when she was bargaining over the price of grain or cloth. "I have an alternate proposal for you. I will give your master an ox in exchange for a bull—and he must provide the butchering. And my men get to keep the blood of the bull. How does that sound to you?"

The Celt frowned, opened his mouth to speak, then shut it.

Caeso gazed at Marcus in surprise.

"A beef ox"—Emrys shook his head in obvious confusion—"for a bull? A bull that could sire hundreds of cattle? What kind of bargain is that?"

A poor one. But if you take it . . . Marcus scratched his nose again. "You see, Vilicus, we have many miles yet to march today. Turning aside for the night will cost us half a day's distance." He shrugged his shoulders. "No. Please give your master the news of victory, but if you will pardon me, I must—"

"Yes, yes." Emrys nodded quickly, though he still scowled. "I accept your offer. I accept in the name of Spurious Aquillius."

Marcus grinned. He extended a hand to the man. "Very good."

Emrys shook Marcus's hand, staring at the symbolic sealing of the bargain with apparent astonishment. "I shall ride ahead and inform my master . . . so we may prepare for your arrival."

"No," said Caeso. "You'll ride with us, with the century."

Marcus shook his head. "It is well enough, Prooption. Let him go."

"But he could warn—"

"We can trust him." Marcus locked eyes with his friend. "Trust *me*."

Caeso's eyes widened in sudden understanding. He nodded slightly. "Are you certain?"

Yes, Caeso. It is a prophecy. Marcus nodded. "I *know* we can put our faith in Vilicus Emrys."

Caeso saluted. "Yes, Option."

Marcus turned back to the steward. "Before you leave us, I must inform you that we have a princess traveling with us."

The steward gaped at him. "A princess? Of Rome?"

Marcus shook his head. "No. She is of . . . this land. I would think it a great kindness if your master would allow her to join us for the feast and if he would provide her with suitable lodgings for the night."

The Celt nodded gravely. "I will inform my master. It shall be as you ask."

"Thank you. I have one more request."

Emrys raised his eyebrows. "Another re—" He appeared to collect his battered composure. "Yes?"

Marcus scratched his nose again. And he grinned in anticipation.

♦ ♦ ♦

"Why do you think," asked Maelona, "that these wicked men, these murderers and infant stealers, serve Arawn?" Maelona once again rode behind Marcus on the back of Gaius the Warhorse.

Her arms encircled his waist, and her hands—clasped against his belly—were comforting and exhilarating at the same time. "I don't simply think they do. I know it, because my God told me."

"Your God speaks to you? Christus speaks to you? I thought you said you were not a priest. Have you seen Christus face-to-face?"

Marcus chuckled. "It's not like that."

"But you said . . ."

"Last question first. No, I have never seen Him. And no, I have never heard the voice of Christus. But yes, the Holy Spirit sends words into my mind."

"And you write these words in your book?"

"Yes."

"And the last words you wrote . . . they were about the priests? Priests of Arawn murdering infants?"

Marcus nodded, though he doubted she could see it. At the moment, he would've rather spoken of happier things, happier plans. "Yes. That is why I must kill Arawn and his priests. I must put a stop to this." *Then why am I wasting half a day's march to turn aside so we may be regaled by a wealthy Roman farmer?*

How many more innocents will be murdered while I delay?

. . . fear not to go with him.

Trust in the Lord and lean not to thine own understanding. Trust in the Lord.

And besides, the men need their ritual – to shower in the blood of the Bull of Mithras. It is a pagan rite, but it will give them courage in battle.

And I have a feeling they will need that courage.

"They will need that courage?" Maelona asked.

I spoke aloud? Again? What is it about this girl? When I'm around her, I can't control my own cursed tongue!

"Yes," he said aloud—deliberately that time. "When we must fight Arawn—whatever he turns out to be."

"Are you afraid?"

The question itself—and the answer—frightened him. He took a deep breath, held it, and released it. "Yes. I am terrified."

"But you are Audaxus. The hero. The great warrior. You have faced a night-demon. You are fearless. How can you possibly be afraid?"

"I am . . . always afraid."

"Of what are you afraid? Of death? Of pain? Of failure?"

"Yes. All of those." *But failure most of all. I failed to save Gaius Aquillius. I wasn't there when my mother was raped and killed. I should have been home. I failed her. I failed those I love.*

Perhaps I shall always fail them in the end.

And I am probably leading my men to their deaths.

And Maelona. If she comes with me to Annwfyn, she will certainly die as well.

Maelona had been silent while Marcus was lost in his thoughts. Then she squeezed him more tightly. "Then you are the bravest warrior I have ever met. This is why your men love you." She squeezed him again. "I think . . . this, most of all, is why I love you."

"Maelona, I'm going to Annwfyn. We may all die there. But I must go. It is my duty."

"Then I will go with you. I will not leave you. Give me a dagger, and I will wield it."

"You will not go with me into battle." *Into near-certain death.*

"I have fought in battle. Am I not a free woman?"

Marcus ground his teeth in frustration. "Yes, but I'm not taking you into combat."

"You will not prevent me. I will follow you. I will not leave you."

He grinned. "I'll bind you—tie you to a tree."

"You have a curious idea of freedom."

Marcus chuckled.

"And it would not work," she said. "I will chew through the ropes. I will pray to Christus and He—"

"We do not pray to Christus."

"You do not pray?"

Marcus sighed happily, pleased at the abrupt change in topic. "We pray to God the Father, not Christus the Son. But we pray in the name of Christus."

"Then I will pray to God the Father in the name of Christus, and

He will break my bonds." She squeezed him. "And I will follow you into Annwfyn. I will follow you into death. Into the land of the dead."

"I will not allow—"

"I prayed to the gods . . . of my people, of this land. They did not answer me. Not when my family was killed. Not when my . . . purity was stolen. Not when I was a slave to that *dog*."

"That is because the gods of this land are not gods. They are not real." *Then what is Arawn?*

"But then you came, Audaxus. You freed me. You delivered me. Your God leads you. He speaks to you. I do not know your God. But He is my God now. I will pray to Him." She paused. "Marcus?"

"Yes?"

"When I pray to God the Father, must I raise my hands to heaven and shout my prayer as I have seen you Romans do?"

Marcus laughed and shook his head. "No. You can pray wherever you are. Standing. Sitting. Lying down in your bed at night. And you can pray silently, in your heart."

"I have never seen you pray. Do you always pray silently?"

"Most of time. But not always."

"I see. This is a good thing. I cannot hold on to you and lift my hands at the same time." She paused again. "Will you listen while I pray? To be certain I do it correctly?"

He nodded. *She is determined, isn't she?* "Yes. I will listen."

"God the Father," she began, "I pray to You in the name of Christus the Son. Please, God the Father . . . Please. I wish to be pure again." She trembled, and Marcus realized she was weeping. "Marcus says I may be pure again. He says it is possible. But he says only a priest can give me baptism. I beg of You—send me a priest. Make me pure once more." She sobbed. "Please. You speak to Marcus. I know You do. I have seen it when he writes Your words. Please, tell him. Tell him he must marry me. I love him. I will be a good wife to him . . . once I am pure again. Please, command him to marry me."

"Maelona," Marcus said, "it doesn't—"

She squeezed his waist. "I'm not speaking to you. I'm speaking to God the Father. If I make a mistake, correct my mistake. But this is *my* prayer. I am a free woman. I will pray as I choose. I will . . . *beg* as I need. Now, be silent."

He nodded. Silently. But a grin slowly stole its way across his lips.

"Marcus Aquillius Audaxus is a good man. He keeps his oaths. He does his duty, even when it is not what he wishes to do. He is brave, even when he is afraid. That is why I love him. I do not know, I cannot guess why he loves me. But he does. He said so, even though I suspect he did not mean to say it—not aloud—but he did say it. And he does not lie. He is a good man." Sobs wracked her body once more. Her hands trembled against his waist. "I love him. Please. Please tell him it is a good thing to marry me. If he chooses. I was wrong to ask You to command him. That was wrong. I want him to marry me—not just for my protection—but because he loves me, and because I love him. Please, God the Father, please tell Marcus that he may marry me and still keep his oath . . . and fulfill his promise to me. One more thing I must ask. Please help Marcus to be strong. The beautiful, desirable night-demon will come tonight. She will come to claim him. Please help him to be strong. Please, God the Father. The other gods, they do not answer me. Marcus says You are the only God. That I must pray to You in the name of Your Son, Christus. And so I pray. Please answer my prayer."

And then she became silent.

After several long moments, Marcus asked, "Have you finished?"

"Yes."

"Then end your prayer with, 'Amen.'"

"I thank You, God the Father, for listening to me. Amen."

Marcus swallowed hard. "That . . . that was quite a prayer."

"What is 'Amen'?"

"It is a Jewish word. It means, 'Be it thus.' But Aristobulus told me it is also another name for Jesus Christus."

"Who is Aristobulus?"

Marcus smiled. "He is the man, the priest, who baptized me. He is the missionary who taught me of Christus. He has met Christus, face-to-face. Before Christus was crucified."

"Christus is dead?" Alarm shrilled in her tone. "How can you worship a dead god?"

"He *was* dead," Marcus replied, "but after three days in the tomb, He rose from the dead. He lives again. Aristobulus has seen Him since He rose again. Christus paid for our sins with His blood. And because He rose again, we will all rise again after death."

"There are dead Christians walking around, among us?" Wonder was in her voice. And perhaps a touch of fear.

Marcus couldn't help but laugh aloud.

"Why is this funny? Do you know such Christians who were dead and now live again?"

Tenderly, Marcus pressed a hand against hers. "I'm sorry I laughed." He still grinned, however, at her question. "Your question surprised me. No, when we rise again, we go to be with Him, with God and Christus. But it's not just Christians. All men and women—all will live again. However, not all will dwell with God. Only the righteous will dwell in His presence."

"In the Underworld? Is that the word? Underworld?"

"Yes, that is the word, but, no. The dwelling place of God is not under the ground. It is in the heavens."

She pulled back from him again, but she did not pull her hands away. "In the sky? But where would you walk? You would fall to the ground."

Marcus burst into laughter once more.

"Why do you laugh at me? It is a good question. Your beliefs are so strange."

Marcus bit his lip to quiet his mirth once more. "Yes, my lady. It is a good question. I have simply never heard it before. Or thought of it myself. You have a keen mind to ask questions like that."

She snuggled against him—at least as close as his armor allowed. "A keen mind? You mean, a keen mind for a *woman*."

Marcus smiled and pressed his hand a bit more firmly against hers. He curled his fingers under hers. "Princess Maelona, you have a keen mind. An inquisitive mind. Woman or man, it matters not. I can see we will have many interesting, stimulating discussions."

"Yes. When we are married, we may spend many hours in interesting, stimulating discussions. And in love."

A tingling warmth, pleasant and thrilling, spread from her fingers into his, leaping like wildfire into his heart. *Heavenly Father, show me the way. I love her. I have known her for so short a time. But I love her. It is as if we are riding through a pleasant dream.*

I simply do not see how this dream can become reality.

"But first," said Maelona, "God the Father must send me a priest. So I may be baptized. So I may be pure again. Pure. Again. And then you will desire me."

I desire you now, woman.

She squeezed him. "I desire you too."

"I spoke aloud? Again?" *What is wrong with me?*

Her only reply was another, thrilling squeeze.

"My lady, you have cast a spell over me." He grinned as he shook his head. "Perhaps you are a witch after all."

She chuckled. "Ah, so you have discovered my secret at last. You are in my power, Marcus Aquillius. You will do as I command."

"I am your slave, my Princess."

"I do not need or desire a slave. I would be content to have you as my husband." She sighed. "But first, God the Father will send me a priest."

Amen. May it be so. Though where would we find such a man?

"If you do not fall from the sky," she said, "when you rise from the dead, do you have wings, so you can fly? Like Branwen?"

Branwen. Why do we keep coming back around to Branwen? "No. No wings."

"But she has wings. Why?"

"I don't know. Perhaps because she is a demon?"

"She will come tonight. You must be prepared."

Marcus shivered. *How can I possibly prepare?*

"You fear her," Maelona said.

She hadn't stated it as a question, but Marcus answered her nevertheless. "Yes, I fear her."

"That is good. But she is beautiful."

"Yes."

"She does not have . . . I have these ugly orange spots on my skin. Her skin is fair. Pure. I am impure."

"Maelona, I love your freckles—that is what they are called—freckles. They are . . . fascinating."

"Truly? You are teasing me."

"No. Well, perhaps a little. But I could spend all day counting your freckles."

"Now I know you are mocking me." She growled in disgust. "Count my . . . freckles. You would not do such a thing."

"You are correct. I would not. I just realized it would be impossible."

She laughed bitterly. "Because they are so many."

"No. Because I would forever be distracted by your eyes."

She was silent for a while. Then she said, "Marcus, have you always been a Christian?"

"No. I was taught and baptized only five years ago."

"And before that?"

"I worshipped Mithras and Mars as do many legionnaires."

"Then why . . . if you were not Christian . . . why have you not coupled before?"

"Because of my mother."

"She did not want you to have another woman?"

"Of course, she did. She wanted me to marry."

"But you Romans . . . you seem to take whatever woman you choose."

"Not all of us. My mother was the kindest, most loving person I have ever known. My father called her his queen. He died when I was young. I don't remember him well, but I do remember this—he loved her. He not only called her his queen, he treated her as his queen. I think if he had not thought it might anger the gods, he would have called her his goddess. Because he worshipped her. And my mother loved him. That I remember. I decided long ago that I want to treat the woman I marry as my queen, as my goddess. I want the woman I marry"—he curled his fingers through hers—"to love me as she loved him."

"And this is why you never . . ."

"Yes, because I want what they had. That, and nothing less than that."

"Then why did you enlist in the army? If you desired marriage . . . such as your parents had, why enlist in the army where you cannot marry at all?"

"My mother, when she died . . . when she was murdered . . . I wasn't there to protect her. I should have been. I was . . . grief-stricken, so utterly . . . destroyed. I was young. I wasn't thinking clearly, I suppose. I needed to . . . to get away." He paused. "I wanted revenge. To kill, to let out the anger inside me. No one knew who killed her. I couldn't kill *them*. So . . ." He let his voice trail off.

"So you came to my country to kill my people." Her voice was soft, quiet.

"Not your people. Just the enemies of Rome. Wherever, whoever they may be. I was sent here, assigned here. I did not choose Britannia."

She said nothing.

"Maelona, if I had not come to Britannia, I would never have met Aristobulus. I would never have learned of Christus. And . . . I would never have found . . . you."

"Marcus?"

"Yes?"

"This villa . . . whither we are riding . . . Will a priest be there?"

He laughed. "I doubt it. Why would a priest be at the villa?"

"Because I prayed to God the Father. I asked Him to send me a priest. Does He not answer your prayers?"

"Yes, but not always in the *way* I ask. And certainly not immediately *when* I ask."

"Do you think He sent you to Britannia? So you could learn about Christus? So you could save me?"

"I . . . don't know. It is possible, I suppose. I believe God wants us to be happy."

"I think it is possible too. I prayed for a priest. Do you think God the Father will send me a priest?"

"Yes. I believe He will. But in His time, not necessarily when you . . . when *we* want Him to."

"But I need a priest now. I asked for a priest. Perhaps, there will be one at the villa."

Marcus laughed again. "Remember—God works in His time, in His way. Not ours."

"Perhaps . . ." Her voice dropped so low, Marcus could not make out her words.

"What did you say?"

But Maelona said nothing.

"Please," he said, "tell me what you said."

"I said that perhaps God the Father is punishing me for being impure—for not fighting harder to stop the men—for not running away or taking my own life."

"No, Maelona, no. Sweet Maelona, God would never punish you for that. It was not your choice."

"I should have k-killed myself long ago." She was weeping again. "Long ago."

"No. Do not say such things. God loves you. He loves you as you are. He wants you to be happy."

"It would have been more honorable to kill myself. You Romans believe in taking your own life after dishonor. And I have been dishonored. I have nothing left."

"Not all Romans believe this. I do not. Christians do not."

"What do you believe in? What do *we* believe in?"

Marcus smiled and caressed her hand. "We believe in hope."

"Then I will believe in hope. There *will* be a priest at the villa."

"In God's time, Maelona. In . . ." He lifted his hand from hers and pointed. "There it is!"

From behind a low hill, a house had appeared. The villa was white—white columns supported a roof of red clay tiles. A white wall surrounded the estate. A stream of water flowed on the other side of the wall, glittering in the afternoon sun. Seemingly out of place in the midst of the Cambrian countryside, the villa could have been transplanted straight from a Roman estate back home.

And it was huge.

This Spurius Aquillius must be a very wealthy man. I suppose there is great profit to be made in supplying beef to the army.

And the wall! The compound is large enough to house the entire century – wagons and all.

Perhaps there is a bath! *How I would welcome a real, hot bath!*

"So big!" Maelona leaned precariously behind him. "Bigger than my family's home. That is where we are to camp tonight?"

Camp? Marcus grinned. "My lady, tonight we sleep in a real bed." Then he hastily added, "In separate beds. Separate beds."

Maelona giggled.

Then she tickled his belly below his armor.

Marcus yelped and almost lost his saddle. "Don't do that!"

"Are you . . . I don't know the word."

"Ticklish. Yes. Very. Now, don't do that again. Especially when I am on a horse."

Gaius the Warhorse snorted. Then he bellowed out a loud neigh. The horse surged forward, accelerating into a full gallop.

Marcus fought to restrain the stallion. He managed to halt the animal, but Gaius the Warhorse stomped, restive, ready to leap forward again.

"What is the matter?" Maelona cried, obviously terrified.

"My guess is there are mares down there. Mares ready to mate. He smells them."

Marcus gave the reins a hard tug. The warhorse snorted, but he did not kick. Marcus patted the animal's neck. "Good boy, Gaius." *Perhaps you will enjoy yourself there.*

I hope so. I do hope you like it there.

Maelona clung tightly to Marcus. "Horrible beast. He will kill us both. Kick us to death. And then, after we are dead, for good measure, he'll bite my backside again."

Marcus burst into laughter.

"It is not funny!" Maelona cried. "I shall . . . make you ticklish again!"

Which, of course, made Marcus laugh the louder—even though she did not carry through on her threat to make him "ticklish again."

Marcus forced the horse to turn around and return to the marching column of the century.

In order to catch up to their commander, the men were marching at a quick trot. The mule-pulled wagons and their wagoners struggled to keep up.

Once reunited with his men, Marcus led the century away from the road, toward the expansive Roman villa.

A massive, wooden door, large enough to drive a wagon through, marked the entrance to the estate. In the open door, stood a gray-haired man, clean-shaven, and wearing a white toga with gold embroidery. And beside him stood Emrys, the steward. Men and women in Celtic garb were gathered about, but the Roman and his steward were at the center. The Roman smiled and extended his arms in greeting.

"Welcome to our home, brave, victorious soldiers of Rome!"

Marcus dismounted. Then he helped Maelona down from the stallion's back. Maelona clung to him, obviously grateful to be off the "horrible beast." For his part, Gaius the Warhorse was clearly agitated, stomping and snorting.

Two men—grooms, Marcus assumed—rushed forward. They requested the reins in accented but passable Latin. Marcus surrendered the reins, and the grooms led the unruly stallion away.

"Goodbye," Marcus said to the departing beast. *Enjoy yourself.*

Gaius the Warhorse neighed in reply.

Marcus gently disengaged himself from Maelona's embrace. From behind him, he heard Prooption Caeso Lucilius call for a halt. The tromping of the century ceased. Marcus stepped toward the older Roman.

The older man took a step toward Marcus. "I am Spurius Aquillius Rufus," said the man with the gray hair. He bowed deeply. Then he straightened with a groan. "My pardon, my lord. My back has aged along with my head." He chuckled as he ran a hand through his close-cropped hair. "It is an honor to meet the *Heres Patris* of my family."

Heres Patris? He knows? How could he know?

"What is Heres Patris?" Maelona asked in a loud whisper. "It sounds like a title."

Spurius Aquillius laughed and clapped his hands once. "And you must be Princess Maelona! My lady." He bowed again, then groaned once more with the effort of standing upright. "Welcome to our humble home, Option Marcus Aquillius Audaxus and Princess Maelona!" He beamed at them for a moment, then he waggled a finger at Maelona. "But to answer your question, Princess, the Heres Patris is the heir to the head of a great Roman family. And"—he glanced pointedly at Marcus's longitudinal plume—"the option here is, if I am not misinformed, the adopted son of the head of House Aquillius—my house. He is therefore my lord." He bowed again, more cautiously and less deeply.

"Please stop bowing to me," Marcus said, attempting—and not entirely succeeding—to hide his embarrassment and irritation.

Spurius Aquillius smiled. "Then I will bow to the Princess. My lady." He bowed again.

"How did you know I am Heres Patris Aquillius? I became aware of my adoption and inheritance only recently."

The older man started to bow again, but caught himself. "My lord, your adoption has been in process for more than a year. The . . . delicate nature of it required Senatorial approval, but it was inevitable. I have friends in the Senate, and I get news, even here in remote Cambria. How is your father, Gaius Aquillius Regulus?"

Marcus swallowed the lump that suddenly constricted his throat. "I fear your news is old. Gaius Aquillius Regulus was slain in the battle against Boudicca."

The older man's brown eyes grew wide. "No!" Then he nodded once. Twice. Then he bowed low once more. "My lord, Pater Marcus Aquillius," he said, acknowledging Marcus's title. As he rose from the bow, he did not groan, but he clenched his jaw in pain. "I am grieved at the passing of your father. I met him. Years ago. A good man." He pointed through the estate entrance. "Please come inside. We have much to discuss. Your men may camp within our walls. You and your officers will dine with me. You and the Princess will be my guests for the night."

He smiled at Maelona. "My pardon, my lady, but if you will forgive an old man, we must find you a more suitable gown." He winked at Marcus, then clapped his hands with an imperious air.

Four women, all Celts, and none of them younger than middle age, rushed forward. They swarmed past Marcus and took Maelona by the arms.

As they pulled her toward the entrance, she cried, "No! Please! No!" She swiveled her heard toward Marcus. "Please, Marcus! I want to stay with you!"

"Stop!" Marcus commanded. "She is a Princess. She will go or not go whither she chooses."

Maelona wrenched her arms free from the women's grasp and launched herself at Marcus. She wrapped her arms around his armor. "I want to stay with you."

Gently, he took her face in his hands. "All will be well. You are safe here. Please go with them. For me. Please. We'll be together again soon. I promise."

She gazed up at him, searching his face with her haunting, emerald eyes. "I will hold you to that promise, Marcus Aquillius. That promise . . . and all your promises."

Marcus nodded and forced a smile. *I want to marry you, to have you as my bride, my wife. You and no other.*

But I don't know how it could be.

She withdrew her arms and turned away, though she gave him a sorrowful, longing look. One of the women took her arm, but Maelona shook out of the woman's grip. Maelona held her head high. "Dangoswch y ffordd!" she said.

Marcus didn't understand the words—it wasn't Celtic, though he guessed it might have been Cambrian—but Marcus caught the tone of command. *One moment, a terrified girl—then next, a regal princess . . . even if you are dressed in slave's rags. You are a complex woman, Princess. A mystery.*

And I love you with all my heart.

"She is your mistress?"

Marcus jerked his attention back to his host. "Maelona? No, of course not."

"Of course not?" The older man grinned as his eyes followed the princess and her attendants. There was a hint of lust in that grin, but it quickly transformed into a wistful smile. "A pity. She is a beauty. I have . . . *had* red hair myself, but not so red as some of these Celts. And the green eyes. They take some . . . getting used to. But that one. She is"—he sighed—"a beauty. If I were a decade younger . . ." He sighed again. "It is painfully apparent that the two of you love each other. You should marry her. But perhaps, her father does not approve?"

"Her father is dead," Marcus said, his voice flat. *We killed him.*

The old Roman turned his face toward Marcus. "I'm sorry to hear that. Who was he?"

"I . . . I don't know. She hasn't told me his name. He and his family fell at the first Mona assault. Maelona is . . . the only survivor of her clan."

Spurius Aquillius frowned thoughtfully. "That is a shame. They are a wild people—the Celts, especially this Cambrian breed—but they are also a good people. My late wife was . . . of this land. Alas, she gave me no children. I suppose that means this estate will fall to you when I am gone. But for now, at least, as long as you are here, please consider my home yours." He gestured to his steward. "You have met Emrys. He will see to your men."

The steward bowed. "My lord." Any hint of the haughtiness

shown in their first meeting was gone. "If you will pardon me . . ." He bowed again, then strode past Marcus and toward the century.

"Now," said Spurius Aquillius, pointing through the gate, "if you please, my lord?"

Marcus nodded and entered through the gate.

"If I may suggest," said the older man, wrinkling his strong, Roman nose as they walked, "a bath? I have the water heating."

"You have a bath in this place? In the middle of Cambria?"

A wide grin split his host's face. "Yes, my lord, a full and proper bath. Civilization"—he waved his arms expansively—"even in the wilds of Cambria."

♦ ♦ ♦

"May the gods favor you, Marcus," Agrippa Corfidius said, "even if you don't believe in them." The vexillarius eased his newly cleansed body into the steaming water of the *caldarium*, the final and largest pool in the villa's bath—the hot pool. "By Jupiter! Only you could find us a bath in the middle of nowhere. And in the middle of the day."

"Are you complaining, Vexillarius, about cutting today's march short?" Marcus replied, luxuriating in the hot water. "We *are* losing half a day."

The cornicen, Spurius Orcivius, laughed. "*He* might be complaining, but I'm not! By all the gods, this is wonderful. A pity Caeso Lucilius and Nonus Sestius are stuck seeing after the men. Or rather, I'm glad it's them and not me!"

Marcus chuckled at his junior officers. "They'll be along as soon as the men are settled."

"And we're to be feasted tonight," said Agrippa with a sigh. "Meat and bread and fruit and wine! All we're missing are some pretty slave-girls to . . . entertain us."

Marcus shook his head. "You will not treat this villa as a brothel." He was too tired and too relaxed to chastise, at least not to chastise vigorously. "None of the servant girls are to be touched."

"I'll alert the men," said Spurius. "Oo-ooh, in a quarter hour or so."

"I've arranged for that ox of ours to be traded for a bull," Marcus said. "The animal will be butchered tonight for the men to feast on, and the blood will be saved for the rest of you to shower in."

Spurius looked at him askance. "The blood of one bull? There won't be enough to go around."

Agrippa shrugged. "We can just sprinkle a goblet's measure on each man. It should be enough. Mithras will count it sufficient to cleanse us . . . I hope. It's the ritual that counts, correct? Not the amount of blood. It'll be enough to wash away our sins—make us shriven for battle."

"I hope so," said Agrippa. "I have many sins to be washed away before we go fight a cursed Celtic god." He groaned delightedly. "Although, a good drenching in blood would give me another excuse for another bath."

Marcus chuckled. "We are *not* going to have more than eighty blood-soaked men fouling our host's baths."

"So all the men are to be able to use the baths?" asked Spurius.

Marcus nodded and yawned. "All, in turns. One contubernium at a time. Oh, and warn them about the soap."

"Soap." Agrippa shook his head and grunted in disgust. "It seems to work, I suppose, but I prefer the Roman way. Just let me massage olive oil into my skin and scrape the dirt away with a *strigil*. They had several of them hanging on the wall of the *tepidarium*."

Marcus had seen the steel bathing tools known as strigil, hanging on the walls of the warm pool room. And he'd seen a few pots containing olive oil in there as well. A *few* pots. But there had been plenty of balls of soap. "Not enough olive oil to go around. It's precious enough in Britannia. At least, it's precious to Romans. And remind the men that we are guests here. Tell them to act accordingly. No. Tell them I *trust* them to act accordingly. And tell them I *trust* them to keep their hands—and all other parts of their bodies—off the women."

"Ooh!" Agrippa winked at him. "Nice touch." He elbowed Marcus in the ribs. "You *trust* them to behave. You're good at this. I can't think of any other commander in the whole legion who could tell a bunch of battle-weary, woman-starved soldiers to act like . . . like . . . like a band of Christians and truly expect them to do as he bids."

Marcus chuckled. "Just tell them."

Agrippa sighed and closed his eyes. "I will. Just as soon as I finish soaking. Civilization in the middle of Cambria. I could never have imagined it."

Spurius grunted and scratched at his neck. "That soap dries the skin. It's a Celtic invention, no?"

"Germanic, I think," said Agrippa. "Doesn't matter. Nobody is going to complain about it, not when they get to soak in a real bath. Nobody except noble Spurius Orcivius."

Spurius splashed water on the vexillarius. He rose out of the hot pool, the water streaming from his naked flesh. "I'm getting too hot. I'm going to take a dip in the *frigidarium*." He climbed out of the pool and onto the tile floor. "After that, I think I'll be done." He walked quickly toward the cold pool room.

Agrippa shrugged. "You know, that's not a bad idea." He hoisted himself out of the *caldarium* as well. "I've duties to attend to before the feast. I'm looking forward to some real wine!"

Real wine. Marcus sighed. *How long has it been since I've tasted real wine and not just the wretched posca?* He had not sampled the late centurion's wine—not because he didn't want to, for he enjoyed wine in moderation—but because he wished to save it for a celebration after the mission. *After the mission. Assuming any of us survive.*

"Agrippa!" he shouted. "Are you still there?"

"Yes, oh great Option Audaxus!" He came out of the *apodyterium*—the bath's changing room—adjusting the front of his subligar on his waist. "How may I yet be of service, great Audaxus?" He grinned playfully.

I hate that cursed name! "Tell the men I *trust* them to be careful with the wine. We march at first light." He paused. "Rather, tell them we march an hour after dawn. They've earned a brief rest."

Agrippa saluted, but he saluted with a smile. "As you command, Option." Then he turned and walked quickly back to the apodyterium.

Marcus had the caldarium all to himself.

I need to get out soon. I need to check on Maelona.

I can hardly wait to see her in a proper gown.

However, he indulged in the luxurious water for a quarter hour longer.

Must get out. Check on the men.

Find Maelona.

He lowered himself completely under the hot water, immersing his entire body. He held his breath for several moments, savoring the heat on his scalp. *If only there* were *a priest here. Maelona could be baptized in the tepidarium rather than in some cold pond or river or sea.*

He lifted his head out of the water.

As the water streamed past his eyes, he saw her.

Maelona.

And she was not wearing a proper gown. She wore nothing at all.

His eyes grew wide. He stared for but a moment. Then he slammed his eyes shut and turned his head.

"I heard you were in here," she said in her near-perfect, but delightfully accented Latin.

Marcus heard her slip into the water. "My lady! You should not be—"

"This is wonderful! The water is so . . . nice. I washed earlier, when those women took me and . . . They told me the gown—there are *eight* lovely gowns—they belonged to Spurius Aquillius's late wife. But the women said that they were a gift from *you*. Thank you. Thank you. How did you purchase them? Do you have money? Even as an option, the army doesn't pay you well. So, how?"

Please don't come near me. Please. "I t-traded the horse."

"You gave up your horse? For me?"

He heard the churning of the water. "Please, my lady! No closer."

"I'm sorry." She sounded on the verge of tears. "I thought this was the Roman custom—men and women bathing together. You said you had seen naked women before. I didn't mean to offend—"

Marcus risked a glance.

Only her head was visible above the water.

He turned his face toward her, but he pointedly avoided looking below the surface of the water. "Please do not weep."

"I'm not weeping!" Her lips were pursed in anger. And her face was wet—but so was her hair. Still she wiped at her eyes. "I'm not weeping," she repeated more softly.

"Good. I don't want to make you unhappy."

"But it is the Roman custom, is it not? I have not done something improper?" Her hand brushed her cheek again as if wiping away tears.

"Yes, it is . . . fashionable. In Rome. But . . ."

"I am making you uncomfortable?"

He let out a nervous chuckle and averted his eyes again. "My lady . . . Maelona. You must know how I feel about you. I've told you. You must know how you make . . . You are not just another . . . naked woman in a bath to me. I cannot look upon you and not . . . I cannot have you near me like this and not . . ."

"Then you *do* desire me. Truly." There was amusement in her voice . . . and something else—joy. "This makes me happy. Very happy."

"Maelona, I think it would be best if I do not see you . . . in this manner. Not until . . ."

"Not until we are married." Her words completed his.

"Yes."

"Then you *will* marry me. That is what you are saying." It was not a question.

But he answered anyway. "Yes. Someday. I will find a way. I don't know how, but I will."

"I desire you too. But I will leave you now. You may keep your eyes closed until I am gone if you wish."

"Yes. I'll do that." He kept his eyes shut tight as he heard her exit the pool.

"When next you see me," she said as her wet footsteps slapped softly on the tiles, "I will be wearing one of your gifts."

Marcus smiled with eyes closed. "I'm sure you will be beautiful. You *are* beautiful."

"I love you," she said, and Marcus could hear the smile in her delightful voice.

"I love you too, Maelona." *With all my heart and soul and . . .*

My lovely tribulation. My comely pit.

Our Father who art in heaven, hallowed be Thy name.

Father, help me!

Lead me out of temptation. Out of temptation. Temptation.

Show me how I may . . . protect her.

No, I am not being honest. Not with Thee and not with myself.

Show me, Father, I beg of Thee . . . Show me how I may take Maelona as my wife.

Lead me out of temptation.

"May I join you, old friend?" said a strong male voice.

That voice!

Marcus's eyes snapped open.

Before him stooped an elderly man with white hair and a long gray beard. His face was wrinkled with age, but his brown eyes were bright with the light of intelligence. Marcus was struck dumb as he watched the old man clamber slowly, painfully into the water. A smile spread across the bearded face. "Blessed be the Lord God. This feels marvelous." He turned his smile on Marcus. "Well met, my brother. And here, of all places."

Maelona prayed for a priest.

Yea, and the humble prayer of faith shall be answered.

Marcus's tongue was finally loosed as he extended his hand to the elderly Jew.

"Aristobulus!"

Chapter XIV

"For but a moment, thou shalt have the gift whereby thou shalt interpret the words of a song. And by a song shall souls be touched and four shall be won for the Lord."
from the Book of Marcus Scribonius

The princess you mentioned is correct," said Aristobulus, deepening the wrinkles on his already furrowed brow, above bushy, white eyebrows. "Arawn has never required human sacrifice, much less the slaughter of innocents. No, that is nothing like the tales I have heard of him." The elderly Jew stroked his long, gray beard as he sat in a chair in his bedchamber. He tapped his fingers on the desk before him. On that desk lay the remnants of the Sacrament of the Lord's Supper—a small loaf of bread—with some of it broken off—and a half-empty cup of wine.

Upon finishing their baths, Aristobulus escorted Marcus to his guestchamber and then administered the sacred ordinance. It was the first time Marcus had partaken of the sacrament since the last time he'd seen the old Christian missionary—and that was in Dumnonia, three long years before. Three long years since Marcus renewed his baptismal covenant and was once more cleansed from sin through the Atonement of Jesus Christ. It was also the first time for the sacrament since Marcus had taken upon himself the nomen of Aquillius.

Marcus Aquillius truly felt like a new man.

He was aware that outside the house, in the vast courtyard, the rest of the century was attempting to wash themselves clean in the blood of the bull sacrificed to Mithras. He could hear the sounds of the men celebrating their ritual. However, in that humble guestchamber, Marcus and Aristobulus had quietly and humbly consumed the emblems of the flesh and blood of Christus. Although Marcus knew the Mithraism ceremony would help to give the men courage in combat, he believed that true cleansing came only in the name of Jesus Christus.

Spiritually refreshed as Marcus had not felt in years, the Roman convert and the Jewish missionary reminisced and exchanged news.

And Marcus sought counsel for his current mission.

"No," said Aristobulus, "not Arawn. However, this does remind me of the ancient abominations Moloch and Chemosh."

Marcus leaned forward, resting his elbows on the small table, taking care not to touch the bread and the cup. "Moloch and Chemosh? Who are they?"

The old man bit his lip. "They were ancient gods of the Canaanites, worshipped by the Children of Israel during some of our darkest times. These horrors required a sacrifice of children, usually the firstborn. By fire. Moloch, for example, was an iron idol, heated by fire until he was red-hot. The child for the sacrifice was placed into his arms."

"Alive?" Marcus, who had lived through the horrors of combat, shrank away. He felt as if he might vomit up the sacred bread and wine he had so recently consumed.

Aristobulus nodded gravely. "Yes. Moloch . . . and Chemosh, as well, are evil beyond anything you have seen. Although, I believe the Romans encountered a similar monstrosity in Carthage, did you not? But you never served on that campaign. So perhaps you have never heard of that. But Moloch and Chemosh are evil."

"'*Are* evil?' You speak of these abominations as if they are real. As if they are not simply the evil imaginings of the human heart, cruel idols, the work of the hands of men."

The old man shrugged. "Marcus, my brother, do you believe in Lucifer? Do you believe he is real?"

Marcus nodded. "Yes. Because you have told me he is real. The fallen angel. The father of lies. The enemy of men's souls."

"Yes, well, he was not the only angel to fall before the world was. Do you remember this as well?"

"Yes, I do. I remember every word you have taught me."

Aristobulus smiled with no little amusement. "Yes, your extraordinary memory." He pointed toward the ceiling. "A gift from above." He sighed, then rose from his chair and stepped toward the latticed window. "These fallen angels, these servants of Lucifer—they are condemned to walk the earth until the triumphant return of the Lamb of God. They seek, as their master does, to ensnare the souls of men, to lead them down to destruction. In ancient times, Lucifer appeared to the sons of Adam as a being of light and demanded that they worship him as a god. I believe his demonic servants do the same."

Aristobulus turned back to Marcus. "Do I believe Moloch and

others like him are real? Yes. I believe they appear to men and demand worship, leading the sons and daughters of Adam and Eve to damnation by committing monstrous acts in their name."

"So what you are saying"—Marcus rubbed his freshly shaven chin—"is that this Arawn we seek is a demon? Not a pagan god, but an agent of Lucifer?"

"Yes, I think it is possible. Or perhaps even Lucifer himself." The missionary returned to the table, but rather than sitting down, he laid a hand on Marcus's shoulder. "You must be very careful, brother. Hold fast to your faith, for it will be challenged. It will be shaken. *You* will be shaken. It is not your life I fear for—nor for the lives of your companions—but for your immortal soul. Hold fast."

Marcus pointed with a finger at the broken bread and wine—bread and wine that he felt it was improper for him to touch unless it was given to him by one bearing the priesthood of God. "Then ordain me, Aristobulus of the Seventy. Give me the priesthood. Give me the power and authority of God to command the demon, to banish him. With the priesthood, I could . . ."

Aristobulus shook his head slowly, with a sad smile. "No, my friend. The priesthood is not conferred upon those who ask for it simply *because* they ask for it. One must be called of God, as was Aaron. And I have not received any command of the Spirit to ordain you—at least not at this time. Perhaps someday."

Marcus laid his hand atop the old man's. "Then come with us! You could banish this demon, this false god, in the name of Jesus." He fought to keep the desperation, the fear from his voice. "I know you could."

"I'm sorry. I truly am. But the Spirit has called me elsewhere. I must return to my tiny but growing flock in Dumnonia. And to my beloved wife. The Spirit also tells me that you and your companions must face this challenge alone. But remember this, my dear brother—you are never alone."

Marcus forced himself to return the old disciple's sad smile. *But I feel as if I* am *alone. And I'm frightened. So very frightened.*

"Now," said Aristobulus as he withdrew his hand and began to gather up the remnants of the sacred emblems, "tell me more about your princess, this woman who has captured your heart."

Marcus grinned, and his pulse began to race. Suddenly, in his memory, she was there before him again in the bath—naked and glorious. His cheeks reddened at the thought. "She—" He cleared his throat and rubbed suddenly sweaty palms against his tunica. "She wishes to be baptized . . ."

♦ ♦ ♦

It wasn't as if Marcus had never attended a formal dinner before. He had. Once. With his mother, when a neighboring vineyard owner courted her—with an eye to combining the two vineyards. But Marcus was a youth and relegated to the outermost spot on the *lectus summus* —the "high" couch for the lower-ranking guests. His mother reclined on the innermost spot of the *lectus medius*—the "middle" couch reserved for the highest-ranking members of the dinner party. Their host lay immediately next to her on the *lectus imus*—the "low" couch for the host and his family. Thus they lay as the man attempted with all his might to woo Marcus's mother. His attempts were, of course, utterly wasted, for Marcus's mother declared that she had loved only one man in her life—and she would never love another.

That was Marcus's only formal dining experience in a proper *triclinium,* a formal Roman dining room with its three *clinia*—couches arranged like three sides of an open box. Each *clinium* was sized to accommodate up to three diners, reclining and facing toward a *mensa,* a central table where food was supplied by servants continually scuttling back and forth between the triclinium and the *culina,* or kitchen. And at that dinner, Marcus was positioned as the lowest-ranking guest, a slight his mother surely noticed.

However, in the villa of Spurius Aquillius, Marcus was given the place of honor, on the lectus medius, right next to his host. He was, after all, the new heir to the estate and the new Pater Aquillius.

And that made Marcus extremely uncomfortable. *Like a rabbit princeling dining with a pride of regal lions.* The host, Spurius Aquillius, seemed genuinely pleased to entertain Marcus and his four officers. He had provided them all with clean, white, voluminous, woolen *togae* that made lounging on the couches more comfortable than it would have been had they been clad in their tunicae—odiferous from weeks of combat and marching. In fact, servants had confiscated the tunicae and *subligaris* of the junior officers, with the assurance that the clothing would be returned, thoroughly laundered, before the feast was over—whenever that might be. Marcus knew well that a proper Roman feast could last for several hours.

Still, they will need to get the garments hung up in the wind soon if they are to dry by morning.

Marcus noticed that Caeso Lucilius still had a spot of bull blood on his forehead from the ritual that afternoon. Marcus pointed to his own forehead, looking meaningfully at Caeso. The prooption, grinned back at him, not comprehending the gesture. Marcus tried again, mimicking wiping at his forehead. Caeso, still oblivious, lifted his wine cup and nodded to Marcus.

Ah, well. I tried.

Marcus took another sip of wine—properly mixed with water so as not to be *too* potent—and grinned at his host. The wine was excellent as well. *Yes, Spurius Aquillius has been very generous.*

". . . news of your glorious victory is most welcome," Spurius Aquillius was saying—though Marcus found it difficult to put up the appearance of listening attentively. "As you know, of course, most of this part of Britannia never supported Boudicca. Certainly, none of the clans in this part of Cambria." He waved a beef rib at his steward. "Emrys's people were among the first to welcome Roman rule."

The vilicus lay on his belly, devouring a round honey-barley cake. The Celt, dressed in a toga as well, nodded enthusiastically. "We'd been at war with our neighbors for . . . many generations—raiding—stealing sheep, slaves." He grinned. "Women. And we were none the richer for it. Even with Roman taxes, we are far more prosperous than before. Under Rome, we have freedom."

Freedom? "Forgive me, Vilicus, but I assumed you were a slave."

"A slave?" Emrys chuckled. "My family were no better than slaves under our old king. No, I am a free man. All the servants in this villa serve of their own free will. The emperor, Nero Claudius Caesar Augustus Germanicus, has done us no harm. And for the most part, he leaves us alone. Our kings, as long as they obey Roman law, may rule as they choose. For myself and my wife and our children, I choose to serve Spurius Aquillius." He lifted the cake in salute to his master. "We do well for ourselves here."

"Your wife?"

Emrys smiled widely. "Yes, my Gwawr. She is Vilica—the mistress of the house. At the moment, she is attending the"—his hesitation was so slight, Marcus almost missed it—"princess. She will be joining us shortly." He waved around the three couches. "You didn't think this sumptuous feast was for men alone? What's a grand meal without the company of women?" Emrys added a crude—and typically Roman—joke concerning the fact that only males were present.

Laughter came from two of the three couches. The four junior officers, Nonus Sestius, Spurius Orcivius, Agrippa Corfidius, and Caeso Lucilius—crowded together on the lectus summus—laughed with raucous enthusiasm. Nonus slapped the couch several times in appreciation of the ribald humor. From the lectus imus, the host, Spurius

Aquillius, and the steward, Emrys, laughed as well.

But from the middle couch, the lectus medius, where Marcus and Aristobulus reclined, no laughter could be heard. Both Christians exchanged uncomfortable looks. Marcus was embarrassed by the joke and more than a little worried that the elderly missionary might rebuke the host.

However, Aristobulus kept his tongue.

As the laughter died down, Spurius Aquillius said, "Gwawr has been the mistress of this house for years." He clapped a greasy hand on his vilicus's shoulder, staining the man's toga. "And by Venus, if something should ever happen to you, my friend Emrys, I might snatch her up! So, you better watch yourself. You might meet with an unfortunate accident someday and . . ."

Emrys roared with laughter. "You better watch yourself, old man! Now that I know you have designs on my wife . . . And besides, Gwawr would tear your throat out with her teeth if you tried anything. My woman is a feisty one!"

Both men laughed. "To feisty, beautiful women!" cried Spurius Aquillius. He raised his wine cup.

The steward did the same. "To feisty, beautiful women!"

Together, both men downed a deep draught of wine.

They seem more like father and son than master and servant. Is Emrys, perhaps, Spurius Aquillius's bastard?

It would seem so.

Why not adopt him then? And leave the estate to him? "You two seem very close."

The host chuckled. "Yes, Emrys is my good right arm. I wish . . ." He sighed, and an ocean of regret rolled in that sigh. "But you have probably guessed already."

Marcus shrugged, then nodded.

The old man leaned closer to Marcus. "I petitioned the Senate to adopt him. And failed. I don't have the influence your father had in Rome. I'm not a pater. And even if I had adopted Emrys, it would have made no difference. What we do here, the service we provide the military, is vital. The empire would never allow the farm to fall into the hands of a Celt—not even a half-Roman Celt, even if he were formally adopted. Emrys knows this. No, the farm must and will remain firmly in Roman hands."

The old man leaned even closer till his lips were almost brushing Marcus's ear. "When the time comes, when all this is yours, Pater . . . I ask a boon. Please keep Emrys as vilicus and magister pecoris, and

Gwawr as his vilica. And please allow him to provide for . . . my grandchildren."

Marcus nodded and gave the man a kindly smile. "You have my promise, Spurius. Emrys and Gwawr and their children shall never lose their place in this house—not as long as I live."

The old man's eyes misted with tears. "Thank you. Coming from a Christian, I know you will keep your word." He pushed himself up on his elbows, looked past Marcus, and winked. "Your cult is bizarre, Aristobulus, my old Judean friend, but you do keep your oaths."

Behind Marcus, the old Christian replied, "We do as Christus commands, as you well know."

Their host shook his head and grinned. "Aristobulus, I want you to know you came very close, very close indeed to persuading me to become . . . But no, I will remain as I am. I am comfortable serving the gods of Rome. But I thank Juno that there are Christians in this wonderful Roman world." He raised his cup again. "To Christus!" Then he lowered the cup once more and frowned. "But no. You say it is . . . inappropriate." He poured a bit of wine on the floor. "There. That is my drink offering to Christus, whether he wants it or no." Then he took another draught of wine.

Marcus almost chuckled. Almost. *He means well, I suppose.*

A servant, a young Celtic woman with brown hair and soft blue eyes, approached the table in front of Marcus, bearing a platter of apricots and apples. She favored him with a bold smile as she placed the tray on the mensa.

Marcus returned her grin. *Pretty child.*

Spurius Aquillius chuckled. "Don't waste your time on that one, my lord. Not when you have a rare beauty already madly in love with you."

It was Marcus's turn to chuckle as he changed his focus from the girl to the food she'd set before him. "Don't worry. I wasn't even flirting with her."

The girl, having done her task, turned and left the triclinium.

"No," said the older man, "but she was flirting with you. And such flirtations, though they may lead to pleasure for the moment, can also lead to a lifetime of regret. And loss."

"Ah." *Emrys is the son of a servant girl? Born when Spurius Aquillius's wife was still alive?*

Did his wife . . . take her own life when she learned of the infidelity?

Such a scenario was all too common in Roman society.

"My God forbids such things," Marcus said just loud enough for his host to hear.

The man nodded. He sighed. And took another drink. "Good. You do know that, even if something were to happen to my . . . vilicus, I would never dishonor him by taking Gwawr to wife. I just wanted to assure you of that. It was a jest. And it was . . . in poor taste. Sometimes, when I have enjoyed a bit too much wine . . ." A wide grin split his face. "Ah! And speaking of the lovely Gwawr, here she is at last."

Marcus turned his eyes to the front of the room.

A tall, slender woman stood at the entrance to the triclinium. Her hair was the color of dark honey, and her soft eyes were brown, reminding Marcus of a doe's eyes. She wore a sleeveless gown of pale blue. And she was lovely.

But her radiant smile was all for her husband.

"Gwawr, my heart!" Emrys slapped the couch repeatedly, inviting his wife to join him.

"One moment, husband. First, I must present to you all . . ." She paused and motioned to someone out of the view of the diners. "Come forward, Your Highness. Please." She smiled at the unseen person.

And Maelona entered the room.

Every man present, including a few male servants, joined in a collective gasp.

Maelona's gown was of green linen, the color of a meadow in springtime, with wide, voluminous sleeves. The hems of the gown and the sleeves and the neckline were all embroidered with gold. The bodice was drawn tight across her torso by gold lacings at the sides. A simple belt of red leather was looped and tied at her waist. Her red hair had been combed and pulled back. A woven circlet of white flowers adorned her head, and white flowers dotted her hair like daisies on a field of rose petals. Her eyes shone like emeralds, matching her gown.

Her lovely eyes scanned the room, searching. They found Marcus, and her lips opened in a wide smile.

To Marcus, it was as if the sun had broken through the clouds and illuminated the world.

Suddenly, he found it hard to breathe properly.

Maelona's smile faltered.

Say something, fool!

But he seemed to have lost the ability to form words. All he could do was smile breathlessly.

Maelona's smile broadened again. She bowed her head slightly, but Marcus could still see her eyes through her long, pale red lashes.

"By all the gods!" exclaimed Spurius Aquillius. "Princess! You are a vision to make Venus blush with envy!"

Marcus could only nod in helpless agreement.

"Please," said the host. "Join us!" He scooted over in an attempt to make room for her between himself and Emrys.

"Yes." Marcus forced his mouth to obey him at last. "Please. Join us."

Maelona raised her head. "I do not wish to . . . I am grateful, Master of the House, but I ask you to forgive me. My place"—she turned her eyes to Marcus—"is with the man who holds my heart in his hands."

"My lord," said the old Roman, "you are blessed of the gods." Then he added hastily, "And I do believe your Christus favors you as well."

Marcus nodded. "Amen."

Aristobulus chuckled. "You had better marry her, my brother. Paul the Apostle has said it is better to marry than to burn."

And I do *burn.*

As Maelona walked around the back of the couches to take her place and Gwawr lay down beside her husband, Marcus whispered, "There are obstacles. You must baptize her first. And I am not yet a centurion. And I am not posted to a stable place."

"I will teach her tonight," said the Jew. "And baptize her in the morning hours, in the tepidarium, if she is ready. As for the other problems . . ."

"And there is also our mission. None of us may survive."

"Have faith, my brother. God will show you the way."

Maelona clambered onto the lectus medius between Marcus and the missionary. *Please, Heavenly Father. Show me the way.*

Once she was settled, Maelona turned her face toward Marcus. To Marcus's surprise, she was not smiling. Instead, her brow was creased with worry.

"What is wrong?" he asked, dismayed.

"Gwawr"—she pointed at the vilica—"that nice woman . . . she wanted to braid my hair. She said it was the Roman way. That it would please you. Make me beautiful. Make me look like a Roman princess. I . . . didn't want her to. I wouldn't let her. I am *not* Roman. I do not wish to be Roman." She paused and shrugged. "I just want to be Maelona. I am sorry I am not beautiful as I am."

Marcus laughed. How he wanted to kiss her! "Sweet Maelona, you are lovely. Just as you are. You . . . steal the breath from me. Just now.

When you entered the room, did you not hear the gasps from all the men?"

She smiled. "Truly? You are not saying this . . . because you love me?"

He gripped her hand and squeezed it. "Truly. And I do love you. But you are the loveliest . . . I cannot imagine anything . . . anyone more beautiful."

She beamed, and her smile smote his heart like an arrow from the quiver of mythical Cupid. "I love you as well."

Marcus heard a cough.

"Pardon me," said Aristobulus. "I am truly sorry to interrupt this sweet—if somewhat awkward—scene, but Brother Marcus Aquillius! You must introduce me to this vision of beauty."

Marcus quivered. *Father in heaven, I thank Thee.* "Maelona, may I introduce the answer to your prayer. This is Aristobulus, the man who—"

But Maelona had already turned to the man on her left. "You are the priest! Please! You must baptize me. Marcus says you can make me pure again. Please, my lord Priest. Please make me pure."

Marcus lifted up on an elbow, so he could see past Maelona's hair. He grinned at the man who had baptized him. "I told you it was so."

Aristobulus grinned. "Yes, indeed you did." He turned his gaze to Maelona. "My dear, I can baptize you . . . in the morning . . . after we have spoken . . . after you have eaten. If that is what you desire. But it is Christus who shall make you pure once more."

Maelona leaned over and kissed the old Jew's bearded cheek. "Thank you, my lord Priest!" Then she turned her face to Marcus and smiled. "Your God the Father—He answers prayers. Not like . . . the other gods. They are not gods at all, are they?"

Then she turned her attention to the mensa and the food. She let go of Marcus's hands and began cramming food into her mouth.

"Slow down," Marcus said. "You are behaving as if you have not eaten a bite for days." He chuckled nervously, then said more loudly. "We have been feeding her, I tell you truly."

She chewed a mouthful of cake and swallowed. "I must hurry. As soon as this meal"—she turned her face to the host—"and it is a delicious meal. I thank you." She turned back to Marcus, grabbing a slice of beef. "But as soon as this meal is over, I can talk to the priest and learn more of Christus. So I can be baptized." She slumped, frowning. "In the morning. I suppose I should not hurry too much. Not too much. I must . . . allow the priest to eat as well."

"My lady," said Aristobulus, "give me an hour or two, take the opportunity to enjoy the feast yourself. Then you and Marcus and I shall go to my room and feast upon the word of Christus."

For the next hour, they feasted on sumptuous mortal fare. One of the servants sang for them. The song was in Celtic or perhaps Cambrian—Marcus could not be certain, for he understood only a word or two. However, the melody and the singer's voice were sweet and ethereal, the notes themselves conjuring up images of home and lost loves.

Marcus lay on his right side, so he could see the singer. Maelona lay with her back against him. She took his left arm and pulled it around herself. Her fingers intertwined with his. She snuggled against him, her hair against his face. The pleasant, familiar smells of olive oil and wildflowers from her skin and hair filled his nostrils, and he breathed deeply the intoxicating scents.

And Marcus, for the first time in years, was truly happy and at peace.

"Perhaps, my lady," said Spurius Aquillius after the singer had departed, "if you will indulge an old man, might I ask you to sing for us?"

Maelona stiffened against Marcus. "I? Sing?"

The old Roman chuckled. "I know it is a great presumption . . . and perhaps it is also the wine . . . yes, perhaps, the wine . . . but I have never known a Cambrian lady who could not sing to shame a nightingale. It is something in the blood of this land. My Ceinwen . . . my wife. She could sing like a goddess. I think if you could gather together a few hundred Cambrian men and women and unite them in song, you could . . . reshape the world. Princess, would you please honor us with a song?"

Maelona's breath came in trembling gasps. "I have not sung in years. Not since . . ."

Marcus squeezed her hand. "You don't have to do this. You are a free woman. It is your choice."

She took a deep, shuddering breath, held it, and released it slowly. "Yes. I am a free woman. And I choose . . . to sing. But, if you will forgive me, my host, I will not sing for you. I will sing for Marcus Aquillius Audaxus."

With that, she disentangled herself from Marcus.

Marcus was loath to let her go, but he did. In spite of the sense of loss, of emptiness he felt as she climbed off the couch, he was anxious, hungry to hear her sing. *With you, my love, there is always some new delight.*

Maelona walked from behind the couches and stood in the entrance of the room. She appeared to tremble. She cleared her throat once. Twice. She opened her mouth, and a ragged note escaped her. She stopped herself. Then she opened her mouth once more.

And she sang. And her voice was high and lilting, and after some initial quivering, clear and ethereal.

Marcus understood none of the words, not directly. But when Maelona stared directly into his eyes, when she transfixed him with her gaze, it was as if words coalesced in his soul. The feeling was akin to words of prophecy thrilling through his mind.

Forsaken all I've ever known
For thee, for love of thee.
Father, mother, kindred, and home
For thee, and only thee.
But I will never count the cost
That I have paid for thee.
The past, the past is gone, is lost
Now that thou lovest me.

No golden torc do I desire,
Nor jewels in my hands,
Nor great king's hall, nor hearth of fire,
Nor house, nor flocks, nor lands.
The stars of heaven shining bright,
The moon above I see,
Thy strong arms warming me at night
Are all I ask of thee.

And when Death claims me, as He will,
And His fair halls I see,
No endless feasting can me fill
If I cannot have thee.
So when Death parts us at His call,
No magic wine I'll taste,
No joy I'll know in His great hall
'Til 'gain I see thy face.

Throughout her song, Maelona's eyes never left his. Marcus's heart thundered in his chest. *Father, show me the way!*

As the notes faded, Marcus became aware of another sound. The sound of weeping.

For a moment, he thought the sounds came from himself. But though tears leaked from his eyes, he was not the source of the sobbing, hitching sounds. The source was their noble host.

Spurius Aquillius's sorrow filled the triclinium like a cloud of anguish.

Marcus glanced at the other diners. All of them wept. Even the junior officers, who Marcus knew could not have understood the words of Maelona's song.

But the old Roman shook with unbridled grief. "Forgive me, Ceinwen! Forgive me!" He cradled his face in his hands.

Ceinwen? His wife?

And Marcus knew he had guessed correctly—about Spurius, about Emrys, and about the old Roman's dead wife.

He put out a hand and laid it gently on the man's quaking shoulder. "You know there is a path, Spurius. There is a path to forgiveness, to redemption, and to being reunited with your beloved Ceinwen. Aristobulus has taught you. There is a way."

The old man trembled. Then he lifted his tear-streaked face and looked at the Jew. "I'm ready. I'm ready, my friend. Please baptize me. This very night. Now."

The Christian missionary rose to his feet. "Come, my old friend. We shall go to my room. You shall confess your sins. And then you shall be baptized and confirmed a member of the Church of the Lamb of God. And then you shall receive the gift of the Holy Ghost."

Spurius Aquillius crawled off the couch, groaning, putting a hand to his back. The two older men faced each other, the Roman and the Jew. They embraced, and Aristobulus held Spurius as the Roman sobbed afresh.

Marcus got to his feet as well, standing behind the missionary. Maelona hurried over, coming around the couches from the other direction. She took Marcus's hand and knelt at his side. "Please," she said to Aristobulus, "I'm ready too."

As the four of them left the triclinium, headed for Aristobulus's room, Marcus heard, "Please, wait!"

He looked back to see Emrys and Gwawr standing as well. The vilicus and the vilica exchanged meaningful looks, and then Gwawr spoke. "Take us as well. We are ready."

Aristobulus gave them a beatific smile. He bowed and gestured for them to follow. Then the six of them—Aristobulus, the suddenly smiling Spurius Aquillius, Emrys and Gwawr, and Marcus and Maelona left the dining room. Marcus nodded to his junior officers.

They were all staring after him, the shock plain on their faces.

Caeso Lucilius still had the blood on his forehead. He scratched at his forehead in apparent confusion, smearing the blood.

If only you'd join us, my friends. You could really be cleansed from sin.

But Marcus knew that only four would be baptized that night.

For but a moment, thou shalt have the gift whereby thou shalt interpret the words of a song. And by a song shall souls be touched and four shall be won for the Lord.

♦ ♦ ♦

Aristobulus instructed the small flock until about midnight. He took the confessions of the prospective converts—one at a time, in the privacy of his room, while the others waited in the hall. And then, they all proceeded down to the tepidarium. Aristobulus and the four converts—fully clothed, of course—stepped down into the water while Marcus stood on the side. There the old Jew, who had known Jesus Christus in mortality and seen Him after His resurrection, took each of them in turn, raised his hand to the square, said the words of the baptismal ordinance in the name of the Father, the Son, and the Holy Ghost, and then immersed them in the water.

When Maelona came out of the water, her eyes gleaming, her smile broad and sparkling, and her gown and hair soaked, she threw her wet arms around Marcus, pressed her drenched body to him, and kissed him.

And Marcus found himself forced to suppress some less-than-holy thoughts on that very sacred occasion.

Then Marcus watched as Aristobulus laid his veined and age-spotted hands on the heads of the new converts one-by-one, confirmed them as members of the Church of Jesus Christus, and commanded them to receive the Holy Ghost.

Afterward, as Marcus and Maelona walked hand-in-hand to her room and she leaned against him in her wet gown, Marcus could not remember a happier moment in his life. At the door, he gathered her in his arms, lifted her up so her feet were no longer touching the floor. He whirled around once with her in his arms, both of them giggling like children. Then he kissed her, long and tenderly, attempting to keep at bay the passion burning so close to the surface.

She broke the kiss and pressed her lips to his ear. "I love you. Aristobulus told me. You must be a centurion first. I will wait. I will try."

"I love you too. Please, be patient. It is not only that. I don't know where or how we could be together while I'm still in the army." He set her down. Then he cocked his head and smirked at her. "So when Aristobulus explains it to you, you understand? Not when I explain it?"

She laughed. "I can be . . . persistent. Is that the word?"

He grinned. "That's one word for it."

"Are you certain I cannot stay in your room tonight?"

He nodded with a grimace on his face. "I'm certain. Not here. It would not look proper. In the field, we have no choice. But here you will be safe."

"Someday all this will belong to you?"

He shrugged. "I suppose so, but I am a soldier now."

"But this would be a good place to raise our children."

He chuckled. "Already thinking of children, are you?"

"Yes"—she sighed, then winked—"and the joy of making them."

Marcus stared at her aghast. "You just got baptized and already you are thinking sinful thoughts?"

She kissed him quickly and wriggled out of his arms. She gave him a sly, impish grin. "It's not sinful if we are married."

Then she retreated into her room and shut the door.

Marcus stared at that door for several moments.

Princess, you are driving me mad.

"With your jaw hanging open like that, an insect might fly down your throat."

Marcus's head snapped to the left. He wheeled and instinctively reached for his sword. However, he was not wearing a sword. Or a dagger.

Branwen stood before him. She wore a dark-blue, sleeveless Celtic gown. And the sheathed sword of Quintus Aquillius. Her arms were crossed, and she eyed him with a small degree of amusement. "If that . . . freckled child can get you so . . . excitable, you shall be easy prey for me."

Must get her away from Maelona. From everyone in this house. He took a few steps toward her. "What are you doing here?"

She chuckled, but there was little mirth in the low laugh. "I have told you. I am here for you. You will choose me, not that upstart girl."

Marcus heard voices coming down the hallway. He turned his head toward the sound. *Not now! Go away!*

"You needn't worry about them," she said. "I promised you. I gave my word. They are safe."

"But they'll see you!"

"Oh, very well." She grabbed his hand. "Come with me." She dragged him down the hall and into a small courtyard. Then she pulled him into a tight embrace. And immediately frowned in disgust. "Ew! You're all wet! Well . . . Ew!" She growled low in her throat. "No time for that now." Her wings appeared, materializing as if out of the air.

And they shot into the night sky.

Chapter XV

"Pity her not. Nevertheless, thou shalt offer that thou canst give. And thine offering shall be called holy."

from the Book of Marcus Scribonius

"This— This is why one should-d n-never f-fly in wet c-c-clothes." Branwen knelt and blew on the small fire she'd lit, coaxing the insignificant flame to catch in the sticks of wood she'd laid. She shivered violently.

Marcus Aquillius had watched in wonder as the fearsome Daughter of Lilith gathered kindling and twigs, moving at speeds so fast he could not always follow with his eyes. He'd observed in amazement as she broke huge branches and split logs, sometimes with the Roman sword at her hip and sometimes with her bare hands. She spun a dry stick, pushing it down into an indentation in a flat piece of wood—her hands moving so quickly they were a blur. And when the wood smoked, then glowed, and then ignited, Marcus had gasped in astonishment.

But as Branwen knelt and tended the fire, quaking as violently in the cold night air as Marcus himself, his awe bordered on fear. "Y-you're c-c-cold?"

"Yes, I'm c-cold," she snapped back at him. "It's cold, and I'm w-wet—thanks to you—and near t-to f-freezing."

"You c-can feel the c-cold?"

"Men are s-s-so s-stupid." With trembling hands, she laid some larger sticks on the fire.

"I thought you were im-m-mort-t-tal."

"I *am* immortal! I d-don't age. I haven't aged f-for . . . a l-long time. B-but I c-can still d-d-die." She bent and blew on the flames again. "J-just n-not as easily as y-you, you s-stup-p-pid man."

The breeze picked up, whistling through the grove of trees. And while the wind fanned the flames, it also deepened the already bone-deep chill.

Can't she fly us somewhere else? Somewhere warm?

He considered suggesting just that course of action, then quickly decided against it. *We'd certainly freeze to death if we went back up there.*

Marcus had no desire to ever be carried through the air again, to see the ground below him, the huge villa receding into a small rectangle of lights no larger than his thumb, to have the low-hanging clouds misting his hair.

The only other time Marcus had flown in Branwen's arms, he was dying, fading in and out of consciousness. However, on this night, he was fully awake and aware. And utterly helpless.

As they shot through the night sky, the chill air ripped through their wet clothing, quickly sapping the heat from their bodies. And even after they were once again safely on the ground and within the shelter of a forest, the cool breeze became a bitter wind. It was late summer, and yet, both the mortal and the immortal were in very real danger of dying from the cold.

Both of us.

As he watched Branwen shiver over the slowly growing fire, Marcus chose the only course of action that might save their lives—or at least Branwen's life. He removed his still-wet toga. Then, clad only in his damp subligar, he crawled up next to the fearsome—yet suddenly vulnerable—Daughter of Lilith and wrapped his arms around her, using his own shivering body to shield hers from the wind.

She stiffened at his touch. Then she melted, quivering, into his embrace.

Together, they shivered and watched the growing fire in silence.

Eventually, the shivering lessened, then stopped.

Branwen turned her face and stared at his. Marcus, for his part, kept his eyes on the fire. *Don't look into her eyes!* Whenever he had locked his gaze with hers in the past, she had pulled at him, tugged at his will. And Marcus was absolutely certain that if she really tried, she could force him to do her bidding.

She kissed his cheek. Her lips were soft and warm—at least, they were warmer than his face.

Marcus shivered anew. And not only from the cold.

"Thank you," she said, her face still turned toward him, her warm breath on his flesh. "You are truly Audaxus. You would sacrifice your life for anyone. Even me." She pulled away from him. She put two pieces of a split log onto the small fire—a log she'd split using only her delicate-looking, mighty hands. The sap on the wood's exposed inner surface crackled and blazed.

Then she returned to his arms and slipped her own arms around his bare chest. She laid her head on his shoulder. "It is no wonder that she loves you."

"How . . ." Her hair, her skin no longer smelled of the grave. It smelled of woodlands—of trees and leaves and loam . . . and wildflowers. It was a pleasant scent. "How d-do you know Maelona loves me?"

She huffed softly. "I have ears. Far better than your poor mortal ears. I can hear you. I have watched you."

"But how? Where have you been that you can hear us and see us? Why have I not seen you?"

"You never look up." She shrugged, and her hair rubbed against his cheek, setting his flesh tingling. "And I can sit, unseen, on a rooftop and listen."

Nothing we say goes unheard. Or is it only at . . . "But only during the night?"

"For a stupid man, you are quite intelligent."

Marcus heard the smile in her voice. *Careful. You are treading on dangerous ground—dangerous ground that must be trod.* "Why only at night?"

She stiffened. "There are things I cannot tell you. Things you cannot know. Not until you are ready."

Ready? "To become as you are? A . . . Son of Lilith?"

She chuckled. "I apologize most sincerely for calling you stupid."

It was Marcus's turn to chuckle. "Women make men stupid. You turn us into imbeciles." *Especially lovely women like you. And Maelona.*

"It is because you desire us."

Marcus's palms became moist, and his throat became dry.

"You *do* desire me," she said. "Do not try to deny it. I can hear your heart pounding, your pulse racing. And your scent . . . Mmm. Your scent is the perfume of a man consumed by desire."

"I . . ." He swallowed once, twice. "I do not deny it."

"Good. I value your honesty."

"But I also fear you."

She laughed then. She lifted her head and looked at him. While he forcibly kept his gaze toward the fire, she kissed his cheek once more. "Good! You are wise to fear me."

"You could kill me with your hands, rip my head off like you did with . . . the evildoer."

"But that is not the only reason you fear me, is it?"

"No." He took a deep, trembling breath. Held it briefly, then released it. "It is because . . . I do desire you. And I must not."

"No, we cannot control our desires." She paused. "All we can do is choose to ignore them."

"My lady, you are very difficult to ignore."

"Look at me. Please. I promise I will not Persuade you. Your thoughts, your feelings shall be your own. I want to look into your eyes when I say this. Please, Marcus Aquillius. Please look at me."

Marcus swallowed hard. He wasn't simply afraid, he was terrified—terrified of those green eyes, of what she might see, of letting this lovely night-demon peer into his soul.

He turned his face and gazed into those eyes—so like Maelona's. Whereas before Branwen's eyes had been confident, strong, determined, even hard like emeralds glowing with fire. But at that moment, they were as haunted and vulnerable as Maelona's had been when Marcus first met her. Branwen no longer seemed an invulnerable, terrifying goddess of vengeance, but rather a soft, defenseless woman. There were no tears in her eyes, and Marcus wondered briefly if she was capable of tears.

Branwen kept her word—she was not pulling at him, and he did not feel the nigh-irresistible urge to obey her, to please her. But he knew—and he was certain it came only of his own free will—that he had no desire to hurt her. Not in any way.

I owe you my life. He swallowed again.

She smiled, and there was a sadness in that smile—a sadness so profound and sweet, it almost broke his heart.

"I've told you before . . . or perhaps I didn't . . . that no one has ever called me his lady." She blinked, glanced away, then met his eyes once more. "There was a man once. He courted me. He said he loved me . . ." She shook her head, but never broke eye contact. "He said he loved me more than the stars loved the moon. And I believed him. I believed him with all my heart. I trusted him. He promised to marry me, to make me his bride. He promised to love me for eternity."

Branwen closed her lips, and they trembled, but still her eyes were dry. "He made me as he was—as I am now. And I let him. It must be done willingly, by your consent. And"—she sighed, turning her eyes away—"I loved him, truly, with all my young, foolish heart."

She turned her eyes back to his, and her eyes had hardened. "But he lied to me. He took my virtue and my heart, and he lied to me. He already had a wife. In fact, he had two wives. And with me, he had three. I was to be simply one of his growing stable of wives, like horses he could take out and ride at his choosing. But that was not the worst of it." Her eyes softened. And they filled with tears.

"My lady?"

She blinked, causing the tears to spill down her cheeks. "Why are you so kind to me? You are a warrior. An invader of my land. You have slain many of my people. We are supposed to be enemies. And you speak to me as if I were worthy of kindness or honor. I am no one's lady. I have never been anyone's lady. In mortality, I was a farmer's daughter—one of six. I was nothing. No lady. My father could afford no dowry, so I was not able to marry anyone, not unless it was some brute—some farmer or shepherd twice my age—who would beat me and use me until I died giving birth to one of his children. I was no princess such as your . . ." She paused, then gave him a shy smile. "But you speak to me as if I were a princess or a queen. Is it the fear? Is that it?"

Marcus shook his head slightly. "No, my lady. I do fear you. Perhaps that is a part of it, but my mother taught me to treat all women with honor—from the highest empress to the lowest whore in the streets. Because they . . . Because you are all born ladies, regardless of what you may become afterward. You are born to be respected, cherished."

She chuckled once. "This is not your Christus that teaches you this? But your mother?"

"Christus teaches that man is not without the woman, nor woman without the man. We must be one. We must love and cherish one another. But yes, my mother taught me to honor women. So did my father. He treated my mother as if she were a goddess. I want to be like him."

She looked away. "That is . . . That is lovely. I wish . . ." She shook herself, then fixed him with her stare again. "The worst part, Marcus Aquillius, is that my . . . husband . . . if I can call him that . . . there was no ceremony, no ritual—not of marriage, at least. He was my Master, and my Master *owned* me. I was his slave. That is part of being . . . what I am. If I have a Master, I must obey. I have no choice. No choice at all."

So like Maelona. But Maelona is now free. Branwen is not.

She shrugged her shoulders. "And so I killed him. Oh, it took me a very long time—years of searching for ways to get around his commands—but I managed it. I killed him. And then I was free. At least free of him. There are . . . others who may still command me . . . if they can find me. There is one . . . She calls to me from time to time. I can feel it. But she has not commanded me. Not specifically. Not yet.

But if she does command, I must go to her. I have no choice."

"Lilith?"

She nodded. "Yes. But I think . . . I hope she is not truly aware of my . . . . freedom. Not yet. And I must never be found by someone—another of my kind—or she may learn."

"Is that why you need the sword?"

"Brave and kind *and* intelligent. And handsome too." A corner of her mouth lifted in a mocking half-smile. "For a big-nosed Roman."

She sighed and pulled out of his embrace. She put three more logs on the fire. The blaze had finally grown to the point where it warmed the front of them. Then she quickly returned to him and put her arms around him once more.

She was shivering again, her clothes still wet.

He shivered as well. And once again, it was not entirely from the cold. He put his arms around her again, and again she melted into his embrace.

The fire's not enough. It warms only the front. I must hold on to her. For both our sakes.

Keep telling yourself that, Marcus.

It is not merely that type of warmth you seek.

But we are not out of danger. Not yet.

"I tried," she said, her cheek against his chest, "I tried to go on. To find a purpose—a purpose for my life, for my *existence*. My kind—we are driven to slay the evildoers—those who commit violence against the innocent—rapists and murderers, and those who defile and abuse children . . . and others who cannot defend themselves. I must kill them. I found some purpose in defending the defenseless. And I have never . . . taken pleasure from . . . the seduction of the innocent. I never wanted . . . I never want to do . . . what was done to me. But I have taken many lives. And I do not regret the taking of them. I regret only . . . that . . ." She fell silent. And she began to weep in earnest.

Marcus held her more tightly, but he did not press her to continue.

After several long moments, her sobbing quieted. "I'm sorry. I haven't . . . wept like that in a century."

"H-how old are you, my lady? If I may ask?"

"I stopped aging when I had seen twenty-one winters. I had seen another one hundred and two before I . . . before I . . ."

"Before you sealed yourself in that barrow?"

She nodded.

"Why did you do that?"

"Because I had no reason to go on living. And I was too cowardly to take my own life. I could have, you understand. I could have just waited for the Sun to set me aflame."

"So you cannot endure the sunlight at all?"

She lifted her head and looked at him. And she smirked. "So, Commander, you are attempting to learn how you may kill your enemy, are you?"

He shrugged. "I need to know how to protect my men" —*and Maelona*— "against any possible threat. But are you my enemy? I do not mean to offend you. I am very much in your power at the moment."

She raised an eyebrow. "If I wanted to kill you, there is nothing you could do to stop me."

"And yet I wounded you. With my sword." Then he added, "Though you healed yourself very quickly."

"You are, aren't you? You're trying to discover how I may be killed." She started to pull herself from his embrace.

"No," he said. "Not you. You have given me your word. And I believe you will keep it. It is not *you* I fear—well, yes, I do fear you, but I believe you will not kill us—it is others like you. You did mention others."

She nodded, cuddling back against him. "Yes. There are others. I have . . . already slain one—just one of my kind out Hunting, who came to prey upon you and your men. I killed him this very night."

He pulled away and looked at her in shock. "Truly? Tonight?"

She nodded. "Yes. I am watching over you and your . . . companions at night. I cannot guard you during the day. Unless it is very cloudy or raining . . . or snowing . . . and I cover myself completely. Then it is possible to watch you. But to fight? In the daytime? That depends on how dark it is."

"Thank you, Lady Branwen. It is not just I, it seems, who owe you a life."

"Yes, you do owe me your life." She rested her head on his chest again. "And some day . . . some night, I will claim it."

Marcus could not suppress a shudder. "If you make me as you are—"

"You must choose it. I cannot force it upon you."

"Very well. If I *chose* to be as you are then, would I . . . be the same man you now desire?"

"If I make you as I am, perhaps you could stand against Arawn. Together, perhaps, we could stand against Arawn. Otherwise, how will you defeat him?"

"You know of that, do you?"

"I told you—I have ears."

"Yes, I see. Our secret mission is . . . not so secret."

"You told . . . Aristobulus. Yes, that was the name."

"But that was during the day."

"Perhaps it was. But he mentioned it in his prayers in the early evening."

"How . . . How did you find us at night? We had left the road."

"Yes, you did. And that was very inconsiderate of you. I was . . . frightened I'd lost you." She clung to him for a moment in silence. "But I caught your scent on a fortunate breeze."

"My scent?"

She laughed. "Yes, even though you have bathed"—she paused, wrinkling her nose—"that soap stinks, do you know. I would recognize your scent anywhere."

"How? Because your nose is better than . . . a mortal's?"

"Yes, and because I love you."

No. Please. "Lady Branwen, how can you love me? You barely know me. We have . . . spent so little time together."

"We have spent more time together than you know. I have read your book, Marcus Scribonius. I should not have read it. It was yours. But I read it while you dined."

"My book?" Marcus felt a flash of anger. "That is private. It is sacred. Sacred to me."

"I . . . am not sorry. Not truly. Your book . . . it speaks of me. Your god has spoken to you of me."

"Yes." *How dare she? She can do anything she likes, and no one can prevent her. But it is* my *book!*

"But you do not understand all the words, all the sayings. You have said as much."

He felt the anger drain from him. "No. I don't understand . . . most of it. Not yet."

"Then perhaps your god has spoken to you of me more times than you understand."

Marcus sighed. And then he chuckled softly. "That is quite likely."

"Perhaps someday, you will understand those passages that relate to me. When you are mine." She squeezed him. "And you *will* be mine."

No! But even as he denied it, desire surged through him. He wanted to turn and kiss her. He wanted it very badly. *Think of something else!* He pictured Maelona in his mind, her joyful smile after her baptism. "Why . . . why did you leave the barrow . . . when you did? What was it like? Did you simply go to sleep? How long were you there?"

She stiffened at his words. "It was . . . horrible. I tried to Sleep during the day. Yes, I always knew when the day had come. And when night fell. But soon the pain, the hunger kept me awake, even after daybreak. My body wasted away, consuming itself for lack of nourishment. The agony was . . . beyond your comprehension. But I was determined to remain. How long was I there? After the first year, I stopped counting the nights. What year is it now?"

"It is Eight hundred Fourteen *Ab Urbe Condita*."

She trembled. "Six . . . years? That is all? It felt like . . . so much longer."

Marcus found himself stroking her hair, comforting her. He stopped himself. "So . . . um . . . why did you emerge from the barrow, from the tomb?"

"That felt nice," she said. "Please. Continue with my hair."

Marcus swallowed. "Y-yes, my lady." He resumed stroking her hair.

She chuckled—a musical, feminine sound. "I'm not going to bite you, Marcus." She chuckled again, though without mirth. "Not unless you give me permission."

He shuddered again. "Why did you emerge from the tomb?"

She sighed. "It was my own fault. I must not have sealed the entrance as well as I thought. Even as I attempted to starve myself to death, I needed a little air, but I thought I had left only a tiny opening . . . But no. The scent of evil blood called to me. I was so hungry. And I . . . cannot resist the sweetness of evil blood."

Evil blood? "B-but . . . there were no marks. No wounds. How did you . . . kill them?"

"Have you not guessed? When I Healed you—"

"With your spittle, yes. So you . . . *drank* their blood. Then you sealed up the wound with your spittle?"

She nodded. "I lick the wound, and the flesh closes. But I must consume the blood of the evildoers."

"But you did not take the blood of Quintus Aquillius."

"No. I had to kill him, but . . . hungry as I was—starving as I was—saving your life was more important."

"But why?"

"Because you are courageous. You are Audaxus—the bravest man I have ever met. Yours was a life worth saving." She squeezed him tightly. So tightly, it was almost painful. "And you are kind and caring as no man I have ever known. You are so sweet to that . . . girl."

"I love her."

Branwen was silent for several long moments. Then she whispered, "I know. I could . . . kill her. You know that."

"Yes. But you will not. You have given your word." And he knew it was true.

She nodded. "And if I were to kill her, you would never love me. Never."

"Branwen . . ."

"Know this, Marcus Aquillius, I will never be a second wife. Never!" Her voice seethed with anger. And that time, she did squeeze him to the point of pain.

"Branwen!" He grunted. "You are . . . hurting me!"

She jerked back, releasing him. Her eyes were wide with horror. "I'm sorry!"

Marcus gingerly probed his ribs. "I don't think . . . ow . . . anything is broken."

Branwen hugged herself, breathing heavily. "I am so very sorry." She wept, burying her face in her hands. "I have bungled this so badly. I didn't mean to hurt you. I never, never want to hurt you. I said that I love you. And I do. Forgive me. Please?" She lifted her face to him.

Marcus turned his face to hers and saw that her eyes were pleading and wet with fresh tears. "Forgive you?" He laughed softly. And painfully. "For loving me? Lady Branwen, your love is a gift. A gift I will always cherish."

She smiled at him.

Marcus could see both gratitude and longing in that smile. His breath quickened. He inclined his face toward hers. Their lips almost touched.

Then he slammed his eyes shut with a groan.

And pulled away.

"I have given my word." He opened his eyes and met her gaze. *I could love you. I . . . almost do.* "To Maelona. I love her. I will not hurt her." He swallowed. Hard. But he did not look away from those lovely, sad eyes. "You . . . tempt me."

She nodded slowly, never breaking eye contact. "I know. And I know you will not betray her."

I almost did.

Branwen chewed her lip, then shook her head. "And that . . . somehow . . . makes me love you all the more." She looked away, and the tears on her cheeks glistened in the firelight. "I shall not . . . tempt you again." She laid her head upon his chest. "Just, please, hold me a little longer. Stroke my hair. And let me dream."

Marcus gave a shuddering sigh.

They sat in silence, holding one another.

And Marcus stroked Branwen's hair.

After a long while, they both stood and dried their clothes. As they did, they told each other stories of their childhood. For Marcus, these were happy stories, for the most part. Branwen's happy stories were few. She hinted at unhappy times, at her inability to find a proper husband, at the fact that she felt she had aged past her marriageable years—but she stopped short of telling him any more about how she had been seduced and converted to her present state. She did tell him about a profound loneliness that had lasted already for several lifetimes.

Marcus realized he pitied the beautiful, terrifying, immortal creature.

Pity her not.

Does that apply to Maelona or to Branwen? Or does it apply to both?

But I do *pity her.*

And I almost betrayed Maelona.

What would it be like, though, to spend a hundred years alone and afraid?

How can I not pity her?

Pity will be my undoing.

When their clothes were dry, they sat by the fire and held each other once more.

And Marcus stroked Branwen's hair.

"I must go soon. We must march in the morning." He groaned. "In a few hours."

"I know. But it has been so nice to dream."

"Will you . . . take me back now?" He did not want to fly, but he guessed it might take him hours to walk back to the villa. To Maelona.

She began to weep again.

"My lady! What is wrong?"

"I-I can't!"

"What do you mean? You can fly. That's how—"

"I am too weak. If I tried, we would fall from the sky."

"I don't understand."

"My long . . . starvation. It has left me weak. My body . . . consumed itself, for it had nothing else to feed upon. I was . . . almost skeletal."

Marcus tried to imagine the beautiful Branwen as mere skin and bones. "But you are . . . restored now."

"Yes, but . . . other than the first two evildoers, I have not Fed. All my strength has been used following you, protecting you. I am . . . spent. I vowed . . . Long ago, I vowed never to steal blood from an innocent. I have kept that vow. All my long, lonely, cursed . . . I have kept my vow."

"But surely there are cattle, sheep . . ."

"I cannot . . . I mean, I can, but . . . the blood of animals does not strengthen me—not at all. It is like drinking . . . water. No nourishment. I must have human blood. Nothing else." A huge sob wracked her body. "I'm so . . . hungry."

Marcus stiffened. "How much do you need?"

Branwen froze as well. "Do you mean . . ."

"How much do you need to sustain you?"

"You would . . . for me?"

"Will it kill me?"

She sat up, pulling out of his arms. She wiped at her tears. Then she stared at him, awestruck. "You would, wouldn't you? To save me. To save even one such as I. You would give your life . . ."

He nodded. "Yes. May God have mercy on me, but I would."

"You are truly . . ." She shook her head with vigor. "No, it would not kill you. I would need . . . a goblet's portion. No more. That would sustain me for a few days. And my . . . spittle, it would mix with the blood in your veins and restore you quickly. In the morning, you would be refreshed. Completely. You would do this . . . willingly?"

He gave her a grimace of a smile. "Yes, but . . . there will be pain?"

She laughed and dashed away a fresh tear. "For but a moment. Then . . . there will be . . . pleasure." It was suddenly her turn to grimace. "You will enjoy it. You will . . . *beg* me to drain you." Then she shook her head. "But I will not! You have my word."

His smile and his chuckle were weak. "You terrify me, my lady. But if my life will sustain yours . . ." He frowned. "How . . . is it done?"

She smiled. And it was a beautiful, alluring, tempting smile. "Do you trust me?"

He swallowed hard. "Y-yes. Yes. Quite literally with my life."

Her smile broadened, showing her teeth. Two of the top ones, sharp and pointed, extended, becoming wolfish fangs. Her breath quickened, and she licked her lips with a pink tongue. "Then trust me now. You will enjoy this. Almost as much as I."

She leaned toward him, gripped his head in one hand and his

shoulder in the other, and tilted her face over his neck.

Marcus felt her teeth pierce his flesh. There was pain.

And then there was ecstasy.

Joy coursed through him. Even as he felt strength pass from him, he moaned, "More. Please. More."

But, too soon, she pulled away.

He reached for her, pleading, "More!"

She brushed his arms away. "No, my love. No more. Not tonight."

No! I need you. Anything! Anything you ask! "Please! Please. More."

She shook her head. "This joy, this pleasure that you feel . . . it will pass." She shook her head again, but in wonder instead of denial. "Innocent blood is not as sweet as evil blood. But there is something . . . incredibly sweet . . . a different kind of sweetness . . . to blood given willingly. Something . . . holy."

Holy? My blood was . . . holy to her?

Nevertheless, thou shalt offer that thou canst give. And thine offering shall be called holy.

In moments, the euphoria and the sense of longing dissipated, like dew off the morning grass. Marcus shuddered as he regained control of his body. And his will. "I feel . . . weak, but somehow . . . invigorated too."

She nodded. "Once you have slept for a few hours"—she chuckled—"well, the few hours remaining—you will be restored."

Branwen stood, and Marcus watched as she used her sword to scatter the remains of the fire.

Marcus put a hand to his neck. It still felt wet—not sticky, as with blood, but moist as with spittle. However, he could detect no wounds, no marks.

Miraculous.

I've never seen a miracle – not performed by the power of God. Never. Not water turned to wine. Not a healing. Not raising a man from the dead, as our Lord did with Lazarus.

And yet . . . there is this wonder . . . this terrifying, lovely wonder before me. And her power is not from God. It comes from . . . from where?

She even brought me back from death when Quintus Aquillius murdered me.

Where was God's power in that?

What is happening to me?

Our Father who art in heaven, hallowed be Thy name.

What I have seen this night . . . How does it all fit in Thy plan? Where is Thy power in all this?

I believe. I believe in Christus. I believe in His grace, in His power to redeem my soul from hell.

But what does this *mean?*

I cannot doubt the evidence of my own eyes.

I have never asked Thee for a miracle. I have never asked for a sign.

Tonight, I have seen four souls won for Thee. And that is a miracle. I suppose I could call it miraculous.

It was. It was miraculous.

But I go to do battle with a god.

No! Arawn is not a god. There are no other gods.

Perhaps, as Aristobulus said, Arawn is a demon, an ancient evil, an angel who fell before the world was.

But how am I to fight him? I have no power. Not such as I have seen this night in this lovely . . . in Branwen.

But would even her *power be enough to stand against the lord of the dead?*

I have been denied Thy power, Thy priesthood. All I have is . . . my sword . . . and my faith.

My sword cannot slay a demon. And I do not know if my faith is strong enough. I don't think it is. I don't think it can be. Not enough to fight a demon.

Father in heaven, strengthen my faith.

Strengthen me.

I was sorely tempted this night. I could have given in.

I almost did.

I am still tempted.

"Thank you," Branwen said as she worked, interrupting his prayer. She did not look at him as she spread the remains of the fire. She pushed a log aside, and the blaze flared up momentarily. And for that moment, her body was silhouetted through her gown.

Marcus knew the sight would be etched into his memory forever.

When Branwen finished, she approached him, her face cast in deep night shadow. "I will take you back now." She held out a hand to him, and he took it. She lifted him easily to his feet. "Turn around," she said. "I want you to be able to see—to behold the wonder of flight."

He complied.

She put her arms around his chest and pulled him tight against her body. "Don't you dare close your eyes, Audaxus." Her wings unfurled, and Branwen and Marcus lifted slowly into the air.

As they flew, with the clouds above illuminated by the sliver of a spectral moon, the ground below dark—save for the tiny cluster of lights that was the villa—Marcus realized he was not frightened. *Branwen holds me. She will not let me go. I am safe in her arms.* He opened his mouth in wonder and breathed a single word—"Beautiful."

"Yes," she shouted, "it is!"

Marcus had whispered, and she heard him clearly. But Branwen was forced to shout so that he could hear her above the gale of wind howling in his ears.

"Marcus," she cried, "the memory of this night . . . I shall cherish it for eternity!"

For eternity.

An eternity of loneliness.

Pity smote his heart like a spear thrust.

Chapter XVI

"Seek not to return to Rome, for the emperor shall persecute and slay the disciples of the Lamb. Three years shall not pass away before the fires of Rome shall begin the consumption of the faithful. The apostles of the Lamb shall fall, all save the beloved revelator, and with the apostles, the priesthood shall be taken from the church. Lo! Three generations shall not pass away before the children's children shall no longer know the fullness of my gospel. But be thou valiant, my son, for in the time of the Lord, all things shall be eternal, and all that thou lovest shall be restored unto thee."

from the Book of Marcus Scribonius

Lo! Three generations shall not pass away before the children's children shall no longer know the fullness of my gospel.

Marcus stared in horror at the scroll and the words he had written. The prophecy had come to him an hour before dawn, awakening him from his too-brief slumber.

Three generations? The priesthood gone? The children's children shall no longer . . .

A knock at the door startled him, and he nearly knocked the ink bottle off the small desk. He caught it, steadied it, then said, "Yes? Who is it?"

"Aristobulus," came the answer. "May I enter?"

Aristobulus? The very man! In the next shaky breath, Marcus was at the door, unlatching it. He ushered the elderly Jew into his room.

The old man's beard and hair were disheveled, and he wore the toga—now dry—that he'd worn the night before. "The Spirit awoke me. He said, 'Marcus is in need of thee.' I am here. How can I help you, Brother Mar—"

Marcus grabbed Aristobulus by the arm and dragged him to the desk. He pointed to the scroll. "This! What—"

Aristobulus's eyes widened and his mouth opened in wonder. "Is this . . . Is this your book? The book of your prophecies?"

"Yes! But—"

"I have heard of this! You told me you had the gift of prophecy, but I have never seen—"

"But look. Look at this one." Marcus stabbed a finger at the last, lengthy prophecy on the scroll. "I just received this one. And it is . . . terrifying. I don't understand."

"May I?" The old Jew indicated the Roman chair at the desk.

"Yes. But the prophecy . . ."

"Allow me a moment to . . ." Aristobulus's countenance fell as he read. Then he began to nod.

"Does this mean that the Church . . ."

Aristobulus held up a finger. "One moment more. I must read it again."

Marcus held his peace. He waited as the moments stretched. But finally, he could wait no longer. "Does this mean that the Church is . . . dying?"

Aristobulus shrugged, nodded, then shook his head. "Yes and no. The Church is already becoming corrupted. Ravening wolves in sheep's clothing are invading the flock. They are changing the simple truths of the gospel to match pagan ritual, the philosophies of men masquerading as doctrine. Peter has prophesied it. Paul has too. But I had no—"

"You knew?" Anger mixed with Marcus's fear, and both bubbled up in him like bile. He thumped his fist on the desk, causing the ink bottle and the old man to jump. "You *knew* about this?"

The elderly missionary lifted his face. And there were tears leaking from Aristobulus's eyes, running slowly down the wrinkles of his cheeks and into his beard. "Yes, brother. We have known for some time. The Church will become corrupted, the fullness of the truth and the priesthood will be taken from the earth. Soon . . . all too soon, only a remnant will be left—a pale shadow of the true Church. But we did not know how soon. We have been combating the corruption, the apostasy, but . . . we did not know how long we had. Until now." He shook his head and pulled his white hair with both hands. "Three generations! So soon! My poor children! My grandchildren. My little flock!"

"You knew? But why? Why go on? Why go on baptizing and preaching when it's all . . . going away?" He pointed in the direction of Maelona's room. "Why baptize her? Why give her hope? When it will all . . . die?" He put both hands on the desk, bowed his head, and trembled. He gripped the edge of the small table, certain he would fall without its support. He lifted his face to the ceiling and shut his eyes against angry tears. "Why give me hope?"

Aristobulus placed a hand atop his. "Brother, the Lord's purposes are eternal. *We* are eternal. We know it will be lost, that there will be a falling away, but we also know that it will all be restored. Even this prophecy says it will be restored." He tapped his finger on the scroll, and Marcus opened his eyes. "It says, 'in the time of the Lord.' We don't know when, but we know it will all be restored . . . when the world is prepared."

Marcus stood abruptly and wrapped his arms around himself as if protecting his heart. He turned and faced Maelona's room. "Why get baptized at all? Why get married? Even if I have children and grandchildren and . . . They will be lost." *Lost. All lost.*

The word seemed to hang in the air with a finality that made his legs quake and his heart wither in his chest. "Lost."

Aristobulus rose, came to him, and placed a hand on his shoulder. "Nothing is lost to the Lord. All is eternal. And though our grandchildren may not have the fullness of the gospel or the authority and ordinances of the priesthood, it will all be restored."

"But they need baptism, the Holy Ghost, the endowment of . . ."

"Do you know that we are doing, even now, proxy baptisms for our dead? For our ancestors?"

Marcus nodded slowly. "Yes. I have heard of this."

"They lived and died without the knowledge of Christus. Or in the hope of His coming. He is being preached to them even now in the world of spirits, in the world of the dead. And we, the living, are being baptized for them. Why would we do that if they were lost forever? Not even a sparrow shall—"

Marcus wheeled on the old man as rage and fear welled inside him again. "Yes, yes! That's all fine, but I have to fight a god!" He growled in frustration and waved a hand. "And yes, I *know* Arawn . . . or Moloch or Chemosh or whatever he calls himself—I know he's not a god, but how am I . . . What's it all for? If the Church is falling away, becoming corrupted? What's it all for?" He glared at Aristobulus. *Please. Please give me hope. Give me something to hold on to.*

Aristobulus glared right back at him, and the ferocity in the missionary's eyes was terrifying. "What's it all for? We are fighting, brother! All of us. For every soul. For yours. For Maelona's. For Spurius Aquillius's. For Emrys's and Gwawr's. For all of them! And we will lose . . . so many." He shook his head, and tears sprayed from his white beard. "My grandchildren will see the end of it. I weep for the generations that will not know the blessings of the gospel. But their day *will* come! All will be restored. That I know. That I cling to! Anything less would be to give in to the darkness, to tumble into the abyss. And I will not do it! You're frightened? Well, I am terrified! Terrified. My knees quake. My hands lose their strength. Yet I fight on." He paused, panting after his outburst. "I fight on. And so must you, Brother Marcus. Even if you cannot see the end from the beginning, the Lord does!"

Marcus's anger drained like hot water through a sieve. He bowed his head. "Yes, Elder Aristobulus. Forgive my . . . impertinence. Forgive my . . . fear."

The old Jew took Marcus's hand in his. "I haven't your gift for personal prophecy, but this I do prophesy for you, in the name of the Lord Jesus Christus. Of your loins shall come two great warriors, and they shall fight and defeat an ancient evil. And after they have given all, after they have laid down their very lives, then all that you love, your entire posterity shall be restored to you through them. At least, the restoration shall start with them—for your posterity shall be as the sands of the seashore and as the stars of heaven. Be patient, brother. For God knows you, and He loves you. He is mindful of you. And He is mindful of your beloved princess. Rely on the Lord for strength, because your own strength is not sufficient. Be faithful. Be true. Be valiant. Be . . . Audaxus. For that is who you are."

Marcus sighed in exhaustion and resignation. "I hate that stupid name."

Aristobulus chuckled. Then he laughed aloud. "It is a terrible burden, to be sure." He pointed to Marcus's plumed helm. "As is that crest you wear. But you chose neither the name nor the plume. They were chosen for you. Or rather *you* were chosen for *them*. You are the option and you are the valiant. And you were chosen for this mission. You think you were chosen by your legate, but I tell you that you were chosen by God. Many are suffering and dying, and you have been sent to deliver them. And if you are faithful, if you are valiant, you will not fail them."

Marcus chuckled mirthlessly and shook his head. "Is that a prophecy?"

"No." The old man gave him a warm, affectionate smile. "No. That is merely the faith I have in you, Brother Marcus."

Marcus sighed, the escaping breath deflating him. "I would have preferred a prophecy."

They embraced, and then the elderly missionary took his leave.

Marcus set about donning his armor in preparation for the century's departure. Despite having only a few hours of sleep after his night with Branwen, Marcus discovered that the Daughter of Lilith had been true to her word—he felt fully refreshed and restored, as if she had not taken the blood he offered. *I feel as if I could take on an entire horde of the enemy all by myself.*

He turned his attention to his *lorica segmentata*. He wished he could beg Maelona to help him with the breastplate. Lacing the segmented plates together in front and back was difficult, requiring extra effort—and a different procedure—without the help of another set of hands. He thought about going to her, asking her for help, but decided against it.

Let her sleep a bit more.

And please, God, send her sweet dreams.

The brief prayer recalled the words of Branwen a few hours before—*And let me dream.*

And please, dear Father in heaven, grant Branwen some measure of happiness. I owe her my life. All of us owe her our lives.

At last, he finished with his breastplate. He secured his pack and the rest of his gear on his *furca*—there would be no Gaius the Warhorse for him anymore—and made ready to depart. Last of all, he donned his helm. The plume seemed to weigh as much as a mountain.

A lovely holiday, but it's over.

Now, to stop Arawn. Stop him and his foul, murderous priests. Put everything else aside.

For the moment.

Dragging his gear behind himself, he exited the guest room.

And came face-to-face with Branwen.

A wave of tenderness and affection, mixed with just a touch of guilt, washed over him like a dip in the caldarium.

The fearsome Daughter of Lilith favored him with a shy and feminine smile—the kind that spoke of secrets no male could comprehend.

He smiled back at her.

And then he realized from whence Branwen had come—Maelona's room.

"No!" Marcus dropped his *furca* and charged past the Daughter of Lilith, as she uttered a cry of dismay. He ignored her. He had one and only one object in his mind. He bounded through the open door and into the bedroom of his beloved princess.

And found her sitting on the bed.

Alive. Unharmed.

As he stood in the doorway, panting as if he'd just been in mortal combat against all the armies of Boudicca, the expression of shock on Maelona's lovely face transformed into a smile—a smile to shame the sun itself.

"Marcus!" She leapt from her bed and ran to him with open arms.

As she enfolded him in her embrace, her arms barely reaching around his armor, Marcus heard Branwen's voice from behind him.

"You thought I had killed her. Well, I didn't." The bitterness in Branwen's tone smote his heart.

He turned his head, but she was gone. "I'm sorry." *She can hear me. I know she can.*

I hope she can.

"I'm truly sorry, Branwen."

Maelona whispered, "She has to flee. Dawn is coming. But I will tell her you are sorry when next I see her. *If* next I see her."

Marcus pulled back and searched Maelona's eyes. "I won't be able to tell her myself?" *Last night, she said, "I shall not tempt you again."*

Did she mean that she will not . . . that I will never see her again?

Maelona's smile tightened until her lips were a pale line. "No, she'll be . . . keeping her distance. As she should. She told me it would be too . . . painful to be near you. To be near *us*."

"She told you?"

Maelona nodded. "We have spoken. As women. Woman to woman. We have come to an agreement."

"What? What have you agreed to?"

The corners of Maelona's mouth curled upward. "It is . . . between Branwen and myself. It is not for you to understand." Her green eyes sparkled with delight and female mystery.

"But it is an agreement about *me*."

She shrugged and winked at him. "Perhaps."

He attempted to return her grin. And failed. "Women! How am I ever to understand—"

"Option!"

Marcus jerked himself out of Maelona's arms. He spun about to face the doorway.

Caeso Lucilius, the new prooption, stood there in full armor.

"What is it?" Marcus asked.

"You need to come and see this."

"Very well. Lead on."

Caeso Lucilius saluted, then turned and strode quickly away.

Marcus followed as the prooption led him out of the house and into the great courtyard where the men of the century were busy packing up, readying themselves for the day's march. Some of the men stood and saluted as Marcus and Caeso passed. Most simply nodded their heads and continued about their duties.

However, a small group of legionnaires had gathered at the villa gate, along with Spurius Aquillius and Emrys. And beyond them, stood at least a couple dozen men and women in Celtic garb.

At his approach, Spurius Aquillius turned toward Marcus. "My lord Pater!" He bowed slightly, then indicated the assembled crowd of Celts. "These people wish to speak with you. They bear ill—no, that is not the word . . . They bear *horrific* tidings."

The Celts indeed appeared distressed. Several wrung their hands. The women wept, as did some of the men. Some of them wailed and fell to their knees.

One of the men stepped forward and bowed to Marcus. Then he began speaking in his native tongue. He seemed to be pleading with Marcus, making supplication.

Marcus shook his head. "I'm sorry. I don't understand."

Emrys came to his side. The vilicus's face was pale. "If I may, my lord. I can translate."

Marcus nodded.

Emrys began, pointing to the apparent leader of the group. "His name is Pwyll. He says that, three days ago, the priests of Arawn came to their village. They took the children. All of them. From the age of seven winters, down to babes in arms. They took cattle as well. And some of the younger women. The young wives and the virgins."

Marcus noticed for the first time that the men in the crowd were at least twice as many in number as the women.

One of the women broke from the rest and rushed forward. She threw herself at his feet and sobbed. Several legionnaires drew their swords or their daggers.

Marcus lifted a hand to his men. "Put away your weapons."

The woman threw her arms around Marcus's knees. She bent her head back and gazed up at Marcus with red-rimmed eyes. She spoke to him, blubbering and sobbing.

Emrys translated. "She says, 'They took my babies—my Ceri and my . . . Buddug—I think is the name. They took them. Please go after them. Save my babies.'"

Other women took up the cry, pleading, supplicating, begging. Marcus couldn't understand the words, but the women's anguish shook him as surely as the grieving mother gripping him about the knees.

He bent and gently raised the woman up. "Tell them, we will pursue these wicked men. Tell them, we will save their children and their wives and sisters and daughters if we can. And if we cannot, we will avenge them."

Emrys nodded, then spoke to the crowd.

The crowd quieted somewhat, although the weeping and mourning continued unabated.

"Emrys," Marcus said, "ask them, how many priests of Arawn? Ask what arms they bore. Did they have horses? Ponies? How were the children and the women transported away? Wagons?"

The vilicus relayed the questions and listened to the replies. "They came in the night, my lord. So there is some . . . confusion, some disagreement in the answers. There were at least eighty of them. And they were led by a man who called himself Conwy. He said he is the high priest of Annwfyn. He—"

"Conwy?" squeaked a voice from behind Marcus.

Marcus turned his head to see Maelona, her hand to her mouth.

"Conwy?" she repeated. "Did you say, Conwy?"

Emrys nodded. "Yes, Princess. That was the name."

Maelona was at Marcus's side in a moment. She gripped his arm and gazed up at him in horror. "This Conwy—he was the horrible man my father cast out. He and his handful of followers were evil. They were . . . more than evil. He was the one who said we must make sacrifice to Arawn—sacrifice of children."

Marcus laid a hand over hers. "It sounds like he has found a few more followers. Emrys, what about the rest of it? Weapons? Armor? Wagons? Horses? How many children were taken? How many women?"

The vilicus inquired again and relayed the answers. "Spears and those cursed golden knives. No shields or armor are mentioned. They wore the black robes and hoods. Eighteen children were taken. Four virgins and three young wives. Eleven men and women were slain. Four more were wounded. The priests rode on horses. It sounds as if . . . . Yes, all the priests rode on horses. Not ponies. At least ten wagons, perhaps more."

Marcus growled. "And they are three days ahead of us. But even with horses, their wagons, their captives, and their cattle should slow them down. Which way did they go?"

Emrys asked, and then relayed, "West by southwest—through the hills."

Marcus nodded. "That is more or less where the reports said Arawn was showing himself. Very well." He turned to Caeso Lucilius. "Prooption, tell the men I want them ready to march within the hour. Tell them it will be a long, hard march. We'll leave the wagons here, but tell the wagoners to put packs on the mules. They and their mules march with us."

Caeso saluted. "Yes, Option." Then he strode past Marcus and began shouting orders.

Marcus turned to Emrys. "I want a list of the names, sexes, and ages of each person taken."

The steward bowed, his eyes blazing with righteous indignation. "Yes, my lord. I will see it done immediately."

"Thank you."

Maelona squeezed Marcus's arm. "I'll be ready in moments."

She turned to go, but Marcus stopped her. "No, my love. You shall remain here."

The princess put her hands on her hips and planted her feet in a wide stance. "I am going. I am a free woman. I am going with you."

Marcus shook his head, though he couldn't quite hide a grin at her determination and her courage. "You'll be safe here. I prayed for a way to keep you safe, and—"

"I am going with you."

Marcus shook his head. "You wouldn't be able to keep up. I gave away the horse and—"

"I will march with you. I am strong. I can march fast."

Marcus chuckled. "Not that fast. Your legs are short and—"

Spurius Aquillius coughed. "My lord, if I may. I planned to present the princess with a gift—a strong pony. A gift—in gratitude for that lovely song last night . . . and what came after."

Maelona bowed to the old Roman. "Thank you, my lord."

"Now wait a moment!" Marcus spluttered. "That changes nothing. You are not—"

Maelona raised her chin, looking every bit an affronted royal. "Spurius Aquillius has given me a pony. A proper pony. I'll be able to ride faster than you big Romans can march."

Marcus growled. "You are not coming with us."

She stamped her foot. "I am a free woman, and you cannot prevent me. She said you'd try to stop me. She also said you will need me."

"She? Who? Branwen?"

Maelona nodded once. Decisively. "Yes. She told me—"

"Maelona, she could be trying to get you killed." *To eliminate her rival.*

Maelona's haughty expression hardened. "You are being horribly unkind to her. She saved your life and—"

Marcus grabbed Maelona's arm and dragged her a few paces away from interested eyes and ears. He lowered his voice to whisper. "It's not my life I'm worried about. It's yours."

She shook her head and said through clenched teeth. "She has read your book. Your prophecies. She says that—"

"I know she's read it. But—"

"And Branwen says that your own book says you need me to go with you."

"Branwen does not know what—"

"'When thou shalt face death, face him not alone.' Do you remember these words? How about these? 'Thou must join faith to faith, hope to hope, heart to heart, and hand to hand, else death shall swallow thee, and thou shalt not see the dawn.'" Maelona paused. "Branwen made me commit that to memory. She said it is about you and me facing Arawn together. It is from your book, yes?"

Marcus stared at her, his eyes wide, his mouth agape. "My book?"

"It is from your book. I know I remember it correctly. I repeated it many times."

He nodded slowly, astonished at how quickly she had turned the argument. "Yes. But—"

"'Thou canst not vanquish death by the strength of thine arm. Only faith and faith, love and love, joined together can stand in the halls of the dead.' That was another one. You see, Marcus? You understand? You need *me* to fight him. Otherwise, you will fail." She paused, and she trembled. "Those are the words from your book. The words of your prophecy, yes? I remembered them correctly, yes?"

Marcus began to tremble as well. He took her hand. "Yes. Those are the words."

"There was one more. 'Take thou the hand of a princess under the world and hold fast to it.'—my name means 'princess' in my tongue—'And the night daughter shall stand with thee also. And thou shalt overcome death in the land of the dead.' That is about Branwen. She will be there. She must be there. With us. That is what it means. It can have no other meaning."

Marcus closed his eyes. "I only want to protect you. Branwen should not have . . ." But he knew his arguments were defeated—he had lost.

"And I want to protect you, Marcus." She squeezed his hand. "Look at me. Please."

He opened his eyes and met hers.

Maelona's eyes were fierce—not angry or frightened—but determined. "I am coming with you. These are not my words. These are not your words. They come from above. They come from God the Father. And you and I will obey God."

Marcus swallowed the lump in his throat. *Such courage. Such faith.* He managed a small grin. "And they call *me* Audaxus."

Maelona put her arms around him, clinging to his armored torso. "I am going with you. I am . . . afraid." She lowered and softened her voice. "I know you are afraid too. We shall be Audaxus together. You and I . . . and Branwen. I love you, O, conqueror of my heart. Help me to be brave, and I will help you."

Marcus enfolded her in his arms. "And I love you, my brave princess. It will be as you say. We will face Arawn together." *And Branwen will stand with us.*

"She loves you too."

Marcus stiffened. "I know, but . . ."

"But you have chosen me."

"Yes. I have. And I do. I choose *you*, Maelona." *But Branwen will be with me . . . with us . . . at the end.* And the comfort of that knowledge carried with it a twinge of guilt.

⁂

It was not a drenching rain, but the gentle shower was persistent enough to soak through their *saga*—the red woolen cloaks of the legionnaires. The wool of a *sagum* kept a man's body warm, even when wet. So while the storm wasn't life-threatening, it certainly made for a miserable, draining march.

"Perhaps," said Maelona as she rode her shaggy, brown pony—a sturdy beast named Tegan and probably the best in Spurius Aquillius's stable—"perhaps, the priests of Annwfyn will halt for the day. Perhaps, this storm will allow us to"—she paused, apparently searching for the proper word—"catch them up." She rode the animal skillfully, easily keeping pace with the fast-moving century. She rode beside Marcus as he tromped along the path—it could not be termed a "road"—at the head of his column of men. The wretched path was so narrow, the century was forced to march two-abreast.

"Catch them up?" Marcus mused. "Not in a single day, even if we march forty miles today"—*and we'd better cover at least that much—*

"we'd still be at least a day behind them. At best." He shifted his *furca* to the other shoulder. "But I hope you're right. I hope they do stop for the day. In fact, as wretched as this weather is, I pray it keeps going for a few days."

"Yes!" Maelona cried. "I will pray too. I will pray for the rain to . . . How did you say it? 'Keep going?' Why would we want it to go? Don't we want it to come? To stay?"

Marcus chuckled. "Yes, it does sound funny when you put it that way. Yes, my love. Pray." He lowered his voice a bit, giving it a conspiratorial tone. "Perhaps, you should not say your prayer too loudly. I don't think the men will appreciate anyone praying for more rain."

She laughed.

How he loved the sound of her laughter! *How did I fall in love so quickly? So deeply? It's almost enough to make me believe in Cupid's arrows.*

"Option!" Caeso Lucilius trotted to his side. "Marcus!"

"What is it, *Prooption*?" Marcus emphasized the title as a warning. *You know better than that, my friend – no familiarity in the field.*

The prooption nodded curtly. "Your pardon, Option. But . . ." He turned his head, nodding pointedly in the direction of the woods a few yards to the north. "We're being followed."

Marcus took the cautionary hint from his second-in-command. He glanced to the right, toward the forest, but attempted to make the movement appear casual, incidental.

But he saw nothing. "Where? How many?"

"Just one. Afoot."

Marcus glanced again, but still saw nothing moving in the shelter of the trees. "One man?"

Caeso shrugged. "I've only seen her a few times, and only for a moment or two, but – "

"Her?"

The prooption nodded. "If I had to guess, from the size and silhouette, I'd say it was a woman."

Marcus glanced at Maelona.

The princess, in her wet cloak of forest green, met his eye. "Is she wearing a cloak?"

Caeso huffed once. "In this cursed weather? Of course."

"Is it green," she asked, "like mine? A long one? All the way down to the feet? Hooded?"

The prooption shrugged. "In the shadows of the trees, I can't see the color. It could be green, I suppose. It's not red. I can say that much. And yes, long – down to the feet – and hooded."

Marcus asked, "But you're certain it's a woman?"

Caeso sighed loudly. "I can't be certain. But that's my guess. A few of the men have seen her too. What should we do? Shall I send a few men into the woods to fetch her?"

Marcus locked eyes with Maelona briefly. She shook her head.

Marcus did the same. "No. She's no threat to us."

"Are you . . . certain?" Caeso sounded as if he thought Marcus had lost his reason.

"Trust me, Prooption," Marcus said. "She is no threat. Not to us. We are . . . blessed to have her watch over us. But no one is to approach her."

Caeso nodded. "I do trust you. I'll spread the word. She is not to be meddled with." And with those words, he dropped back.

Marcus took another long glance into the trees.

And he saw her.

Cloaked and hooded in green, she strode under the trees, keeping pace with the men of the century.

Branwen. Watching over us.

Watching over me.

I'm sorry, Branwen, for doubting you. I wish I could tell you. I wish I could tell you how truly sorry I am.

Maybe I can.

"Pardon me for a moment," he said to Maelona. Then he veered from the path, shouting to Caeso Lucilius, "Keep to the path! I'll catch up. I just need a moment."

He marched quickly toward the trees, but he halted short of them.

The hooded figure had disappeared, fading into the shadows of the wood.

"I know you can hear me," he said. "I'm sorry for doubting you. Please, forgive me."

He stared into the trees. *Fool. She may be a Daughter of Lilith, but she's still a woman. And you hurt her.* "I'm sorry. I wish . . . I'm sorry. I need you to know that. I need you to know how grateful I am."

As he turned to go, she stepped into view—still in the shadows, but visible in the darkness. She drew back her hood, and though her face was still cast in shadow, her eyes seemed to shine. "I forgive you, Marcus Aquillius Audaxus. And I will cherish the memory of last night. I love you with all that is left of my heart. And I will love you for eternity. But you have chosen another, and I shall not come between you and the one you have chosen. I shall remain apart, alone. However, know this—when you have need of me, I shall be there, at your side. At the end, I will be there."

Marcus reached out a hand. "Branwen, I—"

Branwen pulled up her hood, and even her eyes vanished into shadow.

"Goodbye, Marcus."

And then she was gone.

Interlude II

"The names of unwilling and penitent shall be had for good and ill."
from the Book of Marcus Scribonius

July 2017 A.D.

Marching back and forth like an avian sentinel, the black bird appeared to be guarding the looming monoliths of stone. It seemed totally unperturbed by the presence of the humans milling about, shooting and posing for photographs on their cell phones or expensive cameras, pointing at one standing stone or other, and talking in subdued voices as if they were visiting Notre Dame. The bird strode slowly along a fairly straight line in the tall grass of the heath, going a few yards one way, before turning smartly, like a soldier, and marching back the other direction. It didn't even glance at the tourists, as if they were beneath its notice. After all, the humans were forced—by a very temporary-looking walkway and its attending rope barriers—to keep their distance from the ruins of the ancient stone circle.

Moira pointed at the winged sentry. "Will ye look at that, laddie! He's nae afraid of us blundering humans."

Carl shook his head. "Nope. Is that a raven?"

Moira couldn't help but smile at the hope in her husband's voice. *What is this obsession with ravens, laddie?* "Nae, laddie. 'Tis but a rook. The rooks of Stonehenge are world-famous."

Carl chuckled. "So world-famous I've never heard of them."

"Well, if it had anythin' tae do with World War Two, nae doubt, ye'd know everythin' there was tae know. Like the beaches of Normandy and the D-Day Memorial yesterday. Ye knew so much about it, ye talked my ear off. And the ears of anyone else who happened to be nearby. Ye were like a wee bairn toddling about a candy store, pointin' out all the varieties of chocolates and caramels."

Carl squeezed her hand and gave her one of his bonny, lopsided grins—a grin which still had the power to set her heart fluttering. "Well, you know, the Royal Air Force almost blew up Stonehenge. They wanted to use it for bombing practice. In fact, it—"

Moira threw back her head and uttered a strangled cry to the overcast heavens. "God spare me from amateur history buffs! Ye do ken I *lived* through World War Two, d'ye nae?"

"Yeah, but you weren't over *here*, now were you?"

She favored him with a dazzling, mischievous grin. "And neither were ye! Ye were nae even born, laddie. Ye were nae sae much as a twinkle in yer grandmother's eye. But"—she heaved a dramatic sigh—"I've ne'er held yer immaturity against ye . . . much."

His grin broadened. "Have I ever told you I have a thing for older women? I just never expected to marry one who was more than two centuries older than me."

Moira narrowed her eyes and pursed her lips in mock anger. "Ach! Ye had better watch yer step, laddie."

"Of course . . . it helps that you stopped aging at seventeen. Well, before you started aging *again*, that is." He chuckled. "I swear you don't look a day over two hundred and fifty."

Her jaw dropped. "Why ye . . . I'm still—biologically speakin'—more than a decade yer junior, my dear ald husband."

"Ooh! Hot, mature, and sexy—triple threat!"

"Ye're nae sae bad yerself . . . for a young pup." She paused, gazing out at the ring of stones. "Ye ken, I have nae ever been here before. Nae once."

He looked at her askance. "Really? Never?"

"Nae. Never. I've been tae stone circles before—they're all over Scotland and Wales. When I was . . . well, searchin' for redemption, I visited holy sites all over the . . . United Kingdom. Including a number of circles. Just nae this one."

Carl took on a thoughtful expression, but Moira sensed some impish intent. "Hm. I can just picture you hanging out in one those barrows out there." He pointed to a pair of earthen mounds well outside the circle. "Then crawling out of the earth at night to—"

She poked him in the ribs. "Oh, ye divil, ye! But can ye imagine? How smelly and stuffy it'd be in one o' those?" Then she herself assumed a thoughtful expression. "I do remember a tale of a Welsh Penitent who buried herself in a barrow—nae here, but in Wales. She was attemptin' to end her life, of course. She did nae succeed, or we would nae know the tale. But can ye imagine such a thing?"

"I don't know." He grinned and winked. "Are you sure she was

Welsh and not . . . Scottish?"

"'Twas nae myself, laddie."

His impish grin faded. He stuffed his cell phone into his pocket, then took her other hand in his. "I love you, my bonnie lassie. I'm the luckiest . . . I've been blessed with the two best women God ever created."

Sharon. Moira almost flinched at the mere allusion to Carl's first wife—his *dead* first wife. *I never met, ye, Sharon Morgan. And when we do meet, after this life, I hope we can be friends. I dinnae ken how I can possibly share this man we both love.*

But if that's what it takes to be with Carl for eternity, then that's what I'll do. I'll be a second wife.

I am a second wife.

"I love ye too, laddie." Her eyes misted with sudden tears. *I love ye so fiercely, I cannae express it.* "Ye . . . a-and our wee ones . . . ye mean everythin' tae me." She squeezed his hands with a passion that in days past might have broken the bones in his fingers. "Everythin'."

He bent his head, and she tilted hers back. And their lips met.

And then they encircled each other in their arms, and they hugged as if, at any moment, their lives might be over.

Mortal life is sae short. Sae very, very short.

They pulled back, only to kiss once more—less fiercely, but more tenderly.

"I hope you don't mind," said a voice with a Welsh accent.

Moira and Carl looked to the other edge of the path that led around the ancient stone circle.

A man stood there. His long, black hair hung to his shoulders. The hair appeared as if it hadn't been combed or brushed in some time. His eyes were deep-set and bloodshot, with dark shadows around them, as if he hadn't slept well in days. He wore a nondescript, blue hoodie. His pants were worn and ripped in spots, and his sneakers appeared to have seen better days. He smelled as if he hadn't bathed in recent memory.

But in his hand, he held a smartphone.

"I hope you don't mind," he repeated, shrugging his shoulders sheepishly. "It was such a pretty picture—two lovers, a husband and wife, kissing in front of Stonehenge. Even on such a gloomy day, it was irresistible. I-I can send you the picture, if you like."

He turned the phone around, displaying the photo.

Moira disentangled herself from her husband's embrace. She held out a hand. "May I?"

But Carl pushed his way in front of her.

Protecting me. Always protecting me.

"That's very nice," said Carl. "May I see?"

The man handed the phone to Carl.

As Carl examined it, Moira stepped slightly to the side to examine the stranger.

Not an addict. He looks the part, aye, but his hands are nae shaking. Just a lad who has fallen on hard times. Or perhaps, he chooses tae dress this way. I thought the "grunge" look was passé.

Either way, I cannae believe he's part of our group, a passenger on our cruise.

He does nae look *like a threat . . .*

"Yes," Carl said, "it's very nice. I'd like to pay you for it, if I may."

The man appeared distressed. "That's not why I took it. I wasn't looking to cause any . . ."

Moira glanced at the photo. "Ye have a talent, laddie. The composition is grand. I agree with my husband. We'd love tae give ye somethin' for it. Are ye a professional photographer?"

He chuckled and gave them an embarrassed grin. He ran his fingers through his unkempt hair. "No. I'm just . . ."

Moira gave him a smile—that in years past—would have caused any man or woman to beg to do her bidding. "Well, perhaps ye should be. I appreciate artistry, and I take great joy in supporting the arts. May we please pay ye for this?"

He looked from Moira to Carl and back again, then nodded. "Sure." He sighed as a huge grin spread across his face. In contrast to the rest of his appearance, his teeth were in good shape—though they needed a good brushing. "How can I send it to you? Email?"

Carl squeezed her hand. He said nothing, but his message was clear—*Don't give out an email address.*

Immediately, Moira was on her guard. *Even on vacation, we need to be careful. First names only, and no other personal information.*

Still holding the fellow's phone, Carl shook it gently. "I think we can just send it via Bluetooth." He examined the stranger's phone and his own. "Yep. Hold on." He fiddled with his phone and then the other man's. "There. It's transferring now. Just a second . . . Got it!" He handed back the phone. "Thank you."

For the briefest of moments, Moira thought she saw a flash of anger in the stranger's eyes. And then it was gone.

Moira dug in her purse and pulled out five twenty-pound notes. She handed them to the man.

He blinked at her, then stared at the money in his hands. He didn't count it, but the fact that he held multiple twenties was not lost on him. "Thank you! I . . . uh . . . Thank you!"

"You're more than welcome, sir," Carl said. He extended a hand. "Thank you."

The man stared at Carl's hand for a long moment, as if he could not comprehend the gesture. Then he grasped Carl's hand and shook it vigorously. "You have no idea what this means to me."

Carl shrugged. "I'm just glad we met. I'm Carl."

The man nodded, still shaking Carl's hand. "I'm Lloyd." Then he let go of Carl's hand and reached for Moira's.

She took the lad's hand and shook it. It felt cold and moist, as if the fellow had been out in the gloomy weather all day. "And I'm Moira."

He nodded, letting go of her hand. "I knew it! You're Carl and Moira Morgan, aren't you?" His eyes opened wide, as if with surprise, but he grinned toothily.

Moira found the combination vaguely unsettling.

Lloyd put a hand to his mouth. "Oh . . . my . . ." He pointed at them, and his hand trembled. "You're the vampires, aren't you? The *former* vampires. The *good* ones. The ones who slew Lilith!"

Chapter XVII

"The son of thy new son shall lead the bereaved to thee, and they shall join thy small band. And yea, though the cost be great, together, thou shalt deliver the stolen."

from the Book of Marcus Scribonius

DCCCXIV *Ab Urbe Condita* (61 A.D.)

Forty miles marching in the rain." With a wooden mallet, Marcus pounded the last of the wooden tent stakes into the ground. "And at best, we're still another day's hard march behind the enemy." He handed the mallet to Maelona. "At least the rain has ceased. For now." He attached and tightened the last tent rope, then sat back on the ground and admired his handiwork—his and Maelona's. Marcus had insisted no other legionnaire was to help erect the commander's tent. Quintus Aquillius, of course, required his soldiers to put up his tent for him. Marcus's mentor, Gaius Aquillius, though he allowed men to help him, did the bulk of the work himself. And Marcus wished to emulate the man he now called "Father."

And he found he enjoyed laboring beside Maelona.

Even the miserable, wet march along the muddy path the Celts dared to call a road had been made pleasant, because he was able to march alongside Maelona on her pony. The two of them—the soldier and the princess—after the encounter with Branwen, chatted as easily as if they had been sharing an intimate walk alone in the woods.

Maelona dusted her hands off and came to sit beside him on the ground. "If you push the men too hard, Marcus, they will not be able to fight when we do catch the priests of Arawn." She gave him a very serious look—the look she always gave him while dispensing advice.

Marcus chuckled. "Who's the military commander here, Princess? You or I?"

She shrugged and gave him a shy smile. "You are, of course, but do not forget that I am not without military experience. I was one of your Mona Witches, remember? I sat in my father's war council. I was older than my brother and would have led when my father . . ." Her expression soured, and she looked away. "Well, that is no matter now. He is dead." She smiled at Marcus. "And I am no longer alone. You can make your own decisions. You are, after all, the conqueror. You are"—she swallowed, and her voice grew husky—"my conqueror."

I love you, woman. You have conquered me. "Good advice is good advice. I am glad to have your counsel, my princess."

She turned her head and looked at him through lowered eyelashes. "Am I your princess then?" Her hand sought his, and their fingers intertwined.

"Yes." Her hand was warm and soft in his. "You are more than my princess. You are my queen."

Her eyes narrowed as if she were upset with him, but an impish smile belied any pretense of anger. "I cannot be your queen until you are my king and husband."

Marcus rolled his eyes. "I will find a way."

Her grin widened to a dazzling smile. "I know you will. I have prayed to God the Father. He will answer my prayer. And besides, Branwen told me your book says we shall marry."

Marcus blinked at her. *Branwen? I don't want to think about Branwen right now.* The memory of stroking her hair as she laid her head on his chest, the memory of feeding her with his blood, and the memory of her legs silhouetted through her gown—these burned in his mind. "Where does it say that? I don't remember it."

"She said you do not understand all you have written."

And therein lies great frustration. "Then show me where it is written."

She frowned, and that time, she appeared genuinely perturbed. But she held on to his hand. "I cannot read. You know this. You promised to teach me, but you have not." She sighed and squeezed his hand. "But you will. You keep your promises."

"So you cannot show me, I suppose. What were the words of the prophecy?"

She shrugged. "I do not know. She didn't tell me. She said only that you will marry me." She glanced away, and her face took on a pensive expression. "She said you have chosen me. She said also . . ."

"What? What else did she say?"

Maelona pursed her lips and shook her head. "No. That is between us—between Branwen and me."

Marcus opened his mouth to question her further, but he shut it once more. *No use asking. She's not going to discuss it.* "Women and their secrets." He'd said it with some irritation, but Maelona gazed at him from under her lashes again.

He found that look very tempting. *And to think I once thought green eyes scary.*

"Is it not our secrets that make us so . . . interesting and alluring?"

He guffawed at that. "Interesting and alluring and *frustrating* beyond all measure!"

She squeezed his hand again. "I must be about preparing your food." She let go of his hand and began to clamber to her feet.

"Not *my* food, Princess—*our* food. We eat together. Still, if you'll prepare the meal, I'll see to the men."

She flashed him a stunning smile, and then she spun away.

He stood, scooping up his plumed helm. As he set the weighty galea upon his head, he turned his gaze toward the camp—and away from the delightful sight of Maelona's retreating figure.

He rose to his feet.

How is it Branwen can understand the prophecies better than I can? He glanced toward the overcast sky, darkening as the dusk of evening stole the light of day.

Our Father who art in heaven, hallowed be Thy name.

I thank thee for these clouds, because without them—and the rain—I would not have been able to . . . beg Branwen's forgiveness.

I do not deny that I feel affection . . . and more for her. But I have chosen Maelona. I love Maelona. I intend to marry Maelona . . . somehow.

But, Heavenly Father, please help Branwen find some measure of happiness too.

And Father, guide me. We are going into battle—a battle I don't know how to fight. A battle I'm not sure I can win. A century against a hundred men on horses?

But somehow . . . having Maelona and Branwen there . . . Somehow, that's important. I just don't know why.

Show me the way. Please.

Marcus watched as the men, exhausted but in good spirits despite the grueling, miserable march, went about setting up camp.

And . . . please, Heavenly Father, strengthen my faith. I'm so . . . afraid.

Please help me to not show fear to the men. Or to Maelona.

I am grateful that Thou hast given me such good and brave fellows.

Show me the way. I—

He heard a scream.

Marcus drew his sword and dropped to a fighting stance, his eyes scanning the camp.

The scream came again, louder than before.

He snatched his shield from where it lay next to his furca and pack.

All the men had drawn their swords—even the support personnel had drawn their daggers. The men looked around frantically, no more able to locate the source of the scream than Marcus.

Maelona came running toward him, her skirt bunched in one hand and a Roman dagger in the other. A small part of his mind wondered where she had gotten the pugio, but a larger part of his mind was grateful the scream had not come from her.

Not Maelona. I thank Thee, Father. Not Maelona.

Once more came the scream, louder and closer.

Where is it? It sounds like it's coming from all around us.

No. Not from around.

From above.

Branwen!

His head snapped up, and he saw her—flying down toward him, her wings flapping, white against the gray sky.

But Branwen was not the source of the scream.

A man dangled below her, his ankle held fast in her iron grip. And the man was screaming as loudly and shrilly as a terrified girl. The pair of them—Branwen and her captive—dropped speedily toward the earth.

She alighted in front of Marcus. The instant her booted feet touched the ground, two things occurred at once—her white wings vanished as if they had never been there, and she dropped the screaming, terrified mortal to the ground with an unceremonious, squelching thump.

The man wore a loose black robe that, while dangling upside-down, had bunched around his armpits. He wore breeches and a Celtic tunic. His short, brown boots were of fine, soft leather. His red beard showed the sparseness of youth.

He screamed once more as he lay on the wet grass, looking wildly about. When his eyes found Branwen, he began to scramble away on his back, like a frightened crab.

Marcus stepped forward and pointed his sword at the man's gut. "Stay where you are!"

The captive's eyes were wide with terror as they flickered from the sword to Branwen and back again. His body quaked, and his voice rose and fell in wordless ululation.

"Stay where you are!" Marcus barked again.

But the man appeared ready to flee, apparently having decided Branwen was the more fearsome threat.

"Peidiwch â symud!" commanded Branwen.

The man on the ground froze as if struck by lightning.

Marcus gazed at the face of the Daughter of Lilith. And she was terrifying, her lovely features contorted in demonic rage.

Just like when she demanded we surrender the "evildoers."

"I doubt he speaks Latin," Branwen snarled through gritted teeth. "Maelona—she can translate for you. You may question him, learn what he knows. But I must . . . go a safe distance away. I will return for his evil blood when you are finished. But don't take too long. And do not deny me. He is mine. His blood calls to me. His evil cries out for vengeance."

And with that, her wings unfurled once more, and she shot like an arrow into the darkening sky.

"Yes." Maelona nodded, clutching her fist to her heart. "I can translate."

The quivering man looked as if he might make another attempt to flee, but he was surrounded by Roman legionnaires, all of them pointing their swords at him. With a wordless cry of despair, he collapsed onto his back, put his fists to his eyes, and wept.

I should feel pity for him. His death is certain. But Marcus could find no pity in his heart. *He has murdered children, sacrificed them to a demon.*

Marcus lowered his sword, but he held it at the ready. "Ask him if he is a priest of Arawn."

Maelona nodded and translated the question.

With a moan of abject despair, the man nodded.

He knows he will die. I'm not going to stand between Branwen and her prey. Not this time.

Not for this monster.

He's a cursed Druid—let a Celt, one of his own people, judge him.

"Ask him where his band is camped."

And so the interrogation began, with Maelona translating the questions and the answers.

At first the answers were halting, almost grudgingly given. The army of priests—for that is what they were—numbered at least one hundred. They were encamped along the road, thirty or so miles to the west-southwest. Their mission was to seize children under the age of eight—by whatever means—and those innocents were to be sacrificed to Arawn when they reached the Gate of Annwfyn. They were also permitted to take women for their own use. This wretch had been out in the woods, about to despoil a virgin captive, when Branwen took him. In addition to the women, the priests were allowed to confiscate cattle and what little wealth the people of the villages possessed.

"Where is Annwfyn? What are its defenses?"

When Marcus asked these questions, the priest began to speak hurriedly, babbling through heaving sobs.

"He says . . . he will not answer," Maelona said. "He is more frightened of Arawn than of you and your swords, or even the monster—I think he is referring to Branwen."

"Ask him again."

Maelona complied, but the man shook his head, screaming, "Na! Na! Na!" He kept repeating this, shutting his eyes and covering his ears.

"I'm sorry, Marcus!" Maelona shouted above the man's wailing. "He's not listening anymore."

"Move back! Make way for me!" The furious voice came from above. Branwen dropped from the darkness, her wings vanishing.

"Leave her alone," Marcus commanded his men. "She is with us."

The men of the century took a step back—in some cases two or three—but they kept their swords drawn.

Branwen gripped the captive's robe near his throat and hoisted the screaming priest two feet into the air. She held the man aloft as if he weighed nothing. Then she fixed him with her eyes.

Abruptly, his cries and struggling ceased. His body went slack as he stared down into the enraged countenance of the terrifying Daughter of Lilith.

"Ble mae Annwfyn?" she growled in a voice like a she-wolf's. "Beth yw ei amddiffynfeydd?"

The priest began to speak. His voice was pleading, supplicating. It was as if he would do anything to please Branwen.

Her power . . . it's horrifying. She can compel a man to do anything.

Marcus shuddered. *She could compel* me *to do anything.*

But she won't. Heaven help me, but I trust her.

When the priest's voice finally trailed off, Branwen, without breaking eye contact with him, asked, "Maelona, did you catch all of that?"

Maelona nodded, trembling. "Yes, but . . ."

Branwen smiled ferociously, her teeth bared, her fangs extended. "Good."

Branwen's wings unfurled from her back, and then she and her victim flew into the damp night air.

As they rose into the darkness, Marcus heard a brief scream.

And then there was silence.

Fighting to keep his voice from shaking, Marcus said, "In one hour, officers to my tent." He turned to Maelona. "I'll need you there too."

She nodded, but even in the shadows, Marcus could see that her eyes were wide with fear.

"We should overtake them tomorrow," Marcus said, "so I must convene a council of war tonight."

He lifted his voice, so all the men could hear. "You've had a hard march today. We'll have another hard march tomorrow. Get some rest. You've earned it. And you're going to need it."

Maelona laid a hand on his arm. "Marcus, this army we're chasing . . . They are but a hundred, but at Annwfyn . . . That man said there are three thousands of them."

Three thousand! That's half a legion.

How can we possibly face so many?

♦ ♦ ♦

"Marcus," said Agrippa, the vexillarius, "you know we will follow you anywhere. If you say, fight, we will fight to the last man." He chuckled nervously. "Is it too late to point out that this was supposed to be a reconnaissance mission, not a combat mission?" He looked at each man of the war council sitting on the ground in the commander's tent. His eyes avoided Maelona's, but they came to rest on Marcus. "Why are we even contemplating fighting half a legion? I don't care if they're a bunch of religious fanatics instead of soldiers. We faced Druid fanatics at Mona. And we won, thanks to you, but . . . Marcus—I mean, Option—we had more men there. A lot more men. Now, we have one century to fight half a legion."

Marcus closed his eyes, took a deep calming breath, then met his friend's gaze. "Because we are not just conquerors here in Britannia. We're not just here to take from this island and her people. We're not just here to build roads and enforce Roman law. We are here to protect these people and keep the peace. *Pax Romana.* That is the dream of Rome."

"But three thousand!" Agrippa countered. "There are eighty-three of us. We'll be slaughtered."

"I have to agree," said Nonus Sestius, the protesserarius. "I don't see how we can possibly win. But"—he grimaced and shook his head—"if Audaxus leads us into battle, no matter the odds, we will follow. *I* will follow."

Caeso Lucilius shook his head. "These are worse odds than we faced against Boudicca. Perhaps if we could choose our ground, as the legate did at . . ."

"To arms! To arms!" The cry of alarm rent the night.

Marcus grabbed his helm and donned it before bursting out of the goatskin tent. The junior officers and the princess followed him.

The century had assembled, though in no particular formation. Every man held his sword and his shield, but many of them were unarmored. Unarmored—and yet they stood between Marcus and whatever threat had appeared in the night.

Marcus spied his kinsman, Septimus Scribonius. "What's going on?" he demanded.

Septimus pointed toward the century. "We see two torches approaching from the road."

"Make way!" Marcus cried. "Let me through!"

The century parted, allowing Marcus to move to the front.

"Form up behind me!" he shouted. While he heard the century forming up in their ranks, he observed the two torches, bobbing in the distance, coming down the path. Two torches only, but Marcus could also see a small host of men following in their wake.

A voice shouted out of the darkness. "Marcus Aquillius! We would speak with you. Marcus Aquillius!"

Marcus lifted his hand, palm open and empty. "I am Marcus Aquillius. Who goes there?"

"Emrys!" cried the voice. "It is I—Emrys! Thank the Lord Christus we found you!"

Emrys? The vilicus?

As the leader of the mob approached, Marcus was able to discern the face of Emrys in the torchlight. The other torchbearer looked familiar as well. After a moment, Marcus recognized him as the leader of the Celts who had come to the villa that morning, begging for help.

Pwyll?

As the host drew nearer, their numbers seemed to grow.

Many more than the group who came to the villa.

There are several times that number!

When Emrys and Pwyll approached to within a dozen paces, the band halted.

"Emrys," Marcus said, "what are you doing here? Who are these people?"

"We're here to fight, Pater Aquillius," said the steward, "alongside you. This is our fight too—even more than it is yours. These are our children, our wives and daughters, our neighbors who were taken. And we will fight for them."

Marcus peered into the darkness. He saw men and women armed with knives, axes, and spears—many of the spears no more than sharpened wooden poles. A few carried scythes. Some carried clubs. At least one was armed with a spade.

As for armor, they had none, save for the occasional torc glinting about a neck here and there. The neck ornaments—though the Celts thought them magical—provided no protection in battle.

They don't have a single shield among them.

He looked at their feet. Emrys wore soft boots, but most of them went barefoot. *Just like Boudicca's army. How did they possibly cover forty miles with no shoes?*

How many of them already have blistered and bleeding feet?

Marcus shook his head. "Go home. You're not soldiers. I . . . admire your courage, but you cannot possibly stand against armed men, some of them on horseback."

Emrys raised his head, and Marcus could see that the man's breathing was labored from the long march. "We will fight. If they come against us with horses, we will plant our spears in the ground and stop them. We know how to stop a cavalry charge."

Marcus stepped toward the steward. "Emrys, why are *you* here? Did you have a child taken? You said nothing of this."

The vilicus shook his head. "No, I did not. But these are my people—my mother's people. Their fight is my fight. Why are *you* here, Marcus Aquillius? These are not your people."

"I'm here . . . We're here to fight for the innocents, the subjects of Rome, to stop a demon and his army of wicked priests." He laid a hand on the vilicus's wet and steaming shoulder. *They have marched hard this day.* "Emrys, we have learned that there are three thousand of them. Go home."

"You are but eighty-three. Ninety-two, if you arm your noncombatants."

"Ninety-*three*!" Maelona brandished her Roman dagger. "Your master gave me this. I will stand with Audaxus! We will fight this evil—this evil that has come up from among us—out of our own people."

Emrys bowed his head, acknowledging Maelona's brave words. Then he lifted his eyes to Marcus. "You need us. We number three hundred and twenty. And even more villages join us as we go. Besides, we will not go home and wait while our children are murdered and our wives and our daughters are raped. We may be few, but we have heard what you, Marcus Aquillius, can do. You faced Boudicca's two hundred and thirty thousand with but ten thousand. And you won."

"Yes, but I am not Gaius Suetonius Paulinus. I am not a brilliant tactician. I'm just a soldier. And you're just farmers. Go home, Emrys."

Emrys shook his head in defiance. "You are Audaxus. I have heard your men call you this name. They speak of you with awe. All we need is for you to lead us. They have taken our children, our wives, and our daughters. Surely God will protect us, for our cause is just. We fight—not for glory, but for our wives and our children."

Marcus noticed for the first time that Emrys's wife, Gwawr, stood behind him, armed with a makeshift spear.

Emrys continued. "God will give us victory. And Aristobulus tells me that you have the gift of prophecy. God will tell you what to do, Audaxus, how you can defeat the hosts of Arawn."

If one more person calls me by that stupid, wretched name . . . "We must march another forty miles tomorrow. You cannot keep up. Your feet must be—"

Emrys laughed, and there was scorn in his eyes. "We marched as far as you. And we sent runners to the villages as we went. Many have joined us. Many more will join us tomorrow."

Marcus shook his head. *Why do I keep losing these arguments? I cannot lose this one. I cannot be responsible for the deaths of these people.* "Emrys, I cannot feed you. We have scant rations for—"

Emrys laughed again. "My master"—Emrys paused, and Marcus felt the unspoken words, the words Emrys dared not utter—*my father*—"Spurius Aquillius has sent ten oxen with us to feed us as we go. We shall eat better than you will." He sighed and shook his head, the scorn draining from his countenance. "No. That is not the way of Christus, is it?" He laughed softly. "I am new to this. No, we will share what we have."

No! I will not be responsible for your deaths! "Emrys, I cannot—"

"All we need is for you to lead us." It was his turn to put a hand on Marcus's shoulder. "God has called you to lead us. Can you not see this? And we will follow your commands without question."

"And if I command you to turn around and go home?"

Emrys smiled. "You will not do that."

Marcus opened his mouth to issue that very command, but the words of a new prophecy seared his mind. And for once, immediately, he understood the prophecy.

The son of thy new son shall lead the bereaved to thee, and they shall join thy small band. And yea, though the cost be great, together, thou shalt deliver the stolen.

Caeso Lucilius stepped up beside him. "Option, why do you hesitate? You can't seriously be thinking of letting them join us. They're just farmers. Send them . . ."

Marcus turned to the prooption, wondering why Caeso had stopped mid-sentence.

"It's happened again, hasn't it?" Caeso said, his eyes widened with awe. "I can see it in your face. You've received another prophecy from your god."

Marcus nodded slowly.

Caeso stood taller, gazing at his commander intently. "What did your god say? What do we need to do? Whatever it is, we will do it."

Marcus turned his face back toward Emrys. "The prophecy says they . . . you will be joining us. It says, together, we will deliver the captives."

A smile split Emrys's face. He turned and shouted something in Cambrian to his troops.

A cheer rose from the small army of farmers. As weary as they were, they sounded elated.

"What did you say?" Marcus asked. "What did you tell them?"

Maelona touched his arm. "He said that your God has promised they will rescue their children, their wives, and their daughters." She beamed at him. Then her countenance drooped. "What is wrong?"

"The prophecy said . . . it said we would deliver them, but the cost of delivering the captives . . . that cost will be great."

Emrys turned back to him, his expression sober. He nodded. "Yes, I will tell them this as well." His expression hardened. "But we will still follow you. We will—with God's help—deliver the captives."

"But, Option," said Protesserarius Nonus Sestius, "they're just farmers."

Marcus nodded, his expression grim. "So was I once. I was just a farmer. So were many of you. Courage can burn in the heart of a farmer, just as it can burn in the heart of a soldier of Rome."

Nonus shook his head, doubt written all over his face. "But half of them are women."

Marcus chuckled. "Have you ever seen a mother fight for her child? I'd rather face a dozen human warriors than one she-bear defending her cubs."

Nonus bowed his head. "Yes, Option." He saluted, fist to chest.

"For the glory of Rome and Audaxus."

"Rome and Audaxus!" repeated one of the legionnaires.

Others took up the cheer. "Rome and Audaxus!"

Marcus tried to stop them. He shouted, but they took no heed. The accolade had sprouted wings of its own and soared into the night sky like the battle cries of a thousand eagles.

The Celts took up the cry as well, but they cried simply, "Audaxus!"

Soon the Romans as well joined them in roaring, "Audaxus!"

Marcus turned slowly, his eyes taking in the sight of the two disparate bands cheering his name—the name he hated and feared.

How many of you will I lose? How many brave men and women—soldiers and farmers, wives and mothers . . . How many will die?

. . . though the cost be great . . .

How many of us will pay that cost?

His eyes scanned the cheering Romans, seeking one man. When he found the combat nurse, he shouted, "Capsarium!" He pointed at the man, and Gaius Publicia nodded.

The capsarium trotted up to his commander.

Marcus put a hand to the capsarium's shoulder. "Go examine their feet. Treat as many as you can."

Gaius Publicia nodded. Then he trotted off to retrieve his supply of salves and medicines.

Marcus turned to Emrys. "We were holding a council of war. You had better join us."

Interlude III

"The unwilling and the penitent shall be in peril because of an act of kindness."

from the Book of Marcus Scribonius

July 2017 A.D.

I swear, if one more person asks to take a picture with us," Carl Morgan muttered in sincere, if somewhat hyperbolic aggravation, "I'm going to shove him or her off this tower." He rested his hands on the walls of the parapet of one of the highest towers of Conwy Castle overlooking the sea and the quaint Welsh village which bore the castle's name.

Moira chuckled and placed a hand on her husband's back, rubbing gently, soothingly. She risked a glance at the middle-aged couple descending the narrow stones of the tower stairs, clinging to the rope that served as the only handrail, still chatting excitedly about having taken selfies "with the vampires." "Ach, laddie, such is the price of fame. Remember, 'twas ye who decided to expose Lilith—and ourselves—to the world on national television. Dinnae take me the wrong way—'twas a brilliant move, but . . ."

Carl grimaced. "Talk about unintended consequences. Lilith spent six thousand years ruling and murdering and corrupting from the shadows, but now she's gone, and the two of us can't even go on a simple vacation without getting mobbed. But as they say, no good deed goes unpunished."

Moira sighed. "I suppose, in many ways, life was simpler when we were vampires." She watched as a pair of seagulls glided below them, slowly circling above the modern bridge that led from the ruins of the thirteenth-century castle and across the River Conwy. The tide had gone out, and much of the river bank was reduced to wet, yellow sand.

"D'ye ken, laddie," she said, "this massive fortress was built by

Edward Longshanks. Aye, now, there was a great scourge to Scotland. Luckily, his son, Edward the Second, was, shall we say, *less* formidable? Still 'tis a bonnie castle"—she sighed—"and a breathtakin' view."

Carl squeezed her hand. "So you approve of my choice for today's 'port adventure'?"

"Aye, laddie. Ye've chosen well. At every turn. I'll nae deny it."

"And you've never been here before?"

Moira shook her head. "Nae. Truth tae tell, I nae ever spent much time in Wales. For the most part, 'twas Scotland and England—anywhere I could learn medicine or sword fightin'. Killin' or healin'. But nae in Wales and nae ever tae Conwy. And by-the-by, 'tis pronounced 'Con-way' and nae 'Con-wee'. Bonnie. Bonnie place ye chose."

Carl favored her with his impish grin. "Whew! I was worried this would be old hat to you. You might even have seen it before it became a ruin."

Moira punched his shoulder playfully. "I'm nae that old, laddie! 'Twas a ruin long before I was born. We had castles in my day, aye, but I dinnae remember many the likes of this. Of course, I was nae invited to castle feasts, ye ken. I was nae but a farmer's daughter. And after—"

Her cell phone vibrated. *Now who'd be a-callin' at this hour? 'Tis three in the mornin' back in Utah.*

Panic seized her, clawing at her gut.

The bairns!

Hands trembling with fear for her children, Moira grabbed her phone from her day bag. Then she saw the caller ID—*Craig L. Foster.*

She shuddered out a sigh of profound relief.

"Who is it?" Carl asked, sounding just as concerned as she had been a moment before. "The kids?"

"Nae, laddie. Nae the bairns. Nae our precious . . . But . . . I do need tae take it."

"A patient? I thought I got the clinic covered."

She slid the virtual button, answering the call, then said into the phone, "Hold just a wee tick, will ye?"

She heard Craig say, "Sure."

Moira lowered the phone, keeping the screen away from Carl's eyes. She briefly considered lying to her husband. *The clinic would aye be a bonnie cover.* "Dinnae fash—" *I have nae used* that *word in decades, now have I?* "Dinnae worry yerself 'bout it, laddie. Nothin' of consequence. Ye go on. I'll meet ye on yon tower." She pointed to the tower on the opposite side of the castle.

He raised an eyebrow. "You're being secretive."

"Ye're one tae talk. After pullin' off this entire trip. Perhaps," she said with a wink and a grin, "I have a surprise o' my own."

He raised both his eyebrows. "Ah-ha-a-ah! Well then, my love, I'll leave you to your secrets. But don't take too long. We're on this cruise to be together. I love you, pretty lady." He kissed her, then he turned and descended the treacherous staircase.

As soon as Moira saw him on the top of the inner wall that ran across the width of the ruined castle, she lifted the phone to her ear once more. "Craig-laddie, 'tis sae late for ye. But"—she didn't even try to conceal the excitement in her voice—"are ye callin' tae say 'tis done?"

"That I am," said her friend, and Moira could hear the grin in his voice. "I *found* it! I found the connection in Olaf Bitling, also known as Olav the Red, King of Mann and the Isles. He married Ingibiorg of Orkney. So it's a royal line of the Nordic-Gaelic kings, who ruled both Dublin and the Isles. Olaf's father was Godfred Crovan—he died in 1095—but that's as far as I got. We think Godfred was a descendant of—"

"But ye definitely found a connection?" Moira glanced in the direction of the tower, but could no longer see Carl.

"Yes! But Godfred is as a far as I can go—at least definitively. As I was saying, we think Godfred is a descendant of Amlaíb Cúarán, King of Northumbria and Dublin, but—"

"Aye, aye. That's grand. Wonderful! Now, how soon can ye have it ready?"

"Well, doing it in *scroll* form will take a little longer . . . but a couple of days at most, I think."

"Perfect. When 'tis ready, I want ye to send it tae Newcastle, tae meet the ship there. We put in there in five days. Ye'll have tae overnight it, but . . ."

"I'll get it done. I promise."

Moira smiled. She could see Carl waving to her from the top of the other tower. "Ye're a treasure, Craig. I cannae thank ye enough. 'Twill make a lovely anniversary gift for my laddie. I'm sorry for the hasty arrangements. I did nae know Carl had this all planned."

"How's it going, by the way?"

"Aye, 'tis grand. Glorious." She sighed. "Romantic! Just what we needed. Carl planned everythin' down tae the last detail. And 'tis all perfect." *Except for my shoes, but I'll nae quibble about that. Though, 'tis still worth a wee bit of teasing.*

"What about the . . . notoriety?"

"Ye know about that?"

"Well, it was actually on KSL news—'Utah's own vampire visits her ancient Scottish homeland.' It was a short personal-interest story. Some pictures of you . . . and Carl—mostly from around here. It was even on Fox News. Probably, KSL got it from Fox, but . . . Face it, Moira, you two changed the world. You saved the world."

Moira groaned. *'Twas a lot more than just the two of us. Sae many lives lost. Sae many good, dear people.* "I do wish ye'd nae put it that way. We did what we did, with God's help. And the cost was dear enough. But . . . Ach, well, that cat's out o' the bag, I suppose. 'Tis all over the ship. Half the people want to take pictures with us. Half point fingers and whisper—nasty things, I think. But I cannae hear them anymore, ye ken. I nae longer have . . . enhanced senses."

"Do you miss it?"

Moira laughed. "Miss bein' a vampire? Miss havin' tae stay out of the light o' the Sun lest I burst intae flame? Miss the taste o' human blood? Miss bein' hunted by Lilith's minions and that daft Brotherhood of Tobias with their vendetta against vampires? Ach, nae! Nae even a wee bit."

"You know that's not what I meant."

Moira sighed and nodded, though she knew Craig couldn't see the nod. "I miss . . . I miss bein' able tae diagnose a patient sometimes on scent . . . or taste alone. 'Tis as if . . . as if I'm half-blind. I wonder about the lives I could save . . . I miss bein' able tae hear a baby's heartbeat—and the mother's heartbeat too—when I deliver a baby. But now I can have bairns of my own. Ye ken how long I wished for a bairn of my own?"

"Two-and-a-half centuries."

"Aye. And now I have my own. Mine and Carl's." Her eyes misted up as she saw Carl waving at her from across the castle. Again. Moira waved back. "I suppose, the thing I miss most is the flyin'. I know Carl misses that the most. He was a pilot, ye ken, and though he can do that now—in an airplane, o' course—'tis nae the same." She sighed. "Aye, I do miss the flyin'. But havin' my wee bairns . . . and the full blessings of the gospel . . . That's worth *any* price. But, now, back tae the matter at hand . . . Ye get it all printed up and ready tae go, and I'll get ye the address so ye can send it tae the ship in Newcastle."

"Sounds good."

"Craig, laddie, I do appreciate all ye've done—ye're a genealogical wizard, ye are. And a grand, bonnie friend. But I must get a-goin', and ye must get yerself tae bed. Now."

Craig laughed. "Yes, Dr. Morgan."

After exchanging a few more pleasantries, Moira ended the call, stowed her phone, and began descending the narrow tower steps. As she clung to the rope secured to the center pillar of the spiral stone staircase, trying to navigate steps that—at least near the center—weren't wide enough even for her petite feet, she saw a young man ascending from the other direction.

A young man in a blue hoodie with torn pants and worn-out sneakers.

He paused on the stairs—which were wider toward the outside of the tower staircase—and he clung to the thick rope on that side. He locked eyes with Moira briefly, intently. Then his eyes flickered away.

Moira smiled at him. "Lloyd? Is that ye, laddie?"

The young man in the hoodie did not return her smile. He pulled his hood lower, hiding his face in shadow, then continued past her, up the stairs.

I'm certain he recognized me.

A feeling of dread crept over Moira.

She glanced up and behind, almost certain she'd see the fellow on the stairs above her, ready to give her a shove. She caught sight of his receding tennis shoes, and that was all.

Moira heard a girlish squeal and swiveled her head. A pair of preteen girls—twin sisters Moira recognized from the cruise—were giggling as they ascended in the wake of the aloof Lloyd.

Moira descended with hasty care to the tower landing. Then she hurried across the high, thick wall-top to the opposite tower, where her husband awaited her.

'Twas he! I know 'twas.

When she reached the top of the tower, she resisted the urge to throw herself into Carl's protective arms. Instead she gave him a weak smile and grasped his hand. She stared across the castle to the tower she'd just left.

And she saw there a hooded figure, standing behind the crenellated parapet.

Moira did not need her erstwhile vampiric senses to discern that the face inside the hood was turned toward them.

"What's wrong?" Carl asked in that hard, stern voice he used when he sensed danger.

I must look as pale as . . . as a vampire who hasn't Fed lately.

Without taking her eyes off the watcher on the other tower, Moira said quietly and distinctly, "D'ye remember that fella who took our picture at Stonehenge? The lad in the hoodie?"

Carl didn't turn around, didn't look at the other tower, but he said, "He's here, isn't he?"

"Aye. On the tower I just left."

"Okay. I won't ask if you're sure, because I know you are."

"I dinnae think he's from the cruise."

"He's not."

Moira tore her eyes away from the hooded figure and looked at her husband. "How d'ye know?"

"Because I asked the concierge *and* security on the ship when we reboarded at Portland. I described him and gave his name as 'Lloyd.'"

"Why would ye've done such a thing?"

The corner of Carl's mouth twitched. "A soldier's instincts. Ever since those jokers with the Brotherhood . . ."

Moira suppressed a shudder at the thought of the fanatical band of hunters—hunters of former vampires—like Moira and Carl. "I thought they disbanded."

"That's what we were told." He paused. "Is he still there?"

Moira looked back to the opposite tower.

The hooded figure was gone.

"Nae."

Carl turned then and surveyed the tower and the wall-top which connected them. "Given the shabby state of his clothing, the way he smelled, and the way he acted, he got my hackles up." He shrugged. "So I asked. Then when we didn't see him at Dublin or Kilkenny, I thought we might be clear. Maybe, he didn't have enough money to get to Ireland."

"Perhaps nae, but now we're here, back in Great Britain, and here he is at Conwy. D'ye think he could've followed us from the port at Liverpool?"

"It's possible. But . . . that'd still cost him money. I don't think he has much."

"He has a hundred pounds." *Which I gave him. Nae good deed goes . . .*

Carl growled softly. He led her away from the parapet and toward the center of the tower roof. He positioned himself so he could see the top of the tower stairs.

Away from the edge, so we cannae be observed. Or shot. Where we can see approaching threats.

"He can't hide a rifle under that sweatshirt," Carl said, "but he could conceal a handgun."

"Or a knife," Moira added.

She didn't cling to her husband for protection. That wasn't in her nature. She'd spent centuries alone, protecting herself. Once upon a time, Moira had been more skilled with the sword than Carl. By far—not that either one of them could carry a sword in the open anymore.

Taking firearms to the United Kingdom or onboard the cruise ship was not even an option.

"Yeah," Carl said, "and we're not as . . . invulnerable as we once were."

We were nae ever invulnerable, but we are certainly more fragile now.

"You know," Carl said, "every once in a while, mortality sucks." He spoke without a trace of humor or irony.

Moira chuckled mirthlessly. "Aye, it definitely has its disadvantages. I'm afraid, laddie . . ." She paused. "Well, I dinnae mean I'm *afraid,* but . . . Well, a healthy dose of fear is . . . aye, well, *healthy* . . . but I do believe we may have ourselves a stalker."

"Yep. I agree. But is he an obsessed fan? Or a murderous fanatic?"

"In the end, laddie, does it make much difference?"

Carl shook his head, his expression hard and grim. "Maybe not much. Either way, we can be just as dead."

Chapter XVIII

"A horse shall bear away two, one willing and one unwilling, and thy secret plans shall be betrayed."
from the Book of Marcus Scribonius

DCCCXIV *Ab Urbe Condita* (61 A.D.)

"I should be marching," Maelona said quietly, "not riding comfortably"—she paused briefly after the word as if to belie its honesty—"on a pony. Those women, those mothers . . . Some of them are old, and yet they march. I should not be so"—she appeared to be searching for the right word—"privileged."

The war council was long over, and everyone, except for the guards, both Roman and Celtic—had retired to their tents and bedrolls or, in the case of most of the Celts, to their sodden woolen cloaks. Marcus and Maelona, alone in the commander's tent, lay in their separate beds. Marcus insisted—more than insisted, he *demanded*—Maelona occupy the piled furs that had once belonged to Quintus Aquillius. That in itself had precipitated an argument—Maelona declared they smelled of the man who had raped her night after night—and Marcus declared he would not have the woman he loved sleeping on a soldier's bedroll. In the end, Marcus won out, but the victory had been costly—Maelona insisted she sleep no more than a single pace from Marcus, rather than across the tent. It wasn't that Marcus didn't want her close by—he did. And that was the problem—he *wanted* her close by.

However, he had to ensure that anyone who might barge into the tent in the middle of the night would be able to see quite clearly that they were *not* sleeping together. A single pace provided that separation—but just barely.

Marcus reached for her hand and found it. "You rode comfortably?" he asked, smiling in the darkness. "I cannot imagine forty miles' ride could possibly have been comfortable. I'd wager your thighs and backside are quite sore."

"If we were married, you could . . . oil your hands and . . . push the hurt away. But we are not."

"No" —he sighed—"we are not."

"Marry me, Marcus. Before we go into battle. Marry me tonight. Write out the marriage contract. I will sign it. You will tell me how to write my name. Marry me now. Please."

He groaned. "I can't! I want to. But I don't have the *right* to marry. Not now. Not yet. Perhaps when we return to the legion, I could—"

"Please stop saying that. How will it be any different when we return? *If* we return . . ."

"I will ask the legate."

"And if he says no?"

"I don't know. Hopefully, he will not."

"Branwen tells me that your prophecies say we will marry. It will happen. I know it will."

Marcus could hear her crying softly, and her hand trembled in his. "Maelona . . ."

"I try to have f-faith," she blubbered, withdrawing her hand. "I try. But I'm so frightened. What if we don't survive this? H-how c-can we be married if one . . . or both of us are dead?"

Marcus almost reached out to her, he almost went to her. *Pity her not. Does that apply to Maelona or Branwen?* "Please don't weep. Aristobulus says that we—all of us—you and I—we are eternal. He says *this* life isn't all there is. I believe him. If one or both of us dies, I believe we can be married by proxy."

She was silent for several long moments. "If I die, I want you to marry Branwen."

"No. My love, no. I am pledged to you. I love you."

"I don't want you to be alone. And she loves you too. Almost as much as I do. Maybe more. No, not more. That is impossible. But she loves you as much as I do. Promise me, Marcus. If I die, you will marry Branwen."

"I will not promise that."

"You must. For me. For my sake."

"But what of you? What if I were to die and you were left alone?"

"There is no other man for me, Marcus. No other. I will not marry. I would go to Aristobulus and serve there, serve his flock as . . . your widow. If not in name, in practice."

"I shall not marry another, Maelona. You are the only woman for me. You are my heart, my princess, my queen."

"Hold me, Marcus. Please?"

"I . . . I can't."

"Not in bed. I know it cannot be in bed. We could sit for a while, on the ground. Just hold me."

Marcus let out a long, shuddering sigh. "I can do that." He pulled back his blankets and sat up. "But we shall sit on your bed. I cannot oil my hands and . . . No, I cannot. But we can sit on your soft furs to comfort your aching backside."

When they were settled on the furs—he sitting upright, and she leaning against his shoulder—she sighed. "Please comb your fingers through my hair, as you did for her."

Marcus stiffened. "She told you of that?"

Maelona nodded, and her mass of curls brushed softly against his neck and cheek. "She told me everything. And because she told me everything, I trust her as I trust you. You did nothing improper. You were honorable to her and to your promise to me. So please, my conqueror, comb your fingers through my hair."

And so Marcus stroked her curls.

♠ ♠ ♠

Dawn brought more additions to Marcus's small but swelling army.

As Marcus and Maelona packed up their tent, Prooption Caeso Lucilius approached, accompanied by Emrys and Pwyll. Marcus observed that Gwawr did not accompany her husband.

It had been explained to Marcus—and the rest of the Romans of the war council—that Celts were comfortable taking commands from a *woman* in wartime. *Like Boudicca,* Marcus thought at the time—though he still had difficulty imagining the lovely Gwawr acting anything like the ruthless rebel queen. *Boudicca became so brutal at the end – and to her own people. Is that what I'd become if I had daughters and they were . . . violated like that? While I was forced to watch?*

He remembered the undirected hatred he'd felt for the unknown fiends who raped and murdered his mother. *If I'd known on whom to focus my rage, what would I have done?*

But experience and training had taught Marcus that rage and hatred didn't make one a good soldier. *If we're to defeat the army of Arawn, I need soldiers who will obey orders. If I had a* month *to train them . . .*

But he didn't have a month. He didn't have a day—not if they were to save the captives before they were sacrificed or raped . . . or both. He knew—they all knew—that once the presence of Marcus's forces was discovered, hostages could be murdered. *I can't train them. And I have only the oaths of these people to bind them to obedience.*

And without relentless drilling and training, nobody knows what he . . . or she will do in the chaos and terror of combat.

Marcus stood as Caeso and his companions halted. Caeso saluted. "Ninety-seven more have joined us. That brings the total reserves to four hundred and seventeen."

Emrys furrowed his brow. "Why do you refer to us as 'reserves'?"

"It is no insult," Marcus said. "You are not frontline soldiers. You will fight, but as I direct. As we agreed. In fact, you may be the first to engage the enemy. Remember?"

Emrys bowed his head in submission. "Yes, Pater." He looked at Marcus with one eye closed. "Should I call you Pater or Commander or Option? I know I should not refer to you as simply Marcus Aquillius."

Marcus grinned as he shook his head slightly. "No, Marcus Aquillius would be inappropriate in a military situation. Option will do."

"But do I need to salute?"

Marcus laughed, caught off guard by the suggestion. "No!" He laughed a bit more. "That *was* a joke, wasn't it?"

The steward grinned even as he shrugged. "Yes, but . . . I don't know how to deal with you. You're going to be my master someday."

Marcus clapped the man on the shoulder. "Hopefully, that day is far off." He nodded his head in the direction of Pwyll. "What's he doing here?"

Emrys's lips drew into a straight line of irritation. "He insisted. He was upset about being left out of the council last night."

"But . . . he speaks no Latin."

The vilicus nodded slightly. "Yes, but . . . he considers me—perhaps rightly—as belonging to the villa and not the village. His . . . wife was taken. He is very worried about her."

"Understandable." Marcus turned to the farmer. "What was her name?"

Emrys answered, "Ffion."

Pwyll's head snapped first to Emrys and then to Marcus. "Ffion." Tears rolled down his sun-browned cheeks.

Marcus said, "We'll save your Ffion." Then he added, still speaking to Pwyll, "Emrys has explained the plan? Your part in it?"

Emrys replied with, "Yes, I did." However, he still translated Marcus's words.

The farmer nodded once more. He eyed Marcus with an expression that flitted between wide-eyed worry and iron-jawed determination. He said something in the local tongue, clearly addressing Marcus.

"What did he say?"

"He says," Maelona replied, appearing at Marcus's side, "that you are brave and noble to fight for a people who are not yours. He says you have great courage to fight against the great god Arawn."

Marcus looked Pwyll straight in the eye. "Tell him, we fight against men and horses, not against a god. Men and horses can be killed. Once they are dead, then we will deal with Arawn—whatever he may be. Tell him, we fight to deliver the women and children. And with the help of God, we will win."

As Maelona translated, Marcus kept his face resolute, his gaze never wavering from Pwyll's. But inside, a storm of doubt and fear threatened to make his hands shake.

. . . though the cost be great . . .

He turned to Caeso and Emrys. "We march within the hour."

The steward bowed his head, and the prooption saluted. Both men said, "Yes, Option."

Pwyll said nothing.

♦ ♦ ♦

As the day progressed, the Celts kept pace with the century, more or less, though they marched well behind. More villagers flocked to them, coming a dozen here, a half dozen there.

And more and more of them came armed with spears. What was better, the makeshift spears—those made of wood and nothing more—were stouter and longer than the thin sticks many of the original group carried.

"I know you wanted heavier spears," Maelona said as she rode and Marcus marched, "but it is as if they are carrying small tree trunks."

Marcus grinned. "I know they're heavy, but we're going to need them."

"Against the horses?"

"Against the horses. You were in the war council—you heard the plan."

"Yes, but . . . sometimes I cannot understand all the . . . military words."

Marcus nodded. "No light infantry can hope to stand against an equally large cavalry charge—and they have two hundred horses. We'd be mowed down, trampled. The battle would be over with the first assault. You're not used to this type of warfare. Ponies aren't as massive as warhorses."

"As massive as . . . the horrible beast."

Marcus chuckled. "Yes, as massive as Gaius the Warhorse."

"And you gave him up for me."

Marcus turned his face to her, and he beamed. "It was worth it to see you in so fine a gown."

She gave him a look of mock disgust. "Men! You think of only one thing!"

Marcus chuckled. "Princess, it's hard to think of anything else when you are around." He grinned widely. "We do think of food as well."

She harrumphed. "But . . . would not the beast have been a help in battle?"

Marcus sobered. "No. He would have been a problem. I cannot command from horseback."

"But you would be so much better rested if you rode."

"As tempting as that sounds, I need to be able to measure my men's strength. It's easy to overestimate that when you haven't marched as they have marched."

She was quiet for some time. Then she asked, "How far have we gone today? How much farther do we have to go?"

Marcus gazed up at the sky—so blue after the previous day's rain. He checked the position of the sun. "It's midday, so . . . twenty miles or so. We have gone over halfway."

"How can you be so certain? From the sun?"

"We are trained to march twenty miles in five hours every day, so the sun and the passage of time can tell me something. But that's not it. I know how far we've marched from the number of steps we've taken."

"You are counting your steps?"

He shrugged. "Yes. That is part of an option's duties."

"But . . . you are the commander now. You have a prooption. Is he not counting?"

Marcus chuckled. "I'm sure he is."

"Then why are you counting? I don't hear you counting."

"Old habits die hard. And I'm counting in my head. It's a trick one learns."

"But we will not attack as soon as we get there?"

He shook his head. "Because we are a vastly outnumbered, inferior force attacking an army on their home ground, we dare not. It would be suicide to attack directly and in daylight, especially after so arduous a march. We will camp a few miles away and prepare for battle at dusk."

"But we have God the Father to help us."

Marcus nodded. "Yes, we do."

"Do you not have faith?"

"I do." *But is my faith strong enough?* "However, God entrusted me with these men and these weapons. And these brave women. He expects me to use every resource I have, every stratagem I have. We can't just march in and expect Heavenly Father to do all the work for us."

And I have been praying for clouds all day. All day.

He raised his eyes to the cerulean heavens.

And not a single cloud has appeared.

Father in heaven. I need the clouds!

Please. Please send me clouds.

But the sky remained blue as sapphires and clear as glass.

And the heavens remained silent.

♦ ♦ ♦

That afternoon, under a maddeningly clear sky, the members of the war council sat before the commander's tent—Option Marcus Aquillius Audaxus, Prooption Caeso Lucilius, Vexillarius Agrippa Corfidius, Cornicen Spurius Orcivius, Protesserarius Nonus Sestius, and Maelona. Emrys and Pwyll had not yet arrived, but the Roman scouts had returned from their reconnaissance mission.

Nearby, the fabro tirelessly wielded his hammer as he reshaped shovels into makeshift choppers, hoes into spears—anything he could do to turn farm tools into weapons. A long line of Celts waited as the capsarium lanced Celt blisters and bound up Celt feet—he'd long ago run out of salves and ointments.

"How many do we have now?" Marcus asked the protesserarius. "How many have joined us now?"

"Five hundred and seventy-one," Nonus Sestius reported. "Farmers and craftsmen and farmwives. They seem to be brave souls—fathers and mothers, fighting for their children, husbands fighting for—"

Marcus nodded. *It's not their courage I doubt.* "How many have spears?"

"Perhaps"—Nonus seemed to be counting in his head—"four hundred. But will that be enough?"

Marcus replied, "It will have to be. What do the scouts report?"

"The enemy is four miles distant. The numbers we got from the cursed priest before he"—Nonus shuddered—"before he *died* appear to be accurate. There are a number of wattle-and-daub huts, one meeting hall. It's a city, all right, but a hastily built one. No fort. No palisade. It's as if they don't see the need to set up defenses—or haven't had the time. There are easily five hundred hostages, kept in a large pen. The children scream. There are too few women to comfort and quiet them."

Nonus swallowed before continuing. "And, Option, at the center of the town, they've erected an iron god. At least, it looks like iron—not wood as we've seen for Druid sacrifices before. The idol is twice the size of a man and has his arms extended, as if to hold a child. Both the god and the earth around it are blackened as by fire. It's just as that bastard described. This is . . . This is far worse than the Burning Man sacrifice we've heard tales of."

"Not just tales," said Caeso Lucilius. "I've witnessed that particular abomination."

Nonus nodded, took a deep breath, and then continued. "Just as the cursed priest said, it appears that they heat up the idol to red-hot, then put the living child in its arms."

Marcus nodded grimly. *Just as Aristobulus described Chemosh and Moloch.* "What about the Gates of Annwfyn itself?"

Nonus Sestius shook his head. "They didn't get a good look, but the gate—and our scouts observed only one—appears to be a narrow opening in a hillside near the city. Against the door is one of those huge stone tables—four standing stones, covered by another stone—like a roof, high and wide enough for a few men to stand under. A pair of armed guards—that's all. It's as if they're not at all worried about anybody getting in. Perhaps what's inside is so . . ." He let his voice trail off.

Marcus nodded. *Perhaps what's inside is so terrifying, nobody would dare enter.*

"But, Option," the protesserarius continued, "if we could take and hold that spot, we'd have the high ground and the hill at our backs."

Agrippa shook his head. "The hill at our backs . . . and the god as well. I, for one, would not choose such a spot."

He's not a god. Not. A. God.

There are no other gods!

Marcus noticed Emrys and Gwawr—as well as Pwyll—standing just outside the circle. The vilicus and the village leader appeared to be engaged in an argument of some kind. Marcus waved to Emrys, indicating that they should join the council. Emrys nodded, and then he and Pwyll approached and sat with the Romans and Maelona.

After the brief interruption, Nonus continued. "There is also a small tor—one of those free-standing hills—overlooking the city. We could make our stand there. Its sides are steeper, and that would slow their horses. That might be the better choice. And it's unwatched from the north. We might approach from the north and be in our ranks before the enemy discovers us."

"Perhaps," said Spurius Orcivius, "but that presumes they will attack us at all. That would *not* be to their advantage. If they have a tactical mind among them . . ."

"Did the scouts observe any archers?" asked Caeso Lucilius.

Nonus shook his head. "No."

Caeso nodded, his expression grim. "Well, at least there's that. But . . . they could still have darts or throwing spears."

"Spears," said Nonus, "they had in abundance. The scouts saw no indication of darts. But plenty of spears."

"Very well," said Marcus, "but the high ground would effectively render those useless."

"Then my counsel," said Caeso, "is to occupy the tor."

"I agree," said Agrippa.

Spurius and Nonus echoed their approval.

"But," Spurius asked, "how do we get them to attack us, and in a timely manner? They could slaughter all the hostages in our sight, and we'd be able to do nothing."

"Taunt them." All eyes turned to Maelona.

"Taunt them?" asked Caeso. "Why would that be effective?"

Maelona's eyes burned with a fierce light. "I know this man, Conwy, who leads them. He will not"—her brow wrinkled as if she were searching for the right word—"permit any challenge to his authority. Taunt them. Taunt *him*. Conwy will attack."

"In what tongue?" asked Marcus. "Does he speak Latin?"

The princess shrugged, then shook her head. "I do not think so."

"Then in your tongue." Marcus nodded thoughtfully. "You know him. Does he know you?"

Maelona grinned savagely. "Oh, yes. I exposed him and his plot to overthrow"—her voice hitched slightly, and her expression softened—"my father. I was the one who got him banished. He knows me. He knows me quite well."

"Then," Marcus said, "you shall be the one to taunt him. But you must be prepared for him to say vile things in return."

Maelona waved a hand dismissively. "What more can be taken

from me? Vile words? Why would I fear those?"

Agrippa eyed her with skepticism. "So you propose taunting this Conwy from the top of a hill? How do you know he will hear you?"

The princess chuckled. "I was one of the Witches of Mona." She gave the vexillarius a wicked grin.

Agrippa recoiled, his eyes wide with shock and fear.

"Yes," Maelona said. "You were there, were you not? You heard how we could shriek and howl."

Agrippa nodded. He opened his mouth to speak, then snapped it shut, swallowed, and simply nodded once more.

Marcus barely suppressed a smile at the junior officer's obvious discomfort. *She scared me too, my friend.* Then Marcus did grin. *She still does, from time to time.* "Then the tor it shall be. That is the plan. The rest of it, how we deploy the villagers, the battle plan is as we laid it out last night."

Marcus waited while Emrys translated the summary of the conversation to Pwyll.

The Celt shook his head and scowled. He spoke quickly to Emrys in a low, angry tone.

Emrys nodded and focused on Marcus. "Pwyll is not satisfied with the role of his people, their part in the battle. He thinks, as he counseled last night—"

"Remind Pwyll," Marcus said, "that he agreed to march under my command. If he has changed his mind, tell him to remain here and guard the camp."

"He's worried about his wife," Emrys replied.

"And that is understandable," Marcus said, "but he obeys my orders, or he remains here. And that goes for anyone else who is unwilling to follow my commands."

Pwyll muttered something in the Cambrian tongue.

Maelona snapped, "Ni wnewch hynny!"

The chief villager's eyes widened, and his mouth hung open.

Maelona continued to speak to him in his native language. It was plain to all that she was angry—her tone was imperious, brooking no disagreement.

Like a princess, a queen.

Pwyll's mouth closed, and his countenance reddened, but he lowered his eyes. When Maelona finished, he bowed his head and humbly said, "Ie, Tywysoges."

Maelona nodded. Keeping her eyes on the Celt, she said, "He will be no more trouble. He will obey your commands without question."

She growled low in her throat. "I dislike being angry. It . . . disagrees with me."

Marcus bit his lip, suppressing a grin. *But you do it so well, my lady.* "We march in one hour. I want to be at the north slope of the tor before nightfall. Nonus, if we approach the hill from the north, how much time will that add to our march?"

Nonus thought for a moment. "There is a forest to the north. We could approach through there—single-file." He shrugged. "Perhaps an hour?"

Marcus nodded. "Very good. Let's go over the plan once more."

"Option," Maelona said.

Marcus was surprised to hear her address him by his rank. "Yes, Princess?"

She grimaced as if embarrassed. "Before we do that, I need to . . . be excused for a moment." She nodded her head in the direction of the newly dug latrine. "I'm sorry."

Marcus gave her what he hoped was a comforting smile. "Certainly. Let's take a supper break, then reconvene in half an hour." He glanced from Caeso to Emrys to Pwyll. "Inform everyone that we march—in combat gear only."

Maelona and the rest of the Celts excused themselves.

The Romans remained.

Once the Celts were out of earshot, Nonus grinned and shook his head. "That woman of yours is incredible! That was . . . amazing. I have to admit, that Pwyll . . . he makes me uneasy. I know he is worried about his wife, but . . . Well, the princess certainly took him to task. Marcus, you are a fortunate man." He put up his hands. "Don't mistake me. Sometimes, she scares me almost beyond reckoning, but . . . What a woman!"

Marcus didn't even try to hide his pleasure. "I'll not argue with you."

Caeso grinned as well, but the grin soon faded. "The last thing we need right now is some type of mutiny. The enemy still has five times our number."

"Agreed," Marcus said. "But if we can take the tor without being noticed, we may negate the advantage of those numbers. Somewhat."

"Since nobody else is willing to talk about it," Spurius said, "what about . . . your winged friend?"

Marcus shrugged. "I wish I knew. She has offered her help, but I've been unable to consult with her, to plan or make specific—"

"To arms! To arms!"

Marcus and his officers leapt to their feet. As one, they drew their swords. Around them, legionnaires snatched up shields and drew their weapons.

"Option!" Septimus Scribonius ran toward them, his own sword drawn. "Option!"

"Speak, man!" Marcus cried.

"The vilicus and vilica are murdered!" Septimus said.

Emrys and Gwawr? "Who?" Marcus demanded. "Who has done—"

"The Celt! Pwyll!" Septimus pointed with his sword.

Marcus could see a pony galloping away, in the direction of the enemy camp, already out of the range of Roman spears. But even as the villain fled, Marcus could see that Pwyll was not alone—another figure lay slumped and bouncing across the front of his saddle.

And before Septimus spoke the words, Marcus knew in his heart who the traitor had abducted.

"Marcus!" Septimus cried. "The princess. He has taken the princess!"

Chapter XIX

"The lamb shall lie at the feet of the black wolf, but her life shall be in her own mouth. Lo, she shall be in the midst of the wolves, and the lamb shall scatter the pack like sheep without a shepherd."

from the Book of Marcus Scribonius

Children screamed in the distance. Women screamed as well.

"Truly, Arawn has smiled upon me."

The melodious voice was familiar—a voice from Maelona's lost youth. But she couldn't immediately identify the owner of the voice. She knew if she could just open her eyes, she would recognize him.

But her eyelids were so heavy. She felt as if she could drift right back to sleep and dream.

Dream of Marcus.

"You have ripened, Princess," said the voice, rousing her once again. "When last I saw you, you were a skinny, gangly child. Now, you are a woman—fully a woman."

I know you, she thought.

Monster. I hate you.

Her eyes fluttered open, and she beheld a face. If it were not twisted with a perverse leer, it would have been a handsome face.

Indeed, once she had thought him handsome. Once, so many of the women of the tribe thought him handsome. He seduced a number of them with his handsome face and his flattering words.

Once, he came so close to seducing her.

But I saw beneath your mask, didn't I? I saw you for the monster you are.

Conwy. High priest of Arawn.

He sat on a Roman-style, wooden chair as if he were a king sitting in court before his subjects.

"Ah, you are awake," he said. "I so prefer you to be awake, Princess."

A half dozen men stood on either side of him, black-robed as Conwy was, but with their hoods pulled low, their faces cast in shadow. Their beards provided the only color in contrast to the solid midnight of their robes and hoods. Conwy's black hood was pulled back, exposing his shoulder-length, curling, brown locks and his short beard. His brown eyes twinkled with delight and malice. And lust.

Maelona attempted to sit up. And failed. Her hands were bound, her arms pulled above her head. A glance showed her hands were tied with leather thongs to a stake driven into the ground. Her legs were free, but with her hands pinned, she could only lie before the villainous priest.

Memories flooded her mind. Paralyzing memories.

Memories of rape.

Of pain and loss and humiliation.

And being utterly powerless.

Reduced to nothingness.

Not again. Not again.

No! Not again!

God the Father, help me.

Help my Marcus. My dear Marcus.

She remembered how Marcus had insisted that he must use what God had given him to achieve victory.

Show me how to use what you have given me.

In the name of Christus. Amen.

She glanced at her feet. *I have my feet. I can kick. But what good will that do? They can hold my feet while they . . .*

No, put that thought aside. Even if it comes to that, I can survive it.

I have survived it before.

"Where"—she moistened her dry mouth—"Where is Pwyll?"

Conwy laughed, apparently surprised by her question. "The traitor? You are concerned for his welfare?" The high priest of Arawn laughed again. "Very well. Bring him to us." He waved. "Bring the traitor and his whore of a wife."

Two of the black-robed priests moved to obey.

Maelona took in her surroundings. She was in a moderate-sized hut, longer than it was wide—like a meeting hall. The walls were of wattle-and-daub construction, the ceiling of thatch. The assemblage of priests was gathered at one end, with an open door at the far end.

Though the sun had not yet set and the air was far from cold, a peat fire burned in the center, the smoke escaping through a hole in the roof. Half a dozen tallow candles burned smokily in iron candlesticks set throughout the hall. The candlesticks were tall but of disparate sizes, as if they'd been stolen from various sources.

The departing priests exited through the door.

Conwy shook his head. "He drugged you with henbane, abducted you, betrayed the battle plan of your dog of a Roman lover . . . And you still ask after him?"

"Pwyll is one of my people." *Not exactly true. He was never under my rule. But he has pledged himself to Marcus. And I stand with Marcus.* "He is mine to protect and to judge. Not yours."

The high priest chuckled. "According to the traitor, you are naught but the Roman commander's whore. Tell me, fair Maelona—does he share you out with his men?" He shook his head and sneered. "You act the princess, but, lass, you are princess of nothing. You refused my advances once, but now, you are mine. And I shall do with you as I will."

Maelona heard low laughter from several of the priests.

The two priests who had left returned, each leading a prisoner by a rope tied to the captive's neck, like a leash or a noose.

Maelona recognized Pwyll, though the man's face was blotched with fresh bruises. The second prisoner was a woman—Pwyll's wife, Maelona assumed. Her gown was torn and muddied, her red-gold hair in disarray, one eye swollen with the purple and green of a ripened bruise. The woman locked her gaze with Maelona's.

Maelona knew the defeated look in the woman's eyes. She knew it well. She'd seen it for years in the bronze mirror of Quintus Aquillius—the look of a woman who had everything stolen from her, the eyes of a woman who had lost every last shred of hope.

"Ffion?" Maelona asked.

The woman's step faltered, her leash became taught. "You know me?"

Maelona shook her head. "No. But I know of you. Be brave. Help is coming."

Ffion bowed her head. "There is no help for me. No help for any of us." Her captor tugged at her leash, and she started forward again. She whispered, "If you fight them, they beat you all the harder."

"Hold fast." *Marcus will come for us.* "Hope is—"

Conwy burst into laughter. "Oh, Princess! The only hope is in Lord Arawn! And you— Your only purpose, in what little life remains to you, is to serve Arawn and his priests." He leaned forward, and his leer widened. His teeth were bared like a wolf about to devour a lamb. "Your only purpose is to serve me."

Terror surged through her, and Maelona fought to keep her body from trembling. *Marcus would not be afraid. Marcus would have faith in Christus.* "I will never serve you." Somehow, she made the words sound brave.

Conwy licked his lips. "But you will, O, sweet Princess of Nothing." He sat up straight and focused on Pwyll. "On your knees, traitor."

Pwyll dropped to his knees and lifted his hands, pleading. "I did as you asked. I have told you all—all their battle plans, even the ones they thought I did not understand."

The plans they thought . . . He understands Latin?

"Please," Pwyll continued, "I have brought you his woman. Please release me. Release my wife! I did as you asked! When you took her . . . I did everything you asked."

One of the priests laughed.

Pwyll's wide eyes turned to the laughing priest, and Maelona could see the despair and certainty in the traitor's helpless gaze.

Conwy rose from his chair. He laid a hand upon Pwyll's head. "Fear not, lad. Your lovely—well, she shall be lovely once more, once the bruises heal—your lovely wife shall live. Her body shall serve us. And her firstborn child shall be sacrificed to Arawn." The high priest reached inside his robe. "You, however, have served your purpose." He smiled widely, then glanced up at the priest holding Pwyll's leash. "Bryn, if you would administer the sacred blow?"

The hooded priest drew back hard on the rope, pulling Pwyll's head back, stretching the traitor's neck. From his cloak, the priest drew forth a golden knife with a man-shaped handle. But rather than bringing the blade to bear, he turned the weapon around in his hand and held it by the blade.

"No!" screamed Ffion, pulling against her leash. "NO!" Her keeper yanked hard on the noose, and Ffion fell to her knees. "No, please! I'll do anything!"

Pwyll, however, said nothing as the heavy golden hilt of the knife struck the top of his head with a sickening crunch. Blood streamed from the wound.

Conwy held a golden knife in his hand as well. "I consecrate this Triple-Death to Cernunnos and Arawn—strangle and strike and cut." He slashed with the gleaming blade at Pwyll's stretched throat.

Maelona shut her eyes, but she was unable to shut out the gurgling coming from Pwyll and the scream coming from Ffion.

And the enraptured sighs of the priests of Arawn.

"Why?" Maelona demanded, opening her eyes and focusing on the face of Conwy, with his mad grin and gleaming eyes. She tried not to focus on the twitching body of Pwyll or the blood that soaked the high priest's robe. "Why? He gave you what you wanted! Why kill him?"

Conwy spoke through his rictus grin of gleefully clenched teeth. "He served his purpose. He is a traitor to his friends. We cannot trust him. And furthermore, I did not *kill* him. I *sacrificed* him. His death is sacred."

"You are mad," Maelona said. "You say you serve the gods? You serve no one but yourself. You serve only your own lusts."

"My own lusts?" He licked his lips, wolflike. "I have one lust I have not served. One that is long, long overdue."

He raised his head. "Out! All of you! I would . . . *speak* alone with the Princess."

"Shall we take the corpse with us?" asked the priest who still held Pwyll's leash.

Conwy shook his head. "No. Leave him. I find the scent of blood, of new death"—he turned his ravening eyes on Maelona—"*enhances* the act."

The priests left the hall, dragging the sobbing Ffion with them.

"Heat up the idol," said the high priest. "I want the Romans to smell burning children when they arrive tonight. And shut the door!"

He removed his gore-soaked robe, revealing a rather ordinary-looking tunic and breeches. "Finally, Princess. After all these years, I shall have you." He removed his breeches. "You're not a virgin anymore, but taking you will be just as sweet. And sweet shall be my revenge."

Maelona tugged with all her strength at the leather thongs that bound her to the earth-driven stake. But she could not move them. She kicked, rolled over, tried to get to her feet so she could pull the stake from the ground.

Conwy kicked her feet out from under her, causing her to crash to the ground, almost knocking the breath from her. As she lay gasping for air, he said, "I find I like it better when you fight."

"Loose my hands, coward, and you shall have a fight!"

He grasped the ankle of one kicking leg, and yanked hard, stretching her flat on the earth, flat on her back. He knelt between her thrashing legs, pinning them apart.

She was trapped.

He bent over her, grinning. "As I understand it, you are quite familiar with being taken against your will." He lifted her skirt. A stream of drool fell upon her chest and neck. "You are quite . . . experienced."

God the Father, deliver me!

♠ ♠ ♠

"But, Option, won't they know we are marching toward the hill?" Marcus Tarquinius, who had been one of the spies and served as guide, marched beside Marcus Aquillius. "That traitor heard the plan. They'll be expecting us, won't they?"

Keep your attention on the coming battle. Do not think of Maelona. Do not think of Maelona in the claws of those inhuman beasts. You can do her no good from here.

He glanced at the clear sky. *Please, God! Send me clouds!* "Yes," Marcus answered. Even he felt out of breath as they moved at a speed near a trot. "That is exactly what they will expect."

"Then why do what they expect?"

"Do you speak Celtic or Cambrian," he snapped, "or whatever cursed tongue they speak here?"

"No."

"Then I cannot command the Celts to do anything but what they have already been told to do. I tried"—Marcus strove to keep the frustration out of his voice—"to draw it out for them, but they didn't seem to understand. All they did was keep repeating, 'Tor.' So the wretched tor it shall be."

Caeso trotted up, then matched Marcus's stride. "Not a cursed man or woman! Nobody speaks a word of Latin. Damn the man! He killed or abducted every single interpreter. What cursed good is an army if they can't understand a word of command? The girl, the princess . . . She didn't teach you any of the benighted tongue?"

"Not a word. She was going to, but . . ."

"Maybe," Caeso said, "if we lead them elsewhere, they'll follow."

"Maybe," Marcus said. "Some might follow, and the rest might go where they were originally told to go. We'd just end up dividing our meager forces. Like as not, they'll meet us before we get there, now that they know we're coming."

Caeso was silent for a moment. "Though we be marching to our deaths, we will stand with you, Audaxus. Your courage will frighten the enemy and lead us to victory." Even as he trotted, he saluted. "For the glory of Rome and Audaxus."

Stop saying that wretched name! I'm not valiant. I'm terrified!

Maelona!

Heavenly Father, protect Maelona!

And let us arrive in time to save the children. Thou hast said we shall deliver the captives. Let it be so.

They know we are coming.

Father, strengthen my faith.

Give me courage.

And protect her. Please protect her.

"Let's pick up the pace," he said.

The Romans and the Celts increased the already grueling pace.

Please, help me to get there in time to save her.

She's alone. She's defenseless.

"If only I hadn't given up the cursed horse."

⸙ ⸙ ⸙

Use what you have.

The words came clearly to Maelona's frantic mind. *You have what you need.*

And in spite of her terror, she suddenly felt calm—as calm as she had felt on the night she was baptized and regained her lost purity.

"I *am* experienced," Maelona said, keeping her voice soft and steady. She had already ceased her useless struggles. "I've had many, so many Roman warriors." She forced a sneer and dropped her voice to a whisper. "I doubt you can possibly compare to them."

His face hovered just above hers, his beard tickling her lips. His hot, sour breath filled her nostrils. "You shall soon know, Princess."

He was taller than her—more than a foot taller.

I can use that. Yes, you monster, move just a little higher. Just a bit more . . .

"Fight me, Princess." His beard covered her mouth. "I enjoy it so much more when a woman fights me." He moved upward, along her body.

"Fight you?" she whispered as his beard brushed past her nose. "Oh, I shall fight you." She gazed at his throat. "And with Christus's help, I shall defeat you."

And with that she turned and lifted her head.

And sank her teeth into Conwy's throat.

She bit hard, tearing and twisting through skin and windpipe and muscles and blood vessels.

Blood from the man's ruined throat spurted onto her face and into her mouth. She turned her head, spitting the gory bite away.

He jerked and rolled away from her, clawing at his neck, his eyes wide with horror. Blood pulsed between his fingers. He turned his face to her.

And in his eyes, she could see the certain knowledge of his own death. His blood mixed with that of Pwyll. In moments, two corpses—murderous priest and hapless victim—lay side by side.

Conwy had not even been able to cry out.

Maelona allowed herself the space of two breaths to collect her strength and her courage.

Thank you, God the Father. In the name of Christus. Amen.

She rolled and twisted herself onto her feet. She grasped the stake that held her to the earth and pulled with all her strength—she pulled with the tingling might that comes with the thrill and terror of battle.

And with a growl of triumph, she ripped the stake from the ground.

Holding the wooden stake as a weapon in one bound hand, she glanced at the closed door.

Still shut.

She scrambled to the gore-drenched cloak that Conwy had discarded. She searched for the golden dagger. She found it in a pocket. The blood on her fingers was already sticky, and the golden dagger was quite heavy—she fumbled, dropping it once, twice as she cut her bonds.

Free at last, she donned the cloak, hooked the clasp at her throat, and pulled the hood low over her head. The cloak dragged along the ground as she moved.

The door will be guarded. Surely, they are waiting outside.

She considered the few windows on the walls—too small, even for her.

She dashed to one of the candlesticks. Holding it aloft, she set fire to the thatch of the ceiling. She moved about the hall, lighting the roof in a dozen places. Then she grasped Conwy's discarded breeches, set them ablaze, and tossed the burning garment on his corpse. The fire spread across the dry areas of his tunic.

She tossed the candle onto Pwyll's corpse. She grabbed Conwy's chair, smashed it, and placed the pieces on the peat fire.

Then she ran for the door.

She crouched low and waited for smoke to obscure the view of the dead. Then she cried in as low and manly a voice as she could muster.

"FIRE!"

A moment later, the door burst open. Several men hurried through the doorway.

The smoke poured out through the open door.

And through the smoke she plunged.

She ran from the burning building and found herself in a busy and crowded town of thatched huts. Men were all around her, yelling, scrambling, carrying buckets of water, pulling off their black robes to bat at the flames.

A gust of wind tore away bits of flaming thatch. Soon another hut was ablaze, and another.

Above the shouts of the priests were shouts of another kind. The screams of the women and children.

Maelona followed that sound.

She dashed into an open field at the center of the town. And halted, quaking with horror.

Before her, at the center of the field, stood the god.

Twice the size of a man, the idol was constructed of a mesh of blackened iron rods overlaid with sheets of the metal. The iron deity stood with arms extended, hands outstretched, ready to accept some horrific sacrifice. The face of the idol smiled benevolently down at its ready, iron hands.

At its feet, a fire blazed. The lower half of the iron horror already glowed red-hot.

Maelona stood, her feet rooted to the spot. In her mind, she imagined a screaming infant being thrust into the glowing arms of the ghastly idol.

But the actual wail of a frightened child snapped her back to reality.

She tore her gaze from the god and followed the sound of the baby. At the other end of the field, stood a large, high-fenced enclosure—like a cattle pen.

And inside—the prisoners.

Women. Children. Babies.

Hundreds of them.

Maelona lifted her skirts and gathered the blood-soaked robe. She sprinted to the gate of the enclosure.

A single guard stood his ground at the entrance, holding a short, leaf-bladed, steel sword. He shouted a word of challenge, but Maelona ignored him.

See the cloak, lad. Don't see how short I am.

Don't see the knife.

Without breaking her stride, she slammed into the guard, driving the golden dagger into the man's guts. She withdrew the knife, twisting it to break the suction as the man's wounded flesh swelled around the blade—just as her father had taught her. She reached up and slashed through the man's throat.

As he collapsed, Maelona kicked him away from the enclosure gate.

She took his leaf-bladed sword, then cleaved the gate latch in two.

Maelona yanked the gate open, and spied a woman cowering away from her, trying to shield a screaming infant in her arms. "No! No!" screamed the terrified prisoner.

"You're free!" Maelona cried. "Run. Spread word. Now!"

Then Maelona turned and fled.

She ran to the nearest horse—a great, black warhorse, tethered to the branch of a tree. The size of the animal was daunting.

A horrible beast.

Stomping down her fear, she slowly approached the horse. It shied away from her, pulling at its tethered reins.

It's afraid of the scent of fire. And blood.

I could discard this horrid cloak.

No. I need it still. It is my safe-passage out of here.

But it's not just the fire and the blood the animal fears.

The beast senses my own thrice-cursed fear.

"Easy, lad," she said as she stowed the golden dagger in a pocket within the cloak. She slipped the sword into her belt. "You're just fine, lad. I'm not going to hurt you. I'm not afraid of you. No, no, I'm not. And you're not afraid of me. No, you're not. We're going to be good friends, you and I."

She untied the beast's reigns and stroked its neck. "I need you, lad. I need to warn Marcus. And you're going to help me."

She approached the animal from the left side, reached up to grasp one of the twin horns of the Roman-style saddle, and hoisted herself into it. She settled herself quickly, then kicked the horse's belly.

The horse snorted, reared, then moved forward.

"Good lad." *Thank you, God the Father. Thank you.*

She kicked the beast again, and the stallion broke into a trot.

Her first thought was to escape, to get back to Marcus.

But then she spied another fenced enclosure. Through the stinging smoke, she saw what she estimated to be about two hundred horses. The beasts screamed and kicked at the high walls of their prison.

The entrance was guarded by two black-robed priests with swords at their belts.

Maelona turned her mount and kicked its flanks. Together, Maelona and the warhorse rode down the two guards, trampling them before they could draw their weapons.

Maelona drew her own sword and hacked at the gate latch. After two blows, the gate was unlatched.

She backed her horse away from the gate.

One of the penned animals pushed the gate open, whinnied, and galloped out. Another horse followed. And then another.

Frightened horses came thundering out of the gate, like a river of unstoppable muscle, bone, and hooves.

Several men foolishly tried to stop the animals. They were crushed beneath the stampede.

No more cavalry!

Maelona spared a glance toward the pen of the prisoners. A savage glee filled her heart as she saw women carrying and leading children as the captives made a dash for freedom. Some of the women carried a babe in one arm and a weapon—a stick, a stone, or a stolen dagger—in the other.

No more sacrifices!

Half the huts in the town were ablaze. The priests of Arawn ran to and fro, like ants escaping a flaming anthill. Some of their cloaks were ablaze.

Fiends! Beasts! May you all burn!

Maelona glanced at the sun to get her bearings, then kicked her steed into a gallop. Men leapt aside as she and her mount raced toward the edge of the town.

"STOP HER!" The voice boomed from behind her, impossibly loud, echoing through the town. "STOP THAT WOMAN!"

Maelona's horse reared.

She fought to keep her saddle. Then she fought to regain control of her mount.

Sudden gusts of wind buffeted her, seeming to come from all sides at once. Her blood-sodden cloak billowed behind her, the hood blown back, exposing her face and hair.

The horse screamed and reared again, nearly throwing her. She gripped the animal's sides with her feet and legs. "Easy, lad. Easy."

The horse no longer reared or kicked, but it trembled beneath her.

"SEIZE HER!" bellowed the voice.

Maelona turned her head.

And she saw him.

Floating in the air above the glowing idol. A man in a black cloak and hood, which seemed to ripple about him like smoke. His bearded face shone white, as did his hand—a hand which pointed at her. His eyes burned red—eyes that seemed to pierce her soul.

"MAELONA!" howled the shining apparition. "COME TO ME, CHILD! EMBRACE ME! YOU CANNOT ESCAPE ARAWN. YOU CANNOT ESCAPE DEATH!"

Her heart thundered in her chest. Fear seized her spine. The air in her lungs congealed.

"Come to me, Maelona!" Arawn beckoned to her with his other shining hand. "Come feast in my halls. Feast and revel. OR BURN IN ETERNAL FLAMES!"

Movement caught her eye, tearing her gaze away from Arawn.

A sea of black surged toward her, a wave of black-robed priests about to crash upon her—crash upon her and drown her.

She could not move. She could not even open her mouth to scream.

Into her mind came a voice, the same voice that had given her the courage to deliver herself from Conwy. *Fly, little one! Fly!*

Her fear died, like a candle flame extinguished by a gust of wind. Maelona turned her horse, kicked its flanks, and galloped out of the town. Out of the town and down the path. To freedom.

I'm coming, Marcus!

Behind her, Arawn bellowed in rage. "YOU SHALL BURN!"

Interlude IV

"In a dark and narrow place on the banks of the Ness shall a Cambrian raise a Caledonian blade. The unwilling shall take a Hibernian stave in his hand, and with it he shall smite the damned."

from the Book of Marcus Scribonius

July 2017 A.D.

Ye could've worn it back to the ship, laddie." Moira squeezed her husband's hand as they strolled through downtown Inverness, Scotland. "Ye did look bonnie in that kilt. Too bad they did nae have the Morgan tartan in yer size. But the Black Watch will do ye nicely. Ye've earned it, bein' former Air Force and all. What d'ye say we go back tae the shop right now, and ye put it back on?"

Carl chuckled. "Not on a bet. Not without bicycle shorts or something on underneath."

"Ooh, ye're too cowardly tae go traditional, are ye?"

"You can call it what you like, but some Scottish . . . uh, traditions are a bit much for me."

Moira squeezed his hand and winked at him as he turned his face to her. "And that's why ye would nae even *try* the haggis, aye?"

Carl stuck his tongue out and shuddered. "Yuck. Sheep stomach stuffed with liver and eyes and . . . who knows what else? No thanks. That's just disgusting. Don't tell me you actually like that . . . stuff."

Moira shrugged, swinging his hand as if they were a pair of children out on a stroll. "Truth-tae-tell, I *do* remember . . . enjoying it. Centuries ago, mind ye. But . . . I cannae bring myself tae sample it now." She grimaced. "But even haggis'd be better'n that awful pizza we just ate. And from a real Italian pizzeria! 'Twas nigh tasteless!"

Carl shook his head. "It was awful. Worst pizza I've ever had. And that includes the Velveeta pizza I made back during my mission in Korea. Talk about disgusting! But that pizza took the proverbial cake. And that so-called milkshake? Pathetic!" He lifted the black walking stick he'd purchased in Kilkenny, Ireland. The stout, knobby cane was made of straight and hard Irish blackthorn—an honest-to-goodness shillelagh. Carl pointed the shillelagh in the direction of the offending pizza shop. "Even microwave pizza is better than that crap, you frauds!"

Laughing, Moira gently pushed the cane toward the sidewalk. "Will ye stop wavin' that Irish . . . *thing* around? People will know ye're a tourist!"

Carl winked and grinned. "Oh, and my accent doesn't give it away?"

"I ken why ye bought it . . . and why ye brought it, but—"

A sonorous wailing interrupted her. Moira squealed with delight. "Look, laddie! 'Tis a wee piper!"

The lad, clad in kilt, could not have been more than twelve—if he was that old. But his bagpipes droned and blew as if the boy were not an inch shy of ten feet tall.

Moira recognized the tune as "The Soldier's Return," but after a quick stanza, it deftly transitioned to "Highland Laddie."

Carl gaped in wonder. "All of that sound coming from that little kid?"

Moira leaned closer to Carl's ear. "Must have a healthy set o' lungs, that one!"

She felt more than heard her husband's chuckle over the blood-stirring piping. He said, "Trust you to look at everything through a doctor's eyes!"

She growled playfully at him. "Ooh, laddie. Ye nae ever stop teasin', do ye? Still, it stirs my blood! Makes me want tae dance." She handed Carl her day bag. "Here now. Hold this fer me!"

She lifted one hand above her head and began to dance a Highland jig. She noticed the eyes of a few men—mostly tourists—eyeing her appreciatively and bobbing their heads in time with the music. A woman began to clap her hands in time with the tune. A few others joined in.

As flattering as the stares of the men and the clapping were, Moira's eyes locked with Carl's. His grin—lopsided, and all gleaming teeth—thrilled her. *I love my laddie!*

By the end of the song, a small crowd had gathered. The synchronized clapping became applause.

Nae! Dinnae clap for me!

She snatched her bag from Carl and pulled out a twenty-pound note. She stepped forward to the wee piper's bonnet which lay on the pavement at the lad's feet. Moira made a great show of placing the twenty atop the few coins she saw in the cap. The lad stared at the money with wide eyes and a growing smile. He bowed to her as she applauded him.

Moira stepped back as she continued to clap. "That was grand, laddie!" She spun around and swept the crowd with her smile. "Was that nae grand? Show him yer appreciation, folks!" She pointed to the cap. "Come on!"

With smiles and shrugs, most of the crowd stepped forward and placed coins in the cap. Even Carl pulled another twenty from his wallet to match Moira's.

Aye! That'll be a grand take for ye, laddie! "Play us another!"

The young piper grinned, worked his jaw for a moment as if loosening it, then gripped the pipe in his lips at the side of his mouth. He tapped his foot four times as he blew into the bag, then he squeezed it, and the upper pipes began to play E-flat in two octaves. The boy tapped four more beats before launching into "Scotland the Brave."

Carl kissed Moira's cheek. "That was amazing! I had no idea you could do that."

Moira gave him a coy smile. "I have nae danced like that in centuries." Her smile faded. "Nae since I . . . left my village."

Carl, his eyes drawn back to the boy with the bagpipes, seemed to have missed her change of mood. "Then it's a good thing we're going back!"

Moira forced a smile. "Aye. 'Tis." *Remember, lassie – there were good times, good memories as well.* Without warning, the face of Donald appeared in her mind. Donald MacDonald—her first love. Long since dead—captured and executed by the English after Culloden. *Nae. I dinnae want tae think of ye, Donald. I love Carl now. For time and eternity. And he loves me. In spite of everything, Carl loves me.*

She sighed inwardly. *But, aye, there are good memories too.*

Think on the good memories, lass.

Dinnae think of why ye chose damnation.

Even though Donald's death was part of why ye chose it.

"'Tis over and gone now."

Carl gazed at her with a quizzical frown. "What did you say?"

She shook her head and sighed. "'Tis nae but ald memories."

Carl's expression softened. "And they're not all . . . good, are they?"

"Let's focus on the good. Today is a good day. A bonnie day." She leaned in and kissed him.

He returned the kiss, wrapping his arms around her—shopping

bags and all. He pulled back and gazed into her eyes. "I love you, Moira. My bonnie, Scottish lassie."

She gave him an impish grin. *Ooh, I think ye're gonna like yer anniversary present!* "Dinnae forget, laddie. Ye are Scottish as well, Mr. *Morgan*."

Their lips met again . . . and Moira lost herself in the kiss—lost herself in the *good*.

The applause pulled her back to reality.

They both looked sheepishly around at the crowd—the much larger crowd. "I think," Moira said, "we should gae now."

Carl chuckled as he grasped her hand and pulled her down the wide, long plaza. "I love how your brogue gets thicker when you're stressed."

"I am nae stressed, ye daft Sassenach lout!"

Carl laughed, and the crowd parted, though not without some cheering and renewed applause.

Already strolling back the way they came, toward the waiting tour bus, Carl asked, "How much time do we have?"

She pulled her phone from her day bag and glanced at it. "Thirty minutes or so. Are ye tired, laddie? 'Tis, aye, been a long day. Cawdor Castle, Culloden, Urquhart Castle, Loch Ness . . . now Inverness."

"Was . . . Culloden . . . difficult for you? We just drove by."

Nae until just a tick ago. Nae really. "I'll nae lie to ye. There are moments. But those moments, good and bad, brought us here. Together. Sealed in the temple o' God. Ye're mine and I am yers. And we have our dear, bonnie, precious bairns." *Which I miss sae much. But I'll nae feel guilty for this time alone with my dear laddie.* "The past is drenched in blood and terror, aye. But we are here. Now. This bonnie, bonnie day."

He squeezed her hand. "You know the absolute worst part of mortality?"

The question was so unexpected, it caused Moira to burst into gales of laughter. When she finally felt as if she could once again utter something intelligible, she said. "Haggis?"

That got him laughing too. "No! Stop it! Not now!" He laughed some more, then wiped tears from his eyes.

"Eel pie?"

He squeezed her hand hard. "Not now!" He laughed, then said through clenched teeth. "Having to go to the bathroom again!"

Moira put a hand to her mouth, trying to hold in her own mirth. "I'm sae sorry, laddie!" She scanned around the street and spied an alleyway to the left, sporting the proper sign. She pointed. "There."

"Let's go. Quick. All this blasted laughing . . ."

"'Let's go?'" she repeated with a grin—which, of course, made her giggle all the more. *Bathroom humor, lassie? 'Tis beneath yer dignity.* And yet, she giggled.

They left the wide street and walked down a shadowed, narrow alley barely wide enough for the two of them to walk abreast. Public restrooms were located near the halfway point of the lane.

Carl growled. "Most uncivilized thing I've ever heard of. Pay toilets. Every-blasted-where in this . . . *bonnie,* native land of yours."

"Beats liftin' yer skirts behind a hedge. Nae that ye'd have skirts, laddie. Unless 'twere a kilt." She began to giggle again.

"Stop! Just when I finally got a good *mad* on to counter my . . ." Grimacing, he shook his head. "Please, God, when we're resurrected, make it so we don't have to use the dang bathroom anymore!" Carl fished two one-pound coins out of his pocket, paid the lass sitting behind a glassed-in, bulletproof—and most likely soundproof—counter, kissed Moira hurriedly, and hissed, "See you in a minute."

Carl disappeared into the men's side, and Moira turned her grinning face toward the ladies' side. *And I thought 'twas women were supposed tae have the wee bladders!*

When she reemerged, she found Carl—shopping bags, shillelagh, and all—waiting for her.

She smiled at him, but her countenance fell when she saw his face.

His expression was hard, the muscles in his jaw clenched. "Take the bags. Quick."

She complied. She didn't need to ask why.

They started walking back up the sloping alley, Carl on the left, Moira on the right. They did not hold hands. After no more than half a dozen steps, she caught the scent as well—the pungent, sour odor of someone who hadn't bathed or worn deodorant for a long while.

Carl whirled to the left, swinging the stout, Irish cane.

As Moira spun to the right, dropping the shopping bags and her day bag, she heard the crack. Not of breaking blackthorn, but of breaking bones.

And after the crack, came the scream.

Lloyd, still wearing the same blue hoodie, clutched at his broken wrist which bent at an angle nature never intended. He dropped to his knees, on the flagstones. And screamed again.

Carl kicked at something. Moira saw a large, Scottish dagger skittering away, down the alley. The weapon made a clinking sound as it skittered across the flagstones and out of Lloyd's reach.

"You broke me bloody wrist!" He cried out again—a sound somewhere between a scream and a roar.

Carl menacingly raised the Irish weapon again. "I'll break the other one too." His voice was calm, matter-of-fact. He could have been discussing the weather.

"Why, Lloyd?" Moira restrained the urge to drop to the assailant's side to examine the wound. "Why did ye try to kill us? Are ye Brotherhood o' Tobias?"

Tears streamed down the young man's face. He began to laugh, a horrible sound caught between hitching sobs. "Brotherhood? No!" He glared up at them, hatred and pain twisting his face. "You took everything from me!"

"What?" Carl asked.

"You killed her! You killed Lilith!"

And the truth hit Moira like a war hammer to the back of her skull. "Ye were a vampire." *Like us.*

"I was a MASTER!" he spat. "I had the WORLD in my hands. I had a Cult, devoted wives, adoring acolytes—"

"Slaves, ye mean!" Moira spat back, rage suddenly boiling up in her gut like lava. "Ye seduced them and made them yer chattel!"

He faltered, looking from one to the other of them. "They *loved* me! I know they loved me. They *worshipped* me!" His rage gave way to wracking sobs. "Now . . . Now it's all g-gone!"

Carl raised the stout cane as if he intended to crack the skull of the former serial killer. "You murdering . . . waste of oxygen. I should kill you right now."

"Do it! I have nothing left. Kill me! I was going to kill you." He lowered his head. "J-just kill me. Please."

"I should kill you." Carl lowered the shillelagh. "It's the least you deserve for what you've done. But . . . I won't. You have a new life now. A chance to start over. Take it."

Moira knelt beside the sobbing, former vampire. "Let me see that wrist, laddie. I'm a physician."

Lloyd's head snapped up, his face contorted in rage. He struck her with the wounded arm.

Moira easily blocked the clumsy blow with her fist. And she heard again the nauseating sound of breaking bone.

Lloyd howled.

Moira backed away, getting quickly to her feet. "I would've helped ye, laddie. Ye are nae longer our enemy. Once upon a time, aye. But nae longer. Gae yer way. Find peace, if ye can."

Lloyd climbed awkwardly upright, using the alley wall for balance, all the while muttering an unbroken stream of vile and blasphemous curses. He turned as if to go down the alley. Toward the dirk.

But Carl blocked his way, holding the cane at the ready as he had so often held a sword. "Don't even think about it, punk."

The former vampire's gaze flickered between Carl and the dagger.

"Don't ye dare, laddie," Moira said, her voice burdened with a sadness so profound it nearly drove her back to her knees. *There, but for Carl and God . . .*

With a soul-deep wail of utter despair, Lloyd turned and stumbled back up the alley, a lost and damned soul dragging himself unwillingly from the shadow back into the light.

Behind her, Moira could hear Carl retrieving the dirk, but her eyes were riveted on the shambling figure of Lloyd as he departed. A puff of breeze carried the man's foul scent to her nostrils. She wrinkled her nose in distaste.

Heavenly Father, help him. Guide that lost soul back to the light.

But in her heart, Moira had little hope for Lloyd. *God will force no man to repentance.*

Carl placed a hand on her shoulder.

She tilted her head, pressing her hair and cheek against his hand. "The poor lad."

Carl growled, holding up the dirk. "That poor lad just tried to kill us. That poor lad is an unrepentant serial murderer."

At the end of the alley, the unrepentant murderer turned the corner and stumbled out of sight.

"Dinnae forget, laddie, I, myself, murdered seventy-two men before I sought repentance."

"Seventy-two men who either raped you or executed your fiancé. Besides, that was in time of war. It's not the same as what he did."

"And I've told myself as much . . . many, many times, laddie."

"I'm just glad you're safe." He pulled her into his arms. "When you knelt to examine his wrist . . ."

She held him tightly. *'Twas ye, laddie. 'Twas ye he tried tae kill first.* "What else could I do? I'm a doctor. But, 'tis nae his body which is in need of the healin'. 'Tis his soul."

Carl nodded. "We'd better head back to the bus."

"Motor coach," she corrected. "They call it a motor coach. Sounds more dignified."

"They call *us* heroes. You may be a hero—"

"Heroine," she corrected. "I prefer the feminine."

He squeezed fiercely. "So do I. At least, in your case."

They remained that way for a very long minute, savoring life—life after coming so close to death. Again.

"We'd better get going," he reminded her.

She nodded.

As they began to stroll back up the alley, Moira noticed that Carl gripped the shillelagh in a white-knuckled fist—at least until they were back in the clear. Back in the sunlight and the crowds.

Moira searched the crowds of shoppers and tourists for a glimpse of a man in a blue hoodie. But Lloyd had slunk away. "Good thing ye brought the weapon. What did ye do with the dirk?"

"Dropped it in the trashcan."

"Dustbin," she corrected absently.

"I wonder," he said, "how many more Lloyds are out there, lurking in the shadows, seeking their revenge?"

A shudder ripped down Moira's spine.

As they walked, she found herself eyeing every shadow.

Chapter XX

"Lo! A rider cometh, bearing glad tidings. The lord of death bringeth fear. The earth shall tremble. The waters shall stand as a bowl overturned. Love shall give thee breath. The valiant woman shall fall. The queen shall arise."

from the Book of Marcus Scribonius

DCCCXIV *Ab Urbe Condita* (61 A.D.)

"*Repellere equites*!" Marcus roared.

The thundering hoofbeats grew louder even as the earth trembled beneath him.

No time for the Celt spears!

The men of the century, in nigh-autonomous movements born of endless hours of training and drilling, dropped their gear and formed up in a square, covering sides and top with their shields. But as fast as they moved, they could've moved more quickly had they not been so exhausted from the long, hurried march.

But move they did.

Marcus allowed himself the briefest moment of pride.

If we can take the brunt of the cavalry charge, perhaps the villagers will be spared the worst of it.

If *they have the sense to gather behind us.*

Close behind us.

But lacking an interpreter, Marcus had no way to communicate with the villagers.

If only we weren't so cursed weary.

Acting almost as one man, the century each took one of their two *pila* and assembled it, inserting the wooden back shaft into the wooden base of the iron front half. Then each man drove the butt of his spear into the ground, placed his right foot upon it, and angled his spear forward, ready to impale a charging horse. The men of the front ranks well knew that they'd be overrun. The men of the second ranks expected to die as well. And most likely the third. But the hope was the men behind them would survive the charge. And that the villagers might be spared.

The square pilum, though a devilishly ingenious throwing spear, made a poor pike. Though the iron spearhead might pierce a horse, the iron half of the shaft would bend, making the spear woefully ineffective at stopping the charge.

Marcus took his place at the front, left corner of the square. He planted his spear. And he braced.

Let me die bravely, Heavenly Father. Let me hold until the last. Let me save the lives of those behind me.

Save Maelona. Please save Maelona.

A woman appeared at his side. The gray-haired villager, her bloody feet bound up in rags, smiled grimly at him. Then she wordlessly planted her wooden spear—a repurposed garden hoe—in the ground, braced it with her blood-crusted foot, and joined the defense.

In moments, three more villagers had taken up position with them to stop the cavalry charge. A glance behind showed dozens more running to join them.

Marcus nodded his plumed head. *Such courage in the face of certain death.*

"Hold fast!" he cried.

And then he saw the approaching horses—death on thundering hooves.

The horses bore down on them, the earth quaking beneath them. Hundreds of massive warhorses.

But they bore no riders.

The herd veered to the right, splashing through the shallows of a nearby pond, and passing on the right side of the astonished but grateful Romans and villagers.

When finally the ground had ceased to tremble, Romans and Celts alike lifted up a wordless cheer.

Was that all *of them? The entire cavalry worth of mounts?*

A hand slapped his armored shoulder. He turned to see Caeso Lucilius laughing, tears of joy streaming down his face.

"By Mithras!" cried the prooption. "I thought we were all surely dead!"

"You know what this means, don't you?" asked Agrippa Corfidius, raising his pilum in triumph.

"It means," cried Nonus Sestius, "that they've lost their entire cavalry!"

"But how?" asked Spurius Orcivius. "How is it done?"

Marcus shook his head in wonder. "I have no idea." He paused, bowing his plumed head. "No, I *do* know." *Forgive me, Father.* "God has preserved us." *I thank Thee!* "But how?"

"I don't care!" cried Agrippa Corfidius, lifting the standard he'd so hurriedly planted in the ground, so he could wield his own spear. "Never question a gift from the gods! Only give thanks."

Marcus nodded. "Amen."

"Option!" shouted Septimus Scribonius. "A rider! A lone rider!"

A rider?

Marcus peered into the cloud of dust left by the stampeding horses. Indeed—a single rider approached atop a black warhorse.

Marcus saw the red hair bouncing and streaming behind the rider. And he could see that she clung to the beast as if it might throw her off at any moment. As if she were terrified of her own, huge mount.

Septimus asked, "Shall we form up, Option?"

Marcus's face split with a grin. "No."

He dropped his spear and sprinted toward her, all his weariness forgotten.

Even as she reigned her horse to a halt, Marcus swept Maelona from the saddle. He held her in his arms as if she were a child. Indeed, she felt light as a babe. He spun about, laughing, weeping, and babbling her name.

She wrapped her slender arms around his neck. "Put me down, you . . . strong beast!" She wept and laughed as well. "Put me down so I can kiss you!"

Grinning madly, he lowered her to her feet.

She grasped his helm in both her hands and pulled his face down to hers.

And his lips embraced hers.

With one hand, she unbuckled his chinstrap, tore his helmet free, and cast it aside.

But their lips did not part. Not for a long while.

A crowd of legionnaires and villagers crowded around them.

Marcus didn't care.

A chant arose. "Maelona! Audaxus! Maelona! Audaxus!"

Marcus didn't care. At that moment, his entire world consisted of only the woman in his arms.

When at last, Marcus lifted his face from hers, he shook his head. "You're alive!"

She grinned with a ferocity in her eyes that reminded Marcus of a lioness. "Yes, I am alive. And I am here. And you are here. And . . . And . . . And I love you."

He nodded, breathless. "And I love you, but . . . how? The horses? That was your doing?"

She nodded. "And more. I freed the hostages. Most of them, I think."

"You . . . freed the hostages? *And* the horses?"

"Yes, my conqueror." Her grin faltered. "Most of them. I'm sure there are women who are being raped inside the huts. But there were hundreds of women and children in a . . . I don't know the word." She drew a square in the air. "I freed them. Some of them will be recaptured, but the priests of Arawn will be busy trying to . . ." Her eyes opened wide in horror.

"What?" Marcus cried. "What is it?"

"Marcus!" She trembled. "I saw him!"

"Who?" *What was the leader's name? Yes. Conwy.* "You saw Conwy?"

She shook her head, but it appeared little different from the tremors that still ran through her. "No, Marcus. Arawn! I saw Arawn!"

At the mention of Arawn, the chanting began to die away.

Marcus scowled. "Then he's real."

She nodded. "Very real. A-and . . . terrifying."

Marcus released her from his embrace, then grasped her by the shoulders. He examined her in detail. "But you? You are unhurt?"

She nodded. "Pwyll is dead. The priests still have his wife. That is why Pwyll betrayed us—to save her. But . . . I must inform Emrys about Pwyll."

"You don't know?" *How could she not know?*

Surely, she was not bound when Pwyll took her.

She shook her head, but the trembling of her body ceased. "Know what?"

"Emrys is dead. Gwawr as well. Pwyll murdered them."

Maelona seemed about to collapse—only Marcus's strong hands held her upright. "No. No. Pwyll. Foolish man. Murdered." Supporting herself once again, she shook her head. "I did not know. He gave me to drink . . ." She growled in apparent frustration. "I only know our word—henbane."

"*Hyoscyami.*"

Marcus turned his head to see Gaius Publicia, the capsarium.

Gaius Publicia nodded. "I know this herb. Sedative. Very fast acting."

Maelona's face reddened with anger. "And like a fool, I drank it. I trusted him." Through gritted teeth, she said, "Well, Pwyll is dead."

"My lady," said the combat nurse, "are you injured?"

She shook her head, wriggling out of Marcus's grip. She faced the nurse. "No, I am unhurt. Thank you, Capsarium."

Gaius Publicia nodded. "I'm sorry, Princess, to ask this, but I don't have time to be delicate." He grimaced in extreme embarrassment. "I would speak with you alone, but . . . Sometimes, even with a woman of . . . your history . . . Sometimes, after a rape, there is injury that—"

She gaped at him. Then she chuckled. Then she laughed. "No, you wonderful, caring man. I am . . . uninjured." She turned to Marcus. "Not that Conwy did not try. He did. But I stopped him. I slew him."

Marcus gripped her shoulders again, staring at her in a mixture of fear, anger, and wonder. "The chief priest? He attempted to . . . but you . . ."

She grinned, showing white, gleaming teeth. The lioness was back. "I ripped his throat out with my teeth." She chomped her teeth together twice for dramatic effect.

Marcus gasped, recoiling a bit.

Maelona raised her voice, shouting something in Cambrian. Marcus caught only "Conwy."

A collective gasp arose from the Celts.

In moments, hurried whispers rippled through the crowd in Latin and Cambrian. "Tore the high priest's throat out. With her teeth!"

"Marcus Aquillius," she said, her toothy grin widening, "a word of advice—when we are married, you would be wise never to drive me to anger. We have a saying—even a kitten has teeth."

Marcus laughed and shook his head. "You are no kitten, Princess. You are a lioness."

She blinked, frowning. "What is 'lioness'?"

Marcus pulled her to his breastplate, laughing. "A huge female cat, the size of a pony. A man-eater." He looked down into her grinning face. "And I shall take care—*great* care with you. I value your happiness and . . . uh, I value my throat."

She pushed upward and nipped playfully at his exposed neck. Then she winked. "Wise man."

"But Arawn, my lady?" asked Caeso. "You saw him? You saw the god?"

Instantly sobering, Maelona pushed away from Marcus. "Yes, I did. Marcus, I suggest you gather your war council. The enemy knows your battle plan."

Marcus turned to the prooption. "Do it." As Caeso turned and shouted orders, Marcus put his hand on Maelona's arm. "With Emrys and Gwawr gone, you are our only interpreter."

She nodded, then shook her head. "Poor Spurius Aquillius. His only son."

Marcus started. *I've been so intent on Maelona's safety, I have taken no thought to mourn for Emrys, Gwawr,* or *Spurius Aquillius.* "Yes. Poor Spurius Aquillius."

"My lady," said Agrippa, "Arawn—what did he look like?"

Maelona shuddered for a moment. Then she straightened, drawing herself up to her full stature, and though she stood nearly a foot shorter than the men around her, she commanded their rapt attention. "He looked like a man. With a black cloak and hood and a full beard. He floated in the air above his—"

"BYDDWCH YN LLOSGI!"

The voice shook the air. The very ground quaked, trembling as if another, even greater herd of horses were thundering by.

But there were no horses. There was only the figure of a man floating in the air.

Arawn.

The demon floated twenty feet above the road. His face shone from beneath his hood as if he were an angel of light shrouded in black. His eyes glowed like red coals. His hands blazed as if with white-hot fire. His voice was as the roar of a thunderstorm. "MAELONA, TRAWIADOL! CYFREITHIWR NGAST! BYDDWCH YN LLOSGI!"

Marcus stumbled. "Maelona!"

She gripped his hand. "I am here!" And she steadied him.

"What is he saying?"

"He says we will burn. He calls me a whore and a traitor bitch."

Marcus ripped his eyes away from Arawn and onto Maelona. Her face was turned toward the demon, her expression grim and determined. "I think he is angry with me."

Such courage. Then he felt the tremor in her hand.

She's terrified.

Just like me.

Such courage.

"YMOSODWCH AR Y GORESGYNWYR RHUFEINIG A'R CHWISTRELLWR TRAWIADOL!"

Maelona's hand squeezed his. "Now he commands to slay the Roman invaders... and the traitorous whore. I do suppose the command is for the villagers, and not us." She raised her fist to Arawn.

"Ewch yn ôl at eich ogof, ysbryd ffug! Nid ydymyn ofni na chi!"

To Marcus, it seemed as if the demon in the air hesitated. The light of Arawn's blazing countenance flickered.

"What did you say?" Marcus asked.

"I told him to go back to his cave. I called him a little spirit. I said we are not afraid of him."

I know you are afraid, Princess. I am too. But Marcus followed Maelona's example. He shouted, "Crawl back to your hole, demon! Your days of terrorizing this people are over. Go back to your master like the cur you—"

"COME TO ME, YOU SPAWN OF A ROMAN WHORE!" roared the demon in perfect Latin. His countenance burned like the sun. "COME TO ME AND BURN! YOU WILL ALL BURN! ALL YOU ROMAN DOGS! OR YOU MAY LEAVE MY LAND AND LIVE! THE CHOICE IS YOURS!" He pointed at the men of the century. "SLAY YOUR COMMANDER, ROMANS, AND SLAY HIS TRAITOROUS WHORE! LEAVE MY LAND, AND YOU SHALL LIVE! STAY, AND YOU SHALL BURN IN ETERNAL FLAMES!"

"Depart!" Marcus demanded. "You have no power here!"

"NO POWER?" Arawn laughed, and his laughter caused the earth to reel under Marcus's feet. "FEEL BUT A SAMPLING OF MY WRATH!" With that, the demon, pointed at the pond.

The waters of the pond swelled and rose, creating a wall, dozens of feet high.

Cries of terror rent the air.

The wall of water crashed upon them.

Marcus was driven to the ground. But even as he fell, Maelona clung to his hand.

In horror, he realized the waters were still above them, still weighing them down. He could see the sun, the sky above him, but only through the water.

Holding his breath, Marcus got his legs beneath him. He kicked off the ground, trying to force his way to the top, to the air.

But he was too heavy. His armor weighed him down.

Maelona floated above him, still clinging to his hand.

His lungs burning, Marcus wrenched his hand free of hers. Then he shoved her upward—up to the air.

The urge to open his mouth, to breathe was unbearable. But he knew, if he opened his mouth, he would drown.

Maelona!

He could see her. Swimming back down to him. So close.

So close.

Too late.

Just as the air burst from his lungs, she grasped his head in one hand and pinched his nose closed with the other. She clamped her mouth over his.

Her hot breath filled his aching, empty lungs, giving him life, if only for a moment longer.

She pushed away from him again, back toward the surface. Marcus, still held to the ground by the crushing water, shoved her upward once more.

But she was slower that time.

She has no air in her lungs! She's heavier!

But in moments, she was swimming down to him again.

Marcus struggled to remove his breastplate, but his fingers couldn't work the buckles and thongs.

Maelona gripped his head, just as he released his breath. Again, she blew life-giving air into him.

How long can we –

The water around them collapsed.

Marcus and Maelona fell to the soggy earth. They lay there in the mud, doing nothing more than greedily breathing gulps of air.

And clasping hands.

"COME TO ME! COME TO ANNWFYN, ROMAN DOGS! COME AND BURN! OR LEAVE MY LAND AND LIVE!" Arawn's laughter filled the air.

Then it faded away.

Marcus opened his eyes, still breathing heavily—as if breathing and breathing alone were the greatest labor he had ever known. He scanned the skies for Arawn.

The demon had vanished.

Marcus propped himself onto one elbow. He gazed at Maelona. "You . . . You saved me."

She managed a weak smile. "Of course. I love you."

A crowd of drenched Romans and Celts had gathered round Marcus and Maelona. The Celts slipped and fell in the soggy mud. The Romans fared little better in the ankle-deep mud, in spite of their hobnailed caligae.

The patch of sodden earth stretched for a hundred paces in all directions. The pond was slowly filling again as the water sought the lowest spot.

But once Marcus was certain Maelona was out of danger, he

looked to his men and to his larger army.

He sat up and gazed around. He spied Caeso Lucilius making his way awkwardly toward them, through the crowd. He resembled a drunken stork.

Marcus called, "Prooption!"

Caeso nodded his head. "Yes, Option."

"Have the men form up. Count our losses."

Marcus squeezed Maelona's hand. "And you, my beloved, beautiful savior—you must now command the villagers. There is no one else. I'm sorry."

Even as she sat, her bedraggled curls hanging in wet clumps, Maelona held her head high. "Before ever I was a slave or your beloved"—she paused—"savior . . . The word can be used for one who saves another, not just for Christus, yes?"

At Marcus's nod, she continued. "Before that, I was a princess and a warrior. I shall see to my army—my portion of *your* army. I shall command them, but I shall do so under *your* command and in *your* name." She climbed to her feet. Though she was muddy and soggy, she stood as straight as any statue of any goddess of Rome. "I shall have a full count for you as quick as I can. Then I shall report to the war council."

She turned and slogged away, into the crowd, shouting commands in the Cambrian tongue and in a voice that brooked no argument. Celt and Roman alike parted before her. The Celts bowed. So too did several of the legionnaires. Maelona paused in front of an old man—a balding farmer with a fringe of white hair—who yet sat in the mud. She knelt, gave her hand to the old man, and lifted him to his feet. She laid a hand on his bowed head, as if she were bestowing a blessing.

Then she resumed giving orders. Her voice was loud and clear—not angry or harsh. Hers was the voice of a woman who knew how to lead.

Marcus watched with a growing sense of awe as the Celts hastened to gather before Maelona. At her command, they began organizing themselves into rough companies.

She rescued herself. She slew the high priest, armed only with her teeth. She freed the hostages. She scattered the horses of the enemy, utterly destroying their cavalry.

She breathed life into me when I was drowning.

And now she transforms a mob into an army.

And in spite of the mud in her hair and on her face, in spite of her tattered and soaked gown, and in spite of whatever vile things she had been forced to endure before that moment, there was no mistaking Maelona's true nature.

In every sense that truly mattered, Maelona had become a queen.

♠ ♠ ♠

"Her name was Rhiain," Maelona said to the assembled war council—Marcus Aquillius, his officers, and, of course, the princess herself. "She was a weaver. A widow. A grandmother. A mother." She paused. "But she was our only death. Some bruises. No broken bones. Rhiain was the only one to fall."

Marcus knew who the casualty was. He hadn't known the name until that moment, but he'd seen the corpse—the gray-haired, old woman with bleeding feet who'd stood beside him. The brave woman who had faced death, shoulder to shoulder with him, when the horses were charging toward them.

Rhiain.

I shall remember Rhiain forever.

Prooption Caeso Lucilius reported, "We—the century—suffered no casualties. Most were just knocked on their backsides. A few cuts and bruises. The only place the water stood more than waist high was over you, Option, and over the princess. A huge dome of water! But only over the two of you. It was as if the god—"

"He is no god!" Marcus snapped.

Caeso nodded. "As you say. It was as if *Arawn* intended to kill only you and the princess. It was as if he considered the two of you to be the greatest threat."

Marcus's lips drew tight over clenched teeth. "And Arawn—whatever he is—shall know *my* wrath."

Agrippa Corfidius cleared his throat. "With all respect, Option, how can you kill a god?" He held up his hand at Marcus's reproachful glare. "That was no goetia. No *man* can do what Arawn did."

Moses did. So did Joshua. So did Elisha.

But they *did it with the power of God.*

However, this demon . . . Why didn't he finish what he began? Why didn't he kill us? "I don't know how he did it." Marcus shook his head. "And I don't care. God or demon, I will face him. And I will destroy his power."

"But he shook the earth!" said Nonus Sestius. "He commanded the waters!"

Marcus fixed Nonus with smoldering eyes. "And *I* command all of you. I command the greatest, bravest soldiers Rome has ever known." As one, the four junior officers sat a little taller than before. "I heard how some of you fought your way into the water, trying to reach us. *And* how the waters held you back." *But only for a time. How long were we in there? It seemed like forever.*

But it was not forever.

Why didn't he kill us?

"And *you* command *me*," said Maelona. She wore a fresh gown—wet but clean. "And I command the villagers."

Marcus gave her a brief smile. "I want us on the march again as soon as we're done here." The others nodded in agreement, but Marcus could detect weariness in their grim, determined faces. "We strike as quickly as we can, while the enemy is still in disarray. They know of our plan to seize and hold the tor. So we must abandon that. We must come up with a different . . ."

Words formed in his mind.

Fear not for the hostages, for none shall be lost, though thy weary and wet people be allowed an hour's rest. They shall wash their clothes and their tired and bloodied feet. They shall eat and drink. Then shalt thou march to the gate of the demon's realm.

Marcus laughed aloud. He slapped his mud-covered knee. *Why can't they* all *be that clear!*

Ah, forgive me, Father in heaven, for my impudence. But . . . I am grateful for the clarity.

"Option?"

Marcus turned his face toward the voice—toward Caeso Lucilius. Marcus quieted his laughter, but his smile remained.

"Option, are you . . ." Caeso's eyes widened, and his jaw dropped. "It has happened again, hasn't it?"

"A prophecy?" asked Nonus Sestius.

Marcus nodded, grinning.

Agrippa Corfidius asked in a voice filled with awe, "What did your god say?"

"He says—" Marcus began.

"Stop!" commanded Maelona. "Write it down first." She indicated Marcus's furca which stood nearby, poking out of the ground, with his pack dangling from it. She quickly got to her feet. She opened the pack and produced the long wooden box. Somehow, the box and its precious contents had escaped the flood.

Marcus nodded. "Yes."

All waited—with varying degrees of patience and silence—while Marcus recorded the new prophecy.

As he sealed the box once more, he said, "We will rest for an hour.

All—and I do mean *all*—will wash their clothes and their feet. We will eat a light meal and drink our fill—of water or posca."

"What about the hostages?" asked Cornicen Spurius Orcivius. "Don't mistake me—I'll be glad of the respite, but surely some have been recaptured. And there would be women scattered throughout the camp."

Marcus shook his head. "None shall be lost."

Spurius raised an eyebrow. "The prophecy said this?"

Marcus nodded.

Spurius's doubtful expression vanished. "Then it shall be so."

Nonus asked, "And after this respite? What then?"

A savage grin split Marcus's face. "Then we march straight to the cursed Gate of Annwfyn. And we shall write in blood above it the name of Rhiain."

Interlude V

"In a dark tunnel, the swordswoman shall find the penitent, and the swordswoman shall call the penitent by her name."
from the Book of Marcus Scribonius

July 2017 A.D.

Henbane." The frail and elderly tour guide talked so softly, Moira could barely make out every third word.

"What'd he say?" Carl whispered.

"Somethin' 'bout henbane," Moira whispered back. "I'm sorry. I *did* think this'd be a good idea." *A tour of the Poison Garden? Irresistible. Nae just as a physician for m'self, but with Carl's fascination with history. Seemed like 'twould be a "win" all 'round.*

Carl took yet another picture with his phone. "Oh, it was a great idea. And if I can just get the right . . . picture, it'll be worth every penny. Well, every pound."

The right picture? Of what? There's just plants in here. All of them poisonous . . . technically. Though in some cases, 'twould be a bit of a stretch.

Like henbane. Ye'd have tae consume a lot of it for it tae be lethal.

And rhubarb.

Carl looked at the latest photo on his phone, and he grinned impishly. "Got it." He handed the phone to Moira.

On the screen shone a somewhat fuzzy image of the tour guide—or more precisely, the tour guide's ear. Or even more precisely, the *huge* tuft of white hair filling and protruding unabashedly from the old gent's ear canal.

Moira jabbed her husband in the ribs. "Ooh, ye wicked thing, ye!" However, she couldn't suppress a giggle. *Have tae admit, I could barely take my eyes off the old fella's ear hair m'self!*

"Worth every pound," Carl said. Then he assumed a dutifully attentive expression as he appeared to listen to every word uttered by the soft-spoken guide.

The Poison Garden itself was a tiny, fenced-off section of the immense, sprawling, and beautiful Alnwyck Castle Gardens. Moira and Carl had paid an extra fee to take the Poison Tour, which was *not* included in that day's Port Adventure.

As long as my laddie's havin' fun, this bein' our last port of call, it is *a win.*

After the Poison Tour, they exited the Poison Garden with its dangerous—and not so dangerous—plants. They strolled toward a massive fountain at the center of the greater garden. Carl pointed toward the two garden mazes. "Care to get lost in the maze with me?"

She squeezed his hand. "Now that sounds like a lovely endin' to the day." She checked her watch. "We'd better hurry. We've got nae more than half an hour before we need tae head back to the motor coach." *And back tae the ship where that lovely anniversary present awaits ye, laddie! I'm sae very excited!*

Carl sighed. "You know, I wasn't that excited about seeing Alnwyck Castle, especially as our last stop."

"Ye prefer the ancient ruins." She lifted his hand to her lips and kissed the back of it. "Ancient like me."

"Well, my love, you've aged remarkably well. Like a fine wine." He grinned. "Not that I've ever tasted any. You know, when I was a kid, I had to clean up a bunch of spilled wine in a grocery store and it really—" He squeezed her hand, and there was an urgency to his grip.

"What is it, laddie?"

"Don't look just yet, but on our right . . . I think we've got *another* one."

Moira forced a smile. "Not our friend Lloyd again?"

"Not unless he's had a sex change. But . . . Okay, look. Quick."

Moira glanced—casually—to her right.

A tallish woman strolled a dozen yards away and slightly behind them, on a path parallel to theirs. Nothing in the woman's bearing or posture caused alarm. No, it was the woman's clothing that caused the fine hairs on the back of Moira's neck to stand on end.

Jeans and a blue hoodie.

Some kind of uniform, perhaps?

Nae, those clothes are common enough.

Moira turned her face forward again, looking away. "She's dressed the same."

"Yep. The hood's so low . . . can't see much. But she just . . ."

"Gives ye the willies, aye?"

"Uh-huh." Carl tapped his shillelagh on the pavement a little harder. "Maybe I'm just being paranoid."

"Aye. But if so, we're both paranoid. And 'tis nae just our own lives at stake, ye ken. What about our bairns at home?"

"Winnie's been alerted. Lorenzo's there as well. I trust Lorenzo to keep them safe. And we've heard nothing from there to alarm us."

Moira nodded. "We—*ye* and *I* were clearly the targets before. I suspect 'tis we are the targets again. Assumin' she's nae just another tourist."

"Did you see her bag?"

Her bag? Moira looked again and stared longer than she should have. The woman carried a long, wide denim bag over her shoulder and against her hip.

With something long and straight weighting down the bottom.

A sword?

As a sword collector and enthusiast—not to mention a master swordswoman—Moira immediately began considering the possibilities. *Short sword—nae a saber. Could be a hanger or a cutlass. The shillelagh will be useless against the weapon itself. Have to strike for the arm or the wrist, and nae the sword.*

Or it could be a pair o' wine bottles. Or a painting print, rolled up in a cardboard tube.

Or it could be a sword.

"Let's head for the maze," Carl said, interrupting her increasingly dreadful musings. "See if she follows. We'll split up at the first branch. Once we get inside, you take the shillelagh. You'd have a better chance with it than me. Between the pair of us, you're better with a weapon."

Moira nodded quickly. "What 'bout you?"

"I've got the advantage of size and strength."

"I suppose ye've got the right of it."

"Just like old times."

Moira let out a soft growl. "The bad old times." She paused, holding him back from the maze. "Before we enter, take a picture, laddie. Of me—but get her in the background and zoom in."

"Sounds good." He pulled out his phone.

Moira struck a pose. An embarrassingly sexy pose. *Must appear tae be totally oblivious.*

Carl fiddled with the focus and zoom. Then he grimaced. "No dice. She turned away." He shrugged. "Maybe it's nothing."

Let's hope 'tis nothin'.

As they strolled—as casually as possible—toward the closest maze entrance, Moira risked another glance back. "She's still there."

The maze itself consisted of tall, thick bushes whose branches met overhead, forming a ceiling, blocking much of the light. Unlike the garden mazes they'd seen at other castles, this one consisted of dark, leafy tunnels.

At the first shadowed fork in the path, Moira took the shillelagh from Carl, and the two of them parted. Carl went to the left. Moira to the right.

Moira traveled fewer than ten paces before she came to another fork.

She pressed herself against the dense wall of foliage, raised the cane above her shoulder, and waited.

And waited.

She tried to quiet her breathing, but she could not control her thundering heart. Instinctively, she imagined projecting a shroud of darkness around herself.

Daft old ninny. Cannae do that anymore.

She must've gone after Carl.

Please, Heavenly Father. Let me be wrong. Let that nae be a sword in her bag.

And let her come after me.

And then she was there.

Still hooded, the woman stood in the path. Her bag was still slung over her shoulder, and Moira was more convinced than ever that the bag contained a sword.

The woman's hands, however, were empty.

From the shadow of the hood, teeth flashed in a grin. "Hello, Moira." The accent was odd. Or old. "How's your bonnie Carl?"

And with that, the woman turned and slipped away into the darkness.

Moira pursued her, holding the shillelagh at the ready, but the woman had vanished.

And then Carl was looming over Moira, nearly colliding with her. "Did you see her?" he asked, breathing hard as if he'd been sprinting through the tunnels to get to her.

Moira looked wildly about. "Aye. Did ye?"

"No. I heard a voice. I came running."

Moira gripped his hand. "Carl, she knows us. She called me by name. And ye by name as well. And laddie, she *is* carrying a sword."

Chapter XXI

"The spoiled flower shall rise and shall become a she-wolf. And, Lo! Her enemies shall flee before her."

from the Book of Marcus Scribonius

DCCCXIV *Ab Urbe Condita* (61 A.D.)

It is as you predicted, Option." Protesserarius Nonus Sestius said, as the shadows lengthened with the setting of the sun. "The scouts report that the enemy is in complete disarray. They appear to be leaderless. The horse pen and the prisoner enclosure are empty." He turned his face toward Maelona. "Princess, you have dealt them a crippling blow. A devastating blow." He bowed his head in deference. "Your actions will save many lives."

Maelona bowed her head in acknowledgement, but she said nothing.

The war council sat upon the ground, a few paces away from the century. The Romans and the Celts had marched at a more relaxed pace after their hour's rest. And though they were still weary, the respite had revived their spirits and their bodies. The villagers were sitting, more or less, in formations of eighty men or women—as an organized army. As they rested, they were busily preparing torches. The Romans took their rest, but they did so in full armor, ready for combat. Both groups ate a hurried and unheated meal—the Romans of precooked bacon and wheat, mixed with olive oil, the Celts of beef strips from the previous night's dinner. The century drank their rations of posca, and the Celts drank water from a stream.

"Actually," Marcus Aquillius said, "Maelona is a princess no longer. She is a queen now. The villagers have appointed her as their queen—at least for the duration."

Nonus glanced from his commander to Maelona, his eyes wide with wonder. Then he bowed his head once more. "Your Majesty."

Maelona nodded again, but she also waved a hand in casual

dismissal. "I serve by the will of the people and subject to the authority of Rome." She shrugged. "And anyway, it is just for now—until the battle is won and Arawn defeated. After that, I wish only to be the wife of a Roman officer. That"—Marcus opened his mouth to protest, but she smiled and silenced him with a finger to his lips—"and nothing more."

Marcus risked a brief smile of his own, then asked, "What about the hostages—the freed hostages themselves?"

Nonus shrugged. "No sign of them. But they're probably hiding in the woods."

Maelona nodded. "That is what they'd do. So many of them have children to care for. So they will hide and make their way home as best as they can."

Marcus said, "That makes sense." He turned back to Nonus. "What about the Gate of Annwfyn?"

"The same as before," Nonus reported. "A handful of guards under the stone roof, but no more."

"Do they know we are here?" asked Agrippa Corfidius. "Just two miles away?"

"We've captured two scouts," Nonus said. "So my guess is yes."

Caeso Lucilius's jaw dropped in shock. "Your guess? You haven't questioned them?"

Nonus shrugged. "Of course, we questioned them, but they aren't talking."

"And so?" Caeso slammed a fist into his palm. "Question them more forcefully."

"No need," said Marcus. "Once the sun is down, we can find out whatever we need from them."

"Ah." Caeso nodded slowly. "Of course." He shuddered. "*She* will be able to get the truth out of them."

Spurious Orcivius uttered a wordless groan. The cornicen's face was pale in the deepening twilight. "Perhaps, if they knew what was coming, they might prefer torture." He appeared as if he might vomit into the end of his cornu.

Marcus shook his head. "Under torture, a man may tell you what he thinks you want to hear—which may or may not be the truth. I'd rather have the truth. We *need* the truth." He waved a hand at Nonus. "Fetch them. Quickly. Before the last rays of the sun are gone."

Nonus stood, saluted, and shouted orders to a legionnaire.

Marcus turned to Maelona. "Torches?"

"At least one for each of my people," she replied. "My hope is they will have two each. Two will be more effective for what you have in mind, would it not?"

"Perhaps. Perhaps not. Two is better, I suppose. Good work."

She nodded.

He had expected a smile. *Not that I expected her to bask in my approval, but . . . as a leader, as a queen, she is all seriousness. As she should be. As I would be.*

What a woman!

"We found tree"—once again, she appeared to be searching for the proper word—"blood . . . We found tree blood to help them to burn."

Tree blood? Ah. "Tree *sap*. You found tree sap."

She nodded. "Thank you. Tree *sap* will help them burn, but oil would be better."

Agrippa frowned. "Even if we gave up all the olive oil in our rations—"

"It would not be enough," Maelona said, shaking her head. "I know. Tree sap will have to do. Tree sap and . . . We are also using beef . . ." She grimaced and waved a hand impatiently. "The white next to the meat."

Agrippa grinned. "*Fat*. Beef fat. Very clever, Your Majesty."

She nodded at the compliment, but she did not smile. "I hope this plan of yours will work, Marcus. Otherwise, all my people will be dead. Otherwise, we shall *all* be dead. Even if the enemy is in . . . *disarray*, I think was the word . . . they still outnumber us."

Two legionnaires—Marcus Tarquinius and Marcus Vivanius—appeared out of the shadows, leading two men clad in the local garb, the long tunics and breeches of the Cambrian Celts.

Marcus had half expected them to be in black robes. *Maybe after dark, but in the daylight, they'd stick out like a Nubian on the streets of Rome.*

Both men had their wrists bound with leather thongs, but neither looked as if they'd been roughly handled—no obvious bruises. The leather bindings were attached to ropes held by the two Roman guards.

Just as I commanded, Marcus Aquillius thought with some satisfaction. *They may not understand the reasons, but they can always be trusted to obey. God the Father, please preserve these good men under my command. Please preserve . . .*

. . . though the cost be great . . .

Please preserve as many as possible of these brave people who have agreed to follow me.

Rhiain was brave. She was valiant. Accept her unto Thyself. Please have the gospel taught to her.

In the name of Jesus Christus, Amen.

"Now," Marcus said, looking up toward the darkening sky, "we wait for—"

Like an angel cast out from heaven, Branwen dropped to earth in the midst of them. Her white, feathered wings vanished as soon as her feet touched the ground. Her gladius—the sword of Quintus Aquillius—was drawn.

Her lovely face contorted with rage. Her fangs were bared, and drool spilled from her lips. Her green eyes blazed with hatred—every bit of it directed at the Druid scouts.

"Gwneuthurwyr drwg!" she spat. "Rydych chi fi!"

Both men screamed. One fell to his knees, his hands raised as if to ward off a blow. The second man collapsed as well.

The legionnaire guards standing on either side of them, also trembled in obvious terror. But they stood their ground.

"Lady Branwen," Marcus said, keeping his voice level and as soothing as possible, "I need to know what these men know."

She turned her face toward him. Her countenance softened. A little. "And then I may have them?"

Marcus paused. *So much depends on this. Perhaps, victory and survival itself.* "My lady, I have seen that you can force others to do your bidding. Is it possible, that these two can be sent back . . . to give a false report? And make that false report believable? I promise you evil blood aplenty before the night is over, but I need these men to return to their superiors and convince them that we have gathered an army of six thousand, rather than six hundred. Can you do that?"

Branwen shuddered. "You . . . know not what you ask."

"I know it will cost you dearly, that it will be painful." Marcus paused. He looked the terrifying Daughter of Lilith directly in the eyes—eyes strained by rage and agony. "And yet, I *do* ask it. Please, Lady Branwen. Will you do this for us?" *For me?*

She took two deep, rapid breaths. Her wings appeared as if she might fly away. Then the wings vanished. She closed her eyes. Her lips tightened into a thin, bloodless line.

And she nodded.

"Thank you, my lady," Marcus said. "Please, make it credible. Just enough to get the evildoers to believe they are outnumbered."

Branwen's lip trembled. "I will . . . do as you ask." She sheathed her sword, then turned her attention to the first kneeling man. She grasped his head with her white-knuckled hands, tilted his head so his face was toward hers. She shook his head suddenly and violently.

His eyes snapped open. And then his mouth as well.

His mouth went slack. And he smiled. He gazed at Branwen with an expression of unabashed adoration, bordering on worship.

Branwen turned her attention on the second man.

A keening wail of abject terror escaped his lips.

She grasped his head, and his wail rose to a high-pitched scream.

His eyes snapped open.

And then he was lost. Lost in Branwen. Hers to command.

Marcus could not suppress a tremor of fear.

No man is safe. No one.

But she promised me.

And yet . . .

The Daughter of Lilith spoke with the two Druid spies for some time in the Cambrian tongue. Her tone was imperious. Their responses were eager, as if they would move mountains in her name.

At last, she bowed her head. "It is done."

She tore away their leather bindings.

The spies seemed to come to themselves, as if awakening from a trance. They crouched low and looked furtively about, but they seemed utterly oblivious to the presence of the Romans and the Celts around them. One gestured to his fellow.

The other man nodded.

Together, they turned and slunk away.

Romans and Celts parted, allowing them to escape, not wishing to break the enchantment.

Marcus cleared his throat. "My lady?"

Branwen turned her terrifying gaze upon him. Her eyes softened. Pain was still visible in those lovely eyes, but there was also tenderness. And longing. And an unmistakable hunger. "Yes, Marcus? What more do you require of me?"

Thank you, Branwen. With you . . . and the help of the Almighty, I think we might actually win.

Against the Druids.

But how to defeat Arawn?

"Lady Branwen, I ask you to join our council of war. I think you may be the key to victory."

She shook her head. "Even *I* cannot slay three thousand."

Marcus gave her a wolfish grin. "You won't have to."

❦ ❦ ❦

Olwenna tugged at the leather thongs that bound her wrists together. Her wrists were also tethered to a stake driven deep into the ground. Even in the lightless hut, she knew her wrists were slick with her own blood. *Should be able to slip at least one hand free. At least one!* The fetter about her left wrist seemed the loosest. She twisted and pulled, and the leather dug into her torn flesh. The needles of numbness in her fingers emphasized the pain in her wrists. She whimpered like a wounded dog. *So close!*

Sounds of the chaos in the darkness outside the hut served only to heighten her sense of urgency. She could hear the cries of men scurrying about like a bunch of frightened rabbits surrounded by a pack of ravening wolves. "The Romans are coming!" and "The Romans are here!" and "We are surrounded!" mingled with screams of terror. Some of the cries and screams terminated with a horrifying abruptness.

These frightened Olwenna. They terrified her.

But what terrified her even more was the thought that *he* might return.

At any moment, the door might open and the beast who called himself Terrwyn might enter. Terrwyn—the monster who had slaughtered her mother, her father, and her older brother right before her eyes. Terrwyn—the fiendish priest who—with the blood of her family still fresh on his hands—had stolen her maidenhood in front of the entire village, claimed her as his slave, and bound and dragged her away to this evil place.

Almost! She yanked, and her hand slid through the thong, almost to the knuckle. *Once more. Just once more—*

The door opened.

No!

A figure—black against black in its priestly robe—slipped through. The door closed again. The bar dropped into place, securing the door.

Olwenna yanked one last time.

Her hand stuck.

She collapsed, sobbing with despair. *No! No!*

The dark figure scrambled over to her, a huge black spider in the blackness, skittering toward her, breathing loudly and rapidly.

A glint of gold.

Knife!

Olwenna shrieked.

"Quiet, you fool!" Terrwyn whispered, his breath hissing between tightly clenched teeth. Terrwyn—it could only be Terrwyn, he whose very name meant "brave."

Olwenna well knew the stench of the man's breath.

He brought the knife to her wrists and sawed through her bonds.

She raised her numbed hands to strike him.

"Take off your clothes!"

The words caught her off guard, and she froze, mid-swing.

"Quick! Take off your gown!" He put the knife to her throat, the cold, sharp gold trembled against her neck. "Now!"

"I c-c-can't with the kn-nife against—"

He uttered a sound very much like a child's whimper.

Then the knife was gone.

"Hurry!" His whisper had become a whine.

What can he want? Surely not . . . in the middle of a battle? But she stripped off her gown as ordered.

He did not order her to remove her undergarments.

Terrwyn removed his cloak. She could see him more clearly as he removed his tunic and breeches—never letting go of his golden knife, never giving her a clear chance to escape.

As he approached her—naked, save for his smallclothes and boots—she shrank back, looking for a clear path to the door.

He snatched up her gown. And put it on himself. Though he was not a large man, and she was not a particularly slender girl, it was a tight squeeze for him. Olwenna had, after all, seen barely fourteen winters.

He was making sounds—strange sounds Olwenna had never heard from her captor. For a moment, she couldn't recognize them. And then she understood.

Terrwyn was sobbing.

He hacked at his beard, hurriedly shortening it, whining as he did so. He appeared to be making an attempt to scrape his remaining whiskers off with the knife, but only succeeded in cutting himself—the gold couldn't hold the sharp edge needed to shave.

At last, he turned himself around, wiping the tears and blood from his face. Then he scrambled for the door.

But the door burst open, the wooden bar snapping like a dry twig.

The doorway was blocked as if by a black cloud. No light could enter through the door.

Terrwyn screamed.

The black cloud vanished.

A woman stood in the doorway. She seemed to have a faint glow about her. Her green eyes burned in a pale face. Her lips dripped crimson.

In her hand, she carried a Roman sword. Blood dripped from the point of the sword.

"You thought you could escape in a woman's gown?" Her voice was a frightening mixture of honey and fire and contempt. "And look! You tried to shave yourself. Even if you had, you putrid boil on a rat's backside, I could've smelled your evil blood from miles away. You could never escape me, pathetic evildoer."

"P-please!" Terrwyn wailed. "Forg-g-give me!"

The terrible apparition pointed her sword at Olwenna, but the woman kept her eyes on the cringing Druid. "Tell me, you vile monster, is this girl your victim?"

Terrwyn glanced at Olwenna, his eyes large with terror. He shook his head at her.

He's pleading with me . . . to deny it?

Olwenna gathered her courage. "Yes. He murdered my mother, my father, my brother. He raped me. He has raped me many times."

The intruder hissed like a snake. "Do you dare deny this?"

Terrwyn quaked, falling to his knees. "L-lies. I d-did no—"

"Take off her gown, worm. I do not want your blood on her clothes."

He shook his head. "Why?" he blubbered. "You'll k-k-kill m-me anyway!"

The woman grinned malevolently. "Oh, yes, I will. But if you do not soil her gown, I will be quick.

"NO!" He made no move to comply.

However, an acrid smell filled Olwenna's nostrils.

"Very well." The woman turned her face to Olwenna, and Olwenna saw genuine pity there. "I'm sorry, child, but the truth is, he's already soiled it."

With that, she fell upon Terrwyn. She did not use her sword.

She lowered her head to his neck.

Terrwyn's final scream cut off abruptly. In moments, he was moaning . . . in *delight*.

After what felt an eternity—but was probably no more than the time it took Olwenna to draw a dozen rapid breaths—the woman dropped the Druid to the earth.

Terrwyn did not move.

"He's not dead," the woman said, "not yet. But he soon will be.

He's too weak to fight you or to be a danger to you. So take back your clothes. Do *not* take his golden knife. Carrying such a blade tonight would be a fatal mistake. Make your escape as best you can. Do *not* go toward the Gate of Annwfyn."

Olwenna's deliverer bent and put a surprisingly gentle hand on the girl's bare shoulder. "I know you're frightened, but this will all be over soon. Return to your people. Some of them are probably outside." She smiled, licking blood from her lips. "You are brave, child. Not like that wretched coward over there. You *will* survive this."

The woman glanced down at Olwenna's bloody hands. "Give me your hands. Quickly, now."

In spite of her fear, the girl extended her hands.

The woman licked around Olwenna's left wrist.

In moments, Olwenna felt a tingling, pleasant warmth spread from her wrist to her heart and through her whole body.

And then came an itching that became nigh unbearable. However, the itch faded quickly, and only the euphoria remained.

The woman licked around the other wrist.

The pleasant euphoria heightened. "Ooh, that feels . . . Argh! The itch!"

But once again, the itching faded, leaving Olwenna basking in pleasing warmth. "Yes . . ."

"Give yourself a moment, but only until your head clears. Then get dressed and run." The woman paused, licking her own lips again. "If it is of any comfort, you are not with child from that brute."

And with that, the deliverer stood. The cloud of blackness enshrouded her once more. The darkness moved through the night, toward the door.

And then it was gone.

Olwenna's odd feeling of pleasure faded. She felt her wrists in the darkness.

The torn flesh had been made whole once more.

She healed me?

She quickly took back her gown from Terrwyn—the man who had taken everything from her.

She hated him. She hated him with all her heart and soul.

But at that moment, she also felt just the smallest measure of pity for him.

He moaned once. His breathing was quick, labored.

Olwenna put on her clothes.

She gave Terrwyn one last look.

His chest moved no more.

Olwenna glanced at the golden knife—the blade that had killed her family. And Olwenna was tempted—sorely tempted—to take it, to arm herself. So she wouldn't feel so helpless.

. . . a fatal mistake.

Abandoning the Druid knife, Olwenna crept to the door, glanced outside . . . and plunged into the chaos.

"The Romans! Surrounded!" Men in black robes ran in many directions, but most ran in one direction—toward the Gate of Annwfyn.

"Arawn! Protect us!" cried one robed priest. A sword appeared out of the night—out of a patch of darkness blacker than the rest. The blade buried itself into the priest's chest.

He fell without a scream.

The sword appeared again, covered with gore.

Another black-robed figure fell.

Olwenna watched in wonder as the sword continued to appear, seemingly from nowhere, only to thrust through one priest after another and vanish into blackness once more.

A man collided with her, knocking her to the ground. He cursed, then raised his golden knife.

The patch of deeper blackness enveloped him.

He screamed. Briefly.

Then he moaned.

The moaning ceased, and Olwenna heard a terrible ripping sound.

A roundish object flew out of the darkness to land at her feet.

The man's head.

Olwenna fled.

Behind her, she heard shouts and screams.

Then she heard other shouts, other voices—bold and confident.

"Attack! For Queen Maelona and Audaxus! Attack!"

The shouts came from all directions, but every voice—male and female—came from far away. From outside the town.

Fresh cries of alarms rent the air. "Surrounded! The Romans are here!"

"For Queen Maelona and Audaxus! Attack!"

Olwenna ran for the edge of the town.

She saw torches ahead—each separated by ten or more paces. The cries of attack came from the torchbearers.

"Help me!" she cried, nearly out of breath. "I'm Olwenna of—"

A man in Celtic garb, bearing a torch, appeared before her. He beckoned frantically. "You're safe, girl! Come here! You're safe." He opened a welcoming arm. He held a spear, but it was pointed up. His other hand held a torch.

Olwenna threw herself into the stranger's embrace, sobbing.

He held her for just a moment. "You're safe."

"Th-thank you."

"What's your name, child?"

"Olwenna."

"Are you brave, Olwenna? Can you bear a torch?"

She looked up into his face—a kindly face. Gray-bearded, bald-pated, with friendly wrinkles around his eyes. "Y-yes," she said. "I am brave." She drew herself up to her full height—coming barely to his shoulder. "And I can bear a torch."

He gave her a smile. He produced a second torch from his belt, lit it, and handed it to her. "Now, spread out. And shout as I do. Can you do that?"

She nodded, taking the firebrand. "Yes. I can do that."

Olwenna turned around, took several paces to the right, placing herself between the old man and an older woman who stood even farther to the right.

The old woman grinned. "For Queen Maelona and Audaxus! Attack!"

Olwenna looked beyond the torchbearers, looking for the attackers.

And was shocked to see that there were none.

There was no army behind them.

A ruse?

A ruse that has the cursed priests running in terror. In terror, right into the arms of . . . her.

Olwenna raised her torch and shouted, "Attack! Attack! For Queen Maelona and Audaxus! Attack!"

Who are Queen Maelona and Audaxus?

Does it matter?

She took a step forward and cried again, "For Queen Maelona and Audaxus! Attack!"

She grinned like a she-wolf as she saw black-robed figures fleeing before her.

They shouted, "Surrounded! To the Gate! Arawn! Save us!"

She laughed for the first time in a month, for the first time since she was taken, since her family was slaughtered. She laughed fiercely. It didn't matter that she had no weapon other than a torch, for her enemies fled before her.

She saw a sword flash out of the darkness. She saw a Druid fall.

The dead man dropped a short sword. The blade was not of gold.

Olwenna's grin widened. She switched the torch from her left hand to her right, then stooped and took up the fallen sword.

A black-robed man turned toward her.

She thrust the sword into his gut.

His eyes widened. He uttered a strangled, inarticulate cry. Then he fell to the earth.

Olwenna laughed in savage joy. "For Queen Maelona and Audaxus! Attack!"

She marched slowly forward with the other torchbearers—vanguards of a nonexistent army.

And the priests of Arawn fled in horror before her.

Interlude VI

"The penitent shall hear my voice, and my voice shall call her home."

from the Book of Marcus Scribonius

July 2017 A.D.

Carl, we must gae hame!" The instant the stateroom door closed behind them, Moira whirled about, gripping her husband's upper arms. "The Spirit is telling me, laddie. 'Tis sayin', 'Moira, ye must gae hame!' It came tae me as clear as the day, as soon as we got ourselves back on this boat."

Carl dropped the shillelagh and his day bag to the floor of the narrow stateroom entrance. He enfolded her in his strong arms. "That woman really spooked you, didn't she?"

"Aye." Moira put her arms around him, swallowing hard, trembling. "Aye, she did."

"But she didn't threaten you. Or me."

"She has a sword, laddie! I'm certain of it. Why else would she have a sword?"

"Maybe it's just a souvenir. I'm surprised you didn't buy one or two or . . . ten." His voice was soothing, calming . . .

But Moira could feel the tension in his body. *He's frightened too.* "Those blades we saw—I already own ones like 'em—that or they were cr-r-rap. Aye. Mostly, they were stainless steel, decorative crap." She tried not to roll the "R" in the word, but the more agitated she became, the thicker her native brogue became. In two hundred and eighty years, she'd never been able to overcome the quirk.

Carl chuckled. "If 'tis nae Scottish, 'tis cr-r-r-rap!"

Moira squeezed him. "Ooh, laddie, ye are a treasure, Carl Morgan. But"—she groaned—"we must go home!" *The bairns!*

The gentle, but unmistakable rumble of the ship's engines shivered through the deck beneath them.

Carl grimaced and shook his head. "We're already underway."

She pulled back and looked up into his face. "Then we'll hire a helicopter. Have it take us direct to Heathrow."

Carl brushed her red hair back from her face. "Before we take that drastic a step, let's pray about it. Together. Okay?"

Moira took two calming breaths. And then a third. "Aye."

She took him by the hand and led him to the small table and sofa by the large porthole. They knelt, still holding hands, and prayed. Moira was the mouthpiece first, and then Carl.

And they listened for an answer.

And the answer came.

Moira shivered.

Carl did as well.

As one, they opened their eyes.

"I need tae go home."

Carl nodded. "Yes." Then he shook his head. "But not to Utah."

"Nae. Tae Scotland. Tae my old village."

"Where it all began." Carl's words came out as a whisper. "But the kids—they're *not* in danger."

Moira's lips twitched, then settled into a thin line. She shook her head. "Nae, the bairns . . . our precious wee ones . . ." A tear spilled from her eye. And she smiled. "They are safe. But, we . . . the twain o' us . . ."

Carl nodded, a grim smile on his face. "We're the ones in danger." He shook his head, and his grim smile broadened. "Won't be the first time. Or probably the last."

Moira shook her head, then nodded firmly. "But we'll face it taegether. As we have always done. Since first ye came tae me."

He reached out and took her in his arms.

And she melted into his embrace, scooting herself into his lap. They were silent for some time.

She kissed him, softly, tenderly. Then she smiled. "Happy anniversary, laddie."

He grinned. "I love you, Mrs. Morgan." He gestured around the stateroom. "In spite of the danger, I hope you're enjoying you're anniversary present."

Moira gasped. *Anniversary present!*

"What is it?"

She glanced at the bed, then favored him with an impish grin. "I have a present for ye, laddie."

She freed herself from his embrace and got to her feet. She took the two steps to the bed. In the center, along with the white bath towels—folded into the shape of two swans with their beaks touching as if in a kiss—was a long, triangular FedEx box.

She snatched it from the bed. *Craig Foster, ye're a marvel!*

She whirled about, grinning from ear to ear. She placed the box in Carl's hands. "Happy anniversary, my bonnie Carl."

Her breath caught. *Bonnie Carl—the words that woman used in the maze.*

He chuckled, gazing at her instead of at the box. "Your 'bonnie Carl?' You've never called me that."

She waved a hand in impatient dismissal. "Just open it, will ye?"

He grinned, then set about opening the box. As he struggled with the clear packing tape, he said, "What I wouldn't give for a knife right now. A *sgian dubh*. I should've bought one in Inverness."

"Ye know we cannae bring weapons aboard the ship. And besides, we have three—nae, four at home. Besides, those in that shop were all crap." *And I did nae roll the "R"!*

"Got it." He pulled open one triangle-shaped end of the box. He tilted the box. He caught the long, cylindrical object as it slid out.

"A scroll?"

Moira had knelt in front of him. "Aye." *I hope ye like it. I really, really do.* "Open it."

A ribbon at the center of the scroll held it closed. Carl untied the ribbon. He slowly unrolled the gift. "Is this real sheepskin?"

"Aye, 'tis vellum." *Just look at what's on it!*

"Wow. It's beautiful." He paused, looking at the unrolled scroll. "It looks like a . . . genealogy chart, but . . . it's weird. Here's you and me at the top. But it's like it's backwards . . . working backwards. Instead of getting wider as it goes back in time, it just shows two lines. Converging on . . ." He squinted at the bottom of the scroll. "Olaf . . . Bitling, a.k.a. Olav the Red, King of Man and the Isles. Married to Ingibiorg of Orkney. His father was Godfred Crovan, died 1095, King of Dublin and the Isles. What is this? We're—you and I . . . We're *related*?"

"Aye!" Moira was bouncing on her heels. "We're cousins. Very, very *distant* cousins. Ye have tae gae back near a thousand years, before we intersect." She pointed at the scroll. "See, here's the Morgan line—yer line—and here's the MacDonald line—mine. O' course, mine is a wee bit shorter than yers. And we're of royal blood. Nae that such matters, but . . . do ye like it?"

He tore his gaze from the scroll to gaze upon her, his eyes wide in wonder. "It's amazing! You did this?"

She shook her head, grinning. "Nae. 'Twas my friend, Craig Foster. The genealogist. The one who works for the Church. But . . . 'twas my idea. I commissioned it."

"It's beautiful. It's amazing! I . . . I don't know what to say."

She bit her lower lip and winked. "Ye dinnae have tae say a thing. Just kiss me, laddie, and then perhaps ye can—"

The phone rang—the stateroom phone that hadn't rung once during their entire cruise.

Moira squeaked.

The phone continued to ring.

Carl grimaced. He began to roll up the scroll.

Still on her knees, Moira scrambled for the phone. She hit the "Speaker" button. "Hello?"

"Moira Morgan?" A woman's voice.

"Aye."

"And this is her husband, Carl Morgan," Carl said, jumping in—to protect his wife. "How can we help you?"

"The Unwilling too," said the voice. "Excellent. The three of us together. On the same ship. At last."

Moira recognized the voice, with its odd, unplaceable accent. *She called Carl the Unwilling.* Fear seized Moira's gut like a claw of ice.

"Moira," the woman continued, "as I'm sure you've guessed, you and I met in the maze at Alnwyck Castle Gardens. Finally, the circle is closing."

And the claw twisted.

Chapter XXII

"Assemble at the broken gate. Ten swords shall slay ten. And, lo! Thousands shall stumble and fall."

from the Book of Marcus Scribonius

DCCCXIV *Ab Urbe Condita* (61 A.D.)

"*Cuneum formate*!" commanded Option Marcus Aquillius Audaxus, and the men of the century lined up behind him in a *cuneus*—the wedge or "V" formation. Marcus stood at the front—the point of the wedge. The junior officers took their places inside, at the back of the wedge. Vexillarius Agrippa Corfidius held aloft the tall standard of the legion. Cornicen Spurius Orcivius bore his battle horn.

Queen Maelona, having set her troops to their task, refused to leave Marcus, even though she could not stand at his side. And so, captured Celtic sword in one hand and Roman dagger in the other, she stood in the center of the Roman junior officers. Protesserarius Nonus Sestius and Prooption Caeso Lucilius stood on either side of her. Privately, Marcus had charged the two of them to protect Maelona at all hazards.

Fully assembled, the legionnaires raised their shields and their swords.

"Forward!" Marcus cried. And the century marched forward into the night.

The line of Celt torchbearers parted for the Romans, then closed behind them once again. Cries of "Ar gyfer y frenhines Maelona ac Audaxus! Ymosodwch!" echoed through the night, along with shouts and screams of terrified and dying priests.

The tactic—which Marcus had borrowed in part from an ancient Hebrew war leader name Gideon—worked, at least thus far. The priests of Arawn appeared to believe they were outnumbered and encircled by an army twice their size.

And Branwen sowed terror among them as well as reaped a

harvest of death and "evil blood."

In spite of the enemy's terror, a ragged but dense line of priests formed in front of the Romans. The priests wielded swords and spears. And they stood between the century and their goal—the Gate of Annwfyn.

Marcus called for a halt. Then he shouted, "Iacite pila!"

As one, the men sheathed their swords. They each assembled one of their two spears and hurled it toward the enemy.

And were rewarded by dozens of screams.

"Iacite pila!" Marcus cried again.

The century assembled and hurled their second and final volley.

More screams.

Then as one, the Romans drew their swords again, pointing their weapons forward.

Marcus called, "Charge!"

Spurius Orcivius echoed the command on his cornu.

And the Romans charged.

Marcus, in the lead, chose his man out of the mob of black-robed priests—a large man with a lethal spear.

Marcus ran straight at him.

Marcus met his opponent's spear, deflecting it with his shield. With the next step, Marcus thrust his gladius into the man's gut—into and up. *Just as Quintus Aquillius did to me.*

He withdrew his blade, letting the dying man fall, and pushed forward to meet the next opponent. That priest likewise fell before the speed and skill of the Roman commander.

By the time Marcus broke through the enemy's disordered ranks, he had counted twenty-seven priests dead by his sword. Though his way forward was unobstructed, he resisted the urge to quicken his pace. Behind him, his men continued to stab and thrust their way through, as the wedge sliced into the enemy forces. Marcus was past the enemy line, but he needed to stay with his men—they needed to move forward as a unit.

Fight as one. Always as one.

As he continued to march, leading his men, he saw it—the great stone table.

Set against a steep hillside, the table gleamed dully in the starlight—four standing stones, each slightly taller than a man, and atop them, a flat slab of stone. Marcus couldn't see it, but he knew that at the back of the table, he would find a crack in the rock face of the hillside—a cave mouth, leading into the Underworld.

The Gate of Annwfyn. The lair of the death lord.

Under the table, stood four priests, each wielding a spear.

Only four. Why so few?

Behind him, the sounds of combat ceased.

We're through!

"Charge!" he roared.

Without breaking the cuneus formation, the century ran up the hillside. All the fatigue of the day's hard march was forgotten as they charged toward their objective.

Marcus dared not risk a glance behind. He knew the enemy would pursue. But in the wedge formation, the commander led, and it was the prooption's duty to watch behind. Marcus placed full faith in Caeso Lucilius. As he always did.

The four guards under the stone table were turned toward them, their spears at the ready.

Surely, they know they have no chance. Run, you fools!

One of the guards tossed his spear. It fell woefully short of the Romans, embedding itself in the steep hillside.

The spear hurler turned and fled into the night.

Marcus saw a cloud of darkness—blacker than the night—enshroud the man. Marcus heard a scream.

Branwen.

The other three guards stood their ground. They shouted in the Cambrian tongue. Marcus caught Arawn's name in those cries.

Religious fanatics. Very well. Die for your evil god.

Three shall attempt to lure thee under the stone. Go not under the stone.

The words of the new prophecy burned in his mind.

"Halt!" he cried, and the century obeyed. Marcus stood barely two paces out of the reach of the three remaining spears—and clear of the stone table.

The three guards shouted at him, thrusting their spears vainly in his direction. But they did not abandon their post.

Suddenly, Branwen was there, under the stone table. She moved so quickly, Marcus could barely follow her actions. Three times she thrust with her sword.

The guards had no time to react. Three screams. Three men fell.

"Branwen!" Marcus shouted. "No! Get back!"

She turned to him, her eyes blazing. But she did not move.

CRACK! CRACK! CRACK! CRACK!

The four pillars of the table shattered.

The table fell.

Right on top of the Daughter of Lilith. Crushing her.

"No!" Marcus ran forward. In madness and grief, he dropped his sword and shield, attempting to shift the massive stone, to get to her. "Help me!" he cried.

The Romans crowded around the massive stone. "As one!" Marcus cried. "Now!"

They heaved.

"Again!"

They heaved. But of course, the massive stone did not move.

"Again!" Marcus cried. He was weeping, but he did not care.

The Romans strove once more to move the stone. But it refused to move.

"Again!" But even as he said the word, he knew they could not save her.

Suddenly, the stone shifted. Rising slightly.

A cheer went up from the men.

"Again, men!" Marcus cried. "Put your backs—"

The huge stone rose into the air—into the air and out of their grasp. It rose above their heads. They stepped back, gaping in awe and horror.

Branwen stood under the stone, holding it up.

She stood on one leg, the other leg was broken, mangled. She lifted with one arm. The other, like her broken leg, was shattered. One side of her face was crushed, her torso misshapen. And she was covered in blood.

With a strangled, gurgling scream, she heaved the massive stone.

The slab flew a few paces and landed, a third of it sinking into the ground.

Marcus stared first at the stone, and then at Branwen. He called her name and took a step toward her.

She extended her good hand, waving him back. "A moment . . . more . . ." she croaked. She wept and cried out as her broken limbs straightened and became whole once more. Her body and face filled out as they also healed.

As soon as her broken form was restored, she let out an agonized scream. She dropped to her knees, her breathing labored, rapid, and irregular.

"Branwen!" Marcus knelt at her side, his knee resting atop the smashed corpse of a priest. Marcus put his arms around her, and he held her close, as she wept and trembled.

With a sob, she put her arms around him.

So much damage. Such agony. And yet, she survives. "Are you still in pain?"

She buried her face in his armored shoulder and shook her head. "I am . . . Healed."

Marcus looked up to see Maelona kneeling beside them. She held the hilt of Branwen's sword in one hand. The blade had snapped off a hand's breadth below the hilt. "Your sword, my sister. I am sorry." In her other hand, Maelona extended her own captured sword, hilt first. "Please, take mine."

Branwen lifted her head and gazed at Maelona. Tears carved rivulets in the blood on her face. "But what will you use?" Nevertheless, Branwen extended her hand and took the sword.

Maelona smiled fiercely. "I have my dagger."

Branwen returned the smile, but there was a profound sadness in her eyes. She pulled herself out of Marcus's embrace. "Thank you, sister, for allowing him to comfort me. I am recovered now. He is . . . yours."

Marcus let go of Branwen—with a degree of reluctance that surprised him. He desired to comfort her after her ordeal. He pitied her. *Beware of pity . . .* But he knew in his heart, his feelings for the Daughter of Lilith had grown beyond mere pity. He turned his gaze to Maelona, and their eyes locked. *I love you.*

I cannot deny I feel something for Branwen as well.

But my love for you is stronger. And so is my promise.

To his surprise, Maelona smiled at him and nodded.

As if she knows the very thoughts of my heart.

He shook himself out of his reverie. "The battle is . . . not yet over." He turned his eyes to the cave mouth—a wide fissure in the side of the hill, like the blacker maw of a black beast, ready to consume them all. "Lady Branwen, I think you should now make your stand here."

She nodded, her eyes avoiding his own. "As you wish."

"I ask you to guard the mouth of the cave." He suppressed a shudder. "To warn us should someone . . . or something emerge from the cave."

Branwen nodded once more. She stood, holding the sword Maelona had given her. "I will guard you." She turned toward the cave entrance. "To my last breath."

"Thank you, my lady. None of this would have been possible without your aid."

Branwen said nothing. She merely turned her back on him and faced toward the entrance to the Underworld.

Remembering another promise he'd made that day, Marcus knelt. He cut a strip of black, gore-soaked robe from the crushed body of one of the guards—a willing sacrifice to the man's evil god. Marcus turned to the cave entrance. Using the cloth as a crude brush, he quickly wrote in large letters on the face of the stone—

RHIAIN

Marcus dropped the bloody scrap of robe and turned back to the battle. "*Testudinem formate*!"

The century arranged themselves into the testudo formation. And just as they had discussed in their war council, the Romans positioned themselves to defend the opening in the hillside. They assembled themselves into a rectangle—ten wide, by eight deep. The spot they occupied was level, except for the broken pillars that had once held the table. However, a pace ahead of the century's front line, the ground sloped steeply downward.

Marcus took his place at the back of the testudo formation, raising his plumed head above the raised shields. He turned his back on the gate to the Underworld. *Anything could come out of there. Anything.*

Arawn tried to lure us under the table. He brought it down. To kill us.

It nearly killed Branwen.

He *nearly killed Branwen.*

Silently, Maelona took her place at Marcus's side.

The priests—those who had not fled . . . or been slain—had gathered into a dark mass of men, swirling at the foot of the hill. They shouted, cursed, wailed in terror . . . but they did not advance toward the Gate.

So many have fled or been killed.

And yet, at least two thousand remain.

The ring of torches was closing in on them. From the distance, Marcus could hear the cries of "Ar gyfer y frenhines Maelona ac Audaxus! Ymosodwch!"

Soon, the enemy would discover the ruse. Soon, they would know that, in spite of their huge losses, the priests of Arawn still outnumbered their foes. And most of their foes were farmers—old men and women, untrained in battle. And exhausted from a grueling forty-mile march.

We're running out of time.

But we hold the high ground. More importantly, we hold a spot that is sacred *to the enemy.*

"I need you to translate for me," Marcus said. "Translate *loudly*."

Maelona nodded. "I can do that. I can raise my voice for you."

"I know. You were a Mona Witch."

"Yes, I was." She chuckled softly. "Perhaps, I still can be."

"Let's pray this works." *Father in heaven, please give us the victory this night. In Christus's name. Amen.* Marcus saw that Maelona's lips also moved as if in silent prayer.

When her lips ceased to move, she looked at him and nodded. "I am ready."

Marcus raised his voice. "Slaves of Arawn!"

Maelona translated, raising her voice as well. "Caethweision Arawn!" And her shrill voice carried very well indeed.

The mob of robed men stopped their cries, turning toward the Romans. The priests' bearded faces were pale in the starlight.

Good. We have their attention. "Your god has abandoned you!"

"Mae dy dduw wedi'ch gadael chi!"

"He cannot defend his own temple!"

"Ni all amddiffyn ei deml ei hun!"

"You are surrounded! You cannot escape!"

"Rydych chi wedi'ch amgylchynu! Ni allwch ddianc!" Maelona added a loud shriek at the end.

Marcus flinched at the unnerving sound. *Just like at Mona.*

Cries of dismay and fear rose from the enemy.

Marcus continued, and Maelona continued to translate—along with the occasional ear-piercing, nerve-shattering shriek.

"You have called upon your god, and he has not answered you. We hold the Gate of Annwfyn! We will desecrate your temple! And I will slay your powerless, impotent god! The mothers and the fathers, the sisters and the brothers, even the grandfathers and the grandmothers of those you abducted, those you murdered, those you raped . . . They surround you. They are coming to kill you. To tear you limb from limb. There are thousands of them. But there are only eighty of us. Perhaps, if you retake the gate, you can hide in the cave."

He paused a moment to let that idea take hold.

"You call yourselves holy men. But I say you are beasts! You murder the helpless and the innocent to feed your evil god. You steal women and virgins and you murder their families, because no woman will have you. You are not men. You are vermin! And like vermin, your only chance of survival is to hide in a cave. And the only way to get to that cave is through us—Queen Maelona and Audaxus of Rome! So, rats? Will it be the army of your victims? Or eighty men and then Annwfyn?"

Marcus held his breath. *Will they take the bait?*

Victory itself depends on this.

Survival depends on this.

"Ar gyfer y frenhines Maelona ac Audaxus! Ymosodwch!" The battle cry came from all sides.

But the priests made no move.

"Ni fyddwch yn ymladd!" Maelona cried. "Nid dynion ydych chi. Nid oes gan ddynion go iawn feddyliau mor fach!"

This brought a chorus of angry shouts from the mob.

Marcus glanced at her. "What did you say?"

A few of the priests started up the hill toward them. Several more followed. And then, all of them were charging up the hill toward the Romans.

Maelona grinned, and there was a wicked gleam in her eyes. "I said they were not real men. I said they all had . . ." She paused, and her lips tightened into a scowl. "I do not know the word in Latin. I should. You would think I would know that word." She growled. "I said they all had tiny man . . . parts."

Marcus laughed. "*That* made them angry?"

Maelona nodded. The wicked grin returned. "It would seem so."

"Cornicen!" Marcus cried. "Sound the signal!"

Spurius Orcivius blew four long blasts on his curved horn.

The torches born by the villagers suddenly went out. The battle cries of the phantom army ceased. Darkness enshrouded the battleground, and an eerie silence smothered the priests of Arawn, like a wet blanket over a campfire.

Yet, the first wave of priests was almost upon the Romans.

"Testudo!" Marcus bellowed.

Spurius Orcivius echoed the command on his horn.

The century stiffened their left arms, bearing their shields, and their right arms, each bracing the man in front. The front rank held their swords ready.

The only sound to be heard was the labored breathing of the priests as they toiled up the hill.

The first wave of priests struck the shield wall.

"Thrust swords!" shouted Marcus.

As one, the men of the front line parted their shields slightly, stabbed blindly at the enemy, then quickly resealed the wall.

Each Roman sword found its mark. Ten black-robed men screamed and fell—downhill.

The dying priests tumbled backward—into the men behind them. This toppled even more of the enemy. And those who fell, collided with the priests behind them.

The effect cascaded down the hill, widening and multiplying, like an avalanche of stones. Here and there a man managed to retain his feet, but the rest fell. By tens. By hundreds.

It worked. Thank God in heaven. It worked!

"Shields and swords!" Marcus commanded.

The men holding shields above their heads, lowered the shields and drew their swords.

"Advance!" Marcus commanded.

The Romans marched forward and down the slope of the hill. They advanced slowly, careful to not trip over the fallen priests. Each man stabbed at the enemy, as the priests struggled to regain their feet. The Romans kept their shields low—a gold dagger in the leg or foot might be crippling or lethal.

And so, they moved slowly downward, gradually widening their lines, dealing death to the enemy.

And the priests of Arawn died. By tens. By hundreds.

Those who attempted to flee—some of them discarding their black robes—found themselves surrounded by a line of villagers—men and women, many of them gray-haired, wielding spears and axes and scythes—sometimes, no more than a club or a knife. The villagers fell upon the fleeing cowards with ferocity and courage.

One young woman, wielding a captured sword, cried, "For my father and my mother. For my brother!" She stabbed and hacked at the enemy. She had no skill, no prodigious strength—only a righteous anger. And the enemy fell before her.

In the end, it was not a battle—it was a slaughter.

The Roman century and the ragged army of Queen Maelona soon found themselves standing on a hillside awash in black-robed corpses and dark blood.

As the victors searched among the fallen—to succor a wounded comrade or to deal a final blow to an enemy—Marcus found his beloved Maelona.

She stood with Caeso and Nonus on either side of her. Marcus gave the two bodyguards a gentle wave, dismissing them. They nodded in understanding, then turned to attend to their duties.

Maelona's hand and her dagger were dark with gore, but her smile gleamed in the starlight, and her eyes shone like emeralds.

They embraced—as best they could without either of them lowering their weapons.

"You are unhurt?" she asked, her face pressed against his segmented breastplate.

"I am unscathed. And you, my dear, sweet queen?"

"I am also well." She lifted her head and grinned. "Or I will be as soon as you kiss me."

He laughed. He dropped his shield, bent his head, and kissed her.

They did not linger over the kiss, however.

"We did it," Marcus said, lifting his head and scanning the hillside. A few torches had been recovered and relit, illuminating the carnage. "It worked. Against all chance, it worked."

"Yes, Marcus. It worked. But there was no chance involved. With God the Father's help, it worked. Just as you prophesied."

"Yes." He grinned at Maelona's words of faith. "With God's help. And Branwen's."

"Yes, with Branwen's help." She pressed herself closer against his armor.

Are you grateful, my love? Or possessive?

Or both?

He gently extricated himself from her arms. "But the battle is not finished. I fear what we just did . . . That may have been the easy part."

She nodded. "There is still the demon."

He turned and gazed up the hillside, toward the Gate of Annwfyn.

The cave mouth and the broken stone table stood silent. Unguarded.

Unguarded?

Branwen was nowhere to be seen.

Terror gripped Marcus. "Branwen!" he cried.

Maelona called Branwen's name as well.

Marcus shouted all the louder.

But Branwen did not answer.

Marcus retrieved his shield. He scanned the night skies for her winged form.

But she was not in the sky.

Marcus charged up the hill, sword and shield in hand.

When he reached the black cave entrance, he saw no sign of her. He shouted her name into the Gate of Annwfyn.

The earth seemed to swallow the sound of his voice.

Branwen did not answer.

He called her name again. And again, she did not answer.

But out of the cave issued a deep voice like an echo, cold as the tomb and filled with loathing—an absolute hatred of all living things. "I have her, Christian. I have your precious Daughter of Lilith. She is mine. Come to me, Roman. Come to me, or she dies. Come to me, and you will die."

Maelona appeared at Marcus's side. She held a lit torch in one hand and her Roman dagger in the other. "Let us enter then. And save Branwen."

Marcus struggled to keep his knees from trembling, as fear seized and twisted his innards. He gripped his sword and shield more tightly, in spite of the sweat and blood that slicked his hands. *What good is a sword or a shield against a demon? But I have no other weapons. I have no priesthood. All I have are these.*

But that was the plan all along, wasn't it? To enter Annwfyn and face Arawn? And Maelona is supposed to stand with me. But why? Why must she go into this horrible place?

I love her, Father. She is precious to me. I cannot take her into darkness, into death. He shook his head. "No, my love. You are staying here. Where it is safe."

She shook her head in defiance. "No! I will not. The prophecy says we must face Arawn together. And together it shall be. I am a free woman. For the moment, I am a queen. I shall do as I choose. As I think best."

Caeso Lucilius trotted up, sword and shield in hand. "I'm coming with you!"

Marcus turned to his prooption. "No, my friend. You are in command here until I return." *If I return. If* we *return.* "I must do this . . . The queen and I must face it alone."

Caeso growled through gritted teeth. "Prophecy?"

Marcus nodded, slowly and decisively. "Prophecy."

The prooption laid a hand on Marcus's shoulder. "And does this prophecy say you will come back? Alive?"

Marcus shrugged. "In all truth, I don't know. But I will go."

"Very well then." Caeso stood taller. He saluted his commander. "Audaxus!" A tear slid down Caeso's cheek. "You are the bravest man I have ever known." He nodded his head to Maelona. "And you, my lady. You have surprised us all."

Marcus returned the salute, fist—with sword gripped tightly—to chest. "Prooption. May God be with you. With all of you."

The prophecy said the cost would be great. "When I return, I want a casualty report. Of *all* our forces."

Caeso nodded. "As you command. You said, '*When* I return.' *When*, not *if*." He managed a small grin. "I'm going to hold you to that, Option."

"Do not worry, Caeso Lucilius," Maelona said, "I will protect him."

Caeso's smile grew. "And I'm going to hold *you* to *that,* Your Majesty." His smile vanished. "May your god go with you. May Christus guard you. I'm going to pray to Him for you."

It was Marcus's turn to wipe away a tear. "Thank you."

The deep voice echoed from the cave again. "Come quickly, Christian. Come quickly, or she dies."

I'm coming, Branwen. We're *coming.*

Arawn said, "Come to me. Come to me and die."

Marcus and Maelona locked eyes for a moment. Marcus tried to think of something to say, but words failed him.

Maelona said, "Together."

Marcus nodded. "Together."

With that, Option Marcus Aquillius Audaxus and Queen Maelona stepped into the darkness.

Into Annwfyn.

And the darkness swallowed them.

Chapter XXIII

"Sword shall pierce her flesh again and again, and though her suffering shall be great, she shall endure. In fire and stone shall she make her offering."

from the Book of Marcus Scribonius

Five hundred paces.

That was what the spies told them while under Branwen's control.

Five hundred paces until we reach Annwfyn.

The tunnel slanted gradually downward in a gentle slope as it wound its way into the earth. The walls, ceiling, and floor were rough and uneven, and Marcus and Maelona were forced to go slowly as they descended. *At least it's wide enough for us to walk abreast. Barely.*

Marcus held his sword and shield at the ready. He knew they'd be useless against a demon. *But we don't know what else might be down here.*

Maelona bore the torch and her dagger. The light from her torch illuminated their way, at least until the next bend in the tunnel. Initially, the walls were coated with moss, but that covering thinned and disappeared altogether by the time they went ten paces. After that, the walls were dry and bare.

Lifeless. Fitting for the realm of the dead.

Stop that! This is not *the realm of the dead.*

Arawn is not *a god – not of the dead or anything else. He's a demon – a fallen, premortal spirit.*

The walls . . . so close. So dark. So small.

Stop that! Think of something else. Think of the battle to come.

But I don't know how to fight him.

What do *I know about him?*

He can cause the earth to quake. He can move water . . . but only for a short time.

Will there be water down there?

More than anything else, Marcus feared what he did not know, the uncertainty of what they would find.

Arawn hasn't even been here very long. He can't have been. Otherwise, his army would have stripped this whole country bare of children and women.

Babies. They were sacrificing babies *to him. Burning them alive.*

And that horrid idol.

Just like Moloch in ancient Israel.

No. Arawn's presence here is recent.

But this tunnel . . . It is not *recent.*

Why would anyone tunnel down here?

The answer soon became apparent as tiny flecks of gold reflected back the torchlight, shining like tiny, golden stars in the darkness. Here and there, the stone had been chipped away in long, irregular lines.

"A mine shaft," Marcus whispered. "They mined gold here—followed the gold downward. Perhaps, that's how they found the cave. It has to be a cave down—"

A ghostly moaning interrupted him.

He froze. "Did you hear that?"

The moaning turned to a high-pitched, keening wail. Marcus glanced at Maelona.

Her eyes were wide with terror, her face dripping with sweat.

And the horrible sound was coming from her trembling lips.

"What is it?" Marcus wanted to hold her, but he dared not drop his weapons.

"I'm s-sorry." Her breathing was too rapid. "The darkness. The . . . tunnel."

The torch in her hand shook.

If she drops that, we'll have no light.

Must calm her. Now. "Are you frightened of the dark?"

She nodded. And the torch nearly did fall.

Marcus dropped his shield and grasped the firebrand, just above Maelona's quivering hand. "You must not drop the torch, my love."

She nodded, swallowing visibly. Then her hand steadied. "I will not drop it. I will . . . do better."

"If you are frightened of the darkness, why did you come?"

She shivered, but her eyes fixed on his without flinching. "You are brave. You are Audaxus. I can be brave too."

He gave her a smile—he hoped it was a reassuring smile. "You have already been brave. So very brave."

"A-and the prophecy says I must come with you." Her already rapid breathing sped up. "I'm just s-so scared. But I *can* face this. I can. I will."

"If it helps, my love, I'm scared too. I'm scared all the time."

She nodded, and the ghost of a smile played at the corner of her lips as she slowed her breathing. "And that is why you are so brave, because you do not allow your fear to stop you. That is why I love you. That is why *she* loves you." She took a deep, shuddering breath, and stood a little taller. "I am ready now."

Marcus shook his head in awe. *Amazing woman.*

He picked up his shield, and they continued down the tunnel. "As soon as we get back to the legion" – *if we get back to the legion* – "I will ask the legate for permission to marry you."

"Then we must hurry and defeat the demon and rescue Branwen and get back to the legion."

Marcus chuckled softly. *Amazing woman.* "Up above . . . You and Branwen—you called each other 'sister.'"

"Yes. We are bound together."

"Bound together?"

"We both love you."

Marcus took the length of two paces to mull that over. "But I can marry only one of you. And I shall marry you." He risked a glance at her.

She was smiling—a secret, feminine smile. "Yes. I know. But she will watch over you from afar. Her love will allow her to do no less. But she will stay away. She will remain alone. And she says she will not marry another. Ever."

Alone? Forever alone? Tears filled Marcus's eyes. His hands were full—he could not dash the tears away, as they spilled from his eyes and down his cheeks.

"You weep for her," Maelona said, "for her sacrifice."

He nodded.

"It is no shame for you to weep. I have seen it. Roman men see no shame in weeping."

He nodded. "But it is a shame among your people?"

She shrugged. "For men . . . sometimes. Not for women."

"But it is a shame for me to weep for *another* woman."

She smiled again. "You love her. I know this. But you are a man who keeps his promises. That is another reason why I love you. It is the same for her. Do not be ashamed of your love for her . . . or her love for you. It is"—she paused, apparently searching for a word—

"honorable, noble, brave, because you keep your promises. It is valiant, Audaxus. And it is valiant and honorable and noble of her to keep her promises as well, though it will be very painful for her. God the Father will reward her for this. I know it. She has read it in the prophecies."

"I love you, Maelona."

"And you will be true to me. I also know this. It is in the prophecies."

"How do you know all this? You can't read."

"No, I cannot. You promised to teach me. But Branwen has read them all. She told me so. And she has promised to stay away from you. So you will not burn for her. And so she will burn a little *less* for you. We have talked. And we have agreed—you are mine. Forever." She paused. "But we must save her first. And conquer the demon."

Marcus had observed that, as long as Maelona was whispering, her fear seemed to diminish. *No, it's more than that. It's her concern for Branwen. Concern for her rival. It's selfless.*

It's Christlike love.

Amazing, magnificent woman.

She frowned. "Shouldn't we be silent?"

Marcus shrugged. "It makes no difference. Arawn knows we're coming. This is the only entrance. It's not as if we could sneak in unannounced."

"How far have we gone?" The torch in Maelona's hand wobbled again, then steadied once more. "Five hundred paces. Have we gone that far? Surely, we must be getting close. But closer means closer to Arawn as well." She shivered. "Marcus, I'm sorry. When the time comes, I will be brave."

You are brave now. "Three hundred and seventy-nine."

She glanced at him in wonder. Then she nodded. "Ah, yes. I remember—part of the duties of an option—to count the paces." She paused. "Perhaps we should go more quickly. But the floor is so . . . I do not know the word."

"Uneven."

She nodded. "Uneven."

"I'm worried about Branwen too," Marcus said, "but we will do her no good if we fall and break our necks or fall on our weapons. Or drop the torch."

"Why does the demon not say something?"

"Perhaps he wants us to be afraid of the darkness and the tunnel."

Maelona drew in a huge lungful of air and shouted, "We are not afraid of you, demon! We do not fear the dark!" Her voice trembled only slightly.

Marcus glanced at her face. Her lips were drawn into a thin smile. *Proud of herself. Pretending to have no fear.*

Just as I pretend. All the time.

"Why does he want us to come?" Maelona asked. "Why not just kill us? He tried to before—with the water."

"I think"—Marcus lowered his voice until it was barely audible—"he wants revenge. We have destroyed his little empire. Our deaths are not enough. He wants to see us suffer."

The floor beneath them reeled. Dust and small stones fell around them.

"And suffer you shall." The deep voice seemed to issue from the cold walls of stone.

So he can hear us. "We are coming." Marcus didn't bother to whisper. "We do not fear you." *Liar.*

"Oh," said the voice, "do you not?"

A scream. Of agony.

Branwen! I'm coming!

Arawn laughed, and the sound echoed, coming from everywhere. "She can endure such pain, such torture. It is quite marvelous to behold. I can stab her immortal body again and again. Forever."

Branwen screamed.

"I can slice her open," Arawn said with hideous glee. "And she will heal. Again and again."

Another scream. And another.

"Delightful," said the demon.

Maelona groaned and sped up.

"No!" Marcus said.

Maelona stopped, breathing heavily.

Marcus caught up with her. "That's what he wants. He wants us to fall. To injure ourselves."

"But Branwen! She is in agony!"

Marcus shook his head, and tears flew from his eyes. "Branwen must endure. She must." *I'm sorry, Branwen!*

In spite of his warning words, Marcus increased his pace as much as he dared. And he counted the steps.

Marcus and Maelona walked in silence, weapons ready . . . and weeping silently.

And Branwen continued to scream. The screams, however, gradually weakened—in pitch and volume and duration.

Please, Branwen. Please endure.

The screams stopped altogether.

He hasn't killed her. Not yet.

Our Father in heaven, please help her to endure. Give her strength!

At last, as the step count neared five hundred, a light appeared in the tunnel ahead.

Marcus and Maelona rounded a bend, and the tunnel opened before them into a vast cavern.

Torches and oil lamps, seemingly without number, illuminated the chamber. The walls and ceiling glittered with flecks of gold. A forest of stalactites and stalagmites protruded from ceiling and floor at the far end of the cavern. A stream of water, four paces wide, gurgled to the left.

The cavern was furnished like some massive feasting hall. Dozens of long tables with benches sat on the right, along with firepits for roasting meat, larders with bags of grain, barrels of fruits, suspended and skinned sheep carcasses, hanging sides of beef, and numerous wineskins. Scores of couches and piles of sleeping furs lay near the feasting area.

But the details of the setting barely registered on Marcus. As a warrior, he took them in, of course, but his eyes focused on Branwen.

She floated in the air near the center of the cave, twenty feet above the floor. She had no wings—she was not flying under her own power. She was held aloft as if by unseen hands. Her eyes were open, but her mouth hung slack. Tears streaked her face. Her breathing was slow and labored. Her gown, crimson with blood, had been slashed open a number of times. Fresh blood dripped from her boots.

And her neck was encircled by three swords forming a triangle—floating as if wielded by magic.

That is how Arawn holds her captive—even one such as her could not survive decapitation.

He and Maelona strode across the rough cavern floor, toward Branwen.

Arawn can shake the earth, he can move the water, he can move objects and people.

Why not us?

"Stay to the right," he whispered to Maelona, "away from the water."

"Yes," said the voice of Arawn, "I control the stream."

The demon appeared, flashing into visibility like the flaring of a sulfur stick. Black-robed and with his hood pulled back, he sat on a throne of fire at the far end of the cave. His hair and beard were black as well, and his eyes burned red like glowing coals. And on his head sprouted stag's antlers. At his feet lay three great hounds, shining white, with crimson ears and noses.

The hounds – they move, they seem to watch us, but they do not attack. Why?

Perhaps –

At his side, Maelona said, "I do not think the dogs are . . . I do not think they are *there*."

Marcus nodded, keeping his eye on Arawn. "Nothing about him is real." Then to the demon he said, "We have come. Release her."

"Go." Branwen's voice was devoid of emotion—except for a profound weariness. "Leave . . . this place. Leave . . . me." She no longer floated in the air. She stood, tall and straight—the three swords still encircling her neck.

She's on the ground. Why? Perhaps he cannot hold her and the swords and make himself visible – not all at the same time. Too many tasks at once?

"I'm not leaving without her."

"Fools!" said Arawn, with a booming laugh. "You were never going to leave here."

"Why, then?" Marcus cried. "Why bring us all the way down here?"

The demon laughed. "To see my glory and my power."

"Behind!"

At Branwen's warning, Marcus whirled around.

A huge man-shape moved quickly and silently toward them—a giant of a man, easily eight or nine feet tall. He carried a round, wooden shield and a long, bronze sword. From below his armpits to below his waist, he wore a large, leather harness, covered with plates of bronze. Upon his head, he wore a simple bronze helm. Bronze greaves armored his shins.

Marcus put himself between the attacker and Maelona. "Stay behind me," he commanded.

The giant, seeing he was discovered, slowed his approach, bending his body in a wary crouch. He held his massive, wooden shield forward, with his sword back, ready to thrust at Marcus.

"Behold," said Arawn, "my champion—Llywellyn."

The giant, Llywellyn, opened his mouth in a feral, wolfish grin. His teeth were jagged and broken, as if he were accustomed to chewing on rocks. Or bones.

A champion? Why does Arawn need a mortal champion? Even one such as this?

"I make you a proposal, Option of Rome," said the demon. "Defeat my champion, and all three of you shall go free. Fall to Llywellyn—"

"If I fall, you still let the women go. Both of them. Unharmed." *He's just sporting with me. But what other choice do I have?*

The demon's laughter echoed through the cavern. "Very well. If you are victorious, I will leave this place. Forever. And the women shall go free."

He has no intention of keeping the bargain. "I accept your proposal, Arawn." *Either way, I still must defeat this brute.*

"Excellent," said the demon.

The giant advanced a step. He spoke, and his voice was deep and surprisingly calm. And he spoke in perfect Latin. "You Romans are taught to fight in units. And you fight extremely well . . . in units. But you are not taught to fight one-on-one, man-to-man. It is not part of your extensive, rigorous training." He thrust his bronze sword at Marcus.

Marcus parried the thrust with his shield, deflecting the heavy bronze. *He's testing me, probing my defense. But a bronze sword that large must be heavy . . . and brittle.* "That is true, giant. It is not part of our training. And you have the size and the reach. You have all the advantage."

"I," said the giant, "have fought many battles. I have"—he made another thrust—"trained well and always one-on-one." He lunged again. And again, his attack was deflected. "I have never been defeated. You shall fall like all the others."

The words of Gaius Aquillius echoed in Marcus's mind. *Watch his eyes. If he's going to move, you'll see it in his eyes first.*

Those intelligent, brown eyes beneath the rim of the bronze helm locked with Marcus's.

He knows. He's watching me.

So far, Marcus had been on the defensive, deflecting tentative, probing attacks from the brute.

Llywellyn's eyes narrowed slightly. He lunged with his shield first, slamming it against Marcus's shield.

The blow should have knocked the Roman on his back. But Marcus, forewarned, sidestepped, wheeled to the right, and thrust his sword into the giant's thigh.

Blood streamed from the wound, but it did not spray or spurt.

Missed the artery!

Llywellyn roared in pain. He stumbled back, stabbing at Marcus with his massive sword.

Marcus led with his own shield, catching the giant's wild sword thrust.

But the bronze pierced Marcus's shield, half of the blade protruding from the back.

With a grunt, Llywellyn yanked his sword up and to the left, ripping Marcus's shield out of his hand. The shield hung on the blade. The giant shook his sword in an attempt to free it.

Marcus lunged, hacking at the massive bronze sword.

And the bronze blade snapped in two, near the handle. The blade and Marcus's shield crashed to the ground.

Out of the corner of his eye, Marcus saw Maelona coming at the giant from behind with her dagger.

"Maelona!" he shouted. "Stay back!"

Marcus drew his own dagger, holding his sword in his right hand and his dagger in his left.

The giant flung his useless hilt away. He swung his own shield back, catching Maelona. She cried out and crumpled to the ground, her dagger skittering away, across the rugged floor.

Marcus snarled. He tensed, preparing to lunge at the giant who'd struck his beloved Maelona. But his mentor's words came again. *Never attack in anger.* Marcus took a step back, attempting to steady his breathing.

The giant leapt at him, shoving with his shield, using it like a battering ram.

Marcus parried with his sword, diving under the massive shield. He whipped his sword around and stabbed Llywellyn in the left thigh with his dagger.

And missed the artery again.

The giant's shield came crashing down toward Marcus.

Marcus leapt back. But he tripped on the rocky floor.

An enormous hand gripped Marcus about the neck, lifting him off the ground.

As the fist tightened around his throat, Marcus brought his dagger up and buried it in his opponent's forearm.

And was rewarded with a spray of blood.

Llywellyn screamed. He dropped Marcus and the round shield to the ground. The giant clutched at his arm, bellowing in pain.

Marcus stumbled for a moment, caught his balance, then stabbed the giant in the thigh once more. Higher, closer to the groin.

And blood spurted from that wound as well.

He's done. Marcus stepped back, out of reach.

Llywellyn dropped to his knees, still clutching at his arm.

"You're correct, giant," Marcus said. "Roman legionnaires are not trained in hand-to-hand combat. But I had a great mentor. He taught me how to fight. And when I've been forced to fight apart from my unit, my mentor's training has saved my life more than once. And now, it has cost you yours."

"Marcus!" Maelona cried. "The river!"

Water crashed upon him, driving him to the ground.

Marcus had barely drawn a little air into his lungs before the flood buried him, crushing him.

Move! Get out! He could see the edge of the water, the limit of the demon's power. *So close!* He started to crawl toward it. The air burned in his lungs.

He saw Maelona near him, under the water as well, struggling to crawl.

He reached for her hand to pull her along with him.

The urge to open his mouth, to breathe—breathe and die—was all-consuming.

No! Hold on!

His sight dimmed as the air in his lungs screamed for release.

Not going to make it!

A strong hand grasped his.

And yanked him out of the water, into the air.

As Marcus drew glorious air into his burning lungs, he looked for Maelona.

She dangled beside him, drenched, but breathing, gulping in air.

Alive! She's alive!

Then he looked up at their savior.

Branwen.

Her wings beating, Branwen carried Marcus and Maelona to the right edge of the cave, away from the water. She deposited them both atop a pile of sleeping-furs.

How did she get free of the swords?

The waters had already collapsed and were draining back toward the subterranean riverbed.

Perhaps, Arawn can't control the waters and the swords at the same—

The three swords flew through the air toward Branwen.

"Branwen!" Marcus tried to shout a warning, but it came out as a croak.

However, Branwen was ready. She batted the swords away, her movements too quick to follow. The weapons clattered to the ground. All save one—she held that sword. Still flying, she turned toward the demon and pointed the sword at Arawn. "You will never catch me again." She gestured toward Marcus and Maelona. "And they are out of reach of your cursed water."

Marcus got to his feet. Weaponless, he faced Arawn.

The spectral hounds were gone—as was the throne of flames.

The demon stood alone on the ground. He still wore a black cloak, but the antlers had vanished.

Marcus forced a laugh. "We have beaten you, Arawn. I have defeated your champion. Your water can't touch us."

"You cannot kill me!" cried the demon in a voice that spoke more of shock than defiance.

"True," Marcus replied. "You were never born. You are a fallen angel, a servant of Lucifer. You have no physical body for me to kill."

The demon roared like a feral beast. "But I shall kill you! You shall suffer as no one has ever—"

"You are finished here," said Maelona, taking Marcus's right hand. "We have slain your evil priests."

Branwen dropped to the ground and grasped Marcus's other hand. "The people of this land no longer fear you, bodiless spirit. Your reign of horror and blood is over."

"I know who you are," Marcus said. "You are Moloch and you are Chemosh."

The demon flinched. "How do you know those names?"

Marcus lifted his head, thrusting his chin forward. "I am a disciple of Jesus Christus."

The demon flinched again. "And so? You have no priesthood. You cannot banish me or you would have done so before now."

Suddenly, Arawn grew. In an instant, he was twenty feet tall, towering over Marcus, Maelona, and Branwen. "I will kill you all."

"Go ahead and kill us," Maelona said. "You have lost. My people above—they do not fear you."

Marcus chuckled. "I understand now. You *need* the priests. Just as you needed a champion. Without mortals to do your bidding, to follow you into damnation, you are nothing. It was *never* about killing us. Killing us would send us into the arms of a loving God. It's about corrupting souls. It's about enticing mortals to commit murder and rape. Even with that poor creature—your Goliath there"—he released Branwen's hand to point at Llywellyn's corpse—"it was about adding yet another murder to his sins."

Marcus grasped Branwen's hand once more, as she declared, "You can kill us, but that is all you can do. You can claim our bodies. But you will never claim our souls for your master."

Arawn snarled at Branwen. "Your soul is already lost. You are a Child of Lilith. You are already damned."

"'The day cometh,'" Branwen said, her voice calm and confident, "'when the daughter of night shall reclaim her own soul.'"

Marcus recognized the words of a prophecy, words he had never understood . . . until that moment. "That was about you?"

Branwen squeezed his hand. "Yes. You have given me hope, beloved Marcus. Such as I never had before." She faced the demon. "My soul shall be my own again. The prophecies of Marcus Scribonius always come true. Always. There is nothing you can do to me."

The demon hissed like a snake. Then he screamed, and in that scream, Marcus heard the anguish of a damned soul. Arawn vanished, but the scream went on and on, echoing, growing, filling the cavern.

The three of them covered their ears.

The hideous shriek cut off abruptly.

Marcus said, "We need to go. Now."

Maelona shook her head, holding him fast by the hand. "No! Gather your weapons. Quickly."

"Why?" Marcus asked.

She said, "The Holy Spirit urges me. I hear it. In my mind. Quickly!"

Marcus spun about, to search for his sword, dagger, and shield.

But Branwen floated before him, wings outstretched. And she held Marcus's shield, upturned. She had removed the broken bronze blade from the shield, leaving a narrow gap. And in the hollow of the shield lay their weapons—Marcus's dagger and sword, Maelona's dagger, and a sword for Branwen.

Marcus gazed at her in wonder. "That was . . . quick."

Branwen grinned. "The queen said to be quick. So I was quick."

They armed themselves, sheathing their weapons. Marcus took the shield in his left hand. "Very well," he said. "Now we can go."

Branwen said, "I can carry you both, and fly up the tunnel."

"Fly?" Maelona looked terrified. "I don't—"

The ground beneath them trembled, causing them to stumble and cry out in panic.

"No time to discuss." Branwen put an arm around each of them, gripping them tightly to her chest.

And they flew—out of the cave, out of Annwfyn, and into the tunnel.

CRACK! BOOM!

Marcus could hear the splitting of massive stones. *The whole cave must be crashing down!*

The rumble of falling rocks grew closer and louder.

Marcus twisted his head to see, but there was no light in the tunnel as they flew. *Branwen can see in this darkness?* They jerked left, then right, then left again. And Marcus knew they must be safely rounding all the turns in the tunnel.

Maelona stifled a scream. "No escape! So close! Dark!"

"Do not fear, sister," Branwen said, her own voice quivering with fear. "Almost there."

Light! Marcus could see it. Dim, but growing brighter. "Almost there!" he echoed.

"The light!" Branwen cried. She slowed, then stopped, setting Marcus and Maelona down. "The Sun!"

She can't go out in the sun!

In the dim light, Marcus could see that Branwen was terrified.

"You go on," she said, covering her face with her hands, as if to shield herself from the faint glow. "I cannot. I must . . . go back, find another exit. Wait until the night."

A stone struck her on the head. She cried out, covering the wound with her hands as fresh blood gushed between her fingers.

Marcus raised his shield over her. More stones crashed upon it. "Maelona! Run! Get out!"

"I won't leave you!" Maelona cried. "Either of you!"

Marcus handed Branwen the shield. "Take it!"

Branwen took the shield from him and held it up. "Go!" Tears glittered, cutting rivulets through the blood and dust on her face. She tried to wipe them away. "I cannot go with you. I must go back. I'm sorry!"

She turned about. Wings sprung from her back, and she flew away, down the reeling tunnel.

Marcus grasped Maelona's hand.

"No!" she cried, trying to twist free of his grip. "Branwen!"

Marcus yanked her around. "We must go!"

Maelona hesitated, then nodded, and together, hand-in-hand, they stumbled toward the exit.

The ground beneath them shook.

"There!" Marcus cried. The exit was before them—twenty paces.

Light. Freedom.

CRACK!

With a great crash of falling stones, the tunnel ahead of them collapsed.

The light vanished.

Trapped!

Stones continued to strike them.

Marcus pulled Maelona beneath him, shielding her body with his armor.

Maelona screamed.

Rocks pummeled his armor and helm, driving him down, sapping the last of his strength.

We're going to die. Crushed.

In the dark.

Stones continued to rain down—Marcus could hear them, but . . . he could no longer feel them striking his armor or his body.

How?

The quaking of the ground ceased. The fall of rocks stopped.

"Branwen?"

"Yes. I am here, Marcus. I . . . should not have left you. Forgive me."

And he understood. She was there. Behind him. Above him. Holding the shield over them. Protecting them.

Marcus forced himself to calm his rapid breathing. "He must think we are dead. Crushed. And we would be, without you."

"If you don't mind," Branwen said, breathing heavily, "I'll sit here. Rest for a bit. I am so . . . weary."

"Wait here?" he asked. "And then what? We're trapped!"

"Give me a moment." She groaned. "And then . . . Then I can dig you out. Do not worry. I shall stay out of the light . . . wait till nightfall. But . . . I'm just so . . . Must rest."

Waiting in the dark, in this small space – Maelona must be terrified.

And I am not just as frightened?

"Maelona?" He put a hand to Maelona's head.

And felt hot blood on her scalp. "Maelona!"

Maelona did not respond.

"She's bleeding," Branwen said. "I can smell it."

"Can you heal her?"

"I can stop the bleeding. I can feel it, smell it. But even I cannot see in this absolute darkness. But let me try." Branwen pushed past him.

Rustling sounds. Slurping.

Branwen sighed. "I have sealed the wound. I can do no more."

Gently, gingerly, Marcus gathered Maelona in his arms. "Wake up, my love. Maelona, please wake up. Please, Maelona!"

The girl did not stir.

"Her heart," Branwen said, "it is not steady. Perhaps . . . Perhaps, if I took some blood . . . my spittle could heal her *inside*, where I cannot feel. But I will not take it from the innocent . . . without permission. I made a vow. And I have never—"

"Take it!" Marcus demanded. "I give you permission!"

"Very well." Her breathing quickened as if with anticipation.

Marcus could almost *feel* her hunger, the ravening drive to consume life. He felt Branwen's hair fall across his arm as she bent over Maelona's neck.

More slurping.

Maelona stirred. She moaned. At first, a moan of pain . . . and then a moan of pleasure.

Branwen withdrew. "I dare not take more. So . . . sweet. Not the sweetness of evil. The sweetness of pure love."

"Thank you." Marcus's eyes filled with tears. "Thank you, my lady."

Branwen sighed and shivered. "Her strength . . . has revived me. I can begin digging now. I don't know how long it will take. And I will go no farther than where the light begins. Then I can finish after nightfall."

Marcus heard her crawling away. Then he heard stone grating on stone as Branwen heaved rocks out of their path.

Maelona stirred. She jerked and gasped. Then she trembled in Marcus's arms. "So dark!"

Marcus hushed her. "Do not fear, my love. I'm here."

She clung to him with quivering hands. "Marcus? Where are we?"

"In the tunnel. Branwen saved us."

"Branwen?"

"I am here, sister," Branwen said.

"Th-thank you!"

"Do not thank me yet," the Daughter of Lilith replied. "We are still . . . several paces from the exit. I am clearing our way of the rocks."

"Maelona," Marcus said, "you told us to bring our weapons. My shield. It protected us. Without it, we'd all be dead."

"And so, sister," Branwen said, "my dear, dear sister . . . You saved us too." She grunted. "I have cleared a pace or so. But we must all move forward, and I will move the rocks behind us as we go."

"We can help you," Maelona said. Her voice shook with fear as she pulled herself out of Marcus's arms. "We can at least move the smaller stones out of the way."

"It is not necessary," Branwen countered. "I can"—she grunted with the effort of moving a stone—"do it."

"No," Maelona said. "I *need* to help. It h-helps . . . with the fear."

"Very well."

Marcus could hear the smile in Branwen's voice.

And so they dug. Working together, they edged up the ruin of the ancient mining shaft.

How long they took, Marcus was unsure. It could have been hours or days—he had no way of judging the time. His dry throat burned for water. His empty belly ached for food. His limbs trembled for lack of rest and sleep. But he labored on.

The three of them labored on—together.

A flash of light. Piercing the absolute darkness, the beam of light was no wider than a pinprick.

Branwen hissed.

Her hand was aflame.

She jerked it back from the light. Her hiss became a scream of pain.

The flames vanished, leaving behind the stench of charred flesh.

And Branwen's soft weeping.

"Branwen!" Marcus and Maelona cried at once.

"No!" Branwen said in a trembling voice. "It will pass. It has . . . already passed. It is astounding to think—all those times Arawn stabbed me, the years I spent starving myself in the barrow . . . Nothing . . . Nothing compares to the agony of burning in the light."

An ache arose, almost a burning, in Marcus's chest—an ache to hold Branwen, to comfort her. But he refrained. "We can wait. Until sunset."

"Thank you," said Branwen with a long, weary sigh. "Sunset . . . It is almost upon us. I can feel it. But the exit . . . it faces west, toward the setting Sun."

"We can wait, sister," said Maelona. "As long as you require."

Demonic laughter filled the small chamber, freezing the blood in Marcus's veins. "You think you have time? You have escape and freedom in your sights, within your reach. You have hope!" Arawn laughed again. "Hope? I allowed you to get this far, so that, at the very last, I can crush your hope. Crush it! As I crush you!"

The tunnel shook violently. Stones fell around them.

Maelona screamed. Marcus cried out as well.

But Branwen made no sound.

As the stones rained around them, Marcus could hear them thundering against wood—the wood of his shield! But no rock struck him.

"Forward!" Branwen cried. "Now!"

Light exploded around them.

Branwen held the shield above with one hand, while she pulled and shoved stones out of their way, widening the opening.

Letting in more sunlight.

Her hand, her arm burst into flame. Her scream of agony filled the chamber, blending with the laughter of the demon.

But still she dug. Stones scattered before her.

The opening widened, giving enough room for the mortals to crawl through.

Flames enveloped Branwen. "NOW!" she howled. She stood back, holding the burning shield over the exit.

Marcus pushed Maelona out, through the hole. He followed her, out into the light of the setting sun. He turned around, reaching back for Branwen. *I'll shade her with my body!*

"NO!" roared Arawn.

The hillside shook, collapsing before Marcus. The ground reeled, and Marcus stumbled like a drunken man.

Strong hands gripped him from behind—Caeso Lucilius pulling him to safety. Agrippa Corfidius likewise restrained Maelona.

"Branwen!" Marcus cried as he was forcibly yanked away from her burning form.

The hillside imploded with a deep boom, as if the earth itself were roaring in its death throes.

Marcus watched in impotent horror. He cried Branwen's name over and over. Maelona stood at his side. Her hand found his.

And they watched. And hope died within them.

When the dust cleared, nothing remained of the Gate of Annwfyn. The hilltop itself had collapsed upon it.

There was no sign of the brave woman who had saved them. There was not so much as a mound to mark her tomb.

. . . though the cost be great . . .

Maelona threw herself into Marcus's arms. They clung to each other.

And they wept.

Chapter XXIV

"The lioness shall return. And she shall claim her rightful prey."
from the Book of Marcus Scribonius

And this is your report, Option?" Legate Gaius Suetonius Paulinus sat at the writing table, in the guest quarters of the villa—Spurius Aquillius's villa. The afternoon had turned chilly, but a small brazier near the window heated the room. The general—who was, of course, still fully armored, save for his helm which sat on the floor next to the desk—thumped his fist on the parchment spread across the table.

Holding his own plumed helm under his left arm, Marcus Aquillius Audaxus stood at rigid attention. He did not look the general in the eye—he knew better than that. Marcus stared at a spot on the wall behind his commander. "Yes, Legate. That is my report."

The legate growled. "When the *noble* master of this *vital* cattle farm sent runners with an *urgent* message, telling me that I needed to come with *all haste*—perhaps to your aid . . . I tell you, Option, if Spurius Aquillius wasn't the man he is—with the senatorial connections he and your adopted father have—I would not have come. But . . . I *have* come."

Poor Spurius Aquillius! Marcus personally delivered the devastating news about the deaths of Emrys and Gwawr to Spurius. Marcus's new "son" took the news about his own son—bastard or not—and his daughter-in-law as Marcus expected. The older man took to his rooms weeping, but not before saying to Marcus, "They are with God the Father and Jesus Christus now. I shall trust in the Lord's tender mercy."

But, shortly after Marcus's arrival at the villa, the legate arrived with a full cohort of soldiers. And he demanded that Marcus report immediately. Fortunately for Marcus—or unfortunately—the option had written his report at night, during their return march.

The legate stood, placing both hands on the desk and leaning forward. His bearded face was no more than a hand's breadth away from Marcus's. "I left the entire Mona campaign in the charge of a tribune, and I came. You were ordered to observe and report—punish a goetia if necessary. But you went far beyond your orders. And what did you observe and report?" He pounded the vellum on the desk. "You present me this wild . . . *tale* of gods and demons. You tell me your commander—that barely-weaned-off-mother's-milk centurion I left in your keeping—*murdered* you, and then this Branwen, this night-demon, brought you back from death? You tell me you lost four men—FOUR men under your command—including your own kinsman, Septimus Scribonius."

Marcus couldn't help but flinch at that one. He rehearsed their names in his mind, just as he had many times each day during the entire march back to the villa. *Mettius Canius and Gwynn—even if they were "evildoers." Marcus Tarquinius and Septimus Scribonius—who fell in battle with the Druids.*

And Rhiain, slain by Arawn.

And Branwen.

Branwen.

Marcus bit his lip, fighting to keep back the tears. *Now is not the time!*

Concentrate on what the legate is saying!

Not on Branwen. Terrifying, lovely, sweet, noble Branwen.

Not now.

The legate muttered something under his breath. Marcus caught only, ". . . so few, considering . . ."

The governor slapped the desk. "Then! Then you freed a slave, and somehow, this former slave gets herself elected *queen* by the locals here. And then, single-handedly she freed all the hostages and scattered the enemy's horses. *You* raised a small army of a few hundred farmers, fought an army of THREE THOUSAND Druids, and achieved victory? Then you fought a GOD—in his own realm—and banished him?"

Gaius Suetonius straightened and turned his back on Marcus. "I tell you, lad, there are more *fables* here than I can stomach." He paused, then lowered his voice. "And none of this—*none* of this can make it into the official record of the legion."

Just like Mona.

"Just like Mona," said the legate, echoing Marcus's own thought. "It simply won't do."

"Every word of it is true, Legate."

Gaius Suetonius wheeled on him. "I do not doubt it. I believe you. Every. Cursed. Word. As fantastic as it sounds, I believe you accomplished all of this—you and these two . . . women. And your valiant men." He shook his head. "But such a tale would require you to report directly to the Senate."

The legate paused, and his eyes narrowed. "Is that what you want? Hm? Look at me, curse you!"

Marcus obeyed. He met the legate's fierce glare. And he did not flinch. But he also did not reply.

"Is that what you want, Marcus Aquillius, to report to the Senate and make a name for yourself there?"

Seek not to return to Rome . . ."No, Legate. I do not seek to return to Rome—now or ever. I wish to remain in Britannia and under your command."

The general chuckled mirthlessly. "Oh, that is what you wish, is it? Serve me loyally? Perhaps, you seek to marry that little queen of yours and make yourself a king and raise an army and challenge—"

"My lord Legate! I would never—"

Gaius Suetonius waved a hand in dismissal and looked away. "No, forget I said that. Your loyalty is not in question. It . . . never was. Your service to the Empire, to the Emperor . . . to *me* . . . has been . . . exemplary. Beyond exemplary. I wish every one of my *centuriones* was your equal."

Marcus blinked.

The legate turned back to Marcus, and the general's eyes softened. "I have some good officers under my command—some *great* officers. But your courage"—he chuckled—"and your brains . . . That was a brilliant tactic at the Gate of Annwfyn . . . Unfortunately, your brilliant tactic at the Gate of Annwfyn will never make it into the official record."

The legate sat in his chair. He stared at the report, then up at Marcus.

"I just don't know what to do with you, Option."

Marcus blinked. "Do with me?"

"Your men, your century . . . They are loyal to you. Fiercely loyal." Gaius Suetonius shrugged. "As they should be. You led them to the realm of the dead and back. And you lost only four of them. They love you, Option. Even the fabro and capsarium."

Marcus swallowed the lump that had formed in his throat.

"And," said the legate, "it is obvious how much you love them." He tapped the table with two thick fingers. "But this cannot go on. I cannot have an entire century more loyal to an option than to a centurion. You must see that. I have a legion to command and a province to govern, and *order* must be maintained, as well as the proper chain of command."

The general stood, and extended a large hand, palm up, toward Marcus. "Surrender your plume, Marcus Aquillius. You can no longer be an option."

Marcus took the space of one deep breath before he moved to obey. Then he detached the longitudinal plume of red-dyed horsehair from the top of his helm. He placed the plume in the outstretched hand of the legate.

Option. Chosen one. I serve only at my commander's pleasure. It can be taken away at any moment.

It has *been taken away.*

But the demotion felt like a fist to his gut.

And worse, stripped of rank, he lost all hope of marrying.

Maelona!

The general set the plume down upon the desk, beside the parchment containing Marcus's report. He thumped it down with a finality that seemed to echo through the small chamber. He gazed at Marcus long and hard, though Marcus did his best to focus on the spot at the back of the wall. Finally, Gaius Suetonius spoke. "What do you have to say to that, Legionnaire Marcus Aquillius Audaxus? You have served Rome and you have served me with honor and distinction, and because I cannot give you credit for your impressive service, I strip you of your rank. What do you have to say, Legionnaire?"

Gaius Suetonius paused, then said, "You may speak freely, Marcus Aquillius."

Many thoughts ran through Marcus's brain—thoughts he dared not utter, though the general granted him leave to speak his mind. Instead, he saluted smartly, right fist to chest. "For the glory of Rome!"

The general burst into uproarious laughter. "For the glory of Rome, is it?" He laughed some more and slapped the table again. "For the glory of Rome. Well, I say it would be a sin against the *gods* to waste talent such as yours or to separate you from such loyal and brave men."

Marcus blinked, then stared back at his commander. "I don't understand, my lord Legate."

The general grinned. "No, you don't." He turned away once more. He strode to the bed and retrieved a dusty, leather saddlebag. Opening it, he turned back to Marcus.

And in the legate's hand was another plume—a latitudinal plume.

A centurion's plume.

The legate presented the plume to Marcus. "You are not yet thirty, but I would be a fool if I waited another day—or another half-weaned centurion's life—on you and your century. Congratulations, Centurion Marcus Aquillius Audaxus!"

Marcus took the plume and, with fingers that trembled only slightly, attached it to his helm. "Thank you, Legate."

The legate smiled widely and laughed. "Well, you've earned it, lad. And I must say that I was greatly amused by the look on your face." He sighed and sat once more. "Sit, Centurion."

Marcus pulled up the other chair in the room and sat across from his commander. He placed his helm with its new plume on the floor to his left.

All mirth had dissipated from the general's face. "Now, tell me about your prophecies."

Marcus gasped. "My lord?"

The legate waved impatiently. "Now is not the time to be coy, Centurion. I have heard rumors of your oracles. And I would deserve to be smitten with madness by the goddess Ira were I fool enough to ignore such a gift from the gods. Or from *your* god."

Marcus suddenly found his mouth dry. "Legate, with all respect, my prophecies are"—*personal, sacred*—"directed at me, for my responsibility, those under my direct command. Not for the legion or the world as a whole."

"But they helped you achieve a great victory." It was not a question, but a statement of fact.

Marcus nodded. "Yes, Legate. But they come unbidden and unexpectedly, and never in answer to my own questions."

The legate nodded slowly. "I see. And you say you have received none for the legion?"

"No, Legate."

"And," Gaius Suetonius's voice lowered to a near whisper, "you have received none for *me*?"

Marcus opened his mouth to reply in the negative, but stopped as understanding dawned on him. "Yes, Legate. There was one. I did not comprehend it until now, but—"

"What is it, man?" the general demanded through clenched teeth.

"It said that my commander—I had assumed that referred to Gaius Aquillius or perhaps Quintus Aquillius, but it never seemed to fit . . . and they are dead, so . . . It said that my commander would be recalled to Rome, relieved of command, because of . . . cruelty."

The legate stared at him, his eyes unreadable. "The punitive campaign against Boudicca's allies."

Marcus hesitated, then nodded. "I believe so, Legate."

"Such a tactic is always a gamble." Gaius Suetonius grunted. "So I am to be relieved of command. I see. Was there more?"

Marcus nodded, but then he smiled. "But your career is far from over, my lord."

"How so?"

"You shall become a consul and a senior legate again within five years, although I cannot say where you will serve."

One corner of the legate's mouth lifted in a half-smile. "Very well, then. I thank you for that, Centurion."

Now. While he's grateful. Ask him for permission to marry! "My lord, I have a request to make."

The general lifted an eyebrow. "Oh, you do?" He grunted. "Sweeten me up and then make demands? I see. For the glory of Rome, eh? Well, what is it?"

Marcus took a deep breath. "I wish to marry."

The governor raised the other eyebrow. "Marry? That queen of yours, the former slave-girl?"

Marcus nodded. "Yes, my lord Legate."

The general gazed at him for a moment, and just as hope swelled in Marcus's breast, the legate shook his head. "You know my policy on this. No married men below the rank of tribune—and I am *not* promoting you to tribune, so you can just put that right out of your head. I cannot allow men in the field to pine for home or, worse, have their families tag along after the legion. I cannot make an exception."

Marcus opened his mouth to object.

The legate raised a hand to stop him. "No, Centurion. No married men in the field. That is final."

No! Please, Father in heaven! Show me the way!

The legate rolled up Marcus's official report. He stood and strode to the brazier. He placed the vellum into the coals. The scroll flared and burned. The smell of burning sheepskin filled the room.

Marcus felt as if hope itself were turning to ash along with his report.

The legate remained by the brazier, watching the immolation of the report. "Our host, Spurius Aquillius—your *son,* now, *Pater* Aquillius—has very correctly pointed out that his operation here is vital to the army in Britannia. During the Boudicca Revolt, he feared that he might be overrun here. And if that were to have happened, his beef would no longer make it into my soldiers' bellies. He has therefore requested that a permanent garrison be established here to guard this farm and his villa. He has offered to provide beef and posca for a century of men. In time, perhaps, we might garrison an entire cohort here. And it might be a wise move to keep a mobile, battle-hardened force in central Cambria, ready to march at a moment's notice to wherever the Empire might need them." He paused. "I have decided to grant Spurius Aquillius's request. You and your men will be garrisoned here. This will be your assignment. Perhaps, your permanent assignment. I fear there will be little hope of promotion beyond, of course, becoming Pilus Prior of the cohort as centuries are added to your command—"

"Permanent garrison?" Marcus could not believe his ears. "Here? That means—"

The legate turned to him, nodding. "That there will be, as I said, little hope of promotion. You would likely remain a centurion for the rest of your career. Do you know what that means?"

A smile split Marcus's face. "It means I can marry—with your permission, of course."

The general's smile was, if possible, wider that Marcus's. "Yes, it means you may marry your queen."

Marcus barely restrained himself from rushing forward to grasp his commander about the shoulders. Instead, he saluted. "Thank you, Legate! Thank you!"

The legate returned the salute, then waived him off. "Go on. Inform your men of their new assignment, and your *son* of his good fortune. And go kiss that lovely queen of yours. If I were you, I would write out the marriage contract this very night. Make it official. Go on! Get out of my room. I leave within the hour. Some of us still have a war to fight!"

Marcus saluted once more, then stooped to retrieve his helm from the floor. He sped out of the legate's room.

Once the door was closed behind him, Marcus donned his plumed helm—the helm of a centurion—then sprinted down the hall to find Maelona.

♦ ♦ ♦

Marcus and Maelona stood in Marcus's guest chamber before the writing desk. A small crowd of men observed from the other side of that desk: Spurius Aquillius—his eyes still red from mourning—officially promoted Option Caeso Lucilius, officially promoted Tesserarius Nonus Sestius, Vexillarius Agrippa Corfidius, and Cornicen Spurius Orcivius all stood at attention. The five men had come to witness. Marcus and his officers all wore their full armor—with freshly washed tunicae—for the occasion.

Maelona wore her green gown. Her red hair fell in waves down her back and over one shoulder. A garland of woven flowers crowned her head.

And she looked every bit a queen.

However, she was not smiling.

Maelona stared at the quill in her hand as if it were a venomous snake. "How do I sign this? You know I cannot write."

Marcus chuckled at her exasperation. "I can guide your hand."

She shook her head. "No. Then it would be you signing for me and not myself."

"Then how?"

She considered for a moment, then gestured vaguely at the marriage contract, written at the bottom of Marcus's scroll—at the bottom of the Book of Marcus Scribonius. "My name is written on here, yes?"

"Yes, my love."

"Then show me. I will copy it."

Marcus smiled. He placed his finger beside her name in the contract. "Here. 'Maelona'—these six letters."

"And where do I sign?"

Marcus pointed to the empty spot awaiting her name.

Maelona nodded, then carefully, laboriously copied her name.

She handed the quill back to Marcus. "And this is all that is necessary? A simple contract? No priest? No clasping of hands? This writing makes us married in the eyes of Christus? And of Rome?"

Marcus took the quill and returned it to its holder on the writing desk. He scattered sand upon the fresh ink, waited a moment, then blew the sand away. *Now that it is dry and official . . .* "Yes. That is all. We are now married."

Maelona squealed with joy. She leapt into his arms and smothered his lips with kisses.

When she finally took time to calm her breathing, she said, "I love you, my conqueror."

He smiled, out of breath himself. "I love you too, my queen. But I think there may be some dispute as to who conquered whom."

He laughed, and she laughed, and she kissed him again.

She declared, "I am a queen no longer. I am the wife of a Roman centurion. I am Maelona, wife of Marcus Aquillius Audaxus. And you are my lord and husband."

Marcus shook his head. "Oh, Maelona, you will always be my queen."

Then she wriggled herself out of his embrace. She turned to their host and Marcus's junior officers. "Thank you for coming. We both owe all of you so very much." She paused, grinning widely and sweetly. "Now, please get out of our bedchamber!"

All the men laughed—including Marcus and Maelona's new "son"—as the bride bustled the witnesses out of the room.

Maelona closed and bolted the door behind them.

She paused, then turned, her movements slow and feline. She advanced toward him.

The lioness has returned.

Amazing woman.

"Well, my lord and husband, Centurion Marcus Aquillius Audaxus of Rome, Pater Aquillius, you are *mine*." She licked her lips. "Now get out of that cursed armor!"

Interlude VII

"On the sea, on a magic ship, in a chamber of blue and green the color of the ocean, the swordswoman shall at last find her quarry."
from the Book of Marcus Scribonius

July 2017 A.D.

"Ach!" hissed Moira, as she gripped Carl's hand more tightly. "Of course—she beat us here."

Should hae picked an aft location, closer to our stateroom.

Carl leaned in to whisper loudly in her ear. "At least it's public."

The nightclub, located on Deck 3, Forward of the Disney Magic, was lit in hues of blue and sea-green to suggest an undersea atmosphere—minus the water, of course—and went by the moniker, Fathoms. And Fathoms was crowded at the moment—for which Moira was grateful. Most of the seating was arranged to face the small stage, where a boisterous comedian told Disney-themed, family-friendly jokes. However, the semicircular back and side wall was lined with intimate alcoves containing booths.

And in one of those booths sat the mysterious woman, still clad in her dark hoodie, with the hood pulled low over her eyes. She waved. It seemed a friendly wave, as if the three of them—Moira, Carl, and the woman who had identified herself only as "a friend"—were old chums, well and surprisingly reunited on a sea cruise.

Moira felt chills rippling up and down her spine. *A friend, aye? And carryin' a sword?*

Carl shook his head. "It feels like the war all over again."

"Aye, laddie. Always in danger, always lookin' over our shoulders for enemies—mortal and immortal." Moira waved back. *Let her know we've seen her, at least.*

"Wish I'd brought the blasted shillelagh."

"Ye'd nae be able tae wield it in here." *Nae. Our protection here is the presence of other people – witnesses.*

The hooded woman waved again.

Carl said, "Let's go."

Together, Moira and Carl started forward.

Hand in hand. As we've always faced the unknown.

As they slowly made their way across the club, Moira scoured the booth and the floor underneath it with her eyes—at least the part she could see.

And she spied it, sitting on the bench beside the woman—the large bag, with the long, heavy object at the bottom. "Look, laddie! On the seat, next tae her!"

Carl hissed, "She's got the sword."

"How'd she get it aboard, d'ye think?"

"How'd she get *herself* aboard?"

Laughter roared around them as the entertainer on the stage finished an apparently successful joke.

Moira leaned up and whispered loudly, "Money. Lots and lots of money."

"Okay. That probably makes her a former vampire. And an *old* one."

"When ye live for centuries and yer livin' expenses are low . . ."

"And you invest wisely." Carl squeezed her hand. "And pay your tithing . . ."

In spite of her dread, Moira chuckled. *Pay yer tithin'!*

When they arrived at the booth, the woman pulled back her hood. "Please sit down." She was a striking beauty, with long, flowing auburn hair and green eyes. And a mysterious smile. "Don't worry. I don't bite."

Her smile widened, showing a mouth full of gleaming, perfect teeth. "Not anymore."

Neither Carl nor Moira made a move to sit.

The woman's smile faded, turning to a smirk. "You've probably noticed the sword. Don't worry. It's not for you. I'm here to *protect* you. To save your lives. I'm here to fulfill a prophecy." Her eyes took on a faraway look and she smiled wistfully. "The last one."

A prophecy? Not the Prophecy – Carl and I already fulfilled that one.

The woman patted the table. "Please, sit. Please."

Carl squeezed Moira's hand, then let go. He slid into the booth—opposite the woman. Moira slid in beside her husband.

The two of them clasped hands once more.

The redhead gave a relieved sigh. "After all this time, all these centuries . . ."

"You know who we are," Carl said, his voice hard, wary. "But who are you?"

Her dazzling smile returned. She reached both hands across the table, palms up—as if she meant Carl and Moira to clasp them. "I'm so pleased to finally meet you—both of you. You saved us all. Now it is my turn to save *you*."

Tears glistened in her perfectly made-up eyes.

"My name is Branwen."

Chapter XXV

"A year and a day shalt thou mourn, and then cometh the night."
from the Book of Marcus Scribonius

DCCCLV *Ab Urbe Condita* (102 A.D.)

Marcus Aquillius plucked one of the tiny, white flowers that dotted the burial mound. He eased himself down on the grass, groaning softly at the pain in his knees, and the old battle wound in his thigh. The grass was still wet from an early afternoon shower. The moisture seeped through the back side of his tunic and coated his bare legs.

The coolness threatened to aggravate the pain in his knees.

"Perhaps," he said, "I should put a bench here—a stone bench, warmed by the sun in the afternoon. It would certainly make the winter visits easier—even if I do have to brush off the snow on occasion."

He put the flower to his nostrils and sniffed.

The sweet fragrance filled his head with memories—sweet memories.

"But sitting here on the grass . . . where I'm able to look at you . . . not *down* on you . . . I never looked down on you."

He sniffed again. The fragrance was weaker. But the memories were still sweet.

"No. This . . . mound of earth is not *you*. Not even the bones beneath. You are with God. Waiting for me." A wistful smile curled his lips. "I miss you, my queen. A year and a day. I must confess, the pain has dulled somewhat. But I miss your emerald eyes, your auburn hair with those glorious streaks of silver, and your sweet smile." He grinned. "And your delightful freckles."

"Grandfather! Grandfather!"

Marcus looked up. He shaded his eyes against the setting sun. He could make out the silhouette of a child on the back of a young pony.

The boy bounced as the pony trotted, the beast not quite always obeying its rider's commands.

"Halt!" cried the boy, pulling sharply back on the reins. Pony and rider slowed and stopped at the side of the mound, a few paces from Marcus. The child patted the beast on the neck. "Good girl!" He beamed at his grandfather. "Isn't she beautiful? And she's my own! My very own. Father said so. I think I will name her Bellatrix. It means "girl-warrior." I think I should name her in Latin, not Cambrian. "Ymadawraig" does not sound as fierce."

Marcus took in the sight of the shaggy pony—what Maelona would have called a "proper pony"—as well as the seven-year-old astride her. "Do you really want a war pony, Wee Marcus? You are too young to join the army."

The boy, named Marcus Aquillius after his grandfather—though his grandfather, and virtually everyone else, called him Wee Marcus—sat tall in his saddle. "I want to be a legionnaire like you, grandfather! I want to serve the Empire and be brave like you! And I want to fight the savages in the north."

Marcus laughed. Heartily. "You have a few years yet before you can go off and be a soldier. And besides, I was not in the cavalry. I was a foot soldier—light infantry. I did not ride a horse" *—or a pony—* "into combat. Not once." He paused. "And as for 'savages in the north,' they are just people, like you and me. People who love their homes and their families and their way of life. Perhaps, someday, they will join the Empire . . . or perhaps they will be forcibly civilized. Or perhaps not. But for now, I am content for them to stay in the north and for us to live here in Cambria, protected by the legions of Rome."

"Then I shall be a legionnaire and defend Cambria!"

Marcus chuckled. "Perhaps, Wee Marcus. Perhaps."

"Grandfather? Will you teach me to fight? With the gladius and the scutum? The pilum? The pugio?"

Marcus smiled and shook his head. "No, lad. My fighting days are over. Perhaps your father—"

"But father says you know the way to fight hand-to-hand. You tried to teach it to him, but he says he could never learn it properly. Will you teach me?"

Marcus nodded slowly. "A man should know how to defend himself. And those he loves." He smiled. "And your father learned well enough, but yes, I will teach you."

"Caeso Lucilius says you were the greatest commander to ever walk the earth. He says you and Grandmother went into Hell itself and fought a demon."

Your grandmother and I and one more. One more. "Caeso Lucilius told you? Did you know that before he was our steward, he was my option? My second-in-command?"

The boy shook his head, his eyes full of wonder. "No!" He jumped down from the pony's back and, holding the reins, led the animal toward Marcus. "I knew he served with you, but . . . Option! Option to the Pilus Prior!" Wee Marcus sat in front of his grandfather, sitting almost, but not quite on the mound itself. And he still clutched his pony's reins. "Is that why he is now your vilicus? Your second-in-command of the villa?"

Marcus nodded. "He is a brave and a true man. A braver, truer man I never knew, although I have known many who are . . . or were . . . his equal. I have been blessed by God with good men."

"There you are!" Emrys Aquillius, Marcus's firstborn and only son and heir to the villa and farm, rode up on a great black stallion—a direct descendant of Gaius the Warhorse. "You little villain!" He tethered his horse to the nearby hitching post.

"But, Father!" whined the child. "You said I could ride her! Bellatrix is mine!" He lowered his head, and muttered, "And I wanted to show her to Grandfather."

And you knew this is where I'd be.

"I'm not angry." Emrys Aquillius squatted beside the boy. He raised his son's chin, so Wee Marcus would look at him. Emrys gave the lad a kindly smile. "I'm just worried. She's a fine pony—Bellatrix, aye? But she needs to get to know you, and you need to get to know her before you go riding her off to battle." He winked.

Wee Marcus's eyes brightened. "Yes, Father. I will . . . get to know her."

Emrys tousled the boy's hair. "Good lad."

"You know," said Marcus, "the most important thing a legionnaire must learn is to follow orders."

The boy nodded, looking thoughtful. "You are trying to say that I must obey my parents. Just like in the commandments."

Marcus laughed, gripping his grandson's shoulder. "You are very intelligent too!"

Emrys gave his father a wry grin. "And intelligence is a very important quality for any commander."

The boy beamed. Then, as with any young child, his attention was quickly drawn elsewhere. He pointed at the long, jagged scar on Marcus's thigh. "Tell me the story of that one, Grandfather! Of the spear thrust that nearly killed you!"

Grandfather and father both chuckled. Emrys said, "You've heard that one before!"

"A dozen times or more!" Marcus laughed.

"Tell me again! Please?" pleaded the boy.

Marcus glanced at the setting sun and the long shadows. "Very well, but quickly. It was five years ago—"

"Right before you retired from the army!" interrupted the boy.

"Yes, we had received reports of bandits along the road to Dumnonia. I took the First Century—"

"Your century." The boy grinned, satisfied.

"I have an idea." Marcus winked at his grandson. "Why don't *you* tell *me* the story, and *I* can interrupt *you*?"

The child, not catching the joke, started right in. "You marched along the road, with the banner of the legion held high!"

Marcus and Emrys exchanged grins as the boy exuberantly told the tale of "Centurion Marcus Aquillius Audaxus and the Dumnonian Brigands."

"And if the spear had been a hair's breadth to the right, it would have severed your artery. But no! You pulled the spear from your thigh and..."

When Wee Marcus finished with, "And the capsarium treated your wound with olive oil and stitched it up. And you limped all the way back to the barracks where Grandmother tended you and lovingly nursed you back to full health."

A wistful smile curled Marcus's lips. "Yes, she did. Your grandmother was an amazing woman."

"She was a queen!" cried the lad.

Marcus chuckled. "At one time."

"But I remember, you called her 'my queen.'"

Marcus sighed. "Now that is the greatest lesson a warrior—or any man—must learn. His wife is his queen. And if he treats her as anything less . . ." Marcus's voice faltered.

Emrys finished, ". . . then he is not a man."

The boy asked, "You always treated Grandmother as a queen?"

"Always." Both Marcus and Emrys said it at the same time.

"Always," Marcus repeated. Tears welled in his eyes. "And she always treated me like a king. I was never a king, laddie, but I was *her* king." The tears spilled down his cheeks. "And I always strove to be worthy of her. Now, she waits for me in heaven, with Heavenly Father and Jesus."

Emrys patted his son on the back. "Why don't you take your pony, your Bellatrix, and show her to Aunt Gwawr and Aunt Branwen?"

"Yes!" squealed the boy. He jumped to his feet, still clutching the reins of his pony, and climbed into the saddle. In a moment, Wee Marcus and Bellatrix were trotting away, toward the villa. He lifted his fist and cried, "For Queen Maelona and Audaxus!"

Marcus looked at his son. "Your sisters have arrived already?"

Emrys nodded. "Yes, they and their families arrived just as our valiant, young warrior rode off on his noble steed." He grinned. "Apparently, my sisters and their guards met on the road and decided to ride together."

"I should go and greet them." Marcus began to rise to his feet, but his son laid a hand on Marcus's shoulder.

Emrys shook his head. "No, father. There will be time for that later. You won't be doing the Naming and Blessing of Branwen's son until tomorrow. And I understand that you are to baptize four more men of the cohort tomorrow as well."

Marcus nodded. "Four more souls won for the Lord. But . . . the Church is crumbling. These" —Marcus thought of many choice words to describe the men who now ruled what was left of the Church in Britannia, but he settled on something less crude—"*wolves* in sheep's clothing that pretend to speak in Christus's name . . ." Marcus growled. "They are thieves and adulterers. The priesthood is lost."

"Not lost, father. You hold the priesthood. Aristobulus himself ordained you before I was born."

Marcus bowed his head. "And I think I am the last true elder on this island. But I was forbidden to ordain another." He paused. "Not even you, my son. And when I die . . ."

"Which won't be for many years . . ."

Marcus shook his head. "And when I die, it will all be lost."

"For a time, father . . . until the Restoration comes. Peter and Paul prophesied it." Emrys lowered his voice. "*You* have prophesied it."

Marcus nodded slowly. "Yes, and we must wait on the Lord. Someday, all things will be restored. Including the sealing keys." He leaned forward and plucked another flower from Maelona's burial mound. "And I shall finally be sealed to your mother for eternity." He inhaled the fragrance of the white blossom. "And to you and all my progeny. It will happen . . . in the Lord's time."

Marcus heard a quiet sob. He turned his gaze on Emrys.

The man was covering his eyes with both hands, and tears dripped from between his fingers. "I . . . miss her."

"I do too, lad." He laid a hand on his son's shoulder. "I do too."

Emrys uncovered his eyes and gazed at his father. "Do you think it will be tonight?"

Marcus nodded. "A year and a day."

Emrys smiled through his tears. "Then I will finally get to . . ."

Marcus shrugged. "We'll see. I'm old now and . . ." His voice trailed off as words failed him.

Emrys glanced at the setting sun. "Then I will leave you . . . and Mother . . . alone."

Marcus said nothing as his son rose, untethered his great gray horse, and rode for home.

And Marcus sat alone, watching the shadows lengthen and fade.

As soon as the final ray of sunlight disappeared, Marcus stood.

"Hello, Marcus."

Marcus turned . . .

And she was there, standing no more than a pace away.

In the twilight, she was as lovely and youthful as ever. And her enchanting eyes brimmed with tears.

"My lady," Marcus said. "I thought you might come."

"I gave you a year and a day to mourn her."

Marcus nodded. "Yes, and I thank you for that. I needed that time."

"I miss her too. I loved her. She was my sister." A sob escaped her. "I'm sorry I was not there—the day she fell. Perhaps I could have saved her. I knew her heart was weak."

"I was not there either. She was out riding. And she just . . ."

"I'm sorry, Marcus."

Marcus shook his head, wiping away hot tears. "No. It was her time. She's waiting for me." He took a long glance at her grave. "I know it."

"I know it too. But that is not why I have come. I have come to claim you as I promised."

"I know, but . . . Look at me, Branwen. I'm an old man. I am not the man you once vowed to claim."

"Oh, Marcus . . . Beloved Marcus, you are *not* the same man. You have grown and matured into an even greater man. But in so many ways, you are still the man I fell hopelessly in love with forty-one years ago."

"But I don't know how much time I have left. And the longer I live, my body will fail. Perhaps my mind. You may be nursing a dotard."

"One year . . . One night or twenty years . . . I will cherish every moment. Every moment with you. I love you, Marcus Aquillius Audaxus, husband of Maelona, father of Emrys, Gwawr, and Branwen, grandfather to . . . many. I love you with all my heart."

Marcus said nothing.

"Do you love me, Marcus?"

He met her eyes and stared into their emerald depths. "You know I do. I have loved you all this time. But not with all my heart. My heart has always been divided . . . between two amazing women. But I was true to one and only one."

"And now you can marry me and be true to us both."

"But how could you still want me? How could you want this old . . ."

She stopped his words with a kiss. "I do want you. One night or twenty years and then forever. I will never—"

Marcus smothered her words with a kiss. He wrapped his arms around her. "I love you, Branwen."

No sooner had the words left his lips than they were aloft, flying in the night air. Branwen's wings beat, but they made no sound. However, Branwen and Marcus flew.

They kissed. Passionately. Then tenderly. Then passionately once more.

At last Marcus pulled back. He looked at the woman—whom he had not seen in forty-one years. "Marry me. Please."

She nodded. "Yes, beloved Marcus, I will. Draw up the marriage contract tonight. In your book, as you did with my sister. Draw it up, and I will sign it."

"I will. Tonight. As soon as you meet my family."

"I know all of them. I have—"

"Watched over us from afar. I am well aware. And I am profoundly grateful. But, they do not know you. And they are very anxious to meet you."

"They want to meet *me*?"

"Yes. They know the stories about you. They admire you. And Maelona has told them many times that someday—or some night, rather—you would be their new mother."

She sighed and smiled. "That . . . makes me so very happy. But, Marcus, my beloved Marcus, there is one thing you must do for me first."

"Anything, my love. Anything. What is it?"

"Baptize me."

Interlude VIII

"The swordswoman shall open the eyes of the unwilling and the penitent to the truth of past and future."
from the Book of Marcus Scribonius

July 2017 A.D.

How did ye escape from Annwfyn?" Moira couldn't help herself. She'd always found the tales of fellow Penitents fascinating. But the story Branwen had been telling Moira and Carl for the past hour—of Option Marcus Aquillius Audaxus and Maelona the slave, princess, and queen, of the battle with the forces of Arawn, of Branwen's selfless love for Marcus—that tale topped them all. "After the cave-in? How did ye survive?"

The comedian, having finished his set, had left the stage, and the Fathoms nightclub was filled with the din of muted—or not so muted—conversations for a while. However, the crowd thinned as passengers with "First Dinner" assignments left. Moira and Carl had the "Second Dinner" assignment—with more adults and fewer children—so there was no need to hurry Branwen's tale. Not yet, at least.

The former vampire, with her pale skin and red hair and green eyes—very similar to Moira's, at least on the surface—frowned. Then she shuddered. "It took me the better part of two years to dig my way out."

"Two years?" Carl and Moira exclaimed together.

Branwen nodded. "I had air to breathe, but nothing else. No light. And obviously, no . . . nourishment. I was buried under tons of rock. And I had just Healed from horrific burning. So I was already weakened. But as time passed, as I starved, I became even weaker and weaker. I had done it before—starved myself—but this time I was expending energy at the same time, attempting to escape. I was in constant agony. Many times, I prayed for death. I prayed to Marcus's God. But death never came."

"Ye poor thing." Moira extended a hand and placed it atop Branwen's. "I'm sae sorry, lassie."

Out of the corner of her eye, Moira could see that Carl still regarded Branwen with a degree of suspicion. *A true warrior. Always concerned for our safety.*

And as he has said many a time, when it comes to a potential threat, 'tis nae the intentions that matter – 'tis the capabilities.

And she has a sword.

A gladius – I wonder how old it is? Could it possibly be the sword of Marcus Aquillius?

Branwen closed her eyes, as if she were drawing inward, reliving the horrors of that time. "But eventually, I saw light – starlight, but it was enough. When at last I emerged from the tomb where Arawn had buried me . . . I had no time to rest. I needed nourishment. I was skeletal, so near death. And fortunately, evil blood was close to hand. There were four of them – a band of Arawn's former priests, some of the few who escaped. They lived in the ruins of the village and preyed upon travelers on the road. They were bandits and murderers and rapists still."

Carl asked, "How do you know who and what they were and what they were doing if you killed them?"

Branwen blinked as she turned her eyes to Carl. "I didn't kill them. I Fed, and I interrogated them. I Persuaded them to go make amends – as much as possible – for their evil ways. I think they were caught and executed by the local people. But I didn't kill them."

"Why not?" Moira asked. "From what ye have said, ye had nae compunction against punishin' evildoers."

Branwen nodded. "True, but during my . . . entombment, I prayed many times. And it was not always for death. Many times, it was for deliverance. I knew Marcus's prophecies. One said that someday I would be wedded to him – after Maelona's passing, of course. I clung to that. I prayed for deliverance. I have never killed an innocent. But as I labored in agony to free myself, to get back to Marcus, I vowed to Marcus's God that I would never kill again – except in battle or in self-defense or in the defense of innocents." She sat up straighter. "And in nineteen-and-a-half centuries, I have never broken my vow."

Carl shook his head. "Nineteen and . . . almost two thousand years! We've never met a vampire that old – except for Lilith herself. Sarah Smythe was the closest, and she was just short of one thousand."

Branwen chuckled softly. "You know, for immortals, we just don't seem to be all that long-lived."

Aye. Most give up after a century or so.

Just as Branwen did, starvin' herself in that barrow.

"So," Carl asked, "what happened then? What happened when you revealed yourself to Marcus and Maelona?"

Branwen smiled sadly. "I never did—not to Maelona . . . and not to Marcus until Maelona, my beloved sister, had been gone for a year and a day."

A year and a day. A very Celtic *span of time.*

Branwen continued. "But I watched over them . . . them and their children and grandchildren. Secretly, from the shadows. They suspected my presence. And suspicion eventually turned to certainty."

Her eyes took on a faraway look, and her lips a wistful smile. "Maelona was barren. In all the years she'd been a slave and during her first year of marriage, she had never conceived. Not once. She'd never missed a cycle. After Aristobulus . . . Did you know he was a member of the *original* Seventy? After Aristobulus ordained Marcus an elder, the two of them—Marcus and Aristobulus—administered to Maelona, gave her a blessing. They healed her. It was, I think, the very first physical miracle Marcus had ever witnessed. After all the supernatural manifestations of demonic power, it was the first time Marcus had seen a demonstration of the power of God. But his faith never wavered. Never. That amazing man . . . Anyway, Maelona finally conceived. She bore twins—Emrys and Gwawr, named after the original vilicus and vilica of the estate. This was a great comfort to Spurius Aquillius, I believe."

Spurius . . . The master of the villa and Marcus's elderly "son."

"You said," Carl prompted, "that they became aware of your presence."

"Yes." Branwen flushed. "I'm sorry, but the memories . . . Yes. You see, little Gwawr had gotten herself lost—wandered away from her nurse. She was only two years old at the time. The entire estate and every legionnaire of the garrison participated in the search, but they could not find her. Of course, once night fell and I became aware of the crisis, it was easy for me to locate the child. She was sleeping in the woods, near dead from exposure. I warmed her, holding her next to my breast. I located the nearest searcher—Caeso Lucilius—wrapped the child in my cloak, and placed her in his path. I called Caeso's name. He found the child and brought her home. He reported that a woman's voice had guided him to the wee lassie."

Branwen smiled at the memory, waving a dismissive hand. "Anyway, that's when they were certain of my presence. After that,

Maelona began weaving clothes for me. She left them for me, in the woods, always with a note of thanks and love. Yes, Marcus taught Maelona to read and write." She smiled. "Marcus always kept his promises. Always."

She closed her eyes, drew in a deep breath, and shuddered. "I love that man!" She laughed. "As if that weren't obvious by now. Maelona left cloaks—with extra-deep hoods and extra-long sleeves to protect me from the light—and several gowns . . . beautiful gowns every year. She also left boots for me. And woolen stockings for the winters."

"She loved you very much," Moira said.

Branwen nodded. "And I loved her. And I loved Marcus. How I loved Marcus! Did you know— Of course, you don't know. He built me a cottage. Deep in the woods. Of stone, with a tile roof—so it could not be burned. And he left firewood. And he set guards over it during the daytime, so I would be safe as I Slept."

She grabbed a napkin from the table and dabbed at tears that spilled from her eyes. "I lacked for nothing that the two of them could provide." She cleared her throat and smiled.

Then her smile vanished, and her lips trembled. Tears streaked her mascara. "Maelona's heart—her gracious, loving heart—failed. She was out, riding her pony. I was Sleeping. I was not there. I could not save her. I would have . . . After that, I gave Marcus that year and a day, and then I came to him."

She smiled through her tears. "And we were wed, that very night—after Marcus baptized me. We had twenty-four years together. Twenty-four *wonderful* years. And yes, there was passion and there was tenderness. We were so happy. So very happy."

Twenty-four years? He was seventy when they married. He lived tae ninety-four? "And he was . . . healthy all that time? No dementia or other . . ."

Branwen shrugged. "Oh, he suffered the normal effects of old age. But he was healthy . . . and vigorous for most of his life. In the last two years, his memory began to fade. Toward the end of his life, he often forgot who I was. He confused me with Maelona. Sometimes, he called me by her name. But I loved him and I cherished him to the end."

Moira could not hold back her own tears. "Such a beautiful story."

Branwen handed her a napkin. "After Marcus's passing, I remained for a few years . . . to see my stepchildren and stepgrandchildren grown and settled. And then I . . . moved on, went into seclusion. I continued to watch over Marcus and Maelona's descendants. And I have to this very day, but they are scattered everywhere. I did the best I could, but I could not be everywhere. I could not be there when . . ." She looked away, biting her lower lip.

"But ye said ye were baptized," Moira said, dabbing at her tears. "How, when ye'd killed sae many? I thought—"

Branwen chuckled. "You thought you were the only vampire to be baptized . . . while still a vampire."

"Aye, I did."

"Well, as I said, I had never taken an innocent life. And frankly, back then, it was quite common to baptize anyone who confessed their sins and repented. When I was *rebaptized* in this dispensation . . . Well, it took a bit longer." She smiled. "But that was a condition I had for marrying Marcus. I would not come to the marriage until I was cleansed from sin. Until I was worthy of"—her voice broke, and she sobbed—"worthy of that man, that good, great, noble, brave man. How I love him! Oh, Marcus. Marcus."

Moira glanced from Branwen to Carl and noticed that Carl was weeping as well.

Carl cleared his throat. "That is . . . a beautiful story. It is, but . . . why are you telling it to *us*? Why are you *here*?"

Branwen looked at him with apparent incomprehension. "Didn't I make that clear? No, I suppose I didn't. Sorry. I'm here, talking to the two of you . . . well, because of the prophecy. Marcus's prophecy. The last one. The only one that is not fulfilled. Not yet."

"And what prophecy is that?" Moira asked.

Branwen smiled and bowed her head. "It says that I would protect the Unwilling and the Penitent from the vengeance of the wicked. I'm here to save your lives."

"Our lives?" Moira was astonished. "Ye're here to defend us? From whom? Or what?" *Lloyd? Or some other former vampire?*

"Hold on," Carl said. "Why would Marcus have received a prophecy about *us*? I thought—for the most part, at least—his prophecies were only for him or his family."

Branwen laughed. And there was joy and wonder in her laughter. "Oh, my dears! I thought you knew. You—both of you—are descendants of Marcus and Maelona. I am your . . . stepgreat-grandmother . . . many, many times over. And I'm here to save you, my children."

Chapter XXVI

"Though thy mind be darkened, yet shalt thou and thy beloved have a moment of light."

from the Book of Marcus Scribonius

DCCCLXXIX *Ab Urbe Condita* (126 A.D.)

Branwen held her beloved husband in her arms as she sat on their bed, the bed they had shared for twenty-four years. A dozen candles shone around the room, their room. *The end is coming,* she thought. *Soon, he will be gone.*

And I will be alone again.

Marcus's breathing was labored and irregular, and Branwen could hear the pounding of his noble heart. *Not much longer.*

Her family had gathered around, most of them sitting on the floor. They had come, all of them, from across Cambria, to witness the end. To be with him.

To be with them both.

Emrys tugged at his gray hair, cropped short in the Roman fashion, but he spoke in the Cambrian tongue. "Is he in pain?"

Branwen shook her head. "I do not think so. I don't think he's aware of much. It is . . . merciful this way." *Heavenly Father, grant him a sweet passage. And a sweet reunion with Maelona. How I will miss him! I thank Thee for every hour we've had together. In Christus's name. Amen.*

Marcus gasped. His eyes fluttered open. They moved about, unfocused. And then they found her face.

She smiled at him, holding back tears. "Hello, my love."

He blinked, and his eyes narrowed. "Who are you?"

The question smote her heart like a dagger. Increasingly, he had not been able to remember her. Her smile tightened, and her lips quivered. "I'm your wife, beloved."

He sighed and smiled at her. "Maelona."

She choked. It was not the first time he had mistaken Branwen for his first wife. His memories of long ago were sharper than those of recent years—the precious years they'd spent together. "No, my love. I'm Branwen." *Do not weep! Don't let his last sight be one of tears.*

Confusion clouded his face. "Where is Maelona? Maelona!"

Branwen forced a smile. "She's waiting for you. In heaven. You'll be with her soon, my love. But I'm here with you now. Branwen. I love you, Marcus."

"Where's Maelona?"

"Mother?" It was Emrys who'd spoken.

"Yes, my son?" Branwen replied, whispering. The tears were so close.

"Give him a moment of clarity." Her stepson, like most of the family, wept. "Please, Mother. You both deserve it."

A moment of clarity. She knew precisely what he meant. Branwen nodded. "I shall try." *Please, let this work.* She bent her head. Her fangs extended. She pressed her lips to his wrinkled neck, feeling the pulse of his sweet blood. She bit down.

And blood filled her mouth. She drank slowly, savoring each drop of his precious life. However, she took only a few mouthfuls. Marcus moaned in ecstasy, his frail body twitching. Then, she licked the wound to seal it. She lifted her head.

He blinked, his eyes unfocused, a groan of pleasure exhaling from his lips.

And then he saw her. "Branwen!" He smiled. "Branwen. My love."

"Marcus, my heart. I am here."

"I'm dying, aren't I?"

She nodded, and her tears fell on his cheek. "Soon. Soon you will go home to God and Maelona. And I will miss you terribly."

He managed a sad smile. His breathing was so shallow. "I will miss . . . you too. You have been . . . my heart, my life for . . . how long has it . . . been?"

She smiled. "Twenty-four years, two months, and seventeen nights. And all of it wonderful, joyful."

A small movement of his head—barely a shake—indicated his disagreement. "You have . . . been forced . . . to nurse a dotard. I . . . warned you."

"I have cherished every moment, as I have cherished you."

"So young. So . . . beautiful. And you stayed with me. An old . . . man."

"Yes, an old man. But the greatest, sweetest, bravest man—old or young—I have ever known."

"You once told . . . told me . . . you would never . . . be a second wife."

"I am so proud, so grateful to be your wife. First or second. Because I have you for my husband. I will never marry another. Never, though I wait a thousand years. Or more. And I love Maelona too. I am grateful to have her for my sister."

A wheeze—but Branwen recognized it for what it was—a laugh.

"You used to . . . frighten me. So . . . terrifying. So lovely. Alluring. Scary."

She smiled.

"Please," he whispered, "watch over them."

"I will do my best, my love. I promise."

"You will see . . . the Restoration of . . . the Church. You will . . . be alone. For so long. I'm . . . so sorry." Tears spilled from his eyes, ran down the sides of his face and into his white hair. "But when the . . . time comes . . . when you're . . . finished here . . . Come to me. I will be . . . waiting. We will . . . be waiting. Come to me."

"I will, Marcus. I love you."

"I love you . . . too." He paused for several shallow breaths. His eyes seemed to lose focus. "Maelona! Maelona!"

It's over.

Our moment of clarity is over.

"Maelona!" he whispered. "I'm coming."

No! He's going! He sees *her!* "Go to her, Marcus." Fresh tears dropped from her eyes to his cheeks. "Go to her."

She bent and kissed his lips softly, tenderly.

And he kissed her back. "Goodbye, my love. Sweet Branwen."

"Goodbye, my heart."

Once more, he whispered, "Maelona. Maelona." He exhaled slowly—one last long breath.

And then he was gone.

Branwen held his body close.

And as her family quietly left the bedchamber to give her some privacy, she wept.

She wept long and loud.

Chapter XXVII

"In the last days, in Britannia, the swordswoman shall preserve the unwilling and the penitent from death."
from the Book of Marcus Scribonius

July 2017 A.D.

Anyone observing the three of them—Moira, Carl, and Branwen—would have assumed they were old and dear friends. Or perhaps close family. Moira and Carl introduced Branwen to dinner companions—or anyone else they met aboard—as Moira's "aunt."

"'Tis true enough," Moira had confided to her husband. "She *is* Maelona's adopted sister."

"Well," Carl had replied, "she's *my* aunt too. But sticking with the story that she's *your* relation will raise fewer questions." He grinned. "And we won't even *try* to go with 'stepgreat-grandmother many times over.'"

When people asked Branwen where she lived, she replied that she'd been born and raised in Wales, and she'd lived in the UK all her life. "Never left—except for this cruise. Not once." Normally, Branwen's accent was . . . unique, difficult to place—she certainly did not sound Welsh. But when speaking with Carl and Moira's acquaintances, she adopted a very convincing contemporary Welsh accent.

Though she was introduced simply as "Branwen," if anyone asked her last name, she beamed and proudly replied, "Aquillius. Branwen Aquillius."

Branwen had managed to pay off enough crewmembers so she could join the Morgans for dinners—occupying an add-on seat—where seating was carefully arranged and assigned with the same four couples. There were only two dinners left on the cruise, and the other three couples readily accepted "Aunt Branwen" into their dinner circle. One woman of that circle asked, quite innocently, it seemed, if

Branwen had also been a vampire.

Branwen laughed it off, and the question was not asked again.

For the remainder of the voyage, the three of them were inseparable, except, of course, when Carl and Moira retired to their stateroom, and Branwen disappeared into a huge "concierge-level" suite. And upon docking at Dover, Carl and Moira learned that Branwen even managed to secure a seat on the Disney Express motor coach back to London Heathrow Airport.

And so, for the entire journey back to London, they continued to chat. Carl and Moira sat together in a row near the back, away from the other passengers so the three of them could talk without raising eyebrows. Branwen knelt on the bus seat in front of them, facing backward, leaning over the back of the seat. Branwen deluged them with questions about their lives—before and after their times as vampires. "I want to know everything! Especially about your children. You know, I always treated my stepchildren and grandchildren and great-grandchildren as my own. And they loved and accepted me."

And as a vampire, Moira thought, *ye could ne'er have any of yer own. And once ye were mortal, ye were still true to your long-dead Marcus.*

And so they talked, with Branwen drinking in every detail. Some things, she had already learned. But of course, some things were new to her.

"Easter Aberchalder?" Branwen was shocked to learn Moira's birthplace. "Easter Aberchalder? Near Inverness?"

"Aye. 'Tis but a wee village. A *wee* village."

Branwen shook her head in amazement. "No wonder I lost track of your branch of the MacDonald line! You seemed to have disappeared from the face of the earth."

"So you *were* seeking us out," Carl said, "trying to find the Unwilling and the Penitent all that time? All those centuries?"

Branwen nodded, but she bit her lip. "I didn't try to follow the Morgan line once it left Britain. I'm sorry, Carl. You see, the prophecy said I would save your lives in Britannia. 'In the last days, in Britannia, the swordswoman shall preserve the unwilling and the penitent from death.' So I stayed here. That's why I didn't come to America when I found out who you were, when you announced your presence to the world. I knew I had to wait *here*." Her eyes brightened. "And when I ran into you at Alnwyck . . . The Spirit sent me there that day, by the way." She winked at Moira. "And there you were!"

"And ye just naturally took along a sword?" Moira asked with a wink of her own.

Branwen shrugged. "Naturally!" She patted the bag on the seat next to her. "Never go anywhere without it. Well, except church and the temple. Oh, don't look at me like that, child. Of course, I've been endowed!"

"It's not that." Carl shook his head in awe. "The sword of Marcus Aquillius! It's amazing that it has survived almost two millennia. Even with great care, the steel should be brittle by now."

Moira recalled how Branwen had shown them the blade—in the privacy of her luxurious shipboard suite, of course. The lovingly polished steel gleamed, without the slightest hint of its antiquity. Moira took the ivory handle, which had never yellowed, in her right hand and slapped the round wooden pommel—also well-oiled and preserved—with the palm of her left. To her astonishment, she was rewarded with a vibration running throughout the blade—there was still some flexibility in the ancient steel!

"I have a theory about that," Moira said as they rode the motor coach to Dover. "When a vampire handles a blade constantly, the *tactile telekinesis*—'tis what Carl dubbed a vampire's ability tae lift and move objects while we touch them—the tactile telekinesis actually strengthens and preserves the blade. D'ye recall how it did nae matter whether a sword was made of the finest carbon steel or the poorest stainless-steel crap"—she unconsciously rolled the "r" in the word—"when 'twas wielded by a vampire? All that mattered was the strength of the *mind*. And skill of the swordsman or woman, of course."

Carl nodded. "You could be right about that."

Moira grinned impishly. "Oh, laddie, ye ken I'm always right!"

Carl returned the impish grin. "Secret of a happy marriage!"

Branwen grinned from ear to ear. "You two! I'm glad you're so happy. After what you've been through, after what you've done, you deserve it. And that explanation works for me—just as long as I can keep my beloved's sword for my own." She pursed her lips thoughtfully. "The scabbard is long gone, of course. I did all I could to preserve it, but . . . Perhaps, you are right about the blade, my child."

Moira couldn't suppress a giggle. "I love it when ye call me that! 'Tis been sae lange . . ." Her expression fell. *Sae lange since I had parents.*

And I am goin' home . . . tae where my mother and father were murdered. And tae where I was . . .

Nae, lassie. Dinnae dwell on it. The Spirit calls me home. And I'm goin' home.

"Moira, what's wrong?" Carl and Branwen asked as one.

Moira blinked. Then she waved her hand dismissively. "Ach. 'Twas nae more than some . . . unpleasant memories. My village . . . Where . . ."

Carl squeezed her hand, and Branwen reached around the seat and patted her knee.

Moira said, "I ken we must go. But I am nae anxious tae be there."

Carl squeezed her hand again. "I think we can take our time. We have to go, but we can make a few stops along the way."

Aye. A few stops. A few days. Tae let me build up my courage.

"How about a day in London?" Carl suggested. "Just like we planned?"

Moira chuckled. "Just like *ye* planned, ye sneaky thing."

"You know me and history." Carl winked at Moira. "Gotta go see the Tower of London!" He looked up at Branwen. "Hey, stepgreat-grandmother many times over? Ever been to the Tower of London? Moira hasn't."

Branwen looked at Moira askance. "You've never been? You, with your love of swords?" Branwen laughed. "Well, you, my child, are in for a treat. Oh, and by the way, I *love* calling you that too." Her lips tightened, and her eyes misted up. "The truth is, I've known you both for such a short time, but I already love you. Marcus and Maelona's children. *My* children."

"You know what?" Carl said. "The feeling's mutual. For an old lady, I mean a really *old* lady, you are pretty darn cool."

Moira nodded. "I feel as if I've known ye all my life."

♠ ♠ ♠

"That is *not* what Boudicca looked like!" Branwen shook her head in disgust as she stared at the bronze monument of the ancient queen and her two daughters riding in a chariot. The huge monument stood near the banks of the Thames in London, within sight of Big Ben's clock tower—now renamed "Elizabeth Tower."

"Ye met her?" Moira asked. "Boudicca?"

"No, I was in the barrow during that period, but—"

Carl gave Branwen a dubious look. "Then how would you know . . ."

Branwen smirked. "Well, my children, for one thing, she and her daughters wouldn't have gone around bare-breasted."

"But the Druids . . ." Carl protested.

"Oh, some women did. A few. To look fierce." Branwen lowered her voice, as people—tourists, mostly—stared. "The fools. I never did. Can you imagine going into combat with your tender . . . *bits* exposed and wobbling around?"

Moira giggled.

Carl grinned. "I can imagine—" He judiciously stopped himself when Moira yanked on his arm.

Men!

Branwen chuckled. "Some idiot men did too—ran around with nothing but a torc around their necks. And their tender bits . . ." She shuddered. "Never mind."

Carl shuddered as well.

"Anyway," Branwen said, "it was nowhere nearly as common as the Romans reported. I think it was just the shock of seeing a few topless women among the warriors."

Moira thought it was high time they brought the original subject around again. "So what else is wrong with it? The monument, I mean?"

Branwen waved at the huge statue again. "Well, for another thing, the chariot is too big, too grand. Like something out of Ben-Hur."

Carl nodded. "I get it. What else?"

Branwen screwed up her face into a grimace. "Well, why build a monument to *her* at all?"

"Because she was a heroine," Carl said. "She stood up and fought against Roman oppression."

"Yes, she did," Branwen said. "And at first, she was fully justified. And victorious. But she became a monster. At the end, she was slaughtering and butchering her own people. What she did to the women of Camulodunum was . . . an atrocity." She paused. "Marcus fought her, you know. He fought in the battle that defeated her. He told me the truth, holding nothing back. Whatever Boudicca started out to do, she became far worse than the enemy she fought. There are lines one must never cross. Not even in war. Marcus taught me that. Marcus held to that—to his principles—all his life."

Moira put an arm around her. "After all this time . . ."

Branwen nodded, dashing away a tear. "I still love him. I . . . burn for him."

Carl and Moira locked eyes, and Moira saw her own burning love reflected in his eyes. *I know just how ye feel, Grandmother.*

❦ ❦ ❦

The drive to Easter Aberchalder took a little over twelve hours, with the traffic and a few stops for food and restrooms. As they turned away from Inverness and headed up into the Highlands, Moira's sense of dread grew and writhed, like snakes in her gut.

Almost home.

It wasn't that anything looked familiar to her—nothing did, except the loch and the burns. *Sae much has changed.*

They traveled in a rented car, a Ford SUV—rented by Carl, but driven by Branwen, since she was the only one of the three with experience driving on British roads. And conversation had faded away to nothing.

Perhaps they sense my mood.

Carl and Moira sat together in the back seat. Carl held Moira's hand, and Moira could sense tension in his muscles. *I'm sae glad ye're here, laddie. I dinnae think I could face it alone.*

They drove through the tiny village of Wester Aberchalder, then across Aberchalder Burn via a tiny, wooden bridge. They turned off the single-lane, paved road and onto a dirt track. They were able to keep sight of the trees that lined the tiny stream—the burn—on their right.

At a small fork in the unpaved road, they arrived at the even smaller collection of farms that comprised Easter Aberchalder. Moira was struck by how truly small the village was. *Even tinier than I remember.*

Branwen drove down and around, exploring the handful of short roads of the village. "Tell me where to stop, child."

Moira acknowledged with a silent nod that she doubted Branwen could see. *I dinnae know what I'm looking for.*

They rounded a small bend. "Stop," Moira said.

Branwen stopped in the middle of the road. There was no shoulder on which to park.

Moira got out of the car. She pointed to a small wooded slope. "These trees were nae here, but . . ."

She walked slowly down the incline, through the woods. Carl and Branwen followed a few paces behind. They didn't try to catch up to her.

This, at the last . . . This I must do alone.

Her eyes swept back and forth. "They would hae taken the stones tae build walls and fences. There may be nothin' left at—"

She stopped.

It was no more than a small pile of rocks—rocks arranged in a shape that once resembled a rectangle. Or the base of a chimney.

Moira dropped to her knees, not caring about dirt getting on her jeans. She expected it all to come back to her—to overwhelm her. The English soldiers, burning everything, bayoneting her mother and father as they did the livestock. Raping her. All of them. The horror, the pain, the emptiness. The rage. The rage that drove her to seek out Sarah Smythe and accept Conversion—vampirism. Damnation.

And the memories were there, jostling like a herd of diseased sheep trying to force their way through a narrow gate—into her mind. Into her.

But those memories stayed at the fringe. Stayed away. She kept them away.

I am nae that person anymore.

Nae, I am *that person. I am Moira MacDonald of Easter Aberchalder. I am the Penitent. Together, Carl and I slew Lilith. And we ended the curse.*

I am that person. And more.

I am Dr. Moira MacDonald Morgan, wife of Carl, mother of Rolf, Sarah, Sergei, and Maighread. I am no longer a Daughter of Lilith—I am a Daughter of God.

"This is it," she whispered. "All that's left of it."

Carl knelt beside her. "Not much to come home to. I'm sorry."

"Nae, the Spirit led me here. For a reason. I dinnae ken why."

She dug her fingers into the earth, dislodging a stone—a broken bit of slate. "This was probably part of the hearth." *The hearth.*

Something clicked in her brain. A memory.

"The hearth," she said, digging with her fingers, finding other bits of broken slate. She pulled them aside.

Carl dug with her. In moments, Branwen knelt on the other side of her and dug too.

As the bits of slate cleared, they had exposed a shallow hole, rectangular, one-and-a-half by three feet. They brushed the dirt away and revealed a flat, rectangular slab of carved granite.

Moira stared at the stone.

"What is it?" asked Carl.

Moira breathed rapidly, her heart thundering in her chest. She dug her fingers into the earth, scraping around the edge. "Clear around it."

In a few minutes, the entire slab was exposed.

"What is it?" Carl repeated.

Moira smiled. "'Tis a lid. Here. From the front, now—help me lift it. Gently."

They dug their fingers in, hooked them under the stone lid, and lifted.

Carl gasped. Under the stone, lay a coffer—a box of stone, sealed with lead along the seams.

And inside the coffer lay two items, wrapped in cloth. One rectangular and thick, and one long and thin.

Moira reached in and pulled out the rectangular shape. Reverently, she laid it on her lap and unwrapped it.

"A book!" Carl whispered with awe. "It looks like a Bible."

Moira nodded, hastily brushing away tears so they wouldn't fall on the precious tome. "Our family Bible. It contains—"

A sob interrupted Moira, but it hadn't come from her. She turned her eyes to Branwen.

The woman was sobbing. She reached into the box and pulled out the long, thin object. "It was lost! So long ago. Lost! Please, God! Let it b-be . . ."

Branwen held the bundle to her chest. "Please!" She lowered it to her lap and removed the wrappings—oil-cloth, they appeared to be.

"What is it?" Carl asked for the third time. "A scroll?"

Branwen nodded and she sobbed, but her tears were tears of joy. "Help me, please. Gently. So gently. Mustn't break the vellum."

Moira set down the precious family bible on its wrappings and set it aside. She and Carl helped Branwen unroll the ancient scroll.

"It looks like genealogy," Carl said. "A family tree."

Branwen nodded. "Yes," she whispered. "Yes!"

The handwriting, the script on the genealogy changed with each line, narrowing as it went back. With each line, the writing faded more and more. And then it ended.

And after the long, long list of names and dates, appeared lines of faded text, printed in a strong, even hand.

Branwen squealed. Weeping uncontrollably, and with a trembling finger, she caressed the letters. Her lips quivered. "Marcus! Marcus! Oh, Marcus!"

"What is it?" Carl asked yet again. "Is it . . . No way! It can't be."

"It is!" cried Branwen through her tears. "The Book of Marcus Scribonius!"

"The prophecies?" Carl eyed the Latin writing with awe. "Marcus's prophecies? In his own hand?"

"Oh, yes!" Branwen nodded. "And so much more. I memorized all the prophecies. But what I'm look— Yes! Here it is. Oh, Marcus. Dear, beloved Marcus."

Moira read the ancient script and she saw the two names written below, one in a different hand from the rest.

Carl read out the second name. "'BRANWEN.' That's you!"

"Carl," Moira said, "it's her marriage contract."

"Finally!" Branwen sobbed. "Finally, I have proof. Proof of my marriage to Marcus!" She turned her joyful, tear-streaked face to each of them in turn. "Don't you understand what this means?"

Moira smiled. "Aye. It means ye can finally go to the temple and be sealed to your husband."

"For all eternity." Branwen closed her eyes. "I thank Thee, Heavely Father. I thank Thee. As Marcus prophesied so very long ago, we will finally be one! I thought it would be after my own death. But it is to be here! Now!"

♦ ♦ ♦

Over the next few days, using Carl's laptop and the less-than-reliable internet connection at their hotel in Inverness, the three of them feverishly cataloged and entered family history records into the Latter-day Saint Family History database. The family Bible contained all of Moira's family tree, as well as carefully transcribed copies of all the contents of the Book of Marcus Scribonius—including the prophecies and the marriage contracts for Marcus and Maelona, and for Marcus and Branwen.

Branwen barely stopped for meals, working through the night until she fell asleep in front of the laptop, her fingers still resting on the keyboard. Carl and Moira helped, of course, but Branwen wanted to make certain they had every connection—down to Carl and Moira's own children.

Moira placed several calls to Craig Foster back at the Family History Department, and all the necessary clearances were hurried through.

And at last, on the first day of August, the three of them journeyed to the Preston England Temple, where Branwen reluctantly left Marcus's precious gladius—hidden inside the big satchel, of course—in the rented SUV. And late that afternoon—with Carl acting as proxy for Marcus Aquillius Audaxus, and Moira acting as proxy for Maelona—after a wait of almost two thousand years, Marcus and Maelona were sealed together for eternity. And then, with Carl once again acting as proxy for Marcus, Branwen was finally sealed to her beloved husband.

And all three of them—Branwen and her two stepgreat-grandchildren many times over—wept unrestrained tears of joy.

Then all three of Marcus and Maelona's children were sealed to their parents. Branwen acted as proxy for her two stepdaughters, Gwawr Aquillius and Branwen Aquillius. They had to enlist the help of a male temple worker to stand in for Emrys Aquillius.

And they wept some more—including the temple worker who'd marveled at the date on the ordinance paperwork.

♦ ♦ ♦

Night had fallen by the time they at last exited the temple. "Of course," Branwen said, "we have to do the work for all of them—all of Marcus and Maelona's descendants. All of my family. My *family*." She sighed, but it came out as a happy sigh. "We have a long, long way to go."

Carl hugged Branwen tight. "Yes, Grandmother. But today was a good start."

Branwen kissed Carl on the cheek. "Yes, my child, today was indeed a good start." She turned to Moira. She took both of Moira's hands in hers. Then Branwen gave in to an utterly girlish urge and bounced up and down while holding Moira's hands. "Oh, Moira! It's like being a new bride all over again."

Moira laughed and bounced along with her. "Congratulations, Mrs. Aquillius!"

Abruptly, Branwen stopped bouncing, and her smiled turned wistful. "Minus the groom, of course. But he's *mine* now. And someday, I'll be with him again. With both of them."

She locked arms with Carl and with Moira. And the three of them strode arm-in-arm to the parking lot and the rented SUV.

Branwen halted, hissing.

"What is it?" Moira asked.

Then Moira saw it—broken glass by the driver's door.

"Get behind me," Branwen whispered.

But neither Carl nor Moira moved. "Whatever it is," Carl whispered, "we face it together." He turned around. "I've got your six."

Watchin' our backs, Moira translated in her mind.

She scanned the darkness. The lights of the parking lot showed their vehicle, the broken glass, the shattered driver's window on the right side—but nothing else, other than a handful of other cars dotting the outskirts of the lot.

Moira approached their car and looked cautiously inside. She could see the rock that had been used to smash the window—it was sitting on the driver's seat. But there was nothing else.

Nothing. Else.

"No!" Branwen whispered. "Marcus's sword!" She rushed forward and bent through the window.

Moira heard a low, sinister laugh, and she and Carl turned toward the sound.

Three men strolled casually toward them. The two on the ends stood taller, were of heavier build. Both wore sweatshirts. But the man at the center wore a dark hoodie, his wrist in a cast—

Lloyd.

"Lookin' for this?" He held up the gladius in his left hand. The ancient sword gleamed in the lights of the parking lot. "Pretty piece, this." The trio of thugs continued to advance. The men on either end carried knives—a meat cleaver on the left and a long butcher knife on the right.

Instinctively, Moira considered their options. *We could run, but Branwen and I are in heels. We could fight, but they have all the weapons.*

I doubt we can talk *our way out of this.*

Branwen straightened up from the broken window. She turned toward the intruders. Behind her back she held a strip of cloth, ripped from the sleeve of her dress, and she quickly wound it about one end of a shard of what appeared to be mirror glass. "You are not worthy to hold that sword."

"Wha'? This sword?" Lloyd laughed, waving it around. "Me? No' worthy?"

Branwen gave him a feral smile, full of gleaming teeth. "Surrender that sword, and I will let you depart with your lives. Otherwise, you are dead men."

"No' worthy?!" Lloyd repeated, apparently enraged.

That struck a sour chord with him.

"Dead men?" Lloyd let out an inarticulate roar. "I was a GOD!"

"No, you weren't," said Carl. "You were a murderous vampire. I gave you a chance once. Now back off!"

The two groups were within a couple of paces of each other. The attackers spread out, encircling their prey. But Moira, Carl, and Branwen—all experienced combatants—instinctively put their backs to each other and assumed fighting stances.

"We got you!" said the man with the meat cleaver. "You're unarmed, ya bastards!"

"Pretend you've got a gun in your purse," whispered Branwen.

Moira gave the slightest nod. "Unarmed?" She opened her purse. "I've got a gun, laddies." She reached in, but she never took her eyes off the man in front of her.

Moira's assailant hesitated.

Branwen let out an inhuman scream, like a banshee of legend.

And as one, Moira, Carl, and Branwen attacked.

Moira leapt at her man, catching his knife hand at the wrist. She lifted the arm, ducked in, and punched the man hard under his armpit. *Hit the nerve cluster! Paralyze the arm.* He yelped, but the knife didn't fall from his hand. Instead, he shoved her to the ground, falling atop her, crushing her, knocking the wind out of her.

He held the cleaver over her neck.

As she struggled for breath, she brought up both hands to keep the knife from her throat. She held the man's wrist up.

But he had the advantage in strength and mass.

And Moira's sight grew dim. *I'm goin' tae die. Carl!*

Her attacker jerked, then rolled off her, the knife clattering to the pavement.

As Moira fought to breathe, finally drawing in a lungful of life-giving air, she saw Branwen standing above her. Branwen's dress was ripped and blood-soaked. She held the gladius in her hand. And it also dripped with blood. In her other hand, she held the improvised knife. It and her hand dark with gore.

Then Carl was at Moira's side, holding her. "Moira! You okay?"

She nodded. "Aye. But 'twas Branwen . . . She killed my man. She saved me."

Moira scanned the area. Lloyd lay on his back, his hands curled in claws over his abdomen. But he did not move. The other two attackers lay in dark pools.

Branwen knelt beside them. She dropped the glass knife. Her hand went to her skirt. The light-blue fabric was now very dark. And very wet. She clutched her inner thigh—high, near the groin.

And blood spurted between her fingers.

"The artery!" Moira cried in a strangled voice. She scrambled to get to her knees. "Carl! Give me yer belt!" *Make a tourniquet!*

But Moira knew it would do no good.

Branwen hunched over. "It's . . . too high. Too high . . . on my leg. Can't stop . . ."

"Please," Carl said. He gently forced Branwen to lie down. "Let her try. She's a doctor." He handed Moira his belt.

Moira bent over the wound, examined it quickly. Then she shook her head. "Nae anythin' I can do. I'm sorry." She applied direct pressure with her hands while the blood spurted around them. Moira knew it was only a matter of moments. "I'm sae sorry."

Lying on her back, Branwen nodded—a small movement of her head. She put a bloody hand to Moira's face, touching her cheek. "I love you." Then she looked at Carl and lifted her hand, but it fell short of his face. "I love you too . . . child." She smiled weakly. She pulled the sword to her chest and clutched it with both hands. Tears fell from her eyes, down her temples, and into her hair. "Twice now . . . I have . . . given my . . . my life . . . for those . . . I love. There was . . . more to . . . the final . . . prophecy. 'And she shall . . . lay her life . . . upon the altar . . . the second . . . time. And at last, she . . . shall find . . . joy.'" She smiled. "Give . . . my life . . . for you . . . m-my ch-children."

Branwen's eyelids fluttered, and her eyes lost their focus. But an expression of joy lit her pallid features. "Yes, Marcus! Yes! I'm coming! I'm coming . . . my love."

"Go to him, Branwen," Carl whispered, his own tears falling on Branwen's face. "He's waiting. You will finally be together. Two thousand years . . ."

"Oh, Marcus," Branwen whispered. "Marcus! Marcus . . ."

And then she was gone.

Carl and Moira held each other.

And they wept—children grieving for their lost mother. But even in their grief, there was joy. For they gazed down upon Branwen's face.

Branwen's open lips were curled in a smile, and upon her breast lay the sword of her beloved Marcus.

The End

Dramatis Personae

Agrippa Corfidius - Vexillarius—standard-bearer—friend to Marcus Scribonius

Aristobulus - Judean tin merchant, Christian missionary, one of the original Seventy

Branwen - Celt—"Daughter"

Caeso Lucilius - Tesserarius—officer of the watch—friend to Marcus Scribonius

Conwy - Druid priest

Demetrius - Calo—Greek herdsman

Emrys - Celt—vilicus and magister pecoris of Spurius Aquillius

Faustus Vivanius - Legionnaire

Gaius Aquillius Regulus - Centurion—pilus prior of the Second Cohort, Legio XIV Gemina—mentor to Marcus Scribonius

Gaius Publicia - Capsarium (combat nurse)

Gaius Suetonius Paulinus - Roman governor (propraetor) of Britannia—legate of Legio XIV Gemina

Gwawr - Celt - vilica of Spurius Aquillius's estate, wife of Emrys

Gwynn - Calo—Celt tentmaker, tanner, butcher

Llywellyn - Druid warrior

Maelona - Slave—former princess and one-time witch

Marcus Lucilius - Legionnaire

Marcus Scribonius Audaxus - Option—recent convert to Christianity

Marcus Tarquinius - Legionnaire

Marcus Vivanius - Legionnaire

Mettius Canius - Legionnaire—"The Ferret"

Nonus Sestius - Legionnaire

Pwyll - Celt—farmer

Quintus Aquillius Lucanus - Centurion—Sixth Century, Reserves, Legio XX Valeria Victrix

Septimus Scribonius - Legionnaire—friend and kinsman of Marcus Scribonius

Spurius Orcivius - Cornicen—horn-blower—friend to Marcus Scribonius

Spurius Aquillius Rufus - Roman cattle farmer

Glossary

Ab Urbe Condita - "From the Founding of the City" The Roman calendar is measured in years starting at the founding of Rome in 753 B.C. This story takes place in 814 Ab Urbe Condita or 61 A.D.

Annwfyn (pr. "ann-OO-vin") - The underworld, the realm of the dead, the kingdom of Arawn.

Apodyterium - The changing room of a Roman bath.

Barrow - Heap of earth over a stone tomb.

Brekekekèx-koàx-koáx - Greek rendering of a frog's croak.

Britannia - Britain.

Burn - stream, brook.

Caldarium - the hot pool in a Roman bath.

Caligae - Roman boots—hobnailed and open—often mistaken for sandals.

Calo (pl. Calones) - "Soldier's slave"—servants owned by the century, rather than by an individual soldier.

Cambria - Wales.

Capsarium - Roman combat nurse, medic, physician's assistant.

Centurion (pl. Centuriones) - Commander of a century, wears a helmet with a latitudinal (left to right) plume.

Century (pl. Centuria) - Military unit composed of eighty men divided into ten contubernia, plus four junior officers and a centurion. Centuria of the First Cohort are composed of one hundred and fifty men, rather than eighty.

Clinium (pl. Clinia) - Wide couches where guests reclined during a formal Roman dinner.

Cognomen - Optional Roman third name, similar to a nickname, bestowed by a third party, may or may not be complimentary.

Cohort - Military unit composed of six centuria.

Contubernium (pl. Contubernia) - Military unit of eight men.

Cornicen - Horn blower, junior officer, blows signals on the cornu, wears a lion skin and head over his armor.

Cornu - Long, three-piece, circular signal horn, blown by cornicen.

Cuneum formate - Command to form a wedge formation, used to penetrate an enemy line.

Cuneus - Roman military wedge formation in the shape of a *V* with the commander at the leading point—used to penetrate enemy lines.

Decimate - Military punishment against a century—option lines up the century and stabs, at random, one man in every ten, i.e., executes one tenth of the century.

Dumnonia - Cornwall.

Fabro (pl. Fabri) - Military engineer, blacksmith, carpenter.

Frigidarium - The cold pool in a Roman bath.

Furca - "Marching pole" carried over the shoulder with a legionnaire's pack and other gear attached to one end.

Galea - Roman helmet.

Gladius - Roman short sword.

Goetia - Illusionist, charlatan, trickster.

Hastile - Option's staff of office, roughly six feet in length, with a wooden ball at the tip—used by the option during marches to keep legionnaires in line.

Heres Patris - Heir to the pater of a great Roman family.

Lectus Imus - The "low" couch where the host and his family reclined while eating at formal Roman dinner.

Lectus Medius - The "middle" couch where the highest-ranking guests reclined while eating at formal Roman dinner.

Lectus Summus - The "high" couch where the lowest-ranking guests reclined while eating at formal Roman dinner.

Legate - Roman general, commander of a legion.

Legio/Legion - Military unit, comprised of ten cohorts, commanded by a legate.

Lorica Segmentata - Segmented steel Roman breastplate, extremely flexible.

Magister Pecoris - Manager of a cattle farm.

Magus - Religious worker of miracles.

Mensa - Table where food is laid in a formal Roman dining room.

Nomen - Roman second name, surname.

Option/Optio - Roman junior officer, second-in-command of a century, "chosen officer."

Orbem formate - Command to form the circular orbis formation.

Orbis - Military formation comprised of legionnaires forming concentric circles around the centurion—employed when the enemy could attack from any side.

Pater - Head of a Roman family.

Pax Romana - The peace of Rome.

Pilum (pl. Pila) - Roman throwing spear—"one-use" throwing spear—the top half of the spear is made of mild steel, the bottom half is made of wood—once it strikes, the steel portion bends under its own weight, so the enemy cannot pick it up and throw it back—after the battle, the Roman fabri would gather up the bent pila and hammer them out straight for reuse.

Pilus Prior (pl. Pila Prior) - "First Spear"—senior centurion of the cohort, i.e., commander of the cohort and his own century.

Posca - Roman drink comprised of wine (or vinegar), water, herbs, and sometimes honey—makes local water safe to drink—standard drink ration of the army.

Praenomen - Roman first name—at this period, there were only eighteen male names in use—therefore the name was almost always tied to the nomen (family name).

Procenturion - Acting centurion, but not officially promoted to that rank—temporarily serving as the commander of a century.

Propraetor - Acting governor of a province.

Prooption - Acting option, but not officially promoted to that rank—temporarily serving as the second-in-command of a century.

Protesserarius - Acting tesserarius, but not officially promoted to that rank—temporarily serving as the third-in-command of a century.

Pugio - Roman dagger—leaf-shaped blade.

Repellere equites - Command to form up in a square formation with shields and spears to repel a cavalry charge.

Sagum (pl. saga) - Cloak worn by legionnaires—made of wool, treated with lanolin (to make it water-resistant) and dyed red.

Sgian Dubh (pr. "SKĀN-doo") - Traditional short Scottish knife, worn in the stocking or boot—the name translates from the Gaelic as "black handle."

Shillelagh (pr. "shil-LAY-lee") - Irish fighting cane, made of lacquered blackthorn.

Soleae Ferreae - Iron shoe for a horse or mule—encases the entire hoof and held in place by leather straps.

Strigil - A Roman bathing tool, constructed of steel, resembling a blunt, flattened hook—used to scrape dirt, sweat, and oil from the skin.

Subligar (pl. subligaris) - A wraparound, linen loincloth worn by Roman men. The feminine version is called a subligia.

Tanad - In Welsh Celtic belief, a creature that exists between life and death, invades and takes possession of a tomb—attempts to lure living subjects into the tomb in order to turn the victim into a tanad.

Tartarus - In Roman belief, the underworld, realm of the dead, a place of torment—roughly the equivalent of Hell.

Tepidarium - The warm pool in a Roman bath.

Tesserarius - Roman junior officer—officer of the watch or guard—carries a clay tablet on which is inscribed the challenge and password of the day—assigns guards or sentries—third-in-command of the century, wears a wolf's skin and head over his armor.

Testudo - Military formation—"Tortoise"—shield wall designed to protect against a superior force—sometimes referred to as a "Roman tank."

Toga (pl. Togae) - Formal Roman robe worn by men and women.

Tor - A lone hill.

Torc - a Celtic neck ornament of twisted copper or gold wire forming an incomplete circle with the opening at the front—thought to give a warrior magical protection in battle.

Triclinium - Formal Roman dining room where three couches are arranged like a letter *U* around a mensa or table where food is set—each guest ate while reclining with their feet toward the outside of the room.

Tunica (pl. Tunicae) - Tunic—military tunics were red so that blood and sweat appear identical.

Vestal Virgin - Virgin priestesses to the Roman Goddess Vesta—served in Vesta's temple in Rome.

Vexillarius - Roman junior officer—standard-bearer—carries the standard of the legion when the century is deployed away from the legion, wears a bear's skin and head over his armor.

Vilica - Mistress of a large estate.

Vilicus - Steward of a large estate.

Acknowledgements

This has been a fun project, but it required a plethora of research. (And yes, I *do* know what a plethora is, thank you.) Dr. Eric H. Huntsman, professor of ancient scripture at Brigham Young University (and one-time professor of classics, particularly Roman history) allowed me to talk his ear off whenever we sat together at Tabernacle Choir at Temple Square rehearsals, broadcasts, concerts, and while on tour this summer. He patiently listened and answered questions, and, for his gracious assistance, I am profoundly indebted. Valerie and Earle Gardner have been my invaluable helpers at most of my weaponry classes over the years. They have helped me hone my presentation. And I believe that there are many things about a sword, dagger, shield, and various other bits of ancient armor and military equipment that can be truly understood only once you've held and wielded such weapons or worn such armor. Valerie and Earle have helped make this possible. And of course, the greatest, deepest thanks go to my lady, my princess, and my queen—my beloved Cindy. She has been my sounding board, my first line of defense in proofreading and editing. She has been my inspiration, and while she is *not* Maelona, Branwen, or Moira, they are all her. (Mull that one over for a while!) And second only to my wife has been my mom. Mable Belt has also been my proofreader throughout this process. David Belt (my dad, not me) provided love and support in every way he could. There are many others—too many others—to list as beta readers, and I know I'm going to forget . . . a lot of them. So, I will list instead only the members of the LDS Beta Readers Dark Fiction group who have critiqued and helped me along the way—Alicia Dodson, Brandon Bluhm, Crystal Brinkerhoff, and Dan Earle. Penultimately, Elizabeth Bentley gave me my start by publishing *The Unwilling* and the rest of *The Children of Lilith* trilogy, as well as *The Sweet Sister*. And now, she's publishing this work (which, if you've read the others, you will know they all tie together now in *The Arawn Prophecy*.) For allowing me to tell this story under the same banner, I am deeply grateful. Many are the hours I've spent praying over this story or sitting in the choir lofts of the Conference Center and Tabernacle, seeking for inspiration. And inspiration has come. Over and over. I thank my Savior for His divine help. To all of you, I thank you from the bottom of my heart—no, not deep enough—from the soles of my caligae.

About the Author

C David Belt was born in the wilds of Evanston, Wyoming. As a child, he lived and traveled extensively around the Far East. In Thailand, he once fed so many bananas to a monkey, the poor creature swore off bananas for life. He served as a missionary in South Korea and southern California (Korean-speaking), and yes, he loves kimchi. He graduated from Brigham Young University with a BS in Computer Science and a minor in Aerospace Studies, but he managed to bypass all English and writing classes. He served as a B-52 pilot in the US Air Force and as an Air Weapons Controller in the Washington Air National Guard and was deployed to locations so secret, his family still does not know where he risked life and limb (other than in an 192' wingspan aircraft flying 200' off the ground in mountainous terrain). When he is not writing, he sings in the Taber-nacle Choir at Temple Square and works as a software engineer. He collects swords, spears, and axes (oh, my!), and other medieval wea-pons and armor. He and his wife have six children (and a growing number of grandchildren) and live in Utah with an eclectus parrot named Mork (who likes to jump on the keyboard when David is writing). There is also a cat, but she can't be bothered to take notice of the parrot, and so that is all the mention we shall make of her.

C. David Belt is the author of *The Children of Lilith* trilogy, *The Sweet Sister*, *Time's Plague*, and *The Arawn Prophecy*. For more information, please visit www.unwillingchild.com.

www.ingramcontent.com/pod-product-compliance
Lightning Source LLC
Chambersburg PA
CBHW030803260626
47169CB00001B/166

* 9 7 8 1 5 1 3 6 4 3 5 6 4 *